THE EMERALD FORGE

MANDA BENSON

-Book three of Pilgrennon's Children-

TANGENTRINE

www.tangentrine.com

www.tangentrine.com

First edition published by Tangentrine 2012
Second edition published by Tangentrine 2024

British Library Cataloguing in Publication Data. A catalogue record for this book is available from the British Library.

ISBN: 978-1-917231-04-6

"There it must be, I think, in the vast and eternal laws of matter, and not in the daily cares and sins and troubles of men, that whatever is more than animal within us must find its solace and its hope."

H.G. Wells, *The Island of Doctor Moreau*

With thanks to J.D. Williams

and D.J. Cockburn

-|-

THE graffiti must have gone up last night. Dana would never have missed this if she'd walked past it yesterday.

A roiling black-and-grey mushroom cloud took up the entire wall, its underside shot through with veins of red flame, upon a background of an infernal red sky and a desolate plain of blackened buildings and burned trees. In the foreground of the panorama, uplit by a red glow and with hair appearing to flow in the hot breeze, had been painted the head and shoulders of a woman with an exaggerated cartoon expression of demonic glee. Her fist was raised in triumph, her face sinister behind dark glasses.

When Jananin Blake had received enough nominations to be elected a Spokesman of the Meritocracy in the first ever vote, critics of the new system had claimed it proved it was unworkable; that voters treated it as a joke, since Blake was a scientist with no experience of politics or interest in taking the role offered, who had only come to public attention because of a viral video and a phenomenal mess left behind by the previous government. The same as how, on that first election, the other nominees included a literal clown, a car enthusiast who presented television programmes, and a revolting Internet celebrity who proclaimed himself to be a racist, misogynist, and homophobe.

They hadn't counted on her agreeing to do it. They hadn't expected her well-reasoned, impartial written analyses on scientific matters being read so seriously by the electorate. They'd never imagined she'd be nominated for a second term.

After the second line-up of spokesmen was voted in, which did not include the clown or the horrible man, but did include Blake and the car enthusiast, who'd demonstrated some strong opinions but also some quite interesting insights on a variety of matters, people stopped saying things like that. They started to take the Meritocracy seriously, and they started to attack Blake and the other Spokesmen for their ideas.

It always hit Dana with a stab of longing and apprehension whenever she recognised Jananin Blake's face on a newspaper or public wall, or when she heard her voice on the radio or television. It wasn't easing over time, either.

If anything, it got harder.

The painting must be one of Boggsy's. Yes, Dana could just make out the cursive signature with the long, curled tail on the *y* on the bottom right corner, highlighted in white against Jananin's shoulder. Boggsy didn't like Jananin. Indeed, Boggsy didn't seem to like any of the Spokesmen for the Meritocracy. Graeme used to say Boggsy was like a mirror, reflecting the Spokesmen's opinions without their high talk. In the last Spokesmen's referendum, people had even voted for Boggsy enough that he — or she — could have claimed a position as Spokesman, but Boggsy was anonymous and had never come forward to claim or reject that right.

Dana took a few steps back onto the grass bank so she could see the image in its entirety. Mentally, she drew a rectangle around it and remembered it as a digital photograph. She'd transfer it to a computer when she got home.

There was a plaque at the bottom of the wall. Dana couldn't read it from this distance, but she knew it had a statement on it saying the surface was a public wall for the expression of the opinions of the public, and something about it being a criminal offence to prevent people from using it, because it was treason to censor the Meritocracy.

Cool pinpricks had begun to flick Dana's face and hands. A sparse rain rustled the dry grass. She glanced up to the sky, at the path behind her. A boy was coming this way, but he was still some distance behind. A tall, fat boy, with thick plastic-framed glasses and dark brown hair cut in a puddingbowl style. The bottom of his shirt hung crumpled over his trousers, and he wore the green-and-gold striped tie of Dana's school, tied so the narrow end was short and the tie so ridiculously long it hung to his knees. He had his coat slung over one shoulder by a finger, and carried his school bag on the other arm.

Earlier that day, Dana had been trying to get through a crowded stairwell to go upstairs to Chemistry, and some older boys had yelled "Falcon Punch!" and shoved a fat boy into her, and laughed and jeered as though pushing fat boys into smaller girls was a new sport. The boy had stared at her before the motion of the throng pulled him out of sight. This boy looked similar, but Dana wasn't very good at recognising people, especially people whom she'd seen only once. It could be the boy was angry with her for being there and making him look bad in front of his friends. It hardly made sense, as it wasn't her fault, but then people rarely did make much sense at school. Best to leave now, and avoid the chance of anything happening.

She didn't look behind as she continued on the path, but she could hear the boy's footsteps, and his presence just a few paces behind made her nervous. She didn't like that boy walking there, able to see her.

Dana's route home brought her through an avenue with cherry trees edging the driveways, and at the end of this avenue was a gate that led to a field of common land and a copse: an alternative route to Pauline and Graeme's house. She would feel much more at ease in the quiet wood with the bird song and the rustle of the trees instead of the noise of traffic and people, and that boy behind her. Dana passed quickly beneath the branches of the cherry trees, climbed up onto the metal stile, and jumped down into the field. She set off across the wet grass confidently, not looking back.

The rattle of the gate behind told her she was followed.

Dana hurried along the uneven path worn in the grass beside the allotments that backed onto the field. A piebald dog behind the hedge barked, making her jump and quicken her pace. The boy had to be following her. Why else would he be coming this way? Dana didn't dare look back. She broke into a run as she reached the bottom of the path. Her course took her across wet grass and under the cover of the trees. She scrambled up the gap worn through the undergrowth and glanced back as she turned onto the main path. The boy was still behind her. She ran.

When she looked back, he still followed, slower than her. Perhaps she could outrun him. Dana knew these woods well, although Pauline was always telling her not to go into them because there might be murderers and rapists lurking there. If she could get enough of a headstart and break off the path, perhaps she could hide in the wood until he'd gone.

She ran on until the path turned a corner and trees blocked the sight of her pursuer, and leapt down into the undergrowth. Her foot landed wrong in the soft soil, her ankle twisted, and sky and ground turned over. Dana sat up, heart pounding. The boy hadn't caught up with her yet, but a nettle had got her on the wrist. She'd pulled in her hands instinctively when she had fallen, and aside from her ankle she couldn't feel that she was hurt anywhere else.

A large tree trunk stood not far from where she had fallen, bracts of burgundy-and-purple-striped fungi sprouting from it. Her ankle ached as she staggered behind the tree and crouched down. From here she could see the wood of the tree was decomposed and spongy, and its core had rotted away to leave an uneven crater formed from its outermost layers of bark. Keeping her knees bent into a crouching position, she crept inside the hollow and looked through a crack in the wood up onto the path.

Presently the boy appeared. He looked about the path ahead, apparently confused, and turned slowly through 360 degrees to scan the woods. Dana steadied her breathing; the boy was standing not ten yards from her, and he might hear it. She felt safe, ensconced inside the dead tree with the smell of mould and soil surrounding her, and she began to think derisive things about the boy, as she often did about people who bullied her. He was a fat, ugly boy, Dana thought, and probably a stupid boy as well from the look of him. He had a double chin and a spotty face, and he was sweating copiously from a brisk walk and a five-minute run on a summer afternoon. The perspiration had wetted his school shirt, and he had breasts like a girl.

The boy was looking at the ground in front of the path. She must have flattened the ferns when she'd fallen. He lifted his head and his eyes looked straight at Dana. Perhaps the boy wasn't as stupid as he looked.

The boy put one foot down off the path. He was coming. For a moment, Dana was paralysed. Then she turned and broke from her hiding place and ran down the hill.

"Oi! *Oi!*" the boy shouted. Dana could hear him crashing through the undergrowth behind her. She ignored the stiff pain in her ankle and weaved her way through brambles, pulling the sleeves of her school jersey over her fists to protect skin and pushing tall stems apart with her arms. She was faster and more agile than the boy chasing her, but quickly she began to see he had other things on his side. She had to use effort to force her passage through the vegetation, whilst he simply followed in the trail she had cleared, and his physical bulk gave him more inertia on the downhill run and made it easier for him to trample anything that did get in his way.

He was almost upon her when she came to the stream. Dana was never sure if it was rightly a stream or a river, or something between the two. It meandered several times around this part of the wood, and she made straight for where she knew a fallen tree bridged it. Dana was up through the gap in the roots and over the tree before the boy knew what was happening. She scrambled over the slimy bark with the water several feet below her, glad she always wore sensible shoes and not the ridiculous bricks Pauline had once suggested she strap to her feet in order to fit in better with the girls at school.

The tree held up the boy, and Dana slackened her pace, panic momentarily giving way to fatigue, but then she blundered into an impenetrable bank of brambles and had to go around, and the boy started gaining on her again. The water doubled back on itself somewhere around here, and upstream of a mini-waterfall it was possible to jump over. Dana could remember a time when the waterfall had been much farther downstream. It had slowly eroded its way up, eating a six-foot gorge backwards into the clayey soil in a process she had learnt about in Geography. She could hear the rush of the falling water now, and she headed for the place where she could cross.

She was running full tilt, and with all the ferns and brambles obscuring it she nearly fell into the gorge. She struggled to stop in time and found herself staring down into a muddy torrent six feet below, scattered with stones, broken plants, and lumps of clay. The waterfall had moved back again; the recent rains must have precipitated it. The water below was deep and fast, swollen by the rain, and Dana imagined someone falling from such a height could easily break a leg, or worse. She couldn't remember how far downstream one would have to walk before there would come a place where it was possible to climb out. When she looked upstream, she couldn't see where the waterfall had moved to, just the gorge going on until the stream's course took it out of view.

She would have to go upstream and find a place to cross. When she turned, the boy was running straight towards her, barging through brambles with his elbows.

"Hey, *Epsilon!*"

Dana turned back and launched herself into a running jump. The muddy gully with its churning brown waters flew past below her. She landed heavily in the wet mud on the other side, bending her knees as she came down and grappling with a tree for stability.

When she looked behind, the boy was standing on the other bank. He stared down at the stream below, before looking back up at her.

Dana began to run up the bank. Slender trees grew vertically from it, impervious to the gradient, and she grabbed at the trunks to speed her ascent. A number of times she slowed to throw a hurried glance over her shoulder, just to check the boy had not jumped and continued the pursuit, but he hadn't. She crested the bank and came out onto the footpath through the woods. She blocked out the raw feeling in her throat, the burning in the muscles of her legs, and the cramp in her side, and kept up a running pace until she was out of the woods and on the path running alongside a cornfield. The path was always strewn with dog turds, and Dana stepped in at least two, too preoccupied with checking behind to pay them due heed.

Epsilon... it was only Ivor who had called her that. It was the name he'd given her before she was born, a label for an experiment...

The path ended with a short alley between a house and a backyard, before leading onto the grassed playing field. Dana shuffled her feet in the grass in an attempt to wipe the dogpoo off her shoes. She checked the time: three minutes to six. She made the last fifty yards across the field and over the street to Pauline and Graeme's house at a run.

Dana rushed into the front porch and closed the door behind her. The hallway was dark and familiar-smelling. Relief enveloped her. Safe, at least for now. She dumped her bag and coat on the hall floor.

Graeme's voice came from the living room. "I expect she'll be back soon," he was saying. "After all, she always wants to watch to see if Demented Badger Woman is on the news. She's *obsessed* with that woman."

A hot prickly feeling crawled up the back of Dana's neck. *Demented Badger Woman* was a mildly unkind name that Graeme called Jananin Blake, because she had black hair that had gone grey at the temples, which he'd compared to the stripes on a badger's face.

"I expect she'll grow out of it," came Pauline's voice. "And anyway, surely a scientist and a political speaker is a much better model for a girl than a singer or a footballer." Her voice became louder as the door to the living room opened. Graeme started when he saw Dana. "Oh, hello, Dana, we didn't hear you come in. You're just in time to watch the news."

"I don't want to watch the news!" snapped Dana, indignant. "And I'm not *obsessed!*"

"*Dana!*" Pauline exclaimed, appearing behind Graeme. Dana looked at the floor behind her, at grubby brown smudges on the carpet where she'd trodden. Great. A shit end to a shit day, and even now she was back home she couldn't escape from people having a go at her. Dana ran upstairs to her room, ignoring Pauline's shout for her to take her shoes off, and slammed the door. She pulled off her dirty, stinking shoes without untying the laces, and threw herself down on the bed.

It felt as though a clockwork mechanism inside her had been wound too tight. She hated school, she hated dog owners who didn't clean up, and she hated not being able to do something as straightforward as watching the news without Graeme and Pauline guessing at her motive and forming judgements on her. She wished, as she often did, that Ivor was still here, and she could go and live with him, and not have to go to school any more. She wished that she could tell Pauline and Graeme that Jananin was her mother, and that she would be allowed to go and visit her, but she couldn't and she wasn't.

There came a knock on the door. "Dana," came

Graeme's voice. "We're sorry for talking about you. Did you have a bad day?"

Dana didn't answer him.

"What are you doing in there?"

Dana turned her head out of her pillow, to look at the desk and at the biscuit tin — one of the fancy ones you get biscuits in for special occasions, with a gold oak leaf pattern on it — that she kept paints and modelling glue in. The overtightened cog inside her slackened a little. She took a deep breath before answering. "I'm making a Hawker Hurricane."

This game had been started by Dana's therapist, who had come up with 'strategies' to help her deal with stress and overwhelming emotions. If Dana had to talk about her emotions, thinking about it only made them even worse, so the therapist had suggested she go somewhere quiet and do something she enjoyed that took up all her concentration. Dana had come up with making Airfix models as an idea for this, so after that meeting, whenever she was feeling overwhelmed she would sit at her desk in her room with the door shut, and paint and glue Airfix models until she felt in control again. If Graeme or Pauline asked her what she was doing, and she told them she was making Airfix models, they were to leave her alone and not disturb her.

Only it had evolved into a kind of code, a private joke. Graeme would ask her what she was doing, and she would say she was making a World War II aircraft based on its size as a comparison to how she was feeling. If she was making a Supermarine Spitfire, then she was just a little bit stressed and would feel better soon. On the other hand, if she was making an Avro Lancaster, it meant she felt really overwhelmed and wouldn't come down for the rest of the day. It meant she could communicate more specifically how bad she felt without Dana having to think or talk about her emotions.

"Oh, that's nice. We've got steak for dinner."

"Don't want any," said Dana.

"All right, I'll keep some for you. You come out when you're feeling better."

Dana heard Graeme go downstairs. She put her hand in her pocket and held Ivor's watch. A hot ache filled her eyes and nose.

She sat up and swung her legs down from the bed, and concentrated on the sensation of the carpet under her feet. After breathing in and out a few times, she got up and went to the desk. Dana arranged the fuses in her pencil tin in ascending order of amperage, standing on their ends on the shelf above the desk. She looked at the ordered calm of the regular, coloured writing on the white middles, and then she opened the biscuit tin and found the pot of enamel paint that was the right colour for painting a Wellington bomber. As she concentrated on reproducing the camouflage patterns on the kit's box, it became easier not to think about what had happened today. By the time she'd finished, it seemed the surrounding room separated her from the boy following her and Pauline and Graeme's disapproval, as though they had become distant.

She heard Graeme's footsteps coming upstairs as she was putting the paint away. He knocked on the door.

"Dana, can I come in?"

"If you want," said Dana nonchalantly. "It's your house."

Graeme came in and sat down on Dana's bed. Dana sat at her desk and put the fuse tin away in the drawer without looking at him.

"It's your house now as well," he said gently. "I'm sorry you came in and heard the end of that conversation we were having. We didn't mean it to sound like what you heard. And besides, it was wrong of us to talk like that. What you like is your choice, and not ours, and not our business to talk about."

Dana shrugged.

"Pauline's gone out with some people from work.

Would you like to come downstairs and have dinner with me?"

"All right, then."

"I recorded the news. If you like, we could watch that too."

"Yes please, Graeme."

Downstairs, Cale was sitting at the dining room table, eating tapioca pudding. Propped up in front of him was one of his music books with his b's and q's written in it. Dana's brother was disinterested in anything musical and refused to play music for anyone. All he did was work out Pi, convert the digits of it into notes, and write them in the book and then play the tuneless string of keys they translated into on his keyboard. He was still working through the decimal places, and Pi in C Major as Graeme called it had built up into six volumes.

The Pen lay on the table next to Cale's bowl. Cale would only write with one kind of pen. The original pen had been a promotional pen with a rubberised grip with holes in it, and the logo of a business printed on a metal barrel coloured a vibrant peacock blue. Nobody knew which business, because the logo and most of the blue had rubbed off. Cale had found the pen on the table and taken it for himself, and had become fiercely possessive of it, keeping it in his pocket at all times when he wasn't using it. Because he tended to write and draw an awful lot, the pen ran out after a month or so. Although it bothered him that the pen didn't work, and Pauline and Graeme explained that the pen needed a refill, and he understood the explanation, he couldn't stand to let anyone else touch the pen to show him how to do it.

In the end, they were all involved in a conspiracy against him. Graeme and Duncan grabbed Cale and took the pen off him, and stood and restrained him by the arms while Pauline took apart the pen, and Dana tried to calm Cale down as he shouted in horror when the spring and the tube inside it came out. But he had been much happier when she returned it to him, working once more. After that, Pauline had asked Dana to secretly examine the pen while Cale was asleep, and Dana had found a manufacturer's name engraved in the metal clip. Pauline had looked this up online and found the manufacturer of the pens, and ordered 50 of them, which was the smallest amount the manufacturer allowed, with *Cale Provine's Pen* printed on them in place of a logo.

As it turned out, it had been a good thing Pauline had ordered 50 of them, because the next time she looked on the website, the pens were gone, and when she emailed the manufacturer, it turned out the model had been discontinued. A lot of the pens were now very worn and grimy, and Cale would habitually take his pen apart and put it back together when he was stressed at school, and this tended to wear out the thread, so they would end up falling apart in his hand.

"Where's Duncan?" Dana asked.

"In his bedroom," said Graeme. "He has his driving test tomorrow, and he's worried about it."

Graeme brought his and Dana's dinner plates into the living room so that they could eat off their laps. Dana started to eat while he sorted out the recorder.

They both sat and ate in silence while the headlines ran. First was another report about electricity and nuclear powerplants, which had featured often on the news recently. Jananin wasn't on it, and Dana was a bit disappointed as Jananin was very keen on nuclear powerplants and often would argue about them in public debates. But they did show a film of a site on Lewis — Dana didn't recognise where, but the scenery was familiar to her — where they were proposing to build a new one.

The next report showed a picture of a graveyard, and Dana didn't pay much attention to the introduction to it.

"...are shocked and disturbed by the desecration of the grave of a young victim of the London Compton bombing. The deceased, a girl estimated to be about fourteen years old and whose identity was never discovered, died from heart failure in the Information Terrorism attack over two years ago."

Dana stopped chewing and stared at the television. It had to be Alpha. No other girls had died in the Compton bomb blast.

"The girl's grave was dug up, and police say the coffin appears to have been tampered with, but that the body remains intact. They can only conclude this is some kind of tasteless joke."

"It's horrible, isn't it?" Graeme must have noticed something in Dana's demeanour. "She was just a girl. They never even found out who she was, and now someone's done that."

Dana couldn't pay attention to the remainder of the news. Jananin wasn't on it anyway, and the realisation that the girl whose grave had been dug up was Alpha shocked her and sent her mind working through a chain of questions. The first reason she could think of for Alpha being dug up was that someone had worked out how to bring her back to life, but she immediately dismissed that as irrational. Alpha had been dead far too long. So what had the news said? That the coffin had been dug up, but that nothing had been removed. Surely after this time, all that would be left of Alpha's body would be bones, and this meant that the police, or whoever dealt with cases like this, had opened the coffin and found what they expected to find, bones, and counted them all and compared them with an inventory of the bones in a human body and found nothing amiss.

But what if something had been stolen, something they hadn't expected to be there: Alpha's transceiver, the same as the one implanted in Dana's brain. If it had been taken, the police who examined the remains wouldn't know, because they'd have no reason to expect it to be there.

Dana began carefully, "Graeme, you know when Bunce

was dead?"

Bunce had been a hamster whom Pauline had brought home one day. Dana had thought it a remarkably uninteresting little animal. For nearly three years it had eaten and drunk and slept and made the living room smell bad. It had a cage with transparent pipes coming out of it so it could climb around in them, and it had always done its business in the pipes, and that made it smell even worse. Pauline kept having to muck it out because no-one else wanted to. Towards the end of the last year, it had become thin and ratlike and balding, and one morning Dana had found it lying on its back in the bottom of its cage, legs in the air like when animals in cartoons are dead, lips pulled back over its ugly yellow teeth.

So Pauline and Graeme held a funeral for Bunce in the back garden, and Dana went with Graeme and Cale to the garden centre to choose a plant to grow on Bunce's grave, because Graeme said they could remember Bunce by the plant, and Bunce would turn into fertiliser in the ground and be good for the plant. Dana chose a plant with green and brown leaves called *Oxalis*, and Bunce must have made really good fertiliser, because nearly a year later there were *Oxalises* growing all over the garden and in the lawn, so that Pauline and Graeme uprooted them and hid them in the compost heap when they thought Dana wasn't looking.

"You know when Bunce was dead, and we buried it in the mud, and you said it would turn into soil and be good for the plant?"

"That's perhaps not something nice to talk about when people are eating," Graeme said.

"Why not?" said Dana.

Graeme put down his cutlery and studied his half-eaten steak for a moment. "Never mind," he said, smiling faintly. "What were you going to ask?"

"You know when people and animals are dead and their skin and their brains and their guts all go rotten and turn into fertiliser, and there's just a skeleton left?"

Graeme took his plate off his lap and set it down on the coffee table. "Yes?"

"Well what if you buried a computer? Would that rot and turn into the soil, or would it stay there like a skeleton?"

Graeme sighed, leaned back on the sofa, and interlocked his fingers behind his head. "Well, I suppose it depends how long it was there. It takes about two years for a dead person or an animal about the same size as a person to rot down to the bones. After a few hundred years, usually the bones have rotted away as well. Some parts of a computer would never rot — the glass on the monitor, I suppose. The metal on it would gradually turn to rust and soak into the soil, but I expect that would take fifty years or more to happen completely. The plastic and the silicon I suppose could last hundreds of years."

"If I buried this," Dana picked up the remote control for the television, "would it still work if I dug it up four years later?"

"I suppose it might. The batteries in it would be flat, though." Graeme's face changed. "Now, Dana, I don't want you going and doing any experiments on stuff in the house. The remote controls are hard enough to find as it is."

"I wasn't going to. I just wondered."

Could it have been Ivor, if he was alive, who had dug up Alpha's grave, in order to get the transceiver back? But this didn't seem like the sort of thing Ivor would do. Ivor had cared about Alpha, and digging up the grave of someone you cared about didn't seem to be a respectful thing to do. In fact, it seemed like a disgusting thing to do.

Dana tried to think of it in terms of what she would do. If someone found a skeleton and identified it as Ivor's, she wouldn't want to look at it at all, not even if there might be something with it that belonged to her and she wanted back. If someone had been dead that long, the remains wouldn't even look like them any more. And besides, if Ivor was alive and he needed another transceiver, he had made them in the first place and could make another. At any rate, he'd said to Dana that implanting transceivers in her and the other children had been wrong, and he'd promised Jananin that he'd never do it again.

Unless he'd lied.

Dana and Graeme talked about other things that were being destroyed by time, like the wreck of a big ship called the *Titanic* that still lay on the bottom of the Atlantic ocean halfway to America, and this made Dana remember the *Atlantic Sonata*, whose route from Southampton to New York must have been the same as the one the ill-fated *Titanic* had taken, and perhaps even then she and Jananin and Ivor had passed directly over her tragic remains and all those who'd died when she sank. She put her hand in her pocket to clutch Ivor's watch.

Graeme told her part of the ship had rusted right through and collapsed not long ago, and the *Titanic* was eventually going to end up as a big rusty stain on the ocean bed. Then they talked about plastic and rubbish in landfill sites, and how the Meritocracy was trying to invent new ways to get energy or extract metals from it, because it took hundreds of years to decompose and it was still there when someone wanted to build a house or make a golf course on it, and how some of the first optical discs ever to have music recorded on them were now unplayable, not because the music back in those days was awful, but because the stuff they were made of had started to degrade and the information stored in it had been lost.

A debate came on the television, involving three women and a man. One of the women was hosting it, and the man was having a difficult time of making his point, because of the other two women, one was a scientist who would make only comments on science, and the other had a loud voice and was just very skilled at talking, and it seemed they had joined forces against him. It caught Dana's attention because part of what they were discussing was to do with the *Induced Meiosis Fertilisation Technique*, which Dana had been hearing more about in recent months, and had come to understand was the same technique Ivor had used to create her from Jananin's ovum combined with a proto-sperm derived from a gene-edited cell from himself, and the same technique that had been responsible for the mammoths in Montana.

The scientist was saying, "The technique was developed by a team led by three women at the MIT in America, about fifteen years ago, who were subsequently awarded the Nobel prize for their work. It's a scientific breakthrough and a huge achievement for women on every level."

The man replied, "I'm not disputing the technique or its benefits. I'm saying we need to have a serious discussion about some of the unintended consequences of it. Fifteen years ago, children were born with a sex ratio of roughly 49 males to 51 females. If you look at the cohort just one year later, after the technique became available, the children turning fourteen this year, the ratio is closer to 40:60. For children being born today, it's even higher."

The loud woman said, "That's because the technique allows a woman who wants to have a child to become pregnant by her female partner, and in these cases the sex of the baby will always be female."

"And this is skewing the sex ratio of children born. In future, women are going to be overrepresented and have far greater electoral power than men in the Meritocracy. Furthermore, the additional merit awarded for having a family is nearly always awarded to the mother, and generally only given to the father or the donor partner if the mother abandons the family."

"That's because the mother's contribution of carrying the child and birthing it, and usually caring for it as an infant, is far greater than what the father or donor can do! A system that awarded merits for siring or donating genetic material to produce children would be far too open to abuse!"

The man raised his hands in a conciliatory way. "I

don't necessarily disagree with the position you're coming from, but there perhaps needs to be more thought put in to ensuring the voices of men and boys are heard moving into the future. I mean, if you go to a school and meet parents, a common nuclear family you'll encounter at the gates is a couple of women with two daughters, who have birthed one each, 'fathered' as such by the other, so they can both claim the family merit from being a mother. A couple in an opposite-sex relationship can typically only claim the credit once by the mother, even when they have two or more children."

The scientist spoke again. "IMFT doesn't just benefit lesbian and bisexual women. It benefits straight couples where the man can't produce viable sperm for whatever reason, as well as straight women wishing to become mothers who aren't able to find a suitable partner in their reproductive window, by giving them more choices and more dignity in requesting donorship from their friends."

"Perhaps we should be asking, in that case, why these women are rejecting the men that are available, and the traditional family, in favour of this?"

The loud woman laughed. "Perhaps it's the *men* who need to ask themselves that? I mean, not even really boring dead-straight women who are only interested in cooking and sewing are going to want men who are sticklers for the kinds of *traditions* that have made women into chattels at worst, second-class citizens at best, throughout most of history. Or who can't even be bothered to put on a clean shirt for a TV interview!"

The man, who had what appeared to be gravy stains splashed down his shirt and tie, snapped in response, "Your remark smacks of misandry and heterophobia!"

The host held up her palms towards the loud woman. "That was inappropriate."

Then Graeme looked at the clock and let out an exclamation, and Dana had to go to bed.

Dana remembered that she hadn't done her homework

when she was getting changed. But then she remembered it was Saturday tomorrow, and that was a good thing as there would be no school. Perhaps she ought to have told Graeme about the boy following her, but it was late, and if she told Graeme and Pauline every time someone was horrible to her at school, there'd never be any time to talk about anything else.

She lay in bed with the lights out for a few moments, fingering the cracked glass face of Ivor's watch, the hands forever frozen at seven minutes and twenty-one seconds to nine, when she and Jananin had fallen into the sea. She thought about the *Titanic*, lost in the depths, and the *Atlantic Sonata*, and she wondered about Alpha's grave and who had dug it up.

-2-

A BREEZE touches your face. The pressing heat of a dark room smothers the drone of a fan.

"It's you again, isn't it?" You feel your own lips moving, not through your bidding. "I remember you. You came to me before, when they were hurting me. Your name's Epsilon, isn't it?"

You know you've had this dream before, many times. It's always indistinct and difficult to remember when you wake, but ever lucid in memory are the countless times it has played out before you when you're living it once again.

You're lying on your back. You can't speak or move your limbs. It's always been this way, in the dream. The only sound you can make is more imaginary than real, like the voice you think you once had, heard down a long tunnel. *Yes, my name's Epsilon.*

You start to move, as though guided by an invisible puppeteer. It's familiar, rather like watching a film, but from the body of one of the actors with all their five senses. A gridded rectangle of yellow light stands out as I push us up into a sitting position. When our legs swing down from the edge of the bed, our feet touch clammy, plasticky flooring. With tentative, unsteady steps, the legs that are both mine and yours carry us to the barred window. Outside, stark lights flood a concrete yard surrounded by wire fence. A prison?

I turn, panning the room with your field of vision. The bars on the window cast squared light upon a bare cell with a mattress upon a metal bedstead in the centre. There are thick straps on the bed, like seatbelts.

Do you remember?

My breathing quickens.

You were a part of this mind, while the body screamed and cried and fought against the straps, alone in the dark. And no-one came, and you pleaded with the other consciousness, against the irrational fear and anger that had overtaken me, to explain to you what was happening. You wanted to help me.

The light from the windows casts a shadow from our body, lengthened and a little distorted, but not greatly unlike the shadow you recall you once had. Tangled curls of hair stand out in a halo around the head, and the mid-thigh-length hem of an unpleasant nylon shift sticks to our skin.

"They say I shouldn't listen to you," I say, my voice weak, reedy, a lot like how you remember sounding some other time — in some other life — they pulled you from the sea. "They say... the voices I can hear in my head..."

The pain and the memories are coming back. I tried so hard to act how they wanted me to behave, just so they wouldn't tie us to that bed and leave us there.

I guide your vision to the dark rectangle of the door. "Epsilon, will you help me escape?"

I will, you think. You don't know who I am, and the vague, unreal feeling of being in the dream makes it difficult to understand, but you're sure, as you always are in these dreams, that I'm held prisoner for something I've not done.

Go to the door.

The padding of feet on the vinyl floor goes unheard over the fan. "The door is locked," I say. Yes, the door's locked. You remember that. That was why we called out for so long, because the door was shut and we couldn't get out, even for a purpose as necessary as using the toilet. You remember the other dreams, after interminable discomfort and pain, how we had been unable to hold on any longer, and the humiliation and the horrible feeling, the silent crying and the self-hating that always followed, and how you told me, furiously, that it was not my fault, that it was the fault of those beastly people who had tied us to the bed.

Where is the key?

"I don't know."

Perhaps it doesn't need a key, you wonder. *Perhaps we should ask it to open.*

"How?"

I'll show you.

I raise our hand, indistinct in the dark. Fingers touch the smooth surface of the door.

Like this. And you unlock the door in the same way you've known to unlock electronic locks for as long as you can remember. The dull click of the mechanism transmits through the surface to fingers that are and aren't yours.

Our hand grasps the doorhandle. The door opens to a corridor smelling strongly of disinfectant. As we step through there's a green LED marking where the swipecard reader that controls the lock is attached to the frame.

I support the heavy weight of the door's closing mechanism so it eases shut silently. The corridor is dark, apart from small windows in doors identical to the one we've just exited through.

Do you know where you're going? you think. *'Cause I can't see anything.*

My left foot reaches forward and feels the way, toes flexing. Loose, gritty material scratches under our soles.

We ought to get downstairs. You recall the window in the room looks down into the concrete courtyard.

We pass the last door-window and reach out with both hands. Our fingertips touch a wood surface. One hand finds a handle. The room behind lies in complete darkness, but from the smell of soap and damp, you know it's a lavatory.

We close the door behind us and with one hand grope in the dark for the cord for the light.

With a dull buzz and a click, a fluorescent tube lights on the ceiling. White tiles cover every surface of the room.

The toilet and handbasin are also white, and a shower with a mildewed beige curtain occupies one side of the space. The fingers on the light cord, you see, are thin and pale, the skin around the nails frayed and reddened as though it's been chewed.

Curiosity overcomes you. *Go to the mirror*, you suggest.

I side-step into the range of the mirror. I look a few years younger than you, about ten or eleven. My face is very pale, and my eyes, although sunken and dark-rimmed, seem unnaturally large for my face. My hair is a tangled mess of loose honey-coloured curls, shoulder length and with no proper structure to its style, as though it was cut very short some time ago and ignored ever since.

You can't remember if you've ever seen what I look like in the dream before. I seem familiar to you, somehow.

There's writing, on our clothes, you notice. The girl in the mirror wears an institutional shift with elbow-length sleeves and a mid-thigh-length hem, similar to one you remembered having to wear... in a hospital? You think you hit your head; you don't remember. It's made from nylon fabric and you can feel I'm not wearing anything underneath it. Orange and green words are printed on the material. My hands pull it up towards our eyes, but either through the vagueness of the dream or some uncorrected defect in my sight, you can't read them.

My eyes begin to move. I'm looking back at the mirror, and the handbasin beneath it. A plastic mug stands there, containing a toothbrush and a disposable plastic razor, like the ones ladies shave their armpits on. My hand reaches and my fingers close on the razor's stem.

What are you doing? you ask.

"I'm escaping."

That's not the way! Please!

"It's the only way."

The hands fumble with the head of the razor. You try, with all your will, to make the fingers obey you, but they won't, and you know now you've tried to do this countless times before, that you cannot alter the events in the dream, like when the film one has seen before is running, and the hero is about to make a terrible, fatal mistake, and wish as one might, the mistake cannot be averted and the hero cannot be saved.

The razor snaps away from its mount and for a moment it lies in our fingers, a sliver of bright metal. Now the hand turns over, hiding the blade, and slashes across the blue-green track of the vein on the inside of our left wrist. You hardly feel the razor, it's that sharp. A gasp comes from our mouth. My hand reaches to clutch the edge of the basin, the razor slipping from my grasp. I knock over the cup, and it and the toothbrush fall to the floor where a pool of dark blood spreads. Strength is running from our legs; the ground meets our knees. The blood covers the floor with sticky heat, but the shock and fear you feel are overpowered by my emotions of triumph and release.

There's a crash. Our head turns to the door. It stands open: a man is there. His face is clear in the stark bathroom light. "Gemma!" he shouts, and in his voice is reproach and anger, and disappointment.

The word stings like a blow to the face. "My name's Gamma!" I defy him. "And I won't be your prisoner any more!"

The room sways, and the scene melts away into darkness.

Dana was suddenly fully alert, her heart racing and her breath rapid. For a moment she was entangled in something and feared she was tied to the bed in the dream, before she realised it was her pyjamas and bedcover all stuck to her skin with sweat, and she was back in her own body, in her own bedroom at Pauline and Graeme's house.

She tried to remember if she'd left the wLAN on; she thought she had. The wLAN, a black box from the telephone company with a few green LEDs on it. Dana didn't know if this was coincidence or not, but every time she had one of these strange dreams, the wLAN was on.

She rose and went to the landing. She hesitated as she looked through the bathroom door, remembering the blood in the dream, but all she saw was moonlight shining on the tiles. Through the open door to the computer room, it was clear by the glowing green spot the wLAN occupied that it had indeed been left on. She felt her way along the wall to where she knew the plug was, and switched it off. Noting the green light had gone, she returned to her room.

Sweat had dried and cooled her, and she got back into bed and wrapped the duvet around herself, pulling it up over her head to enclose herself in the small warm space.

She had often wondered if the dreams were her interpretation of reading some sort of story or account from the Internet in her sleep. Perhaps she'd embroidered her understanding of whatever she was reading with the weird imagination possessed by sleep. She remembered Steve Gideon, stabbed by the yakuza, his blood spreading on Takahashi's hallway mat, hot and sticky and awful, how she couldn't stop it coming out of him and his life draining away. Perhaps it was that memory, combined with something else.

Dana couldn't remember seeing the girl's appearance before, or hearing her name, but neither of these facts seemed particularly novel or unexpected right now. She wondered why, in the dream, she had attributed the girl with the name of Gamma. Perhaps it was something to do with the memory of the boy shouting 'Epsilon' at her the day before. For a moment, Dana wondered if the boy could be Gamma, but Ivor had definitely said that Gamma was a girl. Maybe it was simply that Dana didn't know the identity of the girl, and she neither knew the identity of Gamma, so she had equated them to the same person in her dream.

Dana had a theory that her mind was a lot like a computer, which had to shut down and defragment itself in order for it to work properly, like Cerberus and Steve Gideon's Porpoises had been designed to do. But if dreams were just random memories assembling themselves for sorting during the mind's defragmentation process, why had she dreamed so many times of the girl trapped in the room? Or were the other dreams just part of the dream she had just had — had she indeed dreamt she'd had them — and she'd never had any of the others in the first place, just a disorienting sense of *déjà vu* imparted by the dream she had just had? It was all so vague when she was awake.

*

Saturday was a good day, primarily because there was no school. It was also a good day because it was a post day, and Dana might get a letter. This Saturday, she was hoping to get a catalogue she'd sent off for, from a specialist supplier of carnivorous plants. The supplier it seemed was too old to have a website where people could order plants, so if you wanted plants from him, you had to get them by post.

Pauline and Graeme's garden had always had a damp spot at the bottom, and they'd decided Dana could have that part for herself, to grow whatever she wanted in. Dana wanted to plant *Sarracenia* and *Drosera*, of which there were hopefully several species included in the catalogue she was awaiting. Before she could order the plants, the ground had to be cleared because it had been ignored for a while and was covered in weeds and what remained of the last plants Pauline and Graeme had tried to grow on it. Dana spent the morning with Pauline and Graeme, pulling and digging, and even Cale helped a bit, although he spent much of the time sitting on the back step and watching everyone else work up a sweat, or inside the house, doing something else.

Cale had recently started noticing boys. He looked at other boys' faces and bottoms a lot, and sometimes he thought about young men in ways that made Dana wish he would think more quietly. Cale remained as uninterested as ever in talking to other people, and his fantasies about boys never really involved himself, and Dana wondered often if he'd ever be able to come out of his own head enough to have a real relationship with another lad.

As for Dana, she had never felt any interest in boys, or girls either for that matter. She often wondered if it was something else that was broken about her, like being autistic, or being a runt. It seemed to her as though her body had made a halfhearted attempt at starting puberty, and then given up. She hadn't really developed fatty breasts or hips like most of the other girls at school. She rather hoped something was missing or not formed properly inside her, and the unpleasant enough changes that had happened already would be the end, and she wouldn't have to do any of the other horrible things she'd had to learn about at school.

Pauline would say it was so she could *become a woman*, and that it was nothing to worry about. But Dana didn't want to be a woman. It was bad enough having to try to pretend to be normal without having to pretend to be a woman as well.

After spending a pleasant morning doing the garden, they had lunch, and Pauline and Graeme took Dana to the garden centre to buy some more things they needed (not to buy *Sarracenia* and *Drosera*, because Dana wanted particular species that garden centres don't have). When they got back to the house, there wasn't any post, but sometimes, Dana thought, hopefully, the postman was late on Saturday.

It was late afternoon when she came back into the house to wash her hands in the downstairs loo under the stairs, which also conveniently allowed her to go into the hall and check for post.

There wasn't any, but Duncan had come home, and he was sitting on the bottom of the stairs all hunched up, his discarded trainers lying like mountains on the doormat. His shoulders were shaking, and he did a big sniff.

Dana was about to go away, having realised he had failed his driving test and concerned that it was embarrassing for him, when he said, "Can you do some of that Japanese soup you sometimes make, please?"

Dana went into the kitchen and measured out the water to make miso soup. She'd looked up online how to make it some time ago, having had it often when she was in Fuyūtoshi. It was quite easy to make, but some of the ingredients were a bit difficult to get, and had to be ordered online.

Dana would often look up Fuyūtoshi on the Internet at school. Sato was still the mayor, and it had been the second place in the world to become a meritocracy, after the United Kingdom, or the *Meritocratic Union* of Great Britain and Northern Ireland as it was now called.

The online encylopedias explained that Fuyūtoshi's vote to become a meritocracy and break away from Japan had been the result of many complex things, but the flashpoint that triggered the referendum was a single incident that had come to be remembered by a name that translated into something like 'Magnolia Revenge.' A wealthy family (some eyewitnesses thought they were American) had come to Fuyūtoshi as tourists, and the yakuza had attempted to kidnap a child for ransom, killing one of the adults in the process (some sources claimed it was the child's uncle). A bloody fight had broken out on the streets in broad daylight, and a Japanese agent slew three of the yakuza, with an armed civilian (who had become a local celebrity) killing another. But the remaining three had allegedly been slain by the mother of the kidnapped child herself, who was trained in iaido.

Some special fish stock, made up from a powder; miso paste; a handful of delicious-smelling dried seaweed; a block of tofu cut into cubes; and a few sliced spring onions, and the soup was steaming and ready.

Duncan drank the soup at the table. Dana had explained to him when she had first made it, that you were supposed to eat the bits with chopsticks, and drink the rest out of the bowl, but Duncan had never been able to get the hang of chopsticks, so he ate the bits with a fork. He said he felt a bit better after he'd finished it.

Pauline and Graeme came in, and found out what had happened, and Pauline hugged Duncan, and said she was sure he tried his best, and Graeme said that nearly everyone fails on the first try. As there was a whole pan of miso soup left, Pauline said they might as well have Japanese food for dinner. Dana helped to cook the rice and make sushi. They used avocado, crab, smoked salmon, and cucumber as the fillings for it.

Even Cale liked Japanese food, especially when the miso soup had the soft tofu in it that has a bit of a slimy texture, although he'd still rather have tapioca. Duncan always ended up putting too much wasabi on his sushi and coughing when it got up the back of his nose.

Afterwards, Duncan found a tin of ginger beer, and asked if he could make himself and Dana a whisky and ginger to commiserate. Pauline said that was okay since it was the weekend, as long as he did not put too much whisky into Dana's.

The next day was Sunday, which was good, because it was not a school day, but it wasn't as good as Saturday, because it wasn't a post day. Dana finished her homework and did some more gardening, and did some of her Airfix models.

-3-

ONDAY was a school day, so it was a bad day, but it was also a post day, so perhaps when Dana got home her catalogue would be waiting for her.

The weather was warm, and Dana walked to school with her coat hung over her arm. Her first lesson was History, which she disliked. There was always a peculiar musty smell hanging around the classroom that made it hard to concentrate, and the lessons themselves concerned only things Dana could've pulled off the Internet in less time. The tests in History were never anything more than regurgitating dates and dead people's names and deeds. Dana had never known King Henry the 8th, and barring the unlikely invention of time travel she never would, so she didn't see any point in memorising who he'd been married to and what his opinions on organised religion were.

She sat in her usual place at the back, near the wLAN box. The school wLANs were one of the more positive things about having to go there every weekday. She knew where each one was — there were 36 around the whole school grounds in total — and recognised the distinctive signal of each almost as though they were friends. They were something reassuring in their constancy, at any rate.

The wLAN in the History classroom was called D1B. D, because that was the name of the block where the Art and Humanities classrooms were located, Floor 1, and B to identify it from the other boxes on that floor.

The teacher dictated the title of the lesson, and Dana wrote it in her exercise book. Then he told them to open their textbooks, and commenced waffling on about what was written in them.

Dana's thoughts drifted off, and soon she was surfing

the Internet through the wLAN. First of all, as she did regularly every morning she arrived at school, she ran the name *Pilgrennon* through all the good search engines. As with every other time she'd done it, she found nothing. Then she searched Jananin Blake's name. There were rather more new results this time. Dana simply skimmed over the headlines, not finding anything of particular interest.

Recalling the news broadcast from the night before and her consternation about Alpha, she searched for the Boolean string *+Compton +London +girl + unidentified +grave.*

All of the pages the search brought up were relevant. Dana had learnt very quickly to identify keywords when she wanted to find something. She scanned through the articles in search of the most detailed account, and found an excerpt from a broadsheet newspaper:

COMPTON BOMB VICTIM'S GRAVE DESECRATED

The grave of an unidentified girl who died of a heart condition during the London information terrorist attack was yesterday vandalised in the early hours of the morning. The culprits dug up the grave and broke into the coffin in a baffling act of desecration. Although the coffin had been opened, police have confirmed that the remains were complete and that nothing had apparently been removed from the burial site. Mr Roderick Burrell, the cemetery caretaker, discovered the grave yesterday morning. He commented: "It looked as though the grave had been exhumed with a small mechanical digger, rather than with a shovel, yet there are residential areas nearby and no-one questioned reported hearing any engine noise, and there were no tyre marks in the gateway or on the track leading to the grave. And it looked as though whoever had been there had an enormous dog with them — there were great big paw prints all in the disturbed earth. Police are appealing for anyone with information to come forward.

Dana turned her attention to another article:

COMPTON GIRL DUG UP BY A LION

An expert today identified the prints of a 'giant dog' in the disturbed earth dug from the grave of an unidentified girl who died of unknown causes in the London information terrorist attack as being those of a lion.

"Dana Provine!"

Dana looked up sharply. A snigger ran over the class, like wind rustling the branches in a wood.

"Sorry, what was the question again?"

The teacher glared at her through his grubby horn-rimmed glasses. "I asked you, what year did King John sign the Magna Carta?"

Immediately, she pulled the answer off the Internet. "June 1215."

The teacher did not look pleased, although the answer was correct. "Now pay attention!" he said, and turned back to the board.

Dana had lost the page where she'd been reading about the lion. She expected it was just a tabloid newspaper: most of them, when they did bother to report real news, reported it badly and incorrectly.

After the lesson, Dana went straight upstairs to the nearest girls' toilet. She never liked break-time, and she was worried that she might come across the fat boy who had chased her on Friday. She still had no idea where he'd got the Epsilon name from. The only person who'd ever called her that had been Ivor. It worried her. What if the boy knew more, like about Ivor, and Jananin?

The lavatory stank of cigarettes and excrement, but at least she would be hidden here. As with most of the more remote toilets on the upper floors, there were three cubicles and a line of sinks. Many of the downstairs toilets were large and filled up with girls smoking, swearing, graffiting, and using make-up during the breaks, and Dana never would use these toilets, let alone try to hide in them. She went to the farthest toilet from the door, against the wall. She pulled a piece of paper, a roll of sellotape, and a biro out of her bag. *OUT OF ORDER*, she scrawled on the paper. She pulled out a length of tape and bit it to break it, and taped across the sign, fixing it to the door.

Inside the cubicle, she locked the door and tried not to touch anything. She supposed she would have to think of a way to pass the fifteen or so minutes of break. Some steel part of the school's structure lay between her and the nearest wLAN, D2D, and the only signal she could find was distant and kept flickering off and on.

The door to the lavatories opened with a crash and a twitter of conversation liberally scattered with expletives. Almost automatically, Dana sat on the toilet lid and picked her feet up, holding them out horizontally in front of her. Someone kicked in the door of the cubicle next to her, and it banged against the partition, making the whole stall vibrate. A shadow passed under the door. "No-one in there," said a voice, and the shadow disappeared.

"That's 'cause it's out of order, thicko,"

Dana froze. That was Abigail Swift's voice. Abigail who had attacked Dana in the toilets in primary school, the same Abigail who had hit Dana's head off a sink and put her in hospital. That same Abigail that Dana had punched in self defence, and broken the nose of. Dana had been taken out of that school after what had happened, and taught in Cale's school with the two other most advanced students there, which had worked, until she'd had to start secondary school after summer.

Abigail was in the same year as Dana, but unlike Dana she was tall for her age and had a heavy build with thick ankles and wrists and a solid waist. She had a pasty face with small eyes and fat cheeks, and the crooked nose Dana had given her didn't improve things. She was the kind of girl people called ugly, but only from a distance. Dana and Abigail weren't in any classes together, but whenever she saw Abigail in a corridor or in the schoolyard, Abigail would glare at her, or whisper threats. Everywhere she went, Abigail was accompanied by two other big girls. If they realised she was here, the only chance Dana would stand of escape was if a teacher or a group of older pupils came in.

At the click of a lighter, Dana put her sleeve over her nose and breathed through the fabric. A few seconds later she could smell the stench of the cigarette despite it.

The girls had launched into a diatribe about some teacher called Miss Sullivan. Dana could tell from the voices she could hear that both Abigail's henchgirls were with her, as well as another girl. She was a recent addition, Abigail's *toady*. Quite small and unassuming, but nasty, with a sharp tongue and a knack for clever insults that the other three lacked.

Dana's nose itched. She tried to hold it back, but her eyes started to water. It was no good. She tried to muffle the sneeze in her sleeves, and when she did the gulp at the start of the sneeze the smoky air went in her mouth and lungs. What was worse, she was concentrating so hard on trying to sneeze as quietly as possible, she broke wind loudly at the same time from the pressure.

"What was that?"

"I bet it's that farty little runt Dana Provine!" That was Abigail.

"In Geography we were doing about Japan." The toady's voice. "She kept interrupting the teacher and telling her what food in Japan was made from. Like, she's obsessed with Japanese things. It's not like she'll ever be kawaii, little minger!"

The others all laughed at this.

A loud bang made Dana jump, and the cubicle door shook. "I'm gunna kick the crap outa you, Provine!" shouted Abigail.

Dana got to her feet and backed in between the toilet and the wall. They might kick the door in, or they might try standing on a toilet in the next-door cubicle and climbing over to get her. She had no idea what to do. Cold panic washed over her.

The bang of the main door came again, and an

authoritative female voice announced, "Right, girls! That's enough! Give me that, now. And the others."

"I've only got one, miss," came Abigail's voice.

"Whoever heard of a smoker with only one fag? Empty your pockets, please."

After much complaining and protesting, it sounded as though the teacher was satisfied.

"Miss, but there's someone in that bog, Miss," said one of the henchgirls.

"It's Dana Provine, Miss. She's always hiding in a toilet, with all the other crap," said Abigail.

"Right, the three of you are on detention! For smoking, and swearing. Report to my room after school."

"But we think she should be on detention too."

"There's no-one in that toilet. It says it's out of order."

"Yeh, right, and I suppose it was the farting ghost of the out-of-order toilet, Miss?"

"Outside, now please."

The cursing and sniggering of the girls faded away as they left. The teacher exhaled disgustedly. Dana kept still and silent, listening to the rattle of the window opening, and the noise of the cigarettes being flushed down the toilet. Then there came a loud rapping on the cubicle door. "Come on out then; I know you're in there."

There was not much point trying to hide from the teacher. Dana unlocked the door and opened it slowly.

"What are you doing in there?"

"Mostly just farts, Miss."

"Don't try to be smart, girl. What's your name?"

"Dana Provine, Miss."

The teacher's face softened slightly. Dana didn't know who the teacher was, but Dana's reputation always seemed to precede her with teachers, as though she was some sort of pathetic individual to be pitied. "I don't know why you want to hide in this stinking toilet when you could be out in the fresh air, it being summer and all."

"No, I don't either," said Dana, humbly.

"I'll make sure those other girls don't come back." The teacher left.

Dana's next lesson was science, which she liked. She tried not to think of the lesson she had after that, which was PE. The science teacher, Mr Kell, was a man with square glasses and grey curly hair, and an exuberant attitude that suggested he genuinely enjoyed teaching his subject. Dana sat down in her usual place beside the axolotl tank and arranged her pencil case and her science book neatly on the table as Mr Kell wiped the board clean. Then she copied down the title: *calorimetry*.

"Today we're doing a practical, and you need to organise yourself into groups of between three and four!" he shouted over the hubbub.

The other children leapt out of their seats and rearranged themselves, kicking over stools, dragging the lab benches around, and making noise in general. Dana stayed where she was, hunched over her lab book and trying not to let the noise and commotion overwhelm her. She looked at the axolotl inside its aquarium, a black newt-like thing with a blunt head, and marvelled at how it managed to put up with it. Perhaps it didn't have any ears.

"Come along, Dana," said Mr Kell, stepping down from the board to stand in front of her desk.

"Can't I do the experiment by myself?"

"If I let you do it by yourself, everyone will want to do it by themselves, and there's not enough equipment. Come on."

Dana got up reluctantly and followed him to the nearest group of girls.

"You don't mind if Dana joins you?"

One of the girls rolled her eyes, another scowled, and the third muttered something under her breath.

"There you go, then." Mr Kell pulled over a stool for Dana to sit on.

The experiment they had to do involved setting up some equipment to measure how much energy there was in a peanut. Dana got a heatproof mat, tripod, gauze, and a spike to put the peanut on and set them up on the bench. The other girls in the group just sat on their stools, talking and giggling. Dana fetched a conical flask and put water from the tap in it, and stood the thermometer in the water. Mr Kell came round, handing out peanuts for them to stick on the spikes when they were ready.

"Can I light my peanut yet?" Dana asked, pointing to the peanut on the spike.

"Have you measured the volume of the water and written down the starting temperature?" A commotion interrupted the rest of Mr Kell's answer. A boy behind him had eaten his group's peanut.

When all the groups had set up their apparatus, Mr Kell lit a Bunsen burner on the front bench. Dana lit a splint and carried the flame to her bench, and set fire to the peanut. She watched it turn black, but it kept burning for quite some time. While she was waiting, she started writing up the experiment. One of the other girls took one of Dana's pens from her pencil case and held it over the peanut, melting the plastic.

"Stop it!" Dana shouted, snatching back the pen. "Now the heat from the peanut has gone into the pen instead of the water, and the result won't be accurate!"

The girls tittered and jeered at her. Dana put her pencil case in her lap to stop it from being ransacked any further. When the peanut went out, she measured the temperature of the water and wrote the numbers in the equation to work out the joules of energy in the peanut. The other girls copied her calculation and kept on talking.

She was so engrossed in doing the calculation, she forgot about the time until Mr Kell called out, "Right, put the apparatus back! Your homework is to finish writing up the experiment and to do questions 1-6 on page 138 of the book!"

Then Dana remembered that she had PE next, and she still hadn't sorted out some way of getting out of lunch break, when that boy or Abigail might be looking for her. She grabbed the still-warm conical flask and held it up. "Look, sir!" she shouted, and threw it on the floor, where it broke and splashed tepid water all up the glassware cupboards.

"Dana!" he shouted. "You're on detention this lunchtime!" Mr Kell seized a dustpan and brush and thrust them into Dana's hands. "Pick it up and wait after class."

Dana swept up the conical flask and tipped it into the glass bin, while Mr Kell went round and round the class, shouting at them to get a move on. She waited at her desk after the lab was tidied. The bell went, and the other students filed out.

"What on Earth did you do that for, Dana?" Mr Kell's arms were folded and his mouth was drawn. "I've never seen you be disruptive before. You seem like a bright enough kid, and you're always polite and punctual, but sometimes," he shook his head, "I can't understand you at all."

Dana hung her head. There wasn't anything to say.

"Do you eat your lunch in the canteen, or do you bring your own?"

"I've got sandwiches," Dana said.

"Very well. Report here at lunch and bring your sandwiches. You'll have to help me muck out the axolotl."

Dana was pleased that she was on detention with Mr Kell at lunch. Mucking out the axolotl would be much more interesting than being in the schoolyard trying to avoid being seen by Abigail or the fat boy. Also because Mr Kell had kept her behind to speak to her, most of the children were already in their classes.

Instead of going to PE, Dana went to another part of the block to see if she could find an empty classroom. If she could find one with a wLAN, she could hide there for the lesson and then she wouldn't have to do PE, which she hated. For one thing she hated having to get changed in front of other people, and she hated the teacher watching her and the other kids in the shower and having to see her own and other people's revolting bodies, and for another thing Dana had never had a PE lesson in which she hadn't been called names and thumped, kicked, or hit with the equipment under the excuse of it being part of the subject.

"It's because you're turning into a woman," Pauline had said, again, when Dana had refused to go swimming with her any more. "It's nothing to be ashamed of."

But Dana had thought, *I want to just stay being me.*

She didn't know how Jananin Blake could stand up in front of an audience with her head held high and speak her mind when her body presumably had done all these same disgusting, embarrassing things that entailed being a *woman*.

Dana found an empty music classroom and went in. She was wondering whether she should try to get behind something when the door opened and a man entered. He was a short, fat man she had seen before, and Dana had heard other children refer to him as a music teacher called Slugs. He didn't see her at first, and when he did, he gave a yell and jumped back. "What are you doing in here? You nearly gave me a heart attack!"

"Er, I'm looking for my exercise book, I think I left it here this morning..." her voice trailed off.

Slugs went red in the face. "What rubbish!" he said, tossing his head so his chins wobbled and his forelock quivered. "Get to your class!"

"Sorry, Mr Slugs," said Dana, making past him for the door.

The teacher's face went even redder. "It's *Suggs*, you impudent little... right, you're on detention!"

"But I've already got detention this lunch break, with Mr Kell!" Dana objected.

"Then you'll just have to do it after school! And you'll have to do it with Mr Gordon's lot because I'm busy. Get yourself to physics at last bell. You do know where physics is, don't you?" He glared at Dana.

"Yes."

"What's your name?"

"Dana Provine."

"Now get out!"

When Dana went to the PE rooms, the class had already got changed and gone out. Dana found them on the all-weather pitch. "Dana!" the teacher shouted. "Go back and get your kit on!"

Dana walked as slowly as she could manage back to the changing rooms. When she arrived, there was half an hour of the lesson left. She decided to stay sitting in the reeking sweaty changing rooms and that she would tell the teacher there wasn't time.

When the class came back, the teacher was angry with Dana. She took her aside and spoke to her while the rest of the class used the showers and got changed.

"I've a good mind to put you on detention," the teacher started.

"I've already got detentions off Mr Suggs and Mr Kell," Dana countered.

"Sounds like your attitude is just as bad in your other subjects then. You're consistently late, you're always forgetting your kit, and when you do remember it and bother to turn up, you just stand there and refuse to participate."

"I'm no good at it," said Dana. "I can't understand the instructions."

"What are you, some sort of mental defective?" The teacher glared fiercely at Dana. "A retard could understand the instructions."

"You're not allowed to use that word any more," Dana retorted.

"Shut up, I've had enough of your lip. Get outside, now. I'm going to speak to your head of house."

Dana waited for the bell in the damp, putrid corridor between the boys' and girls' changing rooms. Some of the lessons she could see a point to. Adults needed to understand maths and English, and understand how to use computers properly, and science helped you understand how the whole world worked, and it was interesting too. But PE, what was the point of that, apart from to humiliate people? When in your life would the experience of being kicked and hit with sticks and balls, and having to take your clothes off in front of other people and be in front of them while they take theirs off, be useful to anyone? They didn't even teach martial arts for self defence, or the best technique for running away from rapists and murderers. Dana hated stupid, useless PE, and she really hated that stupid PE teacher.

Her eyes prickled and her vision blurred, and there came a sputtering noise, and a signal in her mind disappeared. She wiped her eyes on her sleeve, and looked at the wLAN B8G box on the wall. The lights on the front of it had gone out, and a thin stream of smoke drifted from it, pooling on the ceiling. Dana tried to pull herself together. It was no use letting herself get worked up, especially not if it broke the wLANs. After all, it wasn't their fault. She tried to concentrate on something positive, and thought of her carnivorous plant catalogue. Assuming the man who ran the mail order sent off the catalogue on the day after he received the SAE, it should have arrived that day. Dana would think about the end of the day, after the detention, when she could go home and decide what *Sarracenia* plants to order.

The bell went and, imagining a spectacular, *Sarracenia*-filled bog garden to rival the ones at the Kew Royal Botanic Gardens, Dana headed off to biology to do her detention. As she pushed through the throng of people, the overwhelming majority of whom were trying to get out instead of in, someone in the crowd grabbed her and shoved her against the wall. It was Abigail. Her two henchgirls stood on either side of Dana, blocking her escape.

"I'm gunna get you, Provine!" said Abigail, forcing her

greasy face into Dana's. "I'm gunna do to you what you did to me, and then some."

"Oi!" someone shouted. It was the teacher from the loos. Abigail and the others disappeared into the crowd. Dana hurried up the steps into the building.

She ate her lunch with Mr Kell and another teacher, trying not to think about Abigail's threat. Then it was time to clean the axolotl tank. Dana first caught the axolotl in a beaker, and stood it to one side. Then she and Mr Kell and the other teacher had to scoop out the water and pour it down the sink, and Mr Kell added a blue solution to some clean water to make it the right pH and get rid of any chlorine and things in it, and they poured that into the tank and put the axolotl back.

The next lesson was Geography, and the class made so much noise the teacher kept all of them in over break, so she didn't have to worry about finding somewhere to hide. The last lesson of the day was English, on the third floor of A-Block. Dana looked out the window while the teacher read two chapters of a boring novel, thinking all the time of home, the mat behind the front door, and how her catalogue was hopefully waiting there for her, in the SAE she'd sent.

-4-

WHEN the bell went, Dana headed for Mr Gordon's physics classroom.

"Mr Suggs sent me," she told him.

Mr Gordon, sitting at his desk marking, waved a hand towards the other kids dotted about the classroom. "Siddown, find some homework to do or something to read."

She ended up sitting behind a short-haired boy who'd shaved a swear word on the back of his head, but had got the *S* in it the wrong way round. She opened her bag, thinking she'd do her History homework, because it was boring and the wLAN at the school was faster than Pauline and Graeme's. She opened her exercise book on the desk and picked up her biro. A wind band was practising somewhere in the building, and discordant snatches of music interfered with her concentration.

"Patrick Moore plays the xylophone," someone sang in a forced basso voice. "Patrick Moore plays the xylophone!"

The teacher looked up from his desk. "Be quiet!"

Dana glanced in the direction the singing had come from. It was a fat boy on the desk in front, two seats to the left of the boy with the shaved head. His mop of brown hair looked the same shape as an unopened mushroom from behind, and the crumpled back of his shirt rode up over a broad back that was pale and spotty, framed by trousers that didn't come up far enough, giving the boy what Pauline used to call a Workman's Cleavage.

She stared hard at the boy, scrutinising his bag and coat. It was the same boy who had followed her yesterday, she was sure of it.

"I don't expect Patrick Moore did play the xylophone,"

said the teacher.

"He did!" the boy had a thick Birmingham accent. "It's on a website, sir!"

Dana bent over her work and leaned her head on her free hand, hoping it would hide her face.

Silence reigned for a few moments. Then, out of the corner of her eye, Dana saw the boy stretch and twist in his chair. He looked round and stopped, and she knew he must have seen her.

"Alpha, Beta, Gamma, Delta, *Epsilon*."

"Will you be quiet!" the teacher snapped.

"I'm doing me maths homework, sir!"

"Well, do it in your head."

"I can't sir, 'cause I'm *styowpid*."

"I don't care if you're stupid, so long as you're stupid quietly!"

Now Dana was starting to worry about how she would evade the boy while getting out of detention. Perhaps she could get out before him and run home, but which way should she go, the normal way or through the woods? If she went the normal way, the boy might be able to follow her, and then he would know where she lived. It might be better to hide somewhere until she was sure the boy had gone, and afterwards go home a completely different way. She put away any hopes she had of getting back in time to read her catalogue.

When the detention was over, she deliberately dawdled while putting her stuff away. The boy dawdled too until it was just the teacher and the two of them left, and after Dana had put all her things away in her pencil case, one by one, he was still there, picking up a heap of little paper circles that had come out of a hole punch. Dana crawled under her desk on her hands and knees as though looking for something.

"Oh, come on!" said Mr Gordon. "You, out!" he ordered the boy. "The cleaners will have to sort that mess out. Don't be so careless in future! What have you lost?" he said to Dana as the boy left the room.

"My pencil sharpener. It's all right, I've found it now." Dana showed him the pencil sharpener in her hand. She got up and put it away.

"Hurry up! Don't you have a home to go to?"

Dana ran out of the classroom. She went straight across the corridor and into the girls' toilet. She waited for exactly ten minutes.

She pushed open the door and surveyed the corridor. It was empty. Dana went to the stairs and through the door. The stairwells had windows all the way down, and from here the yard appeared to be deserted. The building faced east, and the late afternoon sun cast a long shadow upon the yard. In the clear blue sky a distant bird soared, but it caught the sun, flashing like metal. Dana squinted at it. Perhaps it was a small aircraft and not a bird. She hurried down the stairs to the front entrance.

As soon as she was out the door, four girls appeared from behind a building on the northern side of the yard. Abigail, and her henchgirls, and her toady. They came towards her with slow, determined strides, their faces grim, and Abigail punched the palm of her other hand.

Cornered in the toilets, Dana had not stood a chance, but here she could at least try. She jumped off the steps and ran across the yard as the three girls spread out and went for her.

Hands reached for her. Dana swerved and turned again, sprinted for the exit. Far ahead of her, a shadow raced across the all-weather pitch, and a strange note thundered in the air, somewhere between bagpipes and the gut-vibrating noise of a pipe organ. Dana realised the girls had stopped chasing her. She sensed a signal, and looked up to see something gliding down from the sky. The afternoon sun flashed off metal, giving an impression of a steel beak and claws, and enormous wings flexed and tilted to adjust the line of descent, aiming straight for her.

Dana turned and ran back to the school. Abigail and

the other girls screamed and scattered in her wake. Dana raced up the steps; a red light on the swipecard reader told her the door was locked, but it turned from red to green when she told it to unlock. Dana wrenched the door open, threw herself inside, and slammed it behind her. She turned, breathing hard, to see her pursuer alight at the top of the steps. At the braking instant of landing, the creature displayed huge batlike wings with steel vanes, that folded over a serpentine back plated with metal armour, tapering into a long tail, also covered with jointed metal plates, and ending in an arrowtip-like barb. Metal talons clicked on the paving, and a head with a hooked steel beak and steel fangs reared on a long, plated neck, and the amber eyes of some massive beast fixed on her.

Dana backed slowly away from the doors. The windows had chicken wire in the middle of the glazing. Hopefully the thing, whatever it was, would realise this and go away.

Nostrils flared and breath steamed the window. The creature's beak gave one experimental tap on the glass, and then it opened its mouth. Cracks exploded over the window's surface, and a shrill whine became audible, like a dentist's drill. Dana moved back faster as the creature pecked at the window, again and again, until the glass on both sides shattered and the head forced the wire into the building, scattering broken glass over the corridor. Three steel claws hooked over the bottom of the window frame. The foot was followed by another and, with wings furled tightly, the snakelike body began to follow the head into the room. Dana ran up the stairs. There might still be some teachers around. "Mr Kell!" she shouted. She burst into the physics lab. "Mr Gordon?"

Dana ran to the back of the classroom where there was a door to a teacher's office, but it was locked. She ran back to the corridor, but the creature had reached the landing. It lunged for her with its jaws as it forced its way through the doors. Dana screamed for help and ran back into the classroom. She tried to slam the door on the creature, but it just pushed it off, talons digging holes in the linoleum covering the floor.

Dana backed into the classroom and skirted around a desk. She looked at the thing, and it looked back at her. Apart from the membranes of its wings and a few exposed places on the underside of its body and the insides of its two legs, it was completely covered in armour. Long metal spines like knives stuck up from the dorsal line of its neck. A leather collar threaded with electronics boxes was buckled around the neck. She could feel lots of strange conflicting signals. Something was controlling it.

The creature lowered its head and opened its mouth, and a loud bagpipe-organ noise made the windows reverberate. Dana grabbed the fire extinguisher from the wall. She swung the heavy vessel at the creature's head, and it reared up its neck and struck the ceiling, cracking one of the ceiling tiles.

Dana backed away, breathing hard, and fought with the mechanism on the fire extinguisher. There was a plastic pin through it, stopping it from being used. Dana struggled to pull out the pin as the creature came towards her, mouth open, reaching for her with its beak. The pin broke, and she forced the nozzle up with one hand and clamped the two handles together with the other. A cloud of white smoke exploded from the fire extinguisher into the creature's face. Dana yelped and pulled her hand away from the nozzle, which had turned freezing cold. Before the thing could get out the way, she pressed the release valve on the fire extinguisher again and held, until the legs collapsed from under the metal beast and it fell with a crash that sent a tremor through the floor.

Dana dropped the fire extinguisher, gasping. Behind the collapsed monstrosity, someone stood in the doorway. It was the fat boy.

"Mint!" he said.

"Help me! Please!"

The boy jumped over the creature's tail and came over

to Dana.

"Spray the carbon dioxide in its face if it starts to wake up too much," she told him. The boy picked up the fire extinguisher, and Dana went to the side to undo the collar. "Do it, quickly!" The beast's neck had started to writhe. The fire extinguisher roared. Dana held her breath — it wouldn't do for her to breathe in too much carbon dioxide and pass out — and pulled undone both buckles. The collar came away in her hands, an attachment breaking away.

"Wait, now!"

The beast's head lay on one side, and its orange eye rolled senselessly. Its mouth closed and one of its legs flexed, digging its talons into the floor. Dana felt a sudden deluge of panic and fear and incomprehension, as though she'd had just woken up in a strange place with no idea how she'd arrived there. The realisation came to her with a mixture of awe and shock: this was not a machine, one of the computers she came across every day, this was a living mind that could interface, just as she could. That meant someone must have made it, just as someone had caused her to be the way she was, for things such as this didn't come about by natural chance.

There came a shout from the stairwell. Dana and the boy looked at each other. "Quick!" said the boy. "In the store cupboard!"

Dana threw open the store cupboard door. She had been in the physics cupboard before. It was a narrow space, its walls lined with shelves crammed with weights and rules and antiquated little computers and meters. On one shelf towards the back was a small lead safe containing samples of radioactive ores, which she remembered taking out and studying in one lesson, and under the bottom shelf were some smelly bags that contained the camping equipment for the Duke of Edinburgh award scheme. It was supposed to be called something different than the Duke of Edinburgh now, since the Electorate had voted to abolish the monarchy, but Dana couldn't remember what it was, and most people continued to call it the Duke of Edinburgh.

Dana pulled at the creature from the back, while the boy pushed from the front. In this way, they backed it into the cupboard. Dana crawled out between its legs, picked up the collar, threw it inside, and they closed the door. The next moment, the classroom door opened and Mr Kell came in. "What's going on?" he demanded. "There's a window downstairs broken."

A woman teacher appeared; the same one who had intervened earlier that day in the loo. Abigail's crew were behind her. "I caught these four hanging around outside."

"We'll deal with this in the office," said Mr Kell. He led them down the corridor to one of the teachers' common rooms. Dana sat down on one of the shabby chairs arranged around a table with tea and coffee equipment on it. If she could get through this without anyone looking in that physics cupboard, she would need to sneak back in after the teachers had gone, and try to remove the thing and work out what it was, otherwise Mr Gordon would find it there tomorrow morning and there'd be deep trouble.

"Now, I know you're Dana. What's your name again?"

"Eric Cartwright," the boy replied.

Dana turned her head to stare at him. *Eric Cartwright?* She'd known that name before, years ago. Someone calling himself Charon had helped her break into the world Cerberus had constructed around itself, and the name Dana had extracted from his computer had been Eric Cartwright. And she in turn, not wanting to reveal her name had given another, the name Ivor Pilgrennon had given to her and written in to the signal she gave out: *Epsilon.*

Kell wrote the names down on a notepad.

"And that one is Abigail Swift," said the other teacher. She put an odd emphasis on it, as though it was intended to mean something. She prompted the other three, and they gave their names. Kell wrote those down too.

"Now, what's been going on?" he asked. "Dana?"

Dana looked at Eric Cartwright, then at Abigail and her friends, and then at the teachers. Her skin crawled and she felt sick, but even if she'd wanted to be honest, they'd never believe her. She stared fixedly at Mr Kell when she spoke, because Dana's therapist had told her that making eye contact with people makes you appear more trustworthy. "Abigail's been pestering me all day, saying she's going to beat me up. When I came out of detention I saw she was waiting there and I was afraid to go out. They started shouting things through the door because they couldn't open it, and they threw a brick or something at the window and broke it, so I ran upstairs to the classroom, but Mr Gordon wasn't there."

"That's a lie!" Abigail said vehemently. "We never broke no window!"

"They did break the window. I saw them!" Eric's voice startled Dana. She was very afraid he would say something that might inadvertently discredit her lie or draw attention to what had gone on in the physics classroom. "I was in the same detention as her. We were both late out because my hole-punch broke and she dropped stuff under the bench. Mr Gordon will tell you if you don't believe it. I was coming down the stairs and she was in front, and I saw the other girls break the window."

"He's lying too, sir!" Abigail shouted. "What it was, we were hanging around outside, but we were just talking and like, and then *she* came out," Abigail pointed at Dana as though her name was a dirty word that must not be uttered, "and this *thing* came flying down..."

"This thing like a big snake-bird made of metal, with wings and a long tail," chimed in one of Abigail's friends.

"And she ran back into the school through the door, and the thing smashed the window and went after her."

"And it made this sort of trumpeting noise," said the other girl.

Mr Kell frowned. "I did hear an odd trumpeting sound

as I was coming upstairs."

"It probably was a trumpet," said Dana truthfully. "There's a band practising somewhere round here."

"Now wait a minute." The lady teacher raised her hands. "What you are saying, Abigail, is that a — let's not beat about the bush here — a *dragon* flew down and broke the window?"

"It wasn't a dragon, Miss, it was a robot or something. We all saw it!"

Mr Kell looked disgusted. "That is, without doubt, the worst story I've ever heard, in more than twenty years of teaching. You expect me to believe it, when Dana says you broke the window and this boy's account corroborates with hers, when we've got on written record that you have a vendetta against her?"

"I saw these girls behaving threateningly towards Dana at the end of lunchbreak," said the other teacher.

"And it was after school hours as well. That door would have been in autolock mode. There's no way Dana could have opened it from the outside like you described it." Mr Kell wrote something on his notepad. "I think it is crystal clear who broke that window. Any jury would easily see it, and I think your parents will, too." He looked at Dana and Eric. "It's obvious these two are not the ones at fault."

The other teacher got up and opened the door. "Dana, Eric, you can go now." Her voice became sterner. "You four, stay here."

Dana's limbs felt weak and wobbly from the stress of the interrogation and the subsequent relief as she left the room. She and Eric went downstairs without speaking. Eric headed out the back door of the building, where the warm afternoon sun shone through the door, the windows making bright squares on the floor. Dana followed him. She couldn't leave until she'd got back inside and sorted this out, and since he was here she might as well find out if he was Eric from the Cerberus game. If he was, he might be able to stick up for her if Abigail decided to hang around after the teachers let her out, although Dana did wonder if Abigail might leave her alone at least for tonight, if she thought Dana was in control of a 'robot dragon.'

The school's main block formed a right angle to a sort of courtyard, with the road to the teacher's car park completing the square on one side and the building with the science classrooms on the other. In the intersection of the paths that served all three was an unpaved area with a large rhododendron bush growing in it. Normally Dana would have given it a wide berth, because gangs of children used to use it as a smoking hide during break. Now all the other children had gone home well over an hour ago, and the school grounds were deserted. She grabbed the boy by the sleeve of his coat and ducked down under the branches.

The hollow interior of the bush was littered with crisp bags and cigarette butts. Insults and profanities had been carved into the bark of its twisted boughs. Surprisingly, foul language and fumigation hadn't affected the plant in any noticeable way; the leaves were glossy, and it had put forth its usual display of magenta flowers that spring, and the ones too high to be within reach still remained, withered and brown.

"You're Eric Cartwright? *Charon*, from the Cerberus game?"

"And you're Epsilon," he said.

"Why were you following me yesterday?" Dana burst out.

Eric shrugged. "'Cause I thought it was you, but I wasn't sure."

"Why didn't you just ask me?"

"You ran off."

"I thought you were going to attack me or something! You might at least have shouted 'I'm Charon, out of the Cerberus game' or something like that! I might've fallen down that stream and broken my leg!"

Eric suddenly grinned. "I thought you was gunna fly over it, like in the game."

"And howcome you look nothing like you did in the game? I mean, in the Cerberus game, you were a black man with white tattoos and a yellow punk hairstyle."

Eric glanced down at his crumpled shirt and scuffed shoes in a self-deprecating sort of way. "You think if I could look like anyone, I'd choose to look like me?"

Dana checked a stout branch to make sure there was nothing unsavoury on it, and sat down, giving Eric a grudging look. "Thanks for lying to the teachers for me."

"That's all right. Besides, it weren't a dragon, it wer' a wyvern. Dragons have six limbs, and that thing's only got two legs and a pair of wings. 'Though I don't expect they're likely to care about a technicality like that once a teacher opens that cupboard tomorrow morning. It'll likely give the poor git a heart attack!"

"That's why I need to talk to you," Dana explained. "If we wait until the teachers go, we'll have to see if we can get in there and bring it out."

"*We?*" Eric exclaimed. "You're telling me to, like, break into the school with you?"

"All right. Go home if you don't want to. I don't care."

"Uh. Oh, well, I don't mind, really, I mean." Eric turned his head towards the direction of the school, although it was obscured by leaves. "But if we get caught, we'll be in trouble for breaking in as well as lying and hiding a wyvern in the physics cupboard."

After a pause, Dana asked, "How do you know the difference between a wyvern and a dragon anyway?"

"From playing computer games." Eric sat awkwardly on a branch opposite Dana. "It's a machine, isn't it? I wonder where it comes from. Perhaps it's an ANT." He looked at Dana. "ANT stands for Array of NeuroTechnology, and they're a new type of computer that the Meritocracy—"

"I know what an ANT is!" Dana interrupted. "And it's not an ANT anyway."

"How do you know? Have you ever seen an ANT? Do you know what one looks like?"

"It's not a computer, it's something that's *alive*." Dana shifted her seat on the branch. The wyvern — if that was what it was — had been full of pain and fear and panic, and much too complicated to be a computer, even an advanced computer that could learn emotions like Cerberus was. It was true that she didn't know what an ANT felt like, but she knew what Peter and Cale felt like, and she knew what computers felt like, and there was a world of difference between the computer and the others. "Don't ask me how, I just know."

"*Right*," said Eric, in a voice Dana supposed he intended to sound irritating. "What did you say your name was again?"

"Dana."

Eric's expression suddenly changed. "Not Dana *Provine*?"

"Yes," said Dana, starting to get annoyed. "How do you know?"

"You're sort of, what's the word for famous, but in a bad way? *Infamous*. The name Dana Provine is kind of, well, an insult, but I never knew who it actually was before."

"What d'you mean, an *insult*?" Dana snapped at him.

Eric was going red in the face. "Well, boys say things like 'If you can't climb that tree, you love Dana Provine', and stuff like that. I mean, I expect people say it about me as well. I expect girls say, 'If you can't do... whatever it is girls like to do... you love Eric Cartwright,' don't they?"

"I don't know," said Dana coldly. "I don't know any girls."

Eric started to say something else, but the sound of the science block door opening interrupted him. "Shut up!"

The pair sat in silence, listening to the footfall and lowered voices of the two teachers as they made their way past the bush and onto the road. A moment later came the sound of an engine starting up. Dana crouched down to look out through a gap under the bush. The teachers' cars were following each other off towards the exit.

Dana and Eric crept out of the bush through the opposite side. By the time Dana got round to peer out to the road, both cars had already gone. She hurried up the path to the door. The red light showed on the card swipe lock, but the door unlocked at her command.

Dana pulled the door and it swung open. "The teachers mustn't have shut it properly," she told Eric.

"Wait!" He pointed to the corner of the building, from where a CCTV camera observed them with its black lens.

"I don't expect anyone bothers to watch the film out of that every night," she said. "I mean, there'd be no point, unless the building did get broken into and something got stolen or damaged. And we're not going to steal or vandalise, are we, stupid?" Dana was still angry with Eric for saying her name was an insult. She didn't know whether people did watch the CCTV footage. All she did know was that the camera would record only an empty image of the door for the whole time she and Eric were standing in its view, as this was the picture she was overriding it with now. But she didn't want to tell Eric that, and she didn't expect he'd even believe her if she did. She held open the door behind her and Eric followed her in.

The place wasn't so bad when there weren't other children in it, she thought as they climbed the stairs. It was almost peaceful, with the afternoon sun warming the stairwells and corridors. They reached the first landing and crept through the doors, but when they tried the door to the physics classroom, it was locked. Above the handle was a combination lock keypad. Dana checked the school's intranet using a nearby wLAN. There was a database with the combinations for all the rooms in it, and she easily found the entry for this physics classroom.

"I saw a teacher do it," she told Eric as she keyed in the code.

Dana felt for the wyvern's signal inside the cupboard, fearing she might have been wrong about the collar, and that it would attack again as soon as they opened the door. From what she could sense, she was sure it was safe and would do no such thing.

Inside the cupboard, the wyvern did not seem to be so agitated as it had been before. Dana put up her hand and touched the cold metal of its beak. Its nostrils flared, sending a current of air over her hand. Its amber eyes were glassy, protected by solid lenses the size of tennis balls, and there were protective steel shutters retracted into the head above it, but the eyelids were of grey skin, like the nostrils. Behind the tip of the beak there were pairs of protruding metal teeth on either side, the bottom one interlocking with the top one, and both having serrated edges on their contacting sides.

Eric sighed behind her. "It's *amazing*. I wonder who made it."

"Someone was controlling it." Dana picked up the collar off the floor. "Through this. We'd better get out of here." She put her hand on the armour plating of the wyvern's neck. It had no understanding of words, so she projected a feeling of liking and kindness towards it, and visualised the journey out of the cupboard, out of the physics classroom, downstairs, through the door, and to the rhododendron bush. She and Eric walked on either side of the wyvern's head, each with a hand on its metal-plated neck. The stairs creaked alarmingly under the weight of the three of them, and the wyvern had to furl its wings tightly to fit through the back door. Finally, they coaxed it inside the rhododendron bush, where it crouched down, its long body arranged in a curve around the central trunk.

"What are we going to do with it?" Eric said. "We could hide it in my garage for now, but people'll notice if we walk down the street with it!"

Dana had been thinking hard about this all the way down the stairs. The wyvern had been sent for her. Whoever had been controlling it through the collar had commanded it to come here and attack her, even kill her, maybe. And then there was the matter of Alpha's grave. She had to tell someone, and it was no good telling Pauline and Graeme, or a teacher, as she would then have to tell them about Ivor and Jananin, and how she could mentally control computers.

No, she had to tell Jananin. And Jananin was far away, a scientist and a spokesman for the Meritocracy, and she had told Dana she had a family to belong to, and she didn't want to be contacted by her. But Jananin had friends who would be less conspicuous, and there might be a way Dana could get a message to her without risking it being intercepted. Rupert Osric. He had alerted Jananin when Dana had been taken in to hospital.

"There's a man who might be able to help us," Dana said. "He sometimes works at the hospital. If we can go there, we might be able to find out where he is."

"The hospital? Who is he?"

Dana checked the time, and was shocked to realise it was half past five already. "I'll have to tell you later. I've got to go home and have my dinner now."

"Let's meet here at seven." said Eric. "I can sort out transport... but wear sensible clothes... not high heels and a short skirt or anything like that."

Dana had already set off towards home, and she shouted back disparagingly over her shoulder. "I don't wear stupid things like that anyway."

-5-

DANA arrived out of breath, back at Pauline and Graeme's house. She pulled off her shoes in the hallway and ran upstairs to her room.

"Dana, is that you?" Graeme shouted. "Or is it a burglar!"

"It's a burglar!" Dana shouted. She kicked the laundry about the floor until she found a pair of jeans and a long-sleeved T-shirt. She heard Graeme coming upstairs as she threw her school uniform on the bed.

"Can I come in?"

"No! I'm getting changed!"

"You're home very late today."

"I got detention, and then... something else happened."

"Your catalogue came today!"

"Oh!" Dana had completely forgotten about the catalogue. "Wait fifteen seconds!"

Graeme laughed. "All right, then."

Dana counted fifteen seconds as she did up her jeans and pulled her t-shirt on. When she opened the door, Graeme was outside with the catalogue.

"Thank you," she said.

"We're going to have dinner now, so leave it in your room and come down. You can read it afterwards."

Dana quickly pulled her keys, fuses, and Ivor's watch out of her school uniform and transferred them to her jeans. She followed Graeme downstairs. Pauline was setting the plates on the dining room table, and the news was just starting.

"Detention," Graeme mouthed to Pauline.

"Oh, really, Dana!" Pauline chided.

Dana started to cut up her food before anyone else had

been seated.

"Cale? Cale!" Pauline called.

"Oh come on, Dana, don't start without everyone else," said Graeme severely. "It's not polite."

Cale was in the sitting room, lying on his stomach on the floor and working out the next line of notes for Pi in C Major. Dana mentally told him to stop it and come into the dining room.

On the small television in the corner of the room, Jananin Blake was making a brief statment about nuclear powerplants. It didn't matter now if Dana missed the news, because soon she was going to see Jananin Blake in person again! If Graeme and Pauline let her go, of course...

Cale sat down at the table and began to divide his stew, apportioning carrots to one side of his plate and meat to the other. "Honestly," said Pauline, glancing at Cale's plate. "Sometimes I don't know why we bother actually cooking his food." She squeezed behind Cale's chair and sat down.

"Can I go out after dinner, please?" Dana asked.

"I don't see why not," said Graeme with his mouth full.

Dana realised he thought she was talking about the seed catalogue and the *Sarracenias*. "I don't mean out in the garden. I mean, can I go out and see Eric?"

"Who's Eric?" said Pauline.

"Uh, he's my friend," said Dana, uncertainly. Dana knew that Pauline knew that Dana didn't have any friends. But Dana also knew that Pauline lived in eternal hope of her having them.

"How old is he?"

"I think he's in the year above me. He goes to the school."

Graeme put his cutlery together neatly on his plate. "What are you going to do?"

"Hang around?" said Dana, aware that this was how children her own age referred to being in the company of their peers, and also uncomfortably aware that it sounded unnatural and very insincere coming from her own mouth. "There's this biology thing at school. You can go to it sometimes at lunch. Eric and I are doing a project for it, and we were going to look for, uh, ideas to do our project on."

"You mean like a school club?" Pauline asked.

"Ya, like a biology club."

"And it is just you and Eric, not you and a load of Eric's other friends?" Pauline looked at Dana penetratingly.

"I don't think Eric's got any other friends. Most of the people at the biology club haven't." So far as Dana knew, there was no biology club at the school. A prickly heat had begun to crawl up the back of her neck, and she hoped she wasn't going red in the face.

"And the biology club and Eric are more interesting than *Sarracenia* seeds?" Graeme paused to chew. Dana thought he was amused by this from the way his voice sounded, but she wasn't sure. "And watching Demented Badger Woman on the news?"

Pauline glared at Graeme upon speaking his last sentence. "Graeme, she is a perfectly respectable person. Stop being mean to Dana about her! Dana, where are you planning on going with this boy?"

"I'm just going to meet him by the school." This much at least was true.

"In that case I don't see how it will do any harm, if you take mine or Graeme's phone with you, and you get back before nine. What do you think, Graeme?"

"Fair 'nuff," said Graeme, cabbage trailing from his mouth.

Dana ate her dinner as quickly as she could and excused herself from the table. Remembering what Eric had said, she found the most boyish jacket she could: a denim one with heavy metal badges sewn on it. It had belonged to Duncan but he was too big for it now, and he'd given it to Dana. Graeme went with her to the front door. "Here," he said, giving her his phone. Dana put the phone in her jacket pocket and put her trainers on in the porch. "Now, be careful."

"I know." Dana hurriedly tied her laces.

"No, I mean be careful. We don't know who this Eric is. It would've been easier if you'd found some friends of the same sex before you had a boy friend."

"But that's sexist! And Eric's nice, and I don't know any girls that are." It suddenly occurred to her what Graeme might be getting at. "I'm not going to see Eric so I can snog him and do stuff like that! That would be disgusting! He's just a normal friend, like I'm friends with you and Cale!"

"Well, okay then, but be careful anyway."

Dana ran all the way to the school. There was no sign of Eric yet, so she ducked inside the rhododendron bush. The sun was starting to set, and the light filtered through the gaps in the leaves and cast glints of warm colour on the metal plates covering the wyvern's body.

Dana concentrated again on projecting a feeling of benevolence, and reached out slowly and smoothly, and touched the fan of metal blades on the back of its cheek. She ran her fingers along the neck, to where rough, thick skin met steel plates. When she looked at it, this thing that seemed as much machine as beast, she could not help feeling awe and fascination. And she could feel from the wyvern that it was equally interested in her, and it recognised that she too was part machine. It stretched its head towards her and sniffed, nostrils dilating and narrowing with each breath, like those of a horse.

In the distance, a throbbing noise became audible. It sounded like some sort of small, coarse motor, and it was getting closer. Dana sank back into the rhododendron as a motorcycle came down from the school gates and braked to a halt just before the teachers' car park. The rider — it looked like a short plump man beneath the leather jacket — switched off the engine and kicked down a lever to prop up the bike before dismounting. Nothing of his face could be seen beneath his helmet, and he had his arm hooked through a second helmet. He began to walk towards the rhododendron bush. *Surely he won't look in here?* Dana tensed and laid her hand on the wyvern's flank, under the wing joint.

The figure was bending over and reaching out to draw aside the leaves. He was going to look inside the rhododendron. "Are you there?" said a familiar voice, and the visor snapped up to reveal the eyes of a boy, behind thick-framed glasses.

"*Eric!*" Dana was both relieved and annoyed. The wyvern's head jerked up.

"Is it all right?" Eric held out the helmet. "Here, you'd better put this on."

"I think so. Aren't you too young to ride on a motorbike?"

"It's a moped. You're supposed to be sixteen to ride it on the road."

"And how old are you?"

"Fourteen. But the school's private property, so it doesn't count as a road."

"You must have driven it on the road to get here, unless you rode it on the pavement!"

"Well, yes. But it's not like I speed or ride like a prat or anything. If we're going to go to the hospital, we'll need transportation. The buses round here are rubbish."

Dana looked at the moped and thought about Jananin's katana, and the time when Ivor had stolen a helicopter. It wasn't like riding a moped was going to hurt anyone. The helmet was lined with padded material with a furry surface, like car upholstery. It pressed snugly against the sides of her face.

"Do you like Stratovarius?" Eric asked as she came out of the rhododendron.

"Someone else gave it to me." Dana realised he was commenting on the jacket. "Stratovarius are all right, though."

"Have you ridden pillion before?" Eric's words were muffled through the helmet.

"What? Oh, you mean on the back of a bike? No."

"OK. Just get on behind me and hang on to my jacket."

Dana climbed astride the moped behind Eric. She held onto the leather belt at the bottom of the jacket. She quickly looked up the law about riding pillion from the school's wLAN, and it seemed it was allowed if you were under 17, but only if you had permission from your legal guardian, which Dana didn't have. "Do you know where the hospital is?"

"I think so. I'll go slowly up to the gate so you can get used to it. Put your feet up on the footrests."

Eric started the engine, and Dana watched the road go by through the visor. Eric turned right at the gates and began to accelerate. The moped felt unstable, and wind roared past her helmet. Not much of the road ahead was visible, as Eric's shoulders were in the way. A car overtook them and the bike wobbled in its slipstream. Dana pressed her knees into the saddle.

The hospital was busy, with ambulances passing back and forth from the main entrance to a depot outside the main building. Eric steered into the car park and parked the moped in an area with railings containing other bikes. Dana pulled her helmet off and handed it back to Eric.

Up at the hospital entrance, two paramedics burst from the back of an ambulance. They pulled out a stretcher bearing a middle-aged woman with an oxygen mask over her face. Wheeled legs unfolded from under the stretcher to meet the tarmac as it left the vehicle. That must be how she had arrived the last time she had been here, Dana thought. She remembered nothing of the moments between the school lavatories and the arrival at the hospital, because Graeme said she'd had a fit and the paramedics had to sedate her to stop her from hurting herself.

"Let's hurry," she said, and set off at a brisk pace.

"Who is this bloke we're looking for?" Eric asked.

"His name's Dr Osric. He's some sort of a scientist."

Dana pushed open the door to the hospital reception.

People were seated around the waiting room on plastic chairs, not unlike the ones in school. There was a woman behind the desk and two men, porters, in blue shifts, standing by the doors to the wards. She felt for a signal, but the only one she could find was from a wLAN connected to the Internet but not to the hospital's own private network. She noticed one of the people in the room was using a handheld computer; the wLAN must just be here so people could use the Internet while they waited. She knew there was another one, one with higher security, that was used by the hospital staff, as she had accessed it when she had last been here, but the signal was out of range here, probably to make it harder to hack into. Yes, patients' records were confidential, so the wLANs must be set up so they couldn't be accessed in any public areas on the site.

"Eric," she said, "I need to get inside. Can you make a diversion?"

"What do you mean, a diversion?"

Dana motioned to one of the porters. "I need to get into the corridor. Go to the desk and say you want to be in the queue to see a doctor, and try to distract that man so I can get through the door."

Eric frowned. "Oh, all right. If I get caught, I'm telling them you told me to do it, though."

"Okay."

Eric bowed forward slightly, both his hands clutched to his abdomen. He walked in a pained fashion to the desk and stood there until the receptionist looked at him. "I keep being sick," he said. "And it always comes out purple." He made a loud retching noise and lunged over the desk. The receptionist kicked back so her chair scooted across the floor, and everyone in the lobby stared. The porter rushed forward to intercept Eric.

Dana slipped across the room to the unguarded door. There was a card swipe reader to one side of it, but the light turned green when Dana told it to. She opened the door only just far enough for her to fit through, and let it click shut behind her. She stood back against the wall and listened. The commotion in the lobby died down. Once she was sure no-one was coming after her, she turned away from the door and began to walk down the corridor until she sensed a signal. Yes, that was the hospital network she remembered from the time she had been here before.

A number of unused wheelchairs were parked in the space beneath a stairwell. Dana sat down on one of the chairs and concentrated on the wLAN signal. She didn't suppose it would make very much difference if someone came down the corridor and saw her sitting on a chair or standing, but she felt less conspicuous this way.

It didn't take long for her to find Rupert Osric's name on a database of specialist contacts. The name of the company he worked for was also recorded, along with a company phone number. There was no private address given, but there were two out of hours phone numbers, one a mobile and the other a local one.

Dana committed the local number to memory before getting up and making her way back to the foyer. The porter was looking the other way, so she just opened the door and went out. She used the wLAN in the reception area to look up the phone number on the Yellow Pages Internet site, and found where Osric's house was.

"Well, where's this bloke?" said Eric's voice. "Don't just stand there staring into space."

"Oh, he's not here." Dana turned to face the boy. "He doesn't work here tonight, but I've found his address. Let's get out of here."

In the car park as they were walking back to the moped, Eric asked, "You want to go there now, then? You don't think we should ring him first?"

Dana feared that Osric would not believe her if she told him over the telephone that there was a wyvern under a rhododendron bush in the school grounds. "No, let's just go there. He lives in a place called Radford... Se-me-le?"

"Radford Smelly," Eric corrected her. "That's where the posh people live. I'll have to get a map out."

"I can just direct you as we go." Dana had already worked out the fastest route to Osric's house in Radford Semele using GPS. "It'll be faster that way."

After another twenty minutes of wobbling on the back of Eric's bike, and thumping Eric on the shoulders to indicate which way to turn, as neither of them could hear the other through their helmets, they found themselves at a hedge secluding a garden and driveway from the road in a quiet *cul-de-sac*. Eric switched off the engine and kicked down a spring-loaded rubber-footed prong to balance the bike on.

Dana pulled off her helmet and handed it back to him. "This is it." The sun had set and dusk was closing in. Whatever house might lie behind the hedge was completely hidden from the road. The place was too private, foreboding, almost. How might Osric react when he saw her? She didn't want him — or herself — to blurt out something in front of Eric that he might ask questions about, something about Jananin, about what had gone on back around the time of the information terrorist attack on London before the Meritocracy was voted in. "Maybe it's best if you wait here while I speak to him first."

The boy snapped up his visor. "Well, all right then. But I don't see how this is going to help us or the wyvern."

She wondered if Eric was getting annoyed as she walked up Osric's drive. Dana wasn't very good at guessing what other people were thinking. A pang of doubt hit her. Was she doing the right thing? After all, Doctor Osric had been part of the conspiracy that had resulted in Jananin taking her from the hospital.

A security light clicked on as she approached the porch, a blinding glare in her face like the beacon of the lighthouse of Eilean Mor, that cut through the dusk and cast a long shadow behind her. Pinned to the window beside the heavy wood door was a small placard that proclaimed in bold writing: *No Hawkers, No Junk Mail, No Religious Representatives.*

Dana would have hated the idea of going alone to the front door even of someone she knew, but considering this was someone she had met once and probably not made a good impression upon made it even worse. She tried to recall a moment in which Osric had shown any hint of concern towards her, but all she could bring to mind was how clinical he had been and how driven to find out the origins of the device in her head. He'd informed Jananin that Dana was at the hospital; he'd probably watched her sneak out of the back exit and told Jananin where to go so she might catch Dana, and he'd destroyed the CCTV evidence of the incident afterwards.

He told her where I was because she is my genetic mother and she was looking for me, Dana reassured herself, but she knew the truth was not as simple as that.

For a moment she hesitated. She almost went back to the hedge, meaning to ask Eric if he could think of any alternative suggestions. No, she told herself, she had to get word to Jananin about the wyvern. Jananin was the only person she could trust, and Osric was the only one she could contact her through. Osric didn't care about her, but he was loyal to Jananin, and Jananin was the only person Dana felt she could trust with the wyvern.

Dana reached up and banged the brass knocker twice. She stepped back and waited, the security light in her face blinding her. Her pulse thumped in her neck.

She saw the inner porch door open through the window, and the shape of a man, indistinct from the contrast of the spotlight, came to the door. When the door opened, she struggled to fit the face of the man — curly-haired and with metal-framed spectacles — with her own memory from the hospital.

"What do you want?" he demanded. The glare above his head made his face craggy, ravaged with deep lines and hollows.

"Doctor Osric?" said Dana.

Osric's expression changed. "How do you know my name?" He reached to his side and seized the handle of an umbrella. He brandished it at Dana, the lenses of his spectacles flashing, his eye sockets and mouth dark circles in his towering face. "You're trespassing on private property! Leave, or I'll call the police!"

"I'm Dana Provine!" Dana held her hands up in front of her face. "Do you not remember, in the hospital, when I hit my head, and you told Ja—"

Osric had suddenly thrown his umbrella on the floor. "Don't speak that name here, where anyone and his brother may overhear it! What is it you want?"

"Perhaps I had better tell you it in your house," Dana suggested timidly. "If you don't want people to overhear it."

Osric glanced back at his porch, as though he feared Dana's appearance might be a diversion for a burglary. "Very well, then, but don't touch anything."

"There's someone else with me. Can I just get him?"

The man stared down at her, suspicion in his face. "Make it quick."

Dana went back to the hedge. "He says we can come in," she told Eric.

Eric followed her back up the drive and into Osric's porch. Osric did not invite them into his living room nor offer them somewhere to sit. He merely closed the front door and led them into his hallway.

"You can speak now," he said.

There was no light on in the hall, a narrow corridor with a dingy carpet, a coat hanging from the end of the banister, and a telephone sitting on the second stair. Through the various doors leading off could be seen unwashed dishes in a kitchen, an armchair with paperwork strewed about it in the living room.

"We found a, a creature," Dana began.

"A machine," Eric countered.

"A sort of mechanical creature. It flew down from above the school and attacked me, but there was a collar on it that was telling it what to do. We managed to get the collar off it and hide it, but if we leave it there until tomorrow someone will find it."

Osric folded his arms. "What?"

"It's a wyvern," Eric explained. He'd lost the confident air he'd had before, and now he looked insincere, like he was playing a joke on Osric and not managing it very convincingly. "You know, like a dragon but with only two legs."

"It's a weapon… some sort of technology. We need you to tell…" Dana knew she couldn't speak Jananin's name in front of Eric, "…someone about it for us."

"Well," Osric regarded them both through narrowed eyes, "before I tell *someone* about this rather unlikely sounding thing, I will need to see it for myself."

"You'd better come and look at it then," said Dana. "But if we're going to move it, you'll need to get a van."

Doctor Osric's eyes became even narrower. "I can get one. I'll need to go somewhere else first, though."

"You'll have to meet us at the back of the school, then. Have you got SatNav?"

Osric produced a GPS-enabled smartphone from his pocket and let Dana enter the school's postcode.

Dana and Eric walked back to the bike while Osric locked his front door. "Who the hell is he?" said Eric in a low voice. "He's a git."

"He's some sort of scientist who works for the Meritocracy. He knows people in the military and stuff like that. And you're right, he is a git," Dana admitted. "But at least he's listened to us and he's going to come and look."

"Mint." Eric hesitated, a frown deepening on his face. "But what will the people in the army and the scientists and all that do to the wyvern? I mean, what if it's, like, an alien or a cyborg or something, and they kill it so they can dissect it? Like in America, when a spaceship crashed at

Roswell and the government covered it up?"

Dana wasn't sure what he was talking about, or even if it was true. "America is different to England. They don't have meritocratic law there."

"But how do you know what they're going to do?"

A sick, guilty feeling was starting to close on Dana, like an iron fist around her stomach. Jananin would know what to do. Jananin *must* know what to do. There wasn't anyone else she could tell. "It's not like we can keep it hidden even if we don't give it to them. It might be a terrorist weapon. Or it might belong to the military anyway, and we'll just be giving it back."

Headlamps flared behind the hedge, and Osric's car swung into the road and turned away. Eric passed his spare helmet back to Dana. "We'd better go and wait for him, in that case."

By the time they reached the school, dusk had passed into darkness. Eric leaned his bike up close to the wall. The few sodium streetlamps about the grounds were too far apart to illuminate the rhododendron bush well.

"Have you got a torch?" said Eric. "I can't see if the wyvern's still there."

"I can see it. It's okay." Dana couldn't see the wyvern, but she'd been able to tell where it was from its signal since they'd arrived.

Eric shuffled his feet awkwardly, and after a moment said, "If he takes it away, we're never gunna know where it's gone. He'll give it to the government and they'll cover it up and pretend it didn't happen."

"There's no *government*. Besides, we can follow him, find out where he takes it."

"You know what I mean, the Meritocracy's military or whatever it is. And we can't follow him on my bike if he's in a van. It's only a moped."

"We can make him take us with him."

"How can we make him? Besides, there's two of us. There'll only be one passenger seat in the van."

"He'll take me with him."

"Why?"

"Because I have a relative who's a friend of his."

Eric balked. "What, a good enough friend to go off in a van with him, on your tod? What if he's, like, some kind of pervert or something?"

Dana retrieved Graeme's mobile from the pocket of Duncan's heavy metal jacket. She couldn't transmit in the frequency used for mobile phones, but she could use the phone's Bluetooth capabilities to control it and send messages through it. "What's your phone number?"

Eric pulled his phone out of his trouser pocket and Dana copied the number into Graeme's phone's contact list.

"When we get to wherever he's taking it, I'll send you a textmessage with the postcode. Then you can follow."

Eric muttered something to himself as he put away his phone. "I still don't think we should give the wyvern to him. It came to us. There might be a reason for it."

"What reason?"

"Well, something like," Eric gesticulated wildly with his hands, "like it's from an alien civilisation, and there's a war out there that's coming to Earth, and it's on the good side and it's come to warn us, and it's got telepathic powers and it can tell that we're the people who can help it, 'cause we've got mutations we don't know about that give us special abilities."

"Then why did it attack me until I got the collar off it? And it's not from another planet."

"It might have been that we had to fight it to prove our worth to it! And how do you know it's not from another planet?"

"I dunno," said Dana. "You said yourself it's a machine." There was a reason the wyvern had come to her, but Dana was certain it was nothing like any of the reasons Eric was coming up with. Nevertheless, she was starting to doubt her own judgement, and regretting more and more her decision to involve Osric. She had immediately thought of the wyvern as an excuse to contact Jananin, rather than thinking about what might be best for it. She could feel the signal from it the whole time she'd been standing by the rhododendron bush speaking with Eric, and by now she was certain that its mind was nothing less than her own. If only she'd thought about it more before rushing into things.

"It might be a cyborg, with a mechanical exoskeleton to protect it when it travels in space. You know, like the Daleks on *Dr Who?*"

Dana knew it wasn't any of the outlandish things Eric was suggesting, but she couldn't prove it to him without revealing more than she thought was safe, and if this carried on the conversation would just go round in circles. "Have you got any other suggestions of where we can hide it, and how we can get it there?"

Eric's face was barely discernible in the deep twilight, but Dana heard him exhale as he thought his answer over. "No."

Light passed, illuminating Eric and showing a glint of steel under the rhododendron bush where the wyvern hid. A whisper of tyres separated from the noise of the road as a vehicle turned off into the school's drive.

"Then it's too late," Dana said.

The van came slowly to a halt by the bush and the engine switched off. Osric got out without switching off the headlamps.

Dana mentally suggested to the wyvern that it come out. Osric sucked in breath and took a halting step back towards his vehicle at the clank of metal and the emergence of a large indistinct form from the bush.

"You found this, *inside* the school?"

"It flew down," Eric said. "It came into the school and we hid it."

Osric squinted against the headlamps, studying the wyvern's unreal physiology. "But it's made of metal. It couldn't possibly fly."

Eric shrugged. "If you say so." He glanced at Dana before making an obvious point of looking at his watch. "My mum will be expecting me back soon. I'd better go."

Dana watched him ride away, the noise of the bike's motor receding as he disappeared around the corner of the school's main building. Time to face Osric alone.

Osric scowled and said, "You should go home as well. Your parents will probably want you to have a bath or go to bed, or something of that nature."

Dana knew he intended it as an insult, but years of being insulted by bullies had given her a sort of immunity. *Don't rise to it*, Graeme used to say. *It's beneath you. Just ignore them*. Dana had always thought that it surely didn't make sense that she should or shouldn't *rise* to something *beneath* her, and ignoring bullies might all be very well in principle, but in practice what the bullies then do is scream something about being deaf, and hit, kick, or spit when this elicits no response.

Osric didn't seem the sort of person to scream in someone's face, and Dana knew he wouldn't hit her either, because it was taboo for adults to touch children. None of the teachers at the school were allowed to hit the kids, and even in cases when they were forced to restrain them to stop them from attacking each other, they had to fill in special incident forms.

"I'm going with you."

Osric gave a halfhearted laugh. "You aren't."

"How are you going to move the wyvern without me?" she answered.

Osric glared at her.

"You can't control it without me. It doesn't understand instructions. And it doesn't trust you either."

"I see. And is that because you told it not to trust me?"

The wyvern watched Osric and didn't move. Dana could sense a feeling of tiredness emanating from it. It didn't like this man, but perhaps that could be because *she* was emanating dislike?

"Order it to get into the back of the van."

"Only if you'll take me with it!"

Osric glanced between Dana and the wyvern. "Do it and I'll consider it."

"You won't be able to get it out if I'm not there. And it might get frightened and attack you."

The wyvern stretched its neck upwards, the hooked steel beak glinting in the streetlight. Osric took a step back. "Very well." He opened the back door of the van. Dana looked into the empty space within, and imagined going into that place, thinking of it as a safe haven. The wyvern climbed up, the van dipping slightly under its weight, and settled on the floor, turning so its tail curved round to fit.

Dana thought briefly to the wyvern to stay in place and keep calm before he closed the door.

As soon as they were inside the van and the doors were shut, she demanded, "Where's Jananin? Have you contacted her yet?"

"I don't think Jananin Blake would appreciate me divulging that information." Osric turned the wheel to swing the car in a broad circle over the teacher's car park and drove back for the exit onto the main road.

"I have to speak to her!"

"I'll decide that."

Dana looked across at Osric's dishevelled hair and disagreeable scowl, and a pang of jealous irritation struck her. Not only was Osric in the way of what she needed to do, both to keep the wyvern safe and to reach Jananin, but he also represented something she had spent her whole life despairing for. Jananin Blake was her own mother, genetically speaking. Half of Dana was made from the same DNA as her, and yet this foul man knew Jananin better than she did. He probably knew trivial, intimate things about her, like what she preferred to drink, and what colours she chose to paint her house. Things Dana would never know; things that lay forever hidden from her behind the impassive voice-of-reason, Steel-and-Flame persona Jananin chose to present as her public image as a Spokesman for the Meritocracy.

She tried to sense the wyvern, but the metal in the back of the van muffled its signal to the extent they couldn't understand each other.

He drove for about three miles out of Radford Semele, before turning off into an industrial estate. Osric drove up to the main gate, where a steel bar painted with red and white stripes barred the road. He waved a card through the window, to a reader on a post planted in the concrete. The barrier rose to let the van pass.

Osric drove around the back of a blocky white building, down a ramp and into a car park. "You'll need to do something about the security cameras," he said.

Dana could only sense one camera. She remembered the image on it now and set it to overwrite any subsequent images it picked up for the next five minutes.

Osric got out and opened the back of the van. The wyvern stared out at them with its hard, expressionless eyes. When Dana looked at it again, she couldn't stop herself breathing harder. She couldn't quite get her head around this thing existing.

She thought to it about coming out, and it obliged, its metal feet noisy on the concrete as it disembarked from the vehicle.

Osric walked quickly in front, scouring the side of the building facing them and the few squares of light within the larger dark square mass. The wyvern raised its head to the stars. It looked around the car park, with the walls at the edges and the rectangles painted on the tarmac for people to park in, and it didn't understand. Dana reached out to put her hand on the metal plates covering its neck. It felt strange yet oddly secure to be walking with this menacing thing beside her, its long tail swaying side-to-side behind. Perhaps it was the same reason why some older boys around Pauline and Graeme's neighbourhood owned big ugly dogs and took them for walks around the block.

Osric swiped his card in a slot by the door. Inside the foyer, lights flickered on automatically. Dana and the wyvern followed Osric down a corridor and into a laboratory. The room had been built in an L-shape, with machines and large pieces of equipment in the first part, leading to an area with many Perspex-windowed rat cages built in to the walls. Osric walked on.

A big sleek rat looked at Dana with its beady black eyes. She crouched and stuck her finger into a ventilation hole so the rat could smell it. "Do you breed rats as a job?" she asked.

"No, this is a research laboratory. The rats are being fed an experimental drug in their drinking water to see if it has any adverse effect."

"What about after the experiment's finished? Do you sell the rats in pet shops?"

"No, the rats are euthanised and dissected, so we can detect any unintended effects the drug may have had."

Dana looked away from the rat and stood up. "Why?"

"So we can know if the drug is effective, of course. Then, if it is, it can progress on to human trials."

"So it's all right to *kill* them, so people can have medicine?"

"There wouldn't be any medicine for humans or animals if this work was not done."

Dana's face felt hot, and the back of her neck prickled uncomfortably. "I don't think you're a very nice person," she said quietly. She knew she should not speak this way to an adult she didn't know properly, particularly as Dr Osric was her only link to Jananin.

Osric's face became stern. "This is why I don't like children," he said. "They can't see shades of grey."

"I can see in shades of grey!" Dana objected. "And I can see in RGB and CMYK as well!"

"It is pointless me wasting my breath any more. You obviously are closed-minded, not prepared even to try to understand." Osric walked through into the next area, which was laid out with benches covered with equipment and lab books. He pulled out a drawer and picked up a screwdriver. "There appears to be an access panel on the back of the construction. Possibly we can find out more about it if we look inside."

Dana studied the part on the wyvern's shoulders he seemed to be indicating. "What if it hurts it?"

"I shouldn't expect it will. Besides, I'm sure it will make you aware. All you need to do is keep it from interfering with me."

Dana put her hand back on the wyvern's neck and fought down the unease she was feeling, trying to think positive reassuring thoughts instead. Osric turned the four screws holding the plate in position and pried it up. Dana had to stand on her toes to see inside: pipes and metal valves wrapped around slimy biological lumps wrapped in something. Veins and arteries mingled with the plastic-clad wiring running from the metal plates covering the body to the flesh-like material inside. Close to the back of the opening something dark fluttered violently beneath a wrapping of what looked like translucent plastic.

"It's living tissue grafted into a biomechanical shell." As he spoke, Osric's face became distorted, with anger or disgust or something of that sort. "This here is a trachea — a trachea from exactly what I've no idea. And yet it's connected to this." He indicated the system of metal valves. "It looks like the controls on a trumpet, an artificial larynx of sorts. The lungs and the trachea seem to have come from the same animal, but these look like more lungs, and..." His voice tailed off as he glanced upon a plastic cylinder, a foot or so long, clamped firmly in the centre of the wyvern's back. Chemical symbols were printed on its surface. "This is helium. Connected directly to a second pair of lungs with another diaphragm, so far as

I can ascertain."

A memory of a Physics lesson leapt to Dana's mind. "It's like bubblewrap!"

Osric glared at her. "What?"

"They make envelopes out of bubblewrap, because it's light because it's full of air. Helium is *lighter* than air, so if the wyvern has helium inside it, it would make it lighter and it would be easier for it to fly."

"It doesn't work like that. The helium inside the cylinder is compressed so much it will be heavier than air. And even if the lungs were full of helium, it would be like you holding a single balloon. The difference would be negligible. It doesn't make any sense. It's almost like this... machine... was built by an extremely skilled person, to a design by a fool. Either that or it is some kind of prototype that has been expanded upon from an early model. And yet..." Osric raised his hand to his face and rubbed his chin. "Normally, bone marrow manufactures white blood cells. But there don't appear to be any bones, so where in this case does the immune system originate?"

Dana stared into the inside of the wyvern while Osric went to the bench. When he came back, he had a syringe fitted with a needle.

"What are you doing?"

"I'm going to take a blood sample. To see what's going on."

He pushed the point of the needle into one of the pipe-like large blood vessels running down the wyvern's back. When he pulled back the plunger, the liquid that spilled into the plastic tube was not red, but black. He withdrew the syringe and turned back to the table, where he shifted some stuff to find a microscope. After applying a small dot of the black fluid to a glass rectangle on the microscope's plate, he looked through the eyepieces and adjusted the focus wheels for a few seconds.

"Jananin Blake's synapse," he said, straightening and looking to Dana. "And definitely not for a purpose she has authorised. "See for yourself."

Dana stepped around the wyvern and up to the microscope. When she peered into the drop of blood, she saw a coiled worm-like shape, lying inert.

"Is that's what's inside me, connecting my brain to the chip?"

"Yes. Blake programmed a self-replication ability into the DNA of her synapses, so they could repair themselves if they were damaged. The alternative would mean the synapse would need to be replenished every year or so, as they tend to disconnect from neurons and denature eventually. It means that in any living system the synapse is grafted to will shed residual amounts of unattached synapse in the dormant state. It also makes it extremely easy to steal the synapse and graft it into something else."

Dana looked back into the microscope, and started as something dark scuttled across the screen, like a pond skater. "There's something alive in there."

She got out the way to let Osric look. After a moment, it seemed he'd found it. "Looks like some kind of nanomachine. Possibly it's whatever this construct has in place of an immune system, although I've never heard of it before and I've no idea where it might come from."

He stood up straight and stared at his bench, passing a hand over his bottom jaw. "Appalling. This has Ivor Pilgrennon's handwriting all over it."

His words sent a sharp thrill of anticipation up into Dana's chest, and at the same time brought to mind a strange image of Ivor bending over the wyvern and signing his name on it, his signature so familiar although she'd only ever seen him write it once. She turned away from Osric, her heart pounding. Almost without thinking, she put her hand into her pocket to touch Ivor's watch, her fingertip sensing the crack where the face had fractured, its mechanism seizing up in Cape Wrath the last time she had seen Ivor. She had hardly dared to hope, but now Osric had admitted something that seemed to imply Ivor just might still live.

Osric was standing over by the sink now. He had a brown glass jar upside down in one hand and a syringe stuck through the rubber lid in the other hand. He set the bottle down on the bench beside the sink: on the label there was some kind of corporate logo and the words *Sodium pentobarbital 390 mg/mL sodium phenytoin 50 mg/ mL.*

But if Ivor was alive, how had he survived Cape Wrath, and why had the wyvern attacked her, if he had made it?

Osric was walking back to the wyvern now, and he paused to squeeze the plunger into the syringe. A plume of fluid streamed vertically from the needle's tip, dispersing into a fine spray at the summit of its arc, in such a way that it appeared to vanish into the air before it could fall back down to the ground. The image stirred an uneasy *déjà vu* in Dana. Something here was wrong, although she couldn't grasp the memory or make sense of what instinct was telling her.

She felt again for the laboratory's wLAN. It didn't take long for her to break through the security and access the Internet. *Sodium pentobarbital:*

...rapid-onset short-acting barbiturate general anaesthetic...

...commercial animal euthanasia injectable solutions...

Euthanasia: from Greek, meaning 'good death'...

Osric was bending over the open panel in the wyvern's shoulders, and the needle was pointing to the exposed blood vessels within.

"*No!*" Dana lunged for Osric's arm. She grabbed the sleeve of his labcoat and wrenched the syringe away from the wyvern. In the same instant, the wyvern whirled its head about to strike Osric in the side. *Eric come quickly, something bad is happening,* Dana transmitted to the phone in her pocket as Osric blundered into her. She lost her footing and fell, still gripping Osric's sleeve, and he went down on top of her. The impact between the floor and the full weight of the man's body forced all the air out of her lungs, and black spots erupted into her vision. Osric rolled off and thudded to the floor behind her. Despite the pain, disorientation, and a desperate need for air, Dana managed to keep her grip on his arm.

"Get off of me!" Osric shouted.

Dana wrapped both her arms around his, pinning him down, and jacked her knee up into his chest. A discordant trumpet screech penetrated the throb of her own heart in her eardrums. She opened her eyes to see the wyvern's head rearing above her on its segmented metal neck. It was reacting to her; she must have broadcast panic in the instant she'd realised what Osric was doing, transmitted her own fear to it.

She looked back at Osric's arm. He still clutched the syringe in his hand, point down, and as he fought her his arm slipped and the needle grazed the skin on the inside of Dana's wrist.

Dana screamed. Osric immediately realised what had happened and the anger dissipated from his face. He dropped the syringe and staggered backwards, crashing in to some kind of industrial oven that rattled like breaking glass, and heaving in great gulps of air. The wyvern stepped over Dana to straddle her and let out a hollow, metallic hiss, like someone playing a flute wrong.

Heart racing and gasping for breath, Dana tried to send calming thoughts to the wyvern. She rolled over onto her hands and knees and found the syringe Osric had dropped on the floor. The ground felt both sticky and gritty as she stumbled to the sink on her knees and free hand, and pressed the plunger down to discharge the syringe's poisonous load into the plughole.

"You can't... kill it," she forced out between breaths.

Osric's back was pressed flat against the oven. The wyvern watched him. "It's the most humane decision!" he countered. "This is utterly unethical! Whoever did this is wrong! It's like the atrocities during the Cold War. Dogs with extra heads grafted on. Monkeys' brains taken out and kept alive. Experiments like this have been illegal for decades!"

It took a few seconds for Dana to muster the lung capacity to shout her reply: "But it chooses life!"

The force of her outcry for a moment struck fear into his face. He recovered himself. "It's an animal. It doesn't understand..."

"You don't know that it's an animal!"

"It's not a human. There'd be more understanding, more of an attempt at communication. It's an intelligent animal all right, perhaps a primate, but it's not human." Osric shook his head emphatically. "*Look* what's been done to it. It's kinder to put it out of its misery."

"What if it's a human who... who doesn't think to communicate in the same way you and I do?" Dana thought of Cale, how he considered communicating with his voice to be largely irrelevant to him, and how he thought calculating Pi was more important. She thought of Alpha, engrossed in her Tamagotchi, only able to say *No* and *Urh*. "What if it's someone who's damaged, or who isn't old enough to know how to communicate properly?"

Osric opened his mouth and closed it again.

"It still counts as a human." Dana pulled information off the Internet to support her position as she spoke. "It's illegal to euthanise a human unless the human is definitely sane and asks for it and makes a recording of consent. If you kill it and it's human, you'll go to jail for murder."

"I doubt it," said Osric, but his demeanour had changed, and something was there in him that had not been there before. Perhaps it was doubt.

Dana breathed and put her hand out to touch the wyvern's cold metal carapace. *How can I leave you in this place now?* She glanced around the clutter in the lab, at the bits of apparatus and glass and plastic where she assumed Osric must work, and her eyes fell upon the one personal thing that was there: a picture frame containing a simple, stylistic rendering of an owl sitting in the fork of a flowering tree.

"That's Jananin's sigil. It means you're loyal to her, doesn't it?"

Osric looked at the picture uncomfortably.

"I want you to swear on it, that you won't do anything to the wyvern until Jananin has seen it."

"And if she should tell me to destroy it?"

Dana glared up at Osric. "I suppose if she decides that, you'll have to do it. But make sure you tell her what I said properly, and don't just say it's a thing that attacked me. It can think for itself, and when it came it was being controlled by something else. By a collar." She should have brought the collar, but she'd forgotten about it. It was likely still on the floor in the physics store room, although she doubted anyone would notice as it wouldn't look out of place there.

Osric made a disgusted expression.

"Come here and put your hand on it and swear! Or I won't let the wyvern stay here. It broke into a school to get me. It can break out of this lab if it wants to and I tell it to."

Still looking disgusted, Osric edged past the wyvern and put his hand on the top of the picture frame. "I swear on Jananin's drawing..."

"Swear it *properly*. I mean sincerely and everything."

"...not to harm or willingly allow to be harmed this... *thing*."

"Good," said Dana. "Now, where can you hide it where it'll be safe?"

Osric considered for a moment. "There's a coldroom that's broken down in the lower ground floor. It's not scheduled to be fixed until next week. Probably no-one will use it in the meantime. Jananin Blake will have to arrange for it to be collected before then. You had better explain to it that it will have to be quiet."

Osric fixed the loose panel on the wyvern back in place. He led the way and Dana coaxed the wyvern into the lift. He showed them to a thick door with a strong metal handle. The room behind it was windowless and heavily insulated. The wyvern probably wouldn't be noticed here, so long as it didn't make loud noises and nobody came in.

While Osric fetched a bowl of water, Dana made use of her moment alone with the wyvern. She brought to mind Jananin's image and tried to impress upon it a feeling that this person was safe and was going to help, and must not be attacked. She thought about staying here, staying still, and being quiet, and about tolerating Osric, to which she felt a degree of resistance.

Lastly, she put her hand to the wyvern's neck and leaned against its shoulder, closed her eyes, and concentrated.

She pictured Ivor as best as she remembered him, with his spectacles halfway down his nose and a bit lopsided, a few weatherbeaten lines apparent on his forehead from the winds that tore over the Flannan Isles. She remembered his curly, light-brown hair that looked untidy naturally, and that he used to control by parting at the centre and wetting it and combing it flat.

Often these days, she could no longer remember what his voice used to sound like. It was only in her dreams, or in that place between sleeping and waking that isn't quite reality and where cause and effect no longer connect, that he truly felt real to her any more.

Dana sniffed and swallowed to clear her nose and force the cramp out of her throat. The wyvern turned its head to focus on her with one eye, and she knew it had sensed what she felt, but there had been no reaction from it. She had been steeling herself for it to recoil in horror from her memory had Ivor been the one who had built it. But there had been nothing. Either the wyvern had never seen Ivor before, or it didn't remember.

Something else. Dana closed her eyes again and thought back the school, where the wyvern had come down. It did react to this, something like guilt, or contrition, for which Dana forgave it. She tried to get the wyvern to think back, to share with her where it had come from.

Vagueness.

Then, a sense of flying through a clear sky, the sun behind her, sliding to her left as she flew, until it shone full in her face.

Beyond that, a sunrise behind her, a dawn sky streaked with red, and in the midst of it, a great lump of blocky architecture.

And within that...

The wyvern whipped its neck up and away from her with a grating squawk. *Pain.*

Dana had backed to the door without realising it, and now Osric returned with the food and water. "Out," he said, and the door slammed shut between Dana and the wyvern, leaving her with only speculation to make sense of its memory.

"Remember what you swore," Dana told him as they made their way back to the exit.

"I said I'd do it. Don't keep harping on about it." Osric slapped his hand on the button that opened the door and they stepped out into the night air and the noise of an engine. The sound ceased and a helmeted figure ran towards them over the concourse.

"Eric."

"I thought you said you were going home," Osric remarked.

Eric pulled off his helmet. "Where's the wyvern?" he asked breathlessly.

"Oh, it's safe." Osric made an impassive expression. "But you won't be if security finds you up here." He strode away, back towards the car park.

"I got your text message." Eric still hadn't got his breath back. "What happened?"

"Oh, it's..." Dana didn't want to tell him exactly what had happened, didn't want him to say he told her so, and she should have listened to him about Osric not being trustworthy. "It's just that they do experiments in there, and there were these rats."

"I thought he looked like a weirdo. Did you see like, rats being dissected alive, and brains with electrodes all stuck in them?"

"No, nothing like that. Just rats in cages." Dana remembered the phone and reached into her pocket for it. "Oh no!" She hoped that perhaps Graeme had been busy and forgotten, but when she looked at the phone's messages, there were six from him already. She mentally told the phone to text back saying she was coming home now. "I have to get back to Pauline and Graeme's house."

They met little traffic as she rode back to Pauline and Graeme's house on the back of Eric's bike. It was late, and everything had died down by now.

As soon as Eric pulled up at the end of the drive, the door flew open and out came Graeme. "Where the hell have you been?" he demanded as Dana dismounted and pulled off her helmet.

"It's all right, Mr Provine, s'not her fault."

Graeme met Eric's helmet with a glare of disapproval. "My name's Mr Rose."

"Sorry, Mr Rose. We were just hanging around and we saw an old bloke fall over, and we helped him to the hospital. But Dana had to switch her phone off in there so it didn't interfere with the equipment."

"Oh," said Graeme. He paused to reflect, and said, "Aren't you too young to be riding a motorbike?"

"'s alright, just a moped." Eric snapped down his visor and shot off into the night before Graeme could ask anything else.

There wasn't any mention of Alpha's grave on the news that night, nor was there an appearance by Jananin Blake, although a few other Spokesmen were on talking about school reform.

After this, the screen behind the reporter displayed an image of a hooded snake's face, with bright eyes and yellow and grey bands of colour on its scales. "Fourteen

King Cobras and five Komodo Dragons were last night stolen from the reptile house at Whipsnade zoo. Both these species are vulnerable in their natural environments, and the animals taken belonged to a captive breeding programme intended to help preserve genetic diversity. Herpetologists nationwide are concerned for the welfare of the reptiles, and stress that these animals require specialist care and are extremely dangerous. Police are still gathering evidence, but have revealed their chief suspects are private collectors and an animal rights terrorist cell known to be operating in the area. This video was released onto Youtube shortly after the theft was reported."

The screen changed to a low-resolution video of a woman wearing a balaclava mask in a room darkened by tatty curtains. "Humans have no right to enslave non-humans to murder and eat, or torture in laboratories, or force to breed in zoos. These are sentient beings, not walking carrion for human amusement." Through the holes in the woollen mask, the woman's face became distorted with zealous hatred as she spoke. "If someone did liberate the snakes and lizards, and they flee to inhabited places and kill people there, then it is a good thing. Every man, woman, and child who dies is one less filthy human polluting the earth and murdering innocents."

Graeme coughed as he swallowed his dinner. "Has she looked in a mirror lately? I hope the snakes and the lizards go to her house and bite her! That'd serve her right and mean one less *filthy human!*"

Dana thought again of the rats in the cages in Osric's lab. She still didn't think it was right for Osric to do what he did to those rats, although thinking about it now, she couldn't quite rationalise why. The rats' cages were clean and not at all smelly, and they had toys to play with, and food and water. Most wild rats live under the floor in people's houses in dirty nests, and have no toys and not enough food, and die in pain from eating rat poison or being crushed in the jaws of a dog. Perhaps the rats in the lab had a better life, and a better death. She wondered if the way she'd spoken to Osric might have sounded to him like the words of hate coming from this intolerant and unpleasant person on the television, and now she wished she hadn't spoken to him that way.

-6-

THE man stands between us and the window. The pane and the dark bars beyond it are flecked with rain, the thin grey light day offers overwhelmed by glaring strip lights on the room's ceiling. The man's hair is short and grey, his trousers are black, and his white jacket reaches down to the backs of his knees. The walls, floor, and ceiling of the room are all colourless. If the view were on a television screen, it would be impossible to tell if it was in colour or black and white.

The man turns his head to look at me, eyes inscrutable behind his steel-framed spectacles. Something in those spectacles and his long white coat stir a memory in you, something bad, something telling you this man should not be trusted, but you can't pin it down. He folds his arms and begins to speak, his voice made stark and hollow by the unfurnished room's acoustics.

"We have tried *everything*. There is no diagnosis in medical literature that fits the symptoms you seem to exhibit. They are not consistent with the schizophrenia your parents insist you have, nor can they be explained by the autistic spectrum disorder specialists agreed you had before the other symptoms developed. Nonetheless, we have tried practically every drug that's been approved, and even some that haven't, to no avail." His face contorts behind the reflective barrier of his lenses, his hand rising to his chin. "You are not a stupid child. It is almost as if... as though you are *acting* it, as though you do it deliberately, for attention."

You remember someone saying something similar about you, once. You remember how infuriating it is, to have an adult make up lies and rubbish, to tell it to you as an explanation of yourself.

I look at my bare feet and the thin legs engulfed in white jogging trousers on the floor in the room's corner, legs that I know are attached to me, but that don't feel like they belong to me, or you, any more. I don't remember my legs looking that way. The jacket that matches the trousers has a zip down the front, but the tab on the slider is made of round-edged rubber, so it can't be used as a weapon. When I pull at the cuff, the forearm beneath is rutted with scabs and old scars, cross-hatching sketched in my own blood.

I *hate* this body. It's as much as a prison as this room, as these barred windows.

The man's voice cuts into the privacy of our thoughts. "Don't you want your family to take you back? Don't you *want* to be normal? *Leave your arms alone!*"

"There are *things* in my blood."

"There are no *things* in your blood. At least not beyond the usual cells and things that are meant to be in everyone's blood, to protect you from disease and transport oxygen around your body."

I thrust out my arm, pulling the sleeve up past the elbow. My voice comes out shrill and hoarse. "*Look* at it!"

The man looks away instead. Embarrassment. Disgust. He goes to a small table in the far corner and picks up a glass of water, and his hand delves into a plastic jar there. When he comes back to us, he holds out his hand, and in his palm there's a pill shaped like a torpedo, half bright red and half transparent and full of tiny blue spheres. It's the only coloured thing in this white and grey room. It will make the man and the room go away.

The man's spectacles reveal only the reflected glare of the strip light.

You don't trust him.

Don't take it. It could be poison.

Good. I put the drug in my mouth. The water tastes of fluoride, I swallow, and the plastic lump on my tongue is gone.

Why are you letting them do this to you?

It only gets worse if I don't. I've taken this medicine before. It makes things not matter. I forget.

This is wrong. We have to get out of here.

Thoughts grow weak, indistinct. Awareness is being taken away. There's nowhere to go, and even if there were, they'd find out.

You don't understand. Everything you've experienced in this world feels wrong. It all goes against everything you understand to be right and just. If people here can do this to us, there's no telling what goes, what is allowed and considered reasonable. There must be something we can do, somewhere we can get to where we'll be safe, where no-one will look.

I can give up and let go of you, like I have countless times before. Always you'll find me again, always wretched, and always you try to help me with suggestions that don't work. It feels easier not to care, to let you be smothered and lose myself in the oblivion of a dreamless sleep, where I don't have to face what I can't face. But your ideas are seeds endlessly trying to take root. Perhaps this world isn't real, and all I need to do is try for another reality to make it change. Could it still be I have the strength to hope?

Perhaps there is a place like that.

You're slipping away from me. I can barely sense you. I clutch at the memory, in the way stranded people hang on to a rock at high tide, clinging to the last seconds before the currents pull us down. A glimpse caught from the window of a moving vehicle a long time ago. Was there ever a name for it? I cannot recall. Perhaps this sanctuary is mine to call what I see fit, and even if it's not real, if it does only exist in my head, I can at least let myself believe our own lie. There is something comforting in that, something peaceful that stills this constant fear that strains every nerve of me while I'm awake.

The Emerald Forge.

The man's figure becomes hazy and the room gradually darkens.

*

The disorienting darkness made it hard to tell which direction was which. A blurry greenish light became visible. Dana forced her eyes to focus, and the green light resolved into the digits 4:08, a square of curtained window from the streetlights outside Pauline and Graeme's house beyond it.

The Emerald Forge. What did the Emerald Forge mean? Dana stared at the alarm clock and tried to disentangle the unrefined mess of thoughts in her head into something that made sense. Had she been back in Cerberus's world, or something much like it? No, Cerberus was destroyed. All three of it. Were there other games, new games after Cerberus?

In the Cerberus game, the system had recognised things about Dana that she hadn't consciously told it, like automatically rendering its appearance to match hers. It could be the names Gamma and Epsilon had been plucked from her subconscious in the same way. But the Cerberus game had never felt as real as the world she kept encountering in her sleep. Cerberus's world had been obviously fantasy, full of fascinating details made up from complicated codes. This world wasn't. It wasn't that it lacked detail, just that the detail was too well integrated into the whole, and she'd never sensed that code beneath controlling everything. On the other hand, Dana didn't really make a habit out of playing games on the Internet, and this kind of bleak, ultra-realistic scenario might be what people looked for in a game these days. Perhaps fantasies and puzzles had become dated and fallen from favour.

Dana nestled back into the dent in her pillows and pulled the duvet over herself. Eric might know about this sort of thing. She would have to ask him when she next saw him, if she still could remember. She must at least try to remember the Emerald Forge. She wasn't sure what it meant, but just before the dream ended, it had felt as though she had been very close to understanding.

-7-

THE next day was Tuesday, and that morning Dana's concerns about the wyvern and the possibilities its existence might hint at assumed a lesser priority compared to more immediate worries. She still had to get through this day and the rest of the week before the end of term and the six weeks of sanctuary that was the main school holiday. Abigail was still there, and undoubtedly she wanted revenge on Dana for making her look foolish in front of her friends and the teachers.

As she made her way into the front yard and up the steps to the main building and the door where she'd encountered the wyvern, she overheard a conversation between two boys:

"You see that? Abigail Swift broke it."

"A *girl* punched that and *broke* it?"

"And when she got wrong for it, she said a dragon broke it. Ha!"

"Psycho bitch!"

If the news had got out and people were talking about her, Abigail must really be angry. Dana looked around the crowded school grounds, although it wouldn't be now or here Abigail would choose to attack her. It would be during break in the toilets, or after school. Maybe she could come up with a way to escape early for the rest of the week. She hurried past the crowd on the steps and into the building. The corridor was packed with students waiting to go into their registration group classrooms.

"Dana?"

Dana started at the sound of someone shouting her name, but it was only Mr Kell, pushing his way to her through the throng.

"Dana, could I just have a quick word with you in private?" he shouted over the noise the children were making.

He pushed open the door to his science classroom and waved her through. The door clicked shut behind him, muting the racket from the corridor.

"Abigail Swift earned herself a temporary suspension by breaking the door last night. She won't be back at school until the start of the next academic year."

Dana stared at the axolotl where it lurked on the stones flooring its tank, feeling enormously relieved that she would likely not set eyes on Abigail's stupid face for four days and six weeks at least, but not wanting to say anything that might betray the wyvern or her own guilt.

Mr Kell continued. "Over the summer holidays there are probably going to be a number of educational reform topics coming up for referendum. The Meritocracy might finally come up with some coherent arguments from all this background noise of conflicting ideals, and the Electorate might at last have some clear-cut options to choose from."

Dana glanced at him briefly. Perhaps Mr Kell thought the school system would be seriously reformed. Maybe he even thought Dana wouldn't be coming back to this place at all?

"I probably shouldn't talk about myself in front of a pupil, but I am 54, and I've had the misfortune of being a science teacher through some, how shall we say it, *interesting times*. Early on in my career, there was a political furore about the teaching of evolution because a group of people *might be offended* by it. That passed, but then we had another political furore about the teaching of reproduction because some other group of people *might get offended*. These days, the idea of a science teacher being optimistic about his career is a bit cloudcuckoolandish, but I've never given up hope that one day, politics might butt out and I might at least be allowed the golden years of my career to teach in peace. There's a possibility August will be a fresh page, for everyone."

There had not been any referenda yet on school reform, because when people nominated school issues, they complained about so many different aspects of it rather than all focusing on one point as a start of reform that there were never enough votes for any individual referendum on any of the school topics to be carried through. More recently, influential people on the Internet had started to talk about a grammar school system where people would go to different schools depending on their strongest subjects. If Dana did get to go to a science school, it wouldn't mean *no* bullies, but it might mean significantly less bullying. Most of the bullies who targeted Dana seemed to be kids who were bad at science and maths. Or perhaps it wouldn't work at all, and bullies existed in some kind of equilibrium, and if you removed the bullies, more tolerant children would *mutate* to replace them.

"In the meantime, if anything, or anyone, is bothering you, I want you to let one of the teachers know. It doesn't have to be me. It can be a woman teacher if that feels easier for you. It doesn't have to be your registration group teacher or your head of house. Any teacher you like. Will you do that, please?"

"Okay." Dana nodded.

"Good. You'd better get off to your registration group." Mr Kell opened the door again for Dana. Going back into the clamour and crowded mass of bodies was like diving into a fast-flowing river and trying to swim through the rapids. The corridors were a flow of heads, riptides flowing in opposite directions and whirlpools in the stairwells where they surged up to the higher floors. The law in the school was that you had to walk on the left side of the corridor. Dana had always wondered if it was intended to prepare the students for learning to drive when they got to seventeen. Graeme was always saying that schools didn't teach kids anything applicable to life in the real world.

A bigger boy clipped her shoulder and spun her into the opposite current. Dana lost her footing and people swore and shoved into her, but someone's clammy fingers closed on her wrist and spun her back onto the other side. She caught sight of Eric's face obscured by acne and glasses, grinning, before the current bore it away.

It wasn't until after he'd gone that Dana realised a slip of paper had been put in her hand. Rather than risk reading it in the corridor, she put it in her pocket and continued to her registration class.

In registration, Dana always sat in a seat next to the wall, and nobody sat next to her because everyone knew Dana Provine was weird and got bullied, and being seen to associate with her in public was a sure way to invite bullying on oneself. She put her bag on the other seat and opened the note on her lap under the table. It contained only the instruction 'after school' and an address. Dana checked the postcode on GPS. It was easily within walking distance of Pauline and Graeme's house.

Even though it was only Tuesday, Dana suddenly felt overwhelmingly positive. Abigail had been suspended, school would be finished at the end of the week, and she had what she supposed was a friend, which Pauline would be happy about. Yesterday she had found a wyvern, and Osric had sworn not to harm it, and Jananin might still get in touch with her because of that. Ivor might be alive somewhere. It was summer, and she had the whole six weeks ahead to spend at Pauline and Graeme's house enjoying the best weather of the year in peace, constructing her bog garden with Graeme and making ice creams with Pauline and eating them on the lawn.

Duncan had promised to take Dana to go camping one weekend in Devon, where there were fossils and a beach made entirely of shells. She would get to spend time with Cale during the day, when he wasn't engrossed in his own thoughts from being exhausted by interacting with people at the special school he went to. And while they were all out or otherwise occupied, she could make Airfix models and try to dig up more information about Ivor and the wyvern.

Dana's good mood carried her through registration and the morning's lessons, protecting her like a bubble of insulating atmosphere from various insults and rude comments in the corridor. Indeed, it didn't even break when, while queuing in the corridor to go into the school canteen for lunch, a hawking, retching, spitting noise came from someone behind her, and something hit her in the back of the head.

There was a lot of laughter and noise, but Dana had always been told to ignore bullies, so she stood and pretended she didn't notice, resisting the temptation to raise her hand to the back of her hair. She bought her food, found an empty table, and ate, conspicuous of a damp, rubbery sensation in her hair, between the base of her skull and her collar.

In the lavatory, she used a handful of toilet paper to grab hold of the thing and drag it out. It was impossible to do it without pulling it down the entire length of the hair it had stuck to the roots of, a gluey tension resisting all the way. When it at last broke free, it left a dirty off-white clag smelling faintly of spearmint in the toilet paper.

Chewing gum: the same material stuck under every desk, forming revolting beige and grungy pink pustules in every corner and every surface of the school, making the building look as though it was infested with some kind of fungus. She tried to rub it out with more toilet paper, but the residue had left a coagulated tacky wad that felt stiff when she touched the back of her head.

The afternoon's lessons passed without much event. Upon the last bell, she dashed out of the classroom and through the main doors, and ran to the school gates. She took the quickest route back to Pauline and Graeme's house, and as soon as she got there, she ran upstairs without checking to see if anyone else was there. Dana threw her bag and blazer on the bed, pulled off her school trousers and replaced them with her jeans, and unbuttoned her shirt and threw it on the floor as she went from her bedroom to the bathroom. She could sense Cale's signal nearby, and from his bedroom came the tuneless sounds of him bashing at his music keyboard.

A hairbrush and comb lay beside the sink. She grabbed the brush, wet it under the tap, and raked at the back of her hair with it. The chewing gum had by now dried into a hard crust, and all the brush did was stick and hurt.

Pauline's soft tread on the stairs. "Dana, is that you?"

She stepped into the doorway and noticed at once Dana standing in her jeans and sports bra, her hand over her shoulder, the hairbrush knotted up at the back of her head.

"Oh, honestly, Dana!"

"It wasn't me!" Dana objected. "I didn't spit it on myself!"

Pauline took the hairbrush and hurled it into the wastepaper basket on the landing. She did it in rather an exaggerated, melodramatic fashion. She began to pick at Dana's hair with the comb. "The disgusting, filthy swine!" she exclaimed.

"Ow!"

"I'm sorry, love, I don't know how on Earth we're going to get this out."

"Can I go to Eric's house for dinner?"

"Oh, I suppose so. It's a good thing Graeme's going out with his friends from work for dinner tonight. I don't think he approves." Pauline exhaled. "Dana, look, you're not having trouble at school, are you? That girl, Abigail, didn't do this, did she?"

"No, she got expelled. I mean temporarily," Dana quickly corrected. "She broke a window at the school. I don't know who did this."

Pauline shook her head disapprovingly. "She's going to end up in Borstal, that one. Perhaps we could iron it."

Dana didn't want Pauline to iron her hair. She just wanted to get to Eric's house so they could work out what they were going to do about Osric and the wyvern. "I don't mind, really."

"Yes, well you might not, but I'm not having people think I let you not mind! Don't move from that spot!"

She went into the box room with the computer, leaving Dana alone in the doorway between the bathroom and the landing. Dana heard her switch on the computer and type some things. After a moment, she came back out and walked straight past Dana and downstairs. When she came back, she was carrying a jar of peanut butter. Pauline towed Dana over to the bath by her elbow. "Lean over the side."

"Can't you just cut the hair that's manky off?" Dana protested as Pauline slathered a dollop onto the back of her head.

"Then it'll be shorter than the rest and it'll look even worse." Pauline kneaded the peanut butter and chewing gum mixture into Dana's scalp, the pressure of it hurting her chest against the side of the bath. She unhooked the showerhead and switched the shower on. The water ran down her back and made her sports bra wet, and because she was leaning forward the water ran constantly in her eyes and down her nose. When the peanut butter dissolved in the water and ran into the bath, it looked like vomit and made her feel queasy.

Pauline ended up washing her hair three times, first of all in the shampoo Dana normally used, then using Pauline's own expensive and smelly shampoo that was made in France, and then using Graeme's anti-dandruff supermarket's own brand that stank of tar, on the premise that men's shampoo might be 'stronger'.

After she had finished, Pauline dried Dana's hair with her high-powered hairdryer, which was supposed to make ions that are good for your hair. Dana had once asked Mr Kell in a Physics lesson about the ions that came out of the hairdryer, and Mr Kell said he thought they sounded like a load of nonsense made up to sell more hairdryers.

"Where are you meeting Eric?" Pauline asked as Dana was putting on a vest top and a check shirt to stop her shoulders getting burnt in the afternoon sun.

"Just at his house, I think." Dana checked her pockets, making sure she had her fuses and Ivor's watch.

"Well, I hope one of his parents is there. Here, take this." Pauline handed her the mobile phone she'd had yesterday. "And be back by nine."

Out on the street, the sun was very hot, and Dana's damp back was something of a relief. She never liked visiting other people's houses, and she felt even more uncomfortable because her hair was all frizzy and full of static electricity from being washed too much and blow dried, and she couldn't escape the smell of Pauline's shampoo.

This was where the postcode Eric had given her was according to GPS, a quiet street and a semi-detached house of bland 70s design with a tall silver birch in an otherwise desolate front garden. Weeds sprouted from the cracks between the slabs on the driveway, an old-fashioned design with a strip of gravel in the centre, and the full west sun beat down on a buckled garage door with peeling canary-yellow paint.

It was only now she was here that it occurred to her the whole thing might be a trick, and either nothing or something worse would come of it. Not long ago there had been a girl at school Dana had sat next to who had pretended to be her friend, and kept making arrangements to meet her for lunch or out of school and not turning up. Pauline had said, vehemently when she found out, that the girl probably thought it was funny, on account of being a stupid idiot with only half a brain who wouldn't know a funny joke if it jumped out and bit her on the backside.

This was the same Eric she'd solved Cerberus's puzzles with back on Roareim. Surely he wouldn't do stuff like that? He'd seemed very genuine yesterday, but on the other hand, Dana probably had no idea what genuine was compared to what wasn't. Perhaps she wouldn't know *genuine* if it jumped out and bit her on the backside, the same as Pauline said stupid people don't know humour.

A gate at the side of the garage scraped open. Eric peered surreptitiously through the gap. "Hey. Come in."

Dana crossed the drive and went in through the gate Eric held open for her. Perhaps he was her friend, and it felt good that he might be, and to be welcome, but she didn't want to trust that feeling too much just in case it should turn out to be an elaborate trap.

They entered the house through the back door, into an utility room smelling of cat, and indeed there were bowls containing water and little coloured biscuit shapes for the cat to eat on a plastic mat in one corner. Eric showed her to a second door, that led down a step into the garage. However, it didn't contain a car, or a load of gardening paraphernalia and junk like most people's garages did, although Eric's moped was propped up by the large metal door. There was a sofa against one wall with a darts board on the brick above it, and an old CRT telly with a computer console opposite, and a chest freezer against the back wall. Scattered about the rest of the place were boxes of toys, fold-up chairs, an electric guitar and its amp, and dismantled computers and bits.

"This is my lair," Eric explained. He threw himself down on the sofa. He was wearing a heavy metal t-shirt with jeans and trainers.

Dana looked around awkwardly. "Do you, like, *live* in here?"

"Well, sort of. I've got a bedroom and all, an' it's too cold in the winter, but my mum lets me keep my stuff in here and doesn't come in and mess with it or anything." Somewhat flustered and red in the face, he got up again and went over to a fridge on a table next to the freezer. "Anyway, do you want a drink? You can have a lolly instead if you want. Or you can have both; I probably will."

"What are *those*?" A wooden rack holding nearly horizontal bottles stood next to the freezer.

"That's cider I was brewing with my brother. Well, he's my half-brother really. He's gone to University now."

"Isn't that illegal?"

"No, it's not. It's illegal to *sell* alcohol to someone under eighteen, and it's illegal to *buy* alcohol for someone under eighteen, but there's nothing in the law to say a person who's under eighteen can't buy the ingredients and brew their own alcohol and drink it at home in private."

Dana selected a lime ice lolly and chose one of the fishing chairs to sit on. Eric grabbed a tin of pop and another lolly and sat back on the sofa. "What happened to the wyvern in that lab, then?"

"He's going to contact someone who will know what to do." Dana wanted to avoid saying too much. "Someone who works for the Meritocracy."

Eric broke off slurping lemon-flavoured ice to say, "See? Told you they would take it away. Now we'll never hear about it again, and they'll cover it up and hide it in some secret military installation like Area 69 or whatever it's called."

His comment was annoying, not only because of his tone, but because Dana suspected there might be a modicum of truth in it. "Well, it's not about that, is it? It's about what's best for the wyvern. And it's better off with someone who works for the Meritocracy who knows about things like that than it is stuck in the school. I mean, if the teachers had found it in the classroom the next day, they would just have called the police, and the police would have thought it was a bomb or something and destroyed it."

Eric abruptly laughed. "And probably the school with it, so we could start the holidays early." He crunched ice and swigged pop. "So, what were you doing in detention, anyway?"

"Mr Slugs put me on."

"Slugs once put me on detention. He had me doing stupid lines in his office. I farted my guts out and stunk the place up. He never put me on detention again."

Dana laughed. "I wouldn't be able to do that. It never works when I try to get away with things."

"Some teachers you can't pull it off with. I couldn't do it with teachers like Kell or McCafferty; they would say something. But teachers like Slugs don't really have any instincts like that. I mean, he doesn't wear a wedding ring, so I don't think he has kids himself, and he doesn't have any sense of humour, and it says on the school website that he used to have a proper job before he was a teacher, so he must have got the sack and gone into it to get off the dole. They must train 'em in teacher university how to deal with kids misbehaving, but if you do something weird that can't quite be classed as misbehaving, they don't know how to deal with it."

Dana considered this.

Eric indicated the television. "You want to play a computer game?"

"Okay."

"What sort? I've got first-person shooters, MMOGs, fighting games..."

"I want to play a computer game that you have to kill baddies in," said Dana, thinking of Doctor Osric.

"I've got *Pillage and Burn III*," Eric suggested. "You have to ransack settlements and loot them, and you can make yourself better weapons out of the stuff you find."

Dana had played the original *Pillage and Burn* game and its sequel *Pillage and Burn II* when it first came out with Duncan, but Duncan had lost interest in games since he'd got older and started learning to drive, and it wasn't fun without him, and she'd not realised there was another sequel out now. A vague memory about an odd dream came into her mind at his suggestion. "Are there any games around now like the Cerberus game? Online games about exploring worlds?"

"Not puzzle games *exactly* like that. *PB3* is online. You can team up with other people and kill bosses and that kind of thing."

Dana chose her words carefully. "I thought I heard something about a new game online, something about..." It all seemed so distant and hard to remember now, but she was sure there had been something, a name. "Something to do with diamonds or something like that. Forged diamonds, I think."

Eric frowned. "I dunno," he said at length. "Never heard anything like that." He grabbed the computer's keyboard off the floor and typed *forged diamonds game* into a search engine, but there was nothing that came up on the first two pages that seemed to be anything at all related to what Dana could recall.

"I'll give you my email address before you go home, and then you can email me the link if you find it again," Eric said. "I really liked that Cerberus game. I was sorry when it went offline and I couldn't play it any more. And, uh," he looked awkwardly away from her and at the keyboard on his knee, "you were nice to play with. I was kind of hoping I would see you again on that forum so we could play something else together, even if it wasn't Cerberus. I sent you a PM and stuff. But you were never on again."

As he'd been talking, he'd started up the *Pillage and Burn* game he'd mentioned.

"So, why did you never notice me at school before?" Dana asked.

"I only moved here recently and started going to that school. I lived in Dudley before."

"Is that why you talk funny — I mean, differently to other people here?"

Eric snorted. "Are you calling me a Brummie? If me mother comes in while you're here, you'd better be careful you don't call her a Brummie. She's funny about it. She says 'this esn't Brummie, this es Black Countraay!'" Eric selected *two player* and *create new character*. "Here, what do you want?" He dumped a game controller in Dana's lap. "Warrior, thief, wizard, priest…"

"What's a priest?"

"Oh, they're crap. They just heal other people. But if you want to do that, I can make a tank and we can play together." Eric typed *Epsilon* into the character name box, but an error message came up saying it was already taken.

"*Epsilon5*?" Dana suggested.

Eric tried that and it worked. He named his character *Charonn*. A loading screen appeared, a bar filled up with colour, and finally the screen changed to show a split screen of two images of the same computer-generated farm with two characters standing in the middle.

Dana fiddled with the controller. It would have been so much easier just to tell the computer what she wanted her character to do, but if she did that, Eric might notice.

They played for a little while. The purpose of the game, at least for Dana's character, was to keep up with Eric's character as it ran around hitting things with a sword. As the things hit the character in return, the red bar indicating its health shrank, and Dana had to press a button to heal the character and put health back in. Much the same as the original game, but with slightly better graphics.

By now, Dana had started to feel hunger pangs. "Are we going to have dinner? I told Pauline and Graeme I would be having dinner here."

"Sure." Eric frowned. "Why'd you call your mum and dad Pauline and Graeme?"

Dana put the game controller on the floor. "Because they're not my mum and dad. They were my foster parents before, and now I'm adopted."

"Oh. Right. Sorry it didn't work out with your dad. My dad left as well."

"Where did he go?"

"I don't know." Eric suddenly looked solemn. "I think I probably happened by mistake, and I'm not sure my mum really knew him properly. They sort of tried to make it work with him hanging around, but they just argued most of the time." Then he looked at Dana, and a crafty, jocular attitude overcame him. "He's a spy, and he's not allowed to reveal himself to me because he's being hunted by Russian agents. But I expect he'll want me to come with him on missions when I'm eighteen. Actually, *she's* not really my mum; my mother is the Duchess of Essex, and when I was born I was stolen and put up for adoption, but really I'm heir to a fortune and a massive estate with gargoyles on the roof and stables and horses and all that."

Dana laughed. "Well, my mother is a rich and powerful lady, and my father is a mad scientist who made me in a test tube."

Eric laughed. "Mint!"

"If you go north, through Scotland, almost as north as you can go, there are some haunted islands of black rock, called the Seven Hunters. And that's where my dad lives in exile, in a secret bunker built by the Ministry of Defence."

Eric was laughing hard. "Seriously, that's really good. You should write a book or something. Or a computer game."

"What would happen in the computer game?"

"Well, I suppose the character would have to journey to the island, fighting—" and Eric punctuated this by seizing an old TV antenna from a corner and waving it about like an epee, "—sea monsters, and giant squids, and Scotsmen wearing kilts like on *Braveheart!*"

"And if they did," Dana added, pragmatically, "they'd have to take him some toilet paper and some razor blades, 'cause I expect he's run out by now."

In contrast to Eric's raucous laughter that followed, Dana felt a sudden, acute pang of grief. She didn't know where Ivor was, and until Rupert Osric had said what he'd said about the wyvern, she'd believed him to be dead, and she had recurrent nightmares in which she made the journey back to Roareim only to find it cold and abandoned, decaying and in ruin, Peter's fish tank empty in the darkness.

"What's your dad like, then? Does he have wild hair and glasses, and wear a white coat?"

"No. Well, he wears glasses. But he's tall, big. And his clothes are all old and shabby because he can't get to the mainland very often to buy more."

Dana put her hand into her jeans pocket and closed her fingers tightly over Ivor's petrified watch. It wasn't the thought of Ivor being blown up in the helicopter that bothered her most, nor the shocking and unsettling images of him washed up on a beach, cold and drowned, that haunted her mind on nights she couldn't sleep. It was that awful desolation, that emptiness, she felt in the Roareim of her dreams; that great feeling of loss that she'd never hear his voice again, or recognise his smell, or see him stand the way he used to when he was thinking, one hand on the back of a chair or a table, the other on his hip, with his forehead creased and his bottom lip jutting forwards.

Hope yet still kindled in her. Rack the Internet as she might, she had never found any reference to a body being found in the vicinity of Cape Wrath or the Outer Hebrides that would fit Ivor's description from that time or after. There was nothing on any of the classified files she'd been able to find and hack into. There had been an agreement between Ivor and Jananin that he could live in secret, under an assumed identity.

"I wish..." Dana found herself saying, but she noticed Eric watching her, and she suspected he thought it was a joke. She didn't want to make it sound too sincere. "I wish I *knew*. And sometimes I wish I wasn't here. Not because of Pauline and Graeme, because of the school."

Eric shrugged. "You could always skive off." He got up off the sofa and went back to the door. "Let's find something for dinner."

Dana followed him through the utility room and into the kitchen. "You mean, truant? Not go to school?"

"You can forge a note for when you go back in. The main problem is finding somewhere to hide all day where no-one'll find you. If people see kids skiving, they tell the police and then you get caught. Oh, and you ought to say hi to me mum." Eric opened the door on the other side of the kitchen.

"Mum, this is Dana from school."

"Hi," said Dana.

A woman in a dressing gown sitting on a sofa said *hi* and went back to watching television. Eric shut the door when they went back into the kitchen.

"What are good places you can hide?"

"Anywhere people don't go. Which rules out most places if it's summer. Mind you, most of the best places get used by Smith and his lot, and they won't put up with other people hanging out there, and we don't want people from school seeing us anyway."

"Why not?"

Eric shrugged. "They'll think we're, well…"

"What?"

"Going out together."

"It would seem to be largely academic." 'Largely academic' was a phrase Graeme often used in such a situation. "Since they all hate us at any rate, why should they care if they thought we were going out together? It's not as though they can be any… any *horribler* to us because of it."

"You want to put money on it?" said Eric. He had filled the kettle, and now he was getting out some pots of instant noodles.

"If we skived off, we could go and look for the wyvern."

"What, at that weird bloke's lab? We'd be seen for sure there." Eric was making chocolate spread sandwiches.

She thought again of what Dr Osric had said about the wyvern and Ivor's experiments. Then she considered the familiar sensation the wyvern had given her. The wyvern didn't transmit words of a language, or any signal that could be translated and written down as something simple. What it had thought to Dana was an experience, a flight, its great wings beating steadily until the muscles of its shoulders were stiff and aching, a taut, bloated sensation filling its insides, and the colours of the land, from an expanse of nondescript marsh to the sharp geometry of yellow, green, and brown agricultural land, to the grey clutter and haze of cities. She realised what the familiar sensation meant: the wyvern used GPS.

Eric finished making the sandwiches and carried them and the instant noodles on a tray back into the garage. There was a cat in the utility room, but it darted out through its flap when it saw Dana.

"Do you have any road maps?" she asked Eric.

After much rummaging he found a battered AA atlas on a shelf. "Are you going to show me where your dad lives?"

Dana thought that would be a good idea, but when she turned to the map of Lewis, the Flannan Isles weren't shown on it.

"It should be here!" She pointed to the empty space in the pale blue representing the sea. "It's got Gallan Head on it, right there!"

"It doesn't matter," said Eric with his mouth full. "It was a good idea."

"If you look on an Ordnance Survey map, it'll be on there!" Dana said indignantly. "It must be 'cause there aren't any roads, and this is a road map. I suppose it'd be a waste of ink printing a place with no roads."

"You did say it was a secret MoD site. Perhaps they're not allowed to show it on a map."

"Perhaps that's it. Anyway, that wasn't what I wanted to look for. I was thinking about where the wyvern came from."

"How can you work that out from a map?"

Dana was already thinking. The wyvern had conveyed to her the movement of the sun, which rose behind it and moved to its left to set in front of it. That meant the wyvern had been travelling west, but it was no good telling Eric that as he wouldn't believe her. But then she remembered how she'd looked up as the wyvern had flown towards the school, and seen metal glint in the glare, and the yard cool and flooded with the shadow of the school building behind her.

"It came from the east." She knew this wasn't entirely logical, since the wyvern could've made a pass over the school and come back from a different angle, but she hoped Eric wouldn't think to question it. "And I think it came quite a long way."

"Perhaps it came from France."

Dana frowned. "Why would it come from France?"

Eric shrugged. "Because Mum says they smell of garlic and they won't buy our meat or our vegetables."

Dana was sure the wyvern hadn't come from France because it hadn't recalled flying over ocean. She struggled to think of something else that would justify it to Eric. "Osric looked at some of the components inside it," she said at length. "The writing on them was in English. If it'd come from France, it would've been written in French."

"Perhaps it came from Russia."

"Russia's too far away. It wouldn't be able to fly that far."

"Why not? It's a machine, sort of. It's not limited by normal, well, *limits*."

"It has to have come from somewhere over here." Dana covered the other parts of the country with her hands to leave the bulging part of Great Britain's east coast exposed.

Eric leaned back on the sofa and shovelled noodles into his mouth. "If you say so."

She still didn't know how much it was safe to involve Eric, but the idea of going off on her own was daunting. She'd done it before, but that time Jananin had been with her part of the way and given her instructions for much of the rest, and although it was easy to be blasé about it in retrospect, she could still recall how alarming it had been trying to get through the night on Gallan Head, and when she'd managed to strand herself on Roareim. It *had* worked out, but it could have gone horribly wrong.

Dana took a deep breath. "If I skive off to look there, would you come with me?"

Eric paused to consider this. "You do know it's a lot bigger than it looks on a map?"

"Of course I know that!"

He shrugged his eyebrows apologetically. "It's just you don't always appreciate it, not until you learn to drive and get a feel for the roads and the layout of stuff."

Dana felt like shouting at him that she had a perfectly good feel for road layouts, due to her having a military-precision GPS system hardwired into her brain and installed in her imagination.

"We can go on my bike, and I've got a tent we could take, so we could stay there overnight to look. We could do letters to our parents saying we were going on a school trip, so that would be okay, but I don't think we would find anything there."

Dana was sure as soon as she got there, there would be a sign of some sort. She would recognise something from the wyvern's memory, or things would otherwise be made clear, if only she could get closer to the source of the wyvern. And if Ivor was still alive, he'd have a signal to enable her to find him, just like the beacon he'd built to guide her to the Flannan Isles before.

She stared at the keyboard on the floor, thinking about what Pauline and Graeme would say if they knew she was forging a letter so she could lie to them and avoid going to school, in order to travel miles away on a moped, with someone who was legally too young to ride it, to investigate something that might be dangerous and potentially meet with someone who was an Information Terrorist and who had caused a whole load of problems the last time she'd had contact with him.

And who was also the closest thing she had to a father.
"Let's do it. Show me how you write the letters."

-8-

DANA had re-read her forged letter so many times it had become grubby at the edges and worn around the creases. Today, the trials and tribulations of school and its unsympathetic wardens and vicious inmates did not seem so significant compared to what might happen at Pauline and Graeme's house if they could tell from the letter or Dana's manner that it was a trick.

She had already handed in the fake letter with Pauline's forged signature claiming that she would be unable to come in the next day because she had a dentist's appointment. Eric had written a different letter claiming he had to go to a great aunt's funeral, because he said the form tutors might speak to each other and suspect something if they both needed to go to the dentist on the same day. She was less concerned about this, as Eric reckoned a lot of parents couldn't write well and did unprofessional sick notes, but what did worry her was that the letter supposedly from the school, a professional organisation, wouldn't be convincing enough.

She and Eric had started off fooling around and writing silly letters: *Dear Mr and Mrs Rose, Dana has been permanently excluded from school on charges of High Treason and plotting to blow up the Houses of Parliament*, and *Dear Miss Carter, Eric has been found guilty of breaking wind without due care and attention and attempting to Pervert the Course of Justice, and will be duly executed by firing squad at dawn round the back of the PE building.*

After this, Eric had come up with the idea of a school Biology trip, because they were both good at science, and Dana had suggested that the form should have a tear-off strip for a parent or guardian to sign giving permission for the child to go. They had set it out with the tear-off part at the bottom and the school's letterhead copied off a detention form at the top. After some discussion, they had come up with the following letter:

Dear Parent or Guardian,

.... has been selected as a student of particular merit (Dana suggested 'merit', because it was meritocratic) *for a place in the end-of-year Biology field trip to New Forest* (they settled on New Forest by hanging a map of England on Eric's dart board and throwing a dart at it, and finding the nearest appropriate place to where the dart landed). *The coach will depart from the school gates at 9:30 am on Friday 21st and the excursion will involve two nights' stay in a campsite before return at 5:30 pm on Sunday. Please indicate consent by signing and returning the attached slip via your child's registration tutor.*

Eric had forged the headmaster's signature underneath.

Dana lay on her bed, holding the letter over her head and staring at the text as she waited for Pauline and Graeme to return from work. Cale's clanking music drifted in from the next room, and the summer heat beat down on the street outside.

At the sound of the front door opening, she slid off and went downstairs. "Graeme?"

"Hello Dana, did you have an okay day at school?"

When Dana had first come to live with Pauline and Graeme, Graeme had started off asking her if she had a *nice* day at school. But Dana had told him it was impossible for school ever to be nice, so ever since he'd instead asked if she'd had an *okay* day, as that was the best she could hope for.

"I've got invited to a field trip." Dana handed the letter to him, trying to sound as sincere as possible and hoping there was nothing in her demeanour or this mysterious 'body language' thing that neurotypical people are supposed to use to send each other secret messages that would give her away.

She watched Graeme's face with bated breath as he read the letter. When he'd finished, he looked at her and grinned. "Not like you to get all excited about something like a school trip, when you don't like school."

"I know, but I like science!" Immediately after she'd said it, she wondered if she'd been too quick with the answer.

"That's all very well, but you do understand there will be other people going on this field trip as well, and you might have to share tents with them?"

"Only nice people, like Mr Kell and Eric!"

Graeme burst out laughing. "I hope the school doesn't expect you to share a tent with Mr Kell and Eric."

Pauline had come in through the front door, behind Graeme. She nudged him. "Graeme, stop winding her up. I expect there's a woman teacher as well, and she'll be in the tent with the girls."

"Yes, Miss McCafferty." Dana picked the name of a female teacher she knew was well respected at the school. Even if this did work, what would happen if next parents' evening, Pauline and Graeme went up to Kell, or McCafferty, and asked them about the trip? Hopefully they would have forgotten about it by then.

"Hmm, I don't know," Graeme said. "I was planning on trailing around a boring old DIY shop this weekend and buying a new shed, and I need you to hold the nails and spare tools for me..."

Pauline interrupted him with a strident exclamation. "Graeme! Stop being so bloody silly!"

And then Pauline signed the fake letter so Dana could pretend to take it back to school, and the ruse had so far worked in that Pauline and Graeme wouldn't expect her back until the end of the weekend.

On Friday morning, Pauline left to take Cale to school. Dana mumbled a farewell to her in between mouthfuls of her breakfast, and Pauline told her she hoped she would enjoy her trip.

Graeme picked up Dana's bag. He made a noise like he was overexerting himself and dumped it back on the chair. "It weighs a ton! You can't carry that."

"It normally weighs that much," Dana protested. "You try feeling it when I've got PE and Physics and Maths!"

Graeme waved a hand dismissively. "Gimme five minutes and I'll give you a lift in to school and see you off."

Dana stared in horror at his back as he headed out into the hall. If he gave her a lift, to the school, there wouldn't be a coach for him to see off, and he would realise, and the school probably would as well. Whatever happened, Graeme would be angry and she'd have to spend today in school, exactly as she'd planned not to do. She forced down the rest of her breakfast cereal without chewing and followed him upstairs. "It doesn't matter, I can manage."

Graeme let off a sardonic laugh. "You don't want me to embarrass you at school?" He rinsed a plastic comb under the bathroom tap and ran it through his hair and sideburns.

Perhaps she should run with that. "Well, nobody else's dad comes with them at the start of a school trip."

"I bet they do *really*."

Dana was starting to feel the idea was done for and she was going to get caught, but then Graeme's mobile rang from inside his jacket pocket, and he went into his bedroom to answer it.

From what Dana could hear, the conversation he had was brief, and when he came back out he looked flustered, and walked straight past her to the stairs. "There's a problem at work and I'm going to have to go straight there. Sorry, Dana. You'll have to manage without me to embarrass you!"

The door slammed shut behind him, and now Dana was alone, standing still on the landing in the silent house.

Cale would know she was going away. Cale could hear Dana's thoughts, but he kept it to himself. He didn't really see any relevance in confiding in other people. He had his own thoughts, and that was enough for him. It was just the way he was, and the way it had always been since farther back than memory could reach, and it had never occurred to Dana to try to shield what she was thinking from him.

The last time she'd gone away like this, it had been when she'd met Jananin outside the hospital, but that had been very different. Leaving things as they were had not really been an option, at least not one that would have been any easier to deal with than the alternative. This time, there was nothing making her take this risk, other than the urge to find something, somewhere that would give her an answer. If she didn't do it, she'd be safe, and nothing would happen.

If she wanted to, she could send a text to Eric's phone telling him she couldn't come, and that would be the end of the matter.

But then she would never know.

Perhaps they would go there and not find anything, but if they *did* find something, what if it meant something bad? What if the thing she wanted most and the thing she was most afraid of were exactly the same? What *if*...

If Ivor had sent the wyvern after her... if Ivor had been doing something wrong, again, like the experiments he'd been doing that caused her to be born in the first place, that he'd promised Jananin he wouldn't do again.

It must have been a mistake. If it was Ivor behind this, she would be able to find him and stop him, she knew it, and everything would be all right.

She went back downstairs and struggled into her heavy backpack. On the dining table lay the envelope containing her filled-in order form with her selection of *Drosera* and *Sarracenia* plants she was going to put in the garden. If she posted it today, they would probably be delivered next week. She picked it up, remembering a postbox on the route she'd planned.

On the way to Eric's house, she tried to stick to back

alleys and little-used routes away from main roads, in case anyone from school saw her. It wasn't yet nine o'clock, and already the sun beat down hot on the tile roofs, and not a cloud was to be seen in the sky. Her shoulders sweltered under Duncan's heavy metal jacket and the chafing straps of the rucksack.

When she approached the back of Eric's house through the alley, the gate was ajar and the door was unlocked.

"Eric?" She poked her head into the catfood-smelling utility room. The internal door to the garage was open, and he appeared in the doorway.

"Come in, quickly."

Dana shut the door behind her.

Eric stared at the floor where she stood. "What you wearing wellies for?"

Dana glanced at her feet. "I thought you said not to wear impractical things!"

"I didn't mean *that* practical. I mean, who rides pillion on a bike wearing wellies? If the police see us, they're bound to stop us!"

Dana hated it when people seemed to expect her to know something nobody had ever explained was inappropriate as if by some sort of instinct she didn't have. "How am I supposed to know what the dress code is for riding motorbikes? I mean, we're not even old enough to ride motorbikes anyway!"

"Oh, never mind. The police will probably all be hanging around near schools, waiting for them to get out and start chucking paint and eggs and vandalising everything on the last day of term."

Dana threw her bag on the garage floor, sat on Eric's sofa, and pulled her jeans out of her wellies and rolled them down over the rubber so only the foot was visible. "Is that any better?"

"I suppose so. At least it's less obvious now." Eric stuffed Dana's rucksack into one of the bike's panniers. "What did you bring?"

"Sleeping bag, lunch. Other stuff."

"What other stuff?"

"You know, underwear and things like that."

"Oh, right." Eric went red in the face. "I suppose we'd better go now. I've brought extra food, so we should have enough for this evening as well."

He went back into the utility room to lock up, before opening the garage door and wheeling the moped out. Dana waited for him to shut the garage door and get on before she climbed on behind him.

"The A14 goes due east, more or less," said Eric. "Unless you've got any better suggestions, we could try that as a start."

Dana could just about visualise the road, a green line snaking east. Nothing was triggering any memories yet. Perhaps something would remind her once they were closer. Perhaps there might even be another beacon, or something like that. "Okay."

Much of the view ahead was impossible to see from her seat on the back of the bike. Dana tried turning her head to watch the scenery pass, but it made her neck ache. Soon, they were out of the suburbs and tearing along a straight road through the countryside.

Dana began to get stiff from sitting in the same position and hanging on to Eric. The vibrations from the bike's engine and the asphalt under the tyres made her legs go numb. The biker helmet became suffocatingly hot, and the sides of it grew sweaty and pressed uncomfortably on her cheeks. Dust from the road penetrated her jacket and trousers and made her skin feel gritty and sticky. By half past eleven, hunger had turned into a sickly ache in Dana's belly, and Eric pulled over into a layby. When Dana dismounted and pulled off her helmet, her hair was plastered to her head with sweat and felt disgusting.

Eric stripped off his jacket and helmet. "I'm starving. You got the map?"

"No. I thought you had it." Dana didn't need a map to

tell they were in Cambridgeshire. The town of Cambridge itself lay not far to the south, and she could make out the greyish-brown clutter of the city amidst the patchwork of green woodland and fields of crops. Cambridge was where Jananin lived, or at least where she had lived before the Information Terrorism attack on London, and before she became a Spokesman for the Meritocracy. Dana wondered where amongst this city her house might be, what it would be like.

"Bugger. We'd better not have forgotten it."

Traffic whipped past on the road behind. Beyond the low steel barrier at the edge of the layby, a field of sun-burnished grass going to seed waved very slightly in the still, dusty air, a golden sea tinged with violet. Dana spread her jacket on the shorter grass of the embankment to sit on while Eric rummaged through the panniers.

They sat on the bank and ate the food they'd brought, with the map spread in front of them. Even though they'd discussed a plan beforehand and agreed to save some for that night, Dana was so hungry right now it didn't seem to matter any more, and she ate all the sandwiches Pauline had made for her to take, and the fruit and crisps and chocolate, and Eric didn't seem to leave much either.

"Where to now?" Eric said.

Dana gazed at the meadow and the hazy air laden with exhaust fumes and pollen. So far, she hadn't sensed anything. She was tired and aching from being on the bike, and it was starting to look as though this might lead nowhere, and now she couldn't go back home until the excuse they'd made up finished on Sunday. The plan wasn't looking so good now.

When she didn't reply, Eric suggested, "If we go north from here, we could go to the beach. My mum'll never take me because it's too far away and she hasn't got a car, and I suppose it's the weather for it."

Unable to think of any better suggestion, Dana agreed. The idea of a beach heaving with tourists didn't seem appealing, but she supposed the beach might not be a stereotypical one, as the ones in Devon where Duncan had promised to take her, where there were fossils and shells, weren't. After they had finished their food and drunk some water, they put the bags and the map back into the panniers. Dana reluctantly pushed her sticky, constricting helmet back onto her head.

A few hours later, they reached the road GPS reckoned was closest to the sea. However, there was no track leading down to rocky cliffs riddled with faint prints and stains from long-dead sea creatures, nor any shore of shells to hunt through and get painfully stuck to the soles of one's feet. There was not even a path through dunes leading to a sandy beach concealed beneath sun-reddened flesh hanging out of bikinis and hairy grizzled male bodies in garish swimming trunks. All that was there was a flat expanse of waterlogged muck with low hummocks of scrubby grass on it, stretching away as far as the eye could see, and no flat blue horizon of sea laced with white foam anywhere to be seen.

"Oh," said Eric. His eyes looked red and wet, and he took off his biker glove to wipe his nose on the back of his hand. "I'm all right. It's just the pollen." He pointed to the field behind, full of bright yellow flowers that gave off a strong and not entirely pleasant smell.

"What is that?" Dana asked. With no wLAN in range, she couldn't look it up.

"Oilseed rape."

Dana ruffled her hair in an attempt to increase the air circulation around her sweaty scalp. If anything, the day had grown hotter, but a very slight breeze flowed from the marshland and the unseen sea that must lie beyond it to the north. She closed her eyes and inhaled, letting it cool her face. And as she stood there, she sensed a faint, living pulse — a *signal*.

She looked up to the sky. The shape of a hawk hung there, wings stretched wide, shouldering an updraught.

"Look, a bird. I think it's a bird of prey. It looks *big*."

Eric stared up at it. "The biggest bird of prey in Britain is the Golden Eagle."

"It doesn't look golden," said Dana. It looked mostly white from underneath, with a darker colour around the edges. "What colour's a Golden Eagle supposed to be?"

"I think it's sort of brown. Perhaps it's an illegal immigrant eagle."

Dana squinted up at it. "I think it's watching us."

Eric shrugged. "They only eat rabbits and pigeons."

"Not big ones. They carry off whole sheep and stuff. And anyway, that's not what I meant. Look, it's circling round. I'm sure it's watching us."

Dana concentrated on the signal, but there wasn't any two-way communication available to her. She could no more control it than she could control the GPS signal that she used to orient herself and navigate. "It's probably circling on a thermal," Eric suggested. "That's what big birds like eagles and vultures do."

"I mean, what if someone used a bird to spy on people? Like they made the wyvern?"

"Oh, I see. You mean a bird with a camera tied to it. Mint! I remember reading something — I don't know if it really happened, or if it was something in a book or a film — but some spies put lots of expensive cameras and stuff on a cat, 'cause they wanted to use it for spying and that, but when they put it outside it went into the road and got run over!"

"Poor cat!" said Dana. "Perhaps it would be more sensible to use an eagle."

The eagle was starting to drift away. It slipped out of the thermal and began beating its wings slowly. Dana followed it along the side of the road, back in the direction they'd come. This could be the signal, the clue that would guide her to the place the wyvern was made. She didn't want to put the helmet back on and suffer its sticky claustrophobia pressing against her scalp and cheeks, and she didn't want to get back onto the bike and put up with it jarring against her stiff limbs one minute more. Eric wheeled the bike behind her. Each stride eased a little of the stiffness out of her legs.

The bird could fly far faster than she could walk, and it wasn't long before it came away from the road's route and Dana lost both its signal and sight of it against the glare of the afternoon sun.

"Didn't look like a normal bird," said Eric.

"Perhaps it was a falconry bird, and it escaped?" Belatedly, Dana remembered something she'd been told when she went to see a falconry display with Duncan and Graeme. The birds had all had electronic tags on them that allowed them to be tracked on GPS. Perhaps that was all the signal she'd been picking up was.

"We can go birdwatching tomorrow," Eric said. "We need to think about where we're going to camp and what we're going to do about dinner, since we ate all our food for lunch."

The field on the other side to the marshland was lower down than the roads, and Dana could make out what looked like onions growing in the soil there. She climbed down off the road and found herself on the edge of a ditch with a bit of stagnant water in the bottom. "They build a moat round the field to stop people stealing the food and camping in it?"

Eric stumbled down beside her. "It's a dyke. I mean, what the Dutch people built to channel the water out when they drained the fens."

A little farther down the length of the dyke stood a small outcrop of a few trees and bushes. That place might be the most concealed. "Perhaps we could camp in there."

"Okay." Eric looked up the far side of the dyke, to the drooping onion leaves that were starting to turn yellow in the sun. "You know when you go to your grandma's house, and she does roast beef and Yorkshire pudding for you, and you have roast onions with it?"

"I dunno really. I haven't got a grandma." Graeme's mother was the only one still alive, and Dana had only seen her a few times. She lived in sheltered accommodation and got Meals on Wheels.

"I wonder how you make a roast onion."

"In an oven, I expect," Dana suggested. "It's only really barbecues that you can cook on outdoors I think." She could remember when Graeme had made a barbecue and insisted on trying to cook the food without Pauline's help, and it had all been burnt.

"Perhaps we can make barbecued onions."

"We haven't got a barbecue, either."

"On a camping fire, then. That's what you do, when you go camping."

"We could always buy some food," Dana suggested.

"Did you bring money, then?"

Dana hadn't brought any money, and she didn't have any better ideas, so she agreed to give it a go. They each gathered up some brush and dry grass. "We ought to make it somewhere we can put it out quickly if it goes out of control," Dana suggested.

Eric agreed with her. "Let's make it on the other bank. If it sets the grass on fire or something, you can take off your wellies and I can go and fill 'em with water out the dyke."

Crossing the dyke turned out to be easier said than done. They decided it would be easier to throw the firewood across first, rather than trying to scramble across with their hands full, and in this way they ended up scattering most of it on the opposite bank.

Dana went first. She slithered down the bank and jumped across the water, landing on her hands and feet on the opposite side. She climbed up and began to gather the firewood.

Eric jumped too early and slid down the bank into the water. It wasn't very deep, but it didn't look very clean, and it soaked his feet and ankles pretty well and made him swear.

"That's why I wore wellies!" Dana jeered at him.

When he got to the top and took off his trainers, his socks were all brown. He swore and made noises of disgust as he took them off. He wrung them out and started leaping about and flapping them in his hands, like a Morris dancer.

Dana chose a spot concealed from the road by the bushes and trees on the other side of the dyke. Conveniently, a pile of broken bricks and builder's rubble lay nearby. She pulled up the grass and made a ring of bricks and stones to build the fire in. Eric hung his socks on a bush and set to work lighting the fire, while Dana pulled up some fat onions and also some turnips that she found in a field a bit farther down the road.

"We've not brought a pan," she realised when she got back. "How are we going to cook them?"

"I dunno," said Eric. "How do people normally cook things?"

"I think when people have onions they usually cook them in a frying pan in oil."

Eric frowned. "There's some oil in the moped."

"I don't think that's the right sort of oil." Dana thought back to how she'd seen other people cook things: usually at Pauline and Graeme's house, food would be either fried, boiled in water, steamed, or cooked under the grill. Occasionally, cakes and meat were cooked in the oven. The Japanese food Dana knew how to make all involved pans. Even the lobsters and potatoes Ivor had cooked needed a pan to boil in.

Then she remembered a country fair Graeme had taken her to the last summer. The depressing apprehension of the approaching end of the summer holiday had been hanging over her at the time, but she'd forgotten about it because they'd had archery and owls and huntsmen, and shops selling 'tat' as Pauline called it, and people who brewed cider and mead and kept bees, and a man who carved things out of bits of wood. And there had been a whole pig cooked on a spit above an open fire, which was called a hog roast, and Graeme had bought some, in a bun with apple sauce on it. It had been juicy and crisp, and with more flavour than normal roast pork.

"Here, you make holes on either side of the fire, and put sticks in them like cave men did in pictures." She went back to the pile of rubble, where she recalled having seen an old copper pipe. She retrieved it and stuck the turnips and onions on it like a kebab. By the time she'd finished, Eric had the sticks in to support it and the fire going.

They sat and watched the food cooking. It started to go black on the outside, so Dana cut off a piece to see if it was done. The outside tasted burnt, but the inside was still raw and the overall taste was horrible. Eric suggested that they might need turning to make sure they cooked evenly, and he burnt his hand on the hot metal and knocked the spit over so all the food fell down in the ash and dust.

Dana cut up the burnt bits of turnip and onion with the penknife that had been mixed in with the camping gear. At first both of them sat and ate solemnly, and Dana pretended to like it since they had done it themselves from scratch, and she felt an element of pride in their effort.

"Mm," said Eric, "this is a good method of cooking turnips." Then he tried to swallow and retched, and Dana spat out her mouthful of burnt onion, whereupon they both admitted it was foul, and laughed and took great zeal in throwing it in the dyke.

"I don't know," said Dana, exasperated. She thought back to the food Ivor had made on Roareim with a newfound respect. "Maybe it only works on meat. Perhaps we could build a trap and catch a rabbit."

Eric hung his trainers by their laces on the spit over the fire. "I've not noticed any rabbits. And I don't know how to build a trap."

Dana sighed. She knew roughly what a trap should look like, but she was too hot and hungry to think about what to make one from or search for the materials.

"Gypsies, in the olden days, used to catch hedgehogs and roll them up in clay and cook them. The spikes are supposed to come off in the clay. Hedgehogs don't run very fast."

Dana shifted her legs in the uncomfortable position she was crouching. "But then the hedgehogs would still be alive when they were cooked! That's horrible. And I bet they taste awful, anyway."

"Perhaps there's one squashed on the road somewhere."

"Urh!" Dana stood up. She really was very hungry, and the thought of succulent hog roasts, and of lobsters and Ivor's rabbits — she was sure her memory had exaggerated them, as she didn't recall finding them particularly good at the time — was making her mouth water. For the last few minutes, she had been unconsciously aware of an unpleasant rubbery smell, and at this point she noticed it and turned back to the fire, where Eric had left his wet trainers too close to the edge of the burning material. "Your shoes are on fire!"

Eric shouted an expletive and kicked over the spit. He beat the trainers with a stick, although they were not really on fire, merely smouldering and stinking. Dana started to laugh. "You wouldn't laugh, if it happened to you!" Eric objected. It suddenly didn't seem to matter so much that they had come here and not found anything, and that Dana was aching and hungry and the food they had tried to make was inedible.

"Do you like Chinese food?" she asked Eric.

"Course I like Chinese food, but we haven't got any, unless you stuffed a wok in the back of my bike without me noticing." Eric shovelled dusty earth over his trainers and stamped on them to extinguish them.

"I've just remembered something." It might be a bad idea to bring this up. She hadn't tried it since Ivor has asked her to do it for him, and even then she'd known it was wrong, and the security on the machines might have been changed since to make it harder to hack into. Dana had a top-up payment card that would only allow her to pay for items legal for people under eighteen to buy up to the value of the money on it, that she or Pauline or Graeme had paid into it. At the moment the card had nothing on it, but she could probably make the machine that read the card *think* there was money on it. "I think I do have some money, on a payment card. We could go into a town near here and find a Chinese."

"Cool, and thanks." He exhumed his shoes and tried to shake the dust off them. "Even if it's not a very nice Chinese place, it's got to be better than anything we can do."

By now, the day was cooling off and the sun was getting low and ruddy. Clouds of midges had begun to emerge from the marsh and the dyke. Eric grimaced as he squashed his feet back into his wet, muddied, singed trainers.

They rode back towards Spalding, where Dana had found a Chinese restaurant on the Internet via a wLAN she'd sensed coming from someone's house. When they arrived, the man who took the order stared at them, and at the brown water oozing from Eric's shoes, and told them he wouldn't serve them unless they paid in advance. Dana offered him her payment card and, despite her concerns, found she could still interfere with the card reader's signal and make it think she'd paid.

The restaurant had a buffet system where you could take a plate and have as many helpings as you liked. Dana had mussels in black bean sauce, egg-fried rice, sweet & sour pork, and seaweed and crab claws with a skewer of spicy chicken. They sat at a table by a pond with Koi carp in it, where Eric kept pretending to drop bits of rice in the pond for the fish to eat, because he said they looked hungry. For dessert, Dana chose some deep-fried fruits drizzled with sticky syrup, and afterwards they had a pot of jasmine-scented green tea to share, served in thimblelike ceramic cups with no handle, like sencha was served in Japan, which was deliciously refreshing after the heavy meal and very sweet dessert. A lady came around the tables and handed out fortune cookies, and Eric's said *Your trouble will soon pass*, and Dana's said *Wisdom comes from experience.*

By the time they left the restaurant, dusk had fallen. Back at the site they'd picked to camp in, they had to use the torch to assemble the tent, with much difficulty. Dana lay awake in her sleeping bag, staring at the tent's canvas ceiling illuminated by the moonlight behind it, and listened to the sounds of insects and rustling of unidentified animals, and the occasional whisper of a car's tyres on the nearby road. A faint oniony smell permeated the air, and it was starting to make her nose feel clogged. From the regular sound of his breathing, she could tell Eric was already asleep. She ran through the memories the wyvern had given her several times, but nothing she'd seen today triggered any connection. She had been hoping something else might have been implanted in her, something subconscious or otherwise hidden, that she would recognise when she saw something that would trigger it. Now it was looking obvious that wouldn't happen and she had been wrong. The only thing she had seen was the bird, and that might be nothing to do with this. She had only two more days to look for information, and she had no idea where to start.

-9-

YOU can't remember becoming aware of being here again, back in what seems to be a dream you think you've had before. The familiar drone of a fan is barely perceptible. You can sense only a leaden feeling throughout your body, and your eyesight is filled with grey unfocused masses.

Gamma? What's the matter?

My own consciousness is sticky, wrapped around yours like Velcro. It's a while before I can pull together enough that I think is myself to answer. *The medicine must have worn off. You're not supposed to be here.*

Small details become briefly comprehensible: the barred window, and the striped light it throws on the wall opposite. The mattress under my back.

Something's wrong! Try to think!

I'm not supposed to listen to you. That's what they say. You're a symptom; you're part of what's making me ill.

You remember them, men and women wearing white coats, asking probing questions, trying to trap us, nurses in blue uniforms, cold faces, hard hands. *Don't listen to them. You're only ill because they give you bad medicine that hurts you.*

I can think of no reply to this.

They're always telling you that what's in your head is fake, and that what's here is real. What if they're wrong, and it's the other way round? What if this is fake, and we can get out of it and make something else real?

I lie there and I listen to the fan and stare at the stripes cast by the bars on the wall, and my mind is empty. You fear I am ignoring you, that I won't hear. I can't be bothered with the answer. It doesn't matter what's real and what isn't. If I take their medicine, it goes away. I don't have to be me any more. I can just be nothing.

But I can help you get to the place that's safe.

The Emerald Forge? The name kindles some ember trapped deep within me, of a fire I'd thought long extinguished.

The Emerald Forge.

I sit up on the bed with the straps. The motion sets the room heaving and a sick ache starts up in my stomach. Pain shoots through my head and neck.

They give me this stuff, this medicine, to make me better?

Let's get out of here. Let's go to the Emerald Forge, you think.

I wait for the room to stop swimming before sliding my feet off the bed and easing my weight onto the floor. Every step I take sends electric charges of pain lancing up my neck and into my head and eyes.

We tell the door to unlock. The open door to the shower-room stands ahead. A memory stirs, shudders within us.

Not in there. To the Emerald Forge. Down the stairs.

I hold on to the banister as I descend. The stairs are covered with sticky lino with metal grips on the edges that hurt my toes. My legs are weak. I can't remember when I last walked. I think they've been giving me drugs for a long time. I don't remember you being here much.

There's another electronically locked door that leads out into a foyer. Thin light from a window reveals seats and magazines and a big money tree succulent in an urn. You remember the name of that plant. *Crassula.* It looks civilised, not like the unreal side of this world that is more familiar. You wonder if whoever comes here to wait, to sit on these seats and read these magazines, knows what goes on behind the other door, in the deeper parts of the building.

The opposite door leads outside. The horizon is pale,

watery light behind broken cloud, the sun yet to rise.

You tell me the thought that will unlock the door and at last we are out, breathing clean air carrying the chill of early autumn, in the prison-like courtyard you remember seeing from the upstairs window. There's a large metal gate painted black directly opposite the building's exit, but the walls are all made of concrete and topped with barbed wire strung along poles angled inwards.

I look to the eastern horizon where the sky lightens, and stabbing pains shoot through my eyes and jaw. I turn away and blunder into the wall, but the pain is still getting worse. My insides have clenched into a burning knot of agony. I put my hands against the wall, but my legs won't support me, and I'm bending double and sinking to the ground. My mouth is full of slaver and my head spins. My guts lurch and panic grips me. I breathe in and out hard and fast, trying to hold back the urge to vomit. Again I swallow, force it down, but an alarming gargle rises up my throat even though there's no breath there to power my voice. And then it comes again and I can't stop it, and it burns my mouth and it stinks, and this awful greasy acidic slime is all up against the back of my nose and coating my tongue and lips, and running onto the concrete floor.

I cough and I force bitter saliva from the sides of my tongue, spit, trying to wash the taste away.

The sound of a motor comes, the rattle of the front gate moving.

Someone's coming. Quickly! Move!

You urge limbs to move, to coordinate and stand in the way you know, but the muscles of this body are not yours, and I am hunched snivelling and shivering over a pool of sick.

You have to move now. If we stay here, they are going to catch us.

There is a car engine making a noise somewhere near the gate. We are going to get caught, again, and the thought of their hands on me, restraining, forcing, is repulsive. Are we just going to stay here and let it happen, again, because Epsilon keeps vigil while Gamma falls apart?

The engine sound is growing louder. You strain to move, and suddenly something in me gives. *I can't do this. You are better than me.*

Your legs straighten and you're up on your feet, your field of vision swinging with giddy nausea. It's unfamiliar, somehow, as though you did it years ago and it's not as easy as you remember. This body is alien to you, but you know enough to make it work. You make it to the green plastic industrial bins against the wall in four unsteady strides before you fall down, out of sight.

Your vision is swimming and you can't seem to get your eyes to focus. You can just make out the tyres of the vehicle as they pass by, from under the bins. Your sides spasm into another retch, and you feel a hot line track down from the corner of your mouth, but when you try to raise your hand to your face to wipe it off, you can't seem to find the right place to put it. The pain, the cold, and the leaden predawn sky are so much more intense now. Something isn't adding up. How did you get here? You know you came from somewhere, but you can't remember where. You've seen this place before, but it's not yours. When you try to remember your own name, the only word that comes to mind is *Epsilon.*

Gamma?

You can still sense me, but I don't reply.

Gamma, whatever just happened, you have to undo it.

Still no reply. Fragmented memories of another life, somewhere else, start to return: a brother; a family, a man, a woman, and an older boy. You can't remember their names, but you used to know them. *I can't. You have to do this. Not me.*

My reply takes a long time to come. *I'm no good at it. You have it. You keep this. I don't want to be this any more. I don't want to be me; I'd rather not be anyone.*

You feel me withering inside us. What happens if you

become me? You're sleeping now, in the world you know. There are people there who care about you. In the morning, will they find you in bed, unresponsive and in a coma, or something worse? If you have to become someone else, will you cease to be?

Because you're the only one who can make what you want into a reality. Because if you won't be responsible for yourself, no-one else can be expected to. Because you're the only person who can be you.

You pull yourself up by the handle on the back of the bin, and force in a deep inhalation. *I won't help you any more until you stop this.*

The indifference I feel turns to a sharp point of spite. *You let them catch you again, and you deal with it. Your problem now. I'm leaving.*

You begin to count breaths, the way a man you used to know once taught you. *You can't leave. There's nowhere for you to go.*

By the time you have counted to six, breathing becomes less of a conscious effort. When you get to twelve, you're sinking back into the more familiar passive state, and the limbs you feel you no longer control, and everything is becoming as a dream once more.

Okay. Now what?

The gate. There should be an order that will open it.

What is it?

Can you move out slowly so I can get a better look at it?

My hand is shaking, but I put it on the corner of the bin and edge around slowly so we're facing the gate. You feel for the signal, pry at it with your thoughts in the same way you've always known. It only takes a few seconds to work out how to unlock it.

Got it. Before I open it, let's make sure we're not being watched.

I pan slowly across the empty courtyard, searching for signs of life. Nothing can be seen behind the blank windows, and we will just have to hope no-one is there to catch sight of us running the gauntlet from the bins to the gate.

You give the command, and the thin whine of the electric motor starts up, and the gate begins to slide back. *Run now.*

Loose debris on the concrete hurts my feet as I make as fast as I can towards the widening gap. Through the bars I can see a wide flat landscape of farmlands and fields, a road leading to freedom.

As soon as we're through, you give the command for the gate to shut, and the motor's pitch changes as it slides back.

A ditch at the edge of the road comes into view. *Get in it!*

I jump, slip, and fall into a foot of muddy, stagnant water. It stains the white fabric of my lunatic asylum pyjama trousers and sleeves.

You struggle to think over the sensation of my feet sinking into gritty silt. *We need to move. We're not safe until we get away from this place.*

I begin to move along the ditch, which has been dug into the side of the field, probably as some sort of drainage channel. It's slow going. Hopefully, the bottom of the ditch isn't visible from the place we escaped from. The white clothing will surely be conspicuous if anyone does see.

The sound of tyres on the road above fades into hearing range.

Someone's coming.

Keep still. They might not notice. There's nothing else we can do.

A car door slams. I stay in the bottom of the ditch, and we hope together that the person will go away.

A voice behind. A man stands at the top of the bank, looking down. I recognise his face with a jolt of fear, and then you lose contact.

*

When Dana and Eric awoke in the morning, the tent

had partially fallen down by itself.

"Oh well, at least it won't be so much work to take it down," Eric laughed. He opened his rucksack to discover the food he had smuggled out of the Chinese restaurant the previous night had leaked beancurds and yellow bean sauce all over his maps and spare clothes. Dana laughed as he tried to separate what remained unspilled and what remained unsoiled from the mess, making noises of disgust and throwing sticky items on the ground. It was only when she looked away from him that she noticed a glossy grey-black thing with a knobbly texture rippling underneath the long grass close to her feet.

"Hey, look, a snake!"

Graeme had once found a harmless grass snake in a compost bin in the garden, and had picked it up and allowed Dana to stroke it carefully before putting it back. She knew there was only one other kind of snake, called a viper, that was venomous but that very rarely bit and would normally flee from people, and something else called a slow worm that was actually not a snake. Immediately after she spoke she realised something was not right about this snake. The diameter of it was enormous, as thick as her thigh, and she was sure vipers were not meant to be that big, and at any rate, vipers were supposed to be green with a black diamond pattern on the back, and this snake was more of a dark grey with narrow yellow stripes.

Something reared up feet away from her with a noise like someone spitting down a long plastic drainpipe — a neck that flared into a head covered in scaly armour plates, a hood with a throat like corn-on-the-cob. Dana leaned back on her hands and pushed towards the tent with her feet, unable to move fast enough as the head flew at her, and then Eric grabbed her arm and pulled her up the bank and out of the snake's way.

Dana landed at the top of the bank by the tent. Her hand fell on a rock and she flung it at the snake. She rubbed her eyes furiously with her free hand while she searched for another. Dust must have got into them, or the fright of the snake must have done something to her mind, because now it looked like there were far more snakes than just one, all rearing and flailing wildly.

She rolled over onto her knees and found another stone. As she got to her feet and raised her hand to throw it, she noticed something else. At the bottom of the dyke was some great thick brown body with four clawed legs spinning in the mud and a craggy tail churning up the water. The bodies of the snakes seemed to be attached to where the neck of this thing should be.

Eric waddled up beside her bent double. Gripped between his knees and supported by his hands was a lump of concrete masonry with a rusty metal rod sticking out of it. He heaved it forward, into the dyke, and it landed hard on the shoulders of the beast at the bottom, driving it down into the mud. The snakes immediately fell silent and collapsed like puppets with the strings cut.

Both of them stood breathing hard and gazing down into the dyke, where there lay the motionless and headless body of a huge lizard with snakes attached instead where its head should be. Dana realised she was shaking. She took deep breaths and tried to count the snake heads. *Seven.*

"This is mad," said Eric breathlessly. "First it was the wyvern, and then this. They've got to be King Cobras! They're, like, the most poisonous snakes in the world! Someone stole them from a zoo; do you reckon they're the same ones?"

Dana shrugged, out of breath and unable to come up with a response. She stared at the dead lizard and the dead snakes draped over it and trailing in the water. A memory came to mind, the news report with the crazy woman, the reptiles stolen from a zoo. "The body must be a Komodo Dragon."

Eric grimaced. "I saw it on a wildlife programme. Komodo Dragons have saliva so full of bacteria that if they bite you, you get blood poisoning and die. They find a gnu or something and sneak up to it and bite it, and they follow it for days until it drops dead."

"It's not like it can do that anyway," Dana said. "It's got no head, so it can't have any saliva.

"How did they end up sewn together like that? D'you think it's a science experiment that escaped from a secret government lab?"

Dana shook her head. "It's the Meritocracy now, not the government, and I don't think the Meritocracy does stuff like that."

"Maybe the Dutch brought it with them when they came to drain the fens? Bloody foreigners!" He paused for a moment, breathing loudly. "Does stuff like this always happen wherever you go?"

Dana shrugged, trying to be noncommittal. "Something like that." In a way, she wished she could tell him she was the product of an experiment and she could *think* to the wyvern and the computers and stuff. She wasn't sure what he would think if he did tell her. Probably he would either not believe her at all, or go off on another one of his crackpot conspiracy theories about *governments*. He probably wouldn't understand the real conspiracy that had been behind the government when he'd inadvertently helped her attack it in the Cerberus game, and Jananin wouldn't want her telling him that at any rate.

"When I first met you in the Cerberus game, I just thought you were weird, but playing the game with you was really mint. Then I met you in real life and people were saying bad stuff about you, but they were wrong, and it's like real life is as mint as a game. You're awesome."

"Thanks," said Dana. No-one had ever said she was awesome before. It made her feel kind of warm inside to have a friend, to have someone who liked her for who she was. "You're awesome too. Everyone else at the school is, like, well, a dickhead, but you're not like them."

It became conspicuous to her that Eric was standing far too close for comfort, and yet when she turned to face him, he put his hand on her and his face loomed in hers.

Dana stumbled as she pulled away from him. Her foot slid and she fell backwards and scraped the heel of her hand on the ground. "What are you doing?" Stones dug into her fingers as she scrabbled to put some distance between herself and him, moving backwards in an uncoordinated shuffle.

Eric's face had gone red. "I— I thought we were friends."

"Not *that* way!" Dana finally found a footing and stood up.

"What is it, are you, like, a lesbian or something?" Eric's manner had become sneering. His voice was sardonic and unpleasant.

"Yes, I'm a lesbian." Dana didn't really know if she was gay, but she hoped it would make him feel better and stop him from trying what he'd just done again.

Eric glared at her, a bitter expression twisting his face. "You're lying. What is it? Is it because I'm a nerd? Because I'm not *fit* like popular lads, like boys in magazines? Because I don't like sport and I like heavy metal and computer games? Am I just minging?"

Dana stared back at him. She didn't know how to answer these questions, and she didn't know what she wanted, only that she didn't want Eric in her personal space and making her feel that way, and she didn't know how to express this to him in words.

Eric's voice broke into a shrill yell. "You think you're so much better than me! You think the popular lads like Smith and Avery will want you for a girlfriend? They won't! You're just as weird and crap as I am, and you'll not get any better offers."

Without realising it, Dana had been backing away from him. When he shouted, she couldn't stand to look at him any more, and she turned her back on him and walked into the onion field.

"I'm making a Wellington Bomber," she murmured to

herself, but either he didn't hear or he didn't understand.

"Fine! Just walk away from me!" Eric roared behind her.

Dana heard the splash of him throwing something into the dyke, but she didn't turn back. She couldn't deal with people when they got into this state, the same as she couldn't deal with it when she got in a state herself. Normally she would go to her room and make Airfix models, but she couldn't do that here, so she concentrated on the ground she was walking on to try to stop it from overwhelming her.

Eric must have been wanting what some kids did at school, to call themselves *girlfriend* and *boyfriend*. Dana wasn't quite sure what girlfriends and boyfriends actually did, because she'd never seen them at it in school, but she suspected they were either doing or preparing to do what the school taught in Biology lessons and in that stupid subject they called Personal and Social Education that was usually about indoctrinating people not to be racist and pollute the environment. It was *sex*, something crude and mechanical that you had to do in a certain ritual order in a bed, involving inserting parts of other people into one's person, and yet animals somehow managed to do it without attending PSE lessons or reading an instruction booklet with lurid fleshy diagrams. It was something that was revolting and unhygienic and that you could get diseases from doing, and it was supposed to be how normal people, not like her and Cale, who had been made in a test tube by Ivor Pilgrennon instead of in the usual way, were conceived and grew inside a woman in order to turn into people.

She had never even thought about it, at least not as having any relevance to her. It was just one of those things other people did, one of those things she didn't do because she wasn't like other people. It belonged in that side of the world where she didn't trespass. *Women* had sex and got pregnant, and Dana wasn't a *woman* and she didn't have sex and get pregnant. Things like that were alien to her. It didn't belong in the world she lived in.

Dana always hated it when people pretended to be her friends and used her, like the girl who'd thought it was funny to invite her to places and not turn up. People like that made her want to scream and hit something. Now was what she had done to Eric the same as that? Was she a horrible person because she'd only ever thought of using him to help her find Ivor? Because she'd not listened to his ideas about the wyvern when she'd been so keen to use it as an excuse to contact Jananin? Dana had known all her life that other people were not like her, and that other people could be unkind and unsympathetic purely because they did not like that she was not like them, and she supposed she'd always thought she was better than them in a way, because she wouldn't treat someone like herself who was different badly just for being that way. Didn't this just prove that she wasn't?

A choking tension had gathered in her throat. Dana blinked furiously and sniffed hard to clear her nose. What else could she have done? Could she have just let him do that to her, even if it felt revolting and wrong? Perhaps she wasn't really different. Perhaps everyone else saw things exactly as she did, but they were just stronger than her, better at coping, and understood what was the proper impression to make in social situations like that. Perhaps the stuff they taught in biology about sex and about how people are supposed to enjoy it and the stuff they do before it was all lies, a conspiracy to make people accept it, otherwise the species would die out. *Perhaps I am gay.* If a minority of people are gay and a minority of people have autistic conditions, she supposed it might make sense, because both of them are different to what people are told they are supposed to be like.

It had never occurred to her, when she had asked Eric to come here with her, hiding her true motives, he might also have had motives he didn't disclose. She'd had no idea he might be thinking that. She had used him, and she had used the wyvern. The wyvern could be lying dead on some secret Meritocracy scientist's table for all she knew, and it would all be her fault, for not thinking straight, for thinking only about what she wanted and not what others needed more.

She kept walking, and the field of onions gave way to a road, and then to a field of potatoes, that reminded her of the ones Ivor used to grow in Roareim.

Ivor, I wish you were here now. Ivor would have had something to say that would make her feel better. He always did.

Beyond this she came upon a different crop: a wall of tall plants a little bit like bamboo grass with long, lined blades coming from an upright central stalk. Mop-like anemones with stringy fronds coloured a livid burgundy-purple hung from the junctions between stem and leaves. Dana decided they were the maize plants that sweetcorn grew on, or at least something very like them. She pushed in between a gap in the stems and began to make her way into the field.

The maize plants closed ranks around her. Their long stems reached up well above her head, concealing the flat landscape around the field so all that was visible above was blue sky. She continued until she came upon a space on the ground where some of the maize seeds hadn't germinated, and crouched down there.

She put her hand in her pocket and found Ivor's watch and her fuses, and a fortune cookie from the night before, still in its foil wrapper. She took it out and broke it: the slip of paper inside said, *Great fortune awaits you.* Dana knelt on the ground and ate the cracker, and poked the paper slip down a crevice in the dry soil at the base of one of the maize plant stems.

Dana put her cheek and palms to the hard, stony earth. She gradually stretched herself out, finding a natural position where her joints could accommodate the arrangement of the plants. She lay there and gazed at the forest of maize stems and the soil at eye level, holding Ivor's watch in the palm of her hand inside her pocket. There was not even the slightest wind, and the field was still and silent apart from occasional small noises from insects. Dana felt the roots below and the leaves above, ensconcing her in a private chamber away from people. She shut her eyes and breathed, and then she twisted onto her back and studied the bizarre flowers against the backdrop of the intense sky. She drank the water out of her bottle until it was all gone.

Eric wouldn't be able to find her here if he did come looking. There was no point carrying on with this now. She couldn't face him after what had happened. It would be best if she could just find her own way back to Pauline and Graeme's house on buses or whatever she could find. She would be able to get to a wLAN and sort something out. And she could send Eric a text message, explaining that she would go home by herself. She would have to make up something to tell Pauline and Graeme. Maybe she could say a kid on the trip who had a nut allergy ate a peanut sandwich and had to go to hospital, and the whole thing was called off and everyone had to go home.

She found Pauline's phone in her jeans pocket, the other side to the one in which she kept the fuses and Ivor's watch. After taking it out, switching it on, and wiping lint and smeary marks off the screen with her sleeve, she considered how to phrase it.

Hi Eric, not feeling well, going home, pretending trip called off because kid had nut allergic reaction.

Dana could think the message direct to the phone, so she didn't have to mess around with the phone's touch-sensitive keyboard, but she put her thumb to the send button without pressing it, nevertheless. Was there anything else she could say? She wished there was something that would make it as though it had never happened, something that would put things back the way they were before. Whenever she thought of anything to do with Eric, that image of his face looming over her came to mind, a nauseating sensation of horror at someone else intruding on her. Why did he have to do that? It had ruined everything. She couldn't even think of the time they'd fought the wyvern off or the time at his house when they'd played *Pillage and Burn III*, which had been good memories before, without this contaminating it.

She read the message again, and imagined sending it, but something else caught her attention, a signal.

Dana put the phone back into her pocket and rolled onto her knees. The signal grew stronger, and then the form of a hawk broke over the patch of sky visible from her hiding place, and it disappeared just as fast from the opposite side.

She got to her feet quickly. She couldn't see the bird any more, and the signal was already fading, but she could tell it was flying in a straight line. Stuffing her empty water bottle back into her jacket pocket, she began to push on into the maize, following the direction the bird had gone.

It wasn't easy to walk between the plants. Dana turned her shoulder and tried to slip between them, but still they scraped against her, and she soon became very hot and sticky. She was already starting to feel hungry. Noon had now passed and she'd not had any breakfast, and had eaten only a Chinese cracker, and before long she was thirsty as well. Perhaps she should stop and look for a stream or something to fill the bottle from. Pauline always said you shouldn't drink water you find outside, because deer might have wee'd in it and you could get leptospirosis. The day wore on, and Dana didn't find any water, and she became so thirsty that she wouldn't have cared if she'd got leptospirosis.

-|O-

THE sun was low in the sky when Dana reached the edge of the enormous field of maize. She found a dyke there, but unfortunately its weed-choked bottom was bone dry when she slid down to investigate.

She climbed up the other side and sat down there, her mouth burning and dry. Just below her was an untarmacked road, a dirt trail with grass growing in a centre strip where the undercarriages of Land Rovers and farm vehicles had straddled it. Beyond that was a meadow, gold tinged with purple from the summer drought. And yet further away, the setting sun had stained the sky, and the western horizon brimmed with a colour like flame seen through a glass of red wine. There, like an anvil upon the hearth of the sunset, and standing out starkly on the flat horizon, was a building with the shape of a tall rectangle, a few squarish outbuildings clustered around it.

That was it! Dana was sure it was the building from the wyvern's memory. The image she'd seen before had been slightly indistinct, but the impression of the overall shape was the same.

A fence with two strings of barbed wire ran along the edge of the meadow, but Dana could just about fit underneath the lowest one, although she did snag Duncan's jacket once as she crept through. Although the grass was long, it didn't provide cover in the same way the maize had, and she crouched and moved on bended knee and hoped no-one would see her.

She came upon another dirt track that led her to the perimeter fence. A dilapidated gate made from metal mesh had been chained shut across the road. Signs of *Private* and *No Trespassing* had been fixed to the mesh, although the red lettering was faded and the signs were stained from age. The gate sagged so much in the middle, the bottom of it had sunk into the deep ruts tyres had left in the road.

The ruts were so deep Dana fancied she might have been able to crawl under the gate near the posts, and she couldn't sense any signals from CCTV cameras, but the nagging, irrational feeling that someone might be watching her dissuaded her from trying it. She had also begun to notice a very unpleasant odour hanging in the still air. Although she was still some distance from the building, it looked brutish and hideous in the sunset. It was an old, derelict building made of concrete in a blocky, ugly 50s style, and the effects of age and weather had not mellowed it. The façade was cracked and stained where rainwater had run down, and almost green in places where lichens and moss had taken hold. A barren industrial chimney with a broken upper rim stood like an insulting middle finger raised at the setting sun.

Instead, she continued around the perimeter, examining the fence for any gaps she might creep through more surreptitiously. Twice she sensed the signal and again spotted the bird circling in the evening air above the building, and she pressed in to the fence where shrubs and small trees had gained a hold, hoping they would conceal her from it.

She found a gap in the fence where a tree had grown up and torn the wire out from the ground, and slipped through it. The soil within was not meadow or farmland, but a packed-down overgrown wasteground covered in trailing bindweed strands, enormous daisies, ribwort plantains with bobbly seed heads surrounded by halos of pollen-shedding stamens, and brick-red dock flower spikes covered with cuckoo spit.

The building wasn't entirely in the modern concrete style as she'd first thought. The rear part of it was a much older building that had been extended upon, with filthy bricks and tall, dingy windows covered with algae and grime. It looked like an old Victorian workhouse or something of a similar nature from a Charles Dickens book about poverty and misery.

The bird passed over once more. Dana stayed under the brush surrounding the fence and kept perfectly still as it circled in towards the roof of the concrete building, where a figure reached out to it from behind a low barrier. The sun was going down directly behind from Dana's vantage point, and it was hard to make out much detail. It looked to be a large man, and it was only when the bird alighted on his outstretched arm that Dana realised it must be enormous, longer from wingtip to wingtip than a man was tall. It held its wings half open for balance as the falconer drew it in over the edge and disappeared out of view back onto the roof.

Ivor?

There hadn't been long enough to see much, just a glimpse of a silhouette against the ruddy sky, but it had looked like a tall, sturdily built man. Dana's pulse pounded in her throat. There was only one way to find out, and she couldn't turn back now, not after what she'd seen. Dana withdrew her phone from her pocket. If she was to go any closer, it was important she didn't make a noise, and that included if Eric tried to ring her. She switched it off.

She looked up at the blank walls, at the dark windows sunk into the concrete and the tall windows within bricks, so begrimed that nothing could be discerned from within. There could be people watching from there, people she was oblivious to. After checking the sky and the ground in all places she could see, she hurried across the overgrown ground with her body held low. She reached the wall of the older part of the building and crouched so as to keep out of sight of anyone looking out the windows, and shuffled along the brick under the sills. The unpleasant smell she'd noticed from the front of the site had by now become much stronger, and somewhere ahead she could hear a faint whining sound, perhaps some kind of motor running. This got louder and the smell became worse as she approached the corner of the building, and when she reached it and saw beyond, the air was thick with flies.

She'd reached what had probably once been a small courtyard. Perhaps there had been a garden in it at one time, but now it was just weeds forcing up through cracked concrete and dry soil in raised beds within stone partitions. Quatrefoil ponds had been sunk into the ground at each corner, the remains of a central fountain visible in the nearest one, but the stony lining had cracked and the only water that remained was a shallow, scummy puddle in the corner that Dana wasn't tempted by despite her thirst. A pile of rubbish seething with flies leaned against the opposite wall, and as Dana studied it she recognised the things within it as being bones, still with blood and meat on them, reeking from hours of putrefaction in the sun. Some of them looked immense, like they'd come from elephants or something. In school, Dana had learnt that the largest bone in the human body was the femur, the bone inside the thigh, and these were far larger than that, and some looked like curved ribs, almost like the sort of bones she'd expect to see fossilised in a museum from when the dinosaurs went extinct.

In the far wall, the one opposite the entrance to the courtyard, there was a great riveted metal door, ancient with rust and flaking discoloured paint, and it was ajar. As Dana walked to it, her stomach gave a sudden lurch and she quickly put her hand over her mouth at the sight of an enormous vertebra with stringy, blackening flesh sloughing off, as big as an armchair and surely too large to have come even from an elephant. The smell here was very strong and it was hard to breathe without gagging, and the noise of the flies was overpowering.

Behind the gap in the door lay a gloomy corridor, lit only by a light tinged green from a filthy window. The building maintained a chill despite the hot weather outside, and the stone walls sweated.

Dana could still smell the stench from outside, but it lessened as she crept through the building's annexe and past a doorway with no door into a corridor beyond. The place looked like it had not been used in years, and a musty dampness filled it. Stones and bits of glass and rubbish littered the floor. This corridor had no windows, and Dana could barely make out the shape of stairs and a deformed metal hand rail. She paused for a moment, straining her ears for any sounds, but all she heard was her own rapid breathing reflecting off the stone walls, and the drone of flies from outside. She put her hand in her pocket to touch her fuses and Ivor's watch, and looked at the stairs again. Ivor could be hiding here. It was old and derelict, like Roareim, but Dana had never remembered Roareim being as sinister as this. It might have been old and worn-out, and Ivor might have been disorganised in how he kept things, but he'd never been *unhygienic* in the way he lived, or allowed his environment to become filthy.

Trying her hardest not to scratch loose glass and dirt on the steps under her feet and make a noise, she ascended the stairs. The visibility improved on the first floor, thanks to an empty doorway leading to another dirty window. Dana went to it and peered out. It looked down on the courtyard and out upon the meadows of still golden grass flooded with the warm glow of the setting sun. Outside looked like another world.

She continued down a corridor with the upper halves of dirty windows on one side. The windows were mullioned, made up of lots of squares of glass inside a metal lattice, and a number of the panes had fallen out or been broken, and the gaps sent shafts of light thrusting into the greenish murk the intact parts allowed, illuminating empty rooms leading off the other side. Most of these were missing the doors, although a few of them remained hidden behind heavy, prison-like ones.

At the end of the corridor she turned a corner and heard the drone of a fan and an irregular sound of flapping paper. An open door led to a totally different room. Through the doorway it was obvious the window had been cleaned, and the sunset flooded in through it and illuminated shelves of books and a grotesque tigerskin rug on the floor, the hide misshapen over the skull still inside it and with empty holes where its eyes had been, the fur motheaten and balding beige and grey where once had been orange and black. By the window stood a desk with a chair pushed back and a fan running beside it, and on the desk a book lay open, its pages slowly sliding over from the draught created by the fan.

Someone had been here, recently. Dana pulled back from the doorway and checked the corridor she'd just come through, but it remained in its former state of untouched decay.

Then there came a sound like the flapping of wings, from somewhere ahead. Dana pressed in against the wall and looked into another corridor. There were no windows on the side, just one at the end behind her, and a figure was walking away from her, towards the far end, a man with an enormous bird. Dana stepped forward quickly and silently.

It was immediately obvious to her that it wasn't Ivor, and that she had been mistaken. He was too broad, with massive shoulders and an enormous barrel-shaped chest. Ivor had been tall and solidly built, but he'd always had a sort of elegant grace and balance unique to him that this man lacked.

His left hand was clenched inside a leather gauntlet upon which perched the eagle, its great talons digging into the thick hide. Its wings and back were a dark slate colour with lighter stippling and barring, not the brown of the golden eagle Eric had been telling her about.

The enormous bird of prey turned its dark head, fixing upon her with exquisite golden eyes. Dana didn't move, but the man must have heard her or sensed something, and he turned. She must run, get out of here and away from this stranger, but her legs were rigid. She waited, petrified, for the instant he would see her, for the outburst that would come on account of her trespassing here.

The front of his head came into view in the scant light available in the corridor, revealing the skin of the whole of his face and neck to be pocked and distorted. His breath came heavily through thickened, irregular nostrils, and the upper half of his face on one side was just a swollen and sealed eyelid where a scar had been burned, and the other side was a streaky mess of shapeless unmatching skin, as though he had a rasher of bacon stuck to his face.

He had no eyes...

Dana clapped both hands over her mouth, silencing a noise that rose unbidden from her throat. She fought to still her breathing while the man with the horrifying visage stood sightless before her, the bird on his fist staring back at her impassively.

He turned back and walked slowly away, his feet dragging on the concrete floor. Dana shrank back against the wall as soon as she hoped he was out of hearing range. She felt her way to the opening she'd come through and stumbled back to the room with the books. She needed to get away from here, now. There was no telling what was going on here, what she'd just walked into, but her breath would not stop tearing in and out of her lungs, and a susurrating ringing sound had started up in her ears. Her legs and arms were heavy and buzzing pin-and-needle sensations crawled up from the tips of her fingers and toes. Dana leaned against the back wall and slid down to the floor, struggling to block the image of the man out of her thoughts and concentrating instead on the hard textures of stone and concrete and upon the motheaten dead tiger that lay in the vista formed by the two shelves she'd hidden between.

She slowly got her breathing back under control, and the strength returned to her limbs. It wasn't far to the exit, and she visualised the route down, and back past the stinking bones. Her stomach lurched at the thought of them. She'd have to try not to think about that. All she had to do was get up and get out of here, and it would be over, and she could have as much time as she wanted to compose herself.

Over the drone of the fan, footfall became audible on the concrete floor somewhere outside the entrance to the room. Someone was coming.

Dana got up and stood back against the corner between the wall and a shelf, in the place she hoped she'd be least conspicuous. Now it might be too late. She should have gone when she'd had the chance, not come in here where she could be trapped.

As the sound of people approaching grew louder, she sensed something else, familiar, but from where she couldn't pin down.

A signal...

And suddenly, the memories from the dreams she'd been having all came flooding back. Gamma, Pilgrennon's third child, trapped in the nightmare, trying to escape. It wasn't Ivor who had led her here. It wasn't a hidden memory the wyvern had implanted in her. It had been Gamma all along, reaching out to her through the dreams, and she needed Dana's help. Dana quickly thought to her, *Gamma, it's me, Epsilon. I've come to help you. Keep still and don't do anything to draw attention to me.*

Someone stepped into view from the doorway, and Dana found herself face to face with the girl in the mirror in the dream, the girl who had slashed herself with the razor and bled all over the floor even though Dana had tried to stop her. She looked rather older than she had in the dream, about a year older than herself, maybe Peter's age, and the recognition in her expression was mixed with disbelief, and something that might even be fear.

A man rushed into the gap between the shelves. With an awful sense of *déjà vu*, Dana realised his face was also familiar, although she couldn't remember in precisely what way; one of the doctors or nurses from that awful hospital, no doubt. He made a lunge for Dana and caught her wrist, and a deluge of memories from Gamma's dreams, of rough hands grabbing and forcing, rushed to consciousness. Dana threw herself forward into him, and he stumbled back, catching his feet on the dead tiger on the floor. Dana stamped with all the force she could muster on the top of the pathetic beast's head, and its jaw slammed on the man's foot. He shouted out in pain as its fangs perforated his shoe.

Somewhere in front of her, an eagle screamed. "Prendick!" Gamma shouted. Dana looked up. The blind man loomed in the door, the great bird held aloft on his hand, its wings spread for balance. She crouched down and made a dash for the space between his legs, but as though guided by an almost supernatural sense, he reached to intercept her escape.

"Gamma!" she shouted at the girl, who stood there looking shocked, and yet did nothing either to escape or to help her as the two men restrained her. "Gamma, it's Epsilon, remember? We're going to go together, remember? I'm going to help you find the Emerald Forge!"

Gamma stared at Epsilon as the two men held her up. She had the same wavy honey-coloured hair as Dana remembered, and she gave off a signal as distinctive and alive as did Cale and Peter, but she wasn't dressed in the sterile hospital clothes Dana had remembered her wearing. She wore ordinary teenager clothes: marine combat trousers with a vest top and an unbuttoned shirt, and trainers. Dana could sense the incredulity in her signal and expression, and then she did something Cale and Peter had never done. From the signal Dana could sense from her, conscious words took form.

But you only exist in my head?

As soon as it happened, Gamma's expression changed to fury. She forced Dana out of her mind. "This *is* the Emerald Forge!"

The two men dragged Dana along, her feet tripping and scraping on the ground as she struggled against them, back out into the corridor and down a similarly dingy stairwell. At the bottom, Gamma pushed briskly past them and threw open a door that led to a long high-ceilinged room, perhaps where once heavy steam-driven machinery had been situated, around which men in old-fashioned clothes might have toiled. The sudden movement set up a flurry of wings as a number of birds who had been roosting up high on the rafters flapped a startled exit through gaps in another mullioned window at the far end, also algae-stained and with some panes missing, and spanning the whole height of the room.

The sunset streamed through in long shafts of green and red light, like abstract stained glass. Light fell upon grimy brickwork and aged wooden benches bearing glass containers and metal spoons and devices, resembling the equipment from science lessons at school.

Dana had little chance to get a clear look at the clutter, and it passed as more of a vague impression as the two men hauled her down to the far end, where an old ceramic basin stood in the middle of the floor before the window, like a font in some some hellish perversion of a cathedral. What immediately struck her as peculiar was that the basin didn't appear to be plumbed in to anything. There were no taps, and the tarnished copper pipe beneath it stopped short a foot or so from the floor.

The larger man pinioned Dana's arms behind her back while the other tugged Duncan's jacket with the heavy metal badges off her. Heavy hands on her shoulders forced her knees to the concrete floor. "What are you doing?" Dana shouted. She looked to Gamma, who stood aside watching, her face blank. Dana could make nothing out of the signal she gave off. She tried to find a wLAN, a phone switched on, anything that she could use to get help, but there was nothing.

The slighter man made a grab for her wrists. Dana

sank her fingernails as hard as she could into the tendons in the back of his hand. He hissed through his teeth as he yanked his hand back, raising and opening it behind his head, and before Dana had any time to react, the flat of his palm hit her full in the face and she fell back onto the other man. The light from the window became distorted and unintelligible, and by the time she had recovered from the stunning blow, the man had pulled both her arms across the basin and strapped her wrists down to the other side of it with buckled cuffs of thick leather.

He turned and grabbed something from a nearby table, and when he bent over her again in one deft movement, something scratched the inside of Dana's forearm hard, and it was only when blood welled quickly from a puncture in her skin and spilled over the side of her arm that she felt the stinging pain the contact left behind, and realised it had been a blade. She yelled a wordless scream of panic at him as he stabbed the point of the knife into her other arm, but she could not move her arms and she could not rise from the floor.

Her heart pounded and the breath tore in and out of her as she helplessly watched the blood that kept her alive running out and down over the crazed ceramic surface of the glaze and through a hole at the base of the bowl. She had made the wrong choice, and now she was going to pay for it with her life. They were going to kill her here today, and she would bleed to death like poor Steve Gideon had, and she would never see Pauline or Graeme or Cale again, never see Jananin on the news or find out what happened to the wyvern or if Ivor was still alive. And they would all be sad because she was dead, and she had only herself to blame.

The slight man bent down and retrieved something from under the basin: a beaker half-filled with thick red liquid. He carried it to a bench and began methodically setting up a microscope, applying a tiny drop of the blood to a glass slide with a pipette. After a moment he spoke, although his words meant little and they were distorted as though she was hearing them down a long tunnel. "Positive for the moiety."

She caught sight of the faceless man again, the eagle on his shoulder peering down hungrily at the blood, but the light and colour from the windows were fading. The blood staining the basin no longer looked red, and prickling static was encroaching from the edges of her vision, blotting the world out. Over her pounding pulse and rapid breath, a numb oblivion was creeping up her limbs and into her chest and head. She struggled to fight it, to keep her eyes open, to hold onto her memory of Ivor and the thought of Pauline and Graeme at home waiting for her to come back, but the darkness came for her anyway.

-11-

DANA awoke lying on her stomach, in a hazy confusion in which she didn't recall where she was or how she'd got here. A torrid heat pressed her down against a hard mattress. She turned her head, coarse fabric scratching against her cheek. Her mouth burned and her tongue felt as though it was coated with soggy felt. Her forearms were stiff and oddly numb, and when she looked she realised they had been bound with scraps of cream fabric. It was only then she remembered the room with the great window, the blood running out...

A square hole in a concrete wall, blocked off with rusting bars and with little of the glass that had occupied the outer side remaining, cast a rectangle of midsummer sun onto the floor.

She reached down and put her hand in her jeans pocket. Ivor's watch and the fuses were still there, although they'd taken Duncan's jacket with the mobile phone in it. They had taken her wellies away as well, although she had no idea why, and she was lying on the bed in her clothes and socks.

Something in the air was smelly, like dirty little animals in a pet shop. In the far corner by the wall with the window on, a splatter of black deposits covered the floor. On the ceiling directly above hung three or four leathery cocoons, bigger than Dana's fist, but not quite as large as an adult's. As she stared at them, they occasionally squirmed to reveal glimpses of ears and furry heads, or made low twittering sounds.

Against the opposite wall was a lavatory pan with no lid, and on a table next to it stood a metal pitcher and a chipped old glass. *Water...*

She gripped the side of the mattress and hauled her feet off the bed and onto the floor. Sitting upright sent a wave of vertigo crashing through her head, and the room spun for a moment. After her dizziness had eased, she tried getting to her feet and moving slowly towards the pitcher, but everything swayed so much she ended up crouching down and making her way across the floor on hands and knees. She managed to get the glass down off the table and stand it on the floor. She had to hold the jug in both hands and her arms shook so much it spilled dark splashes on the floor all around the glass. She drank one glass, not caring about the lukewarm taste or the shaking of her hand that caused some of it to overflow her mouth and run down her front, and then another, and then half of a third. Then she put the glass on the floor and crawled back to the bed, not caring when she saw the mattress was covered only by a filthy brown pillow inside a disgusting stained pillowcase and a scratchy woollen blanket.

She lay there and breathed for several minutes before the weak dizzy feeling subsided. She needed to do something, she needed to think, and although she sought for a signal, there was nothing. These concrete walls must be filled with metal rods, a Faraday cage as well as a prison. When she looked down at the foot of the bed, the only exit was barred by a riveted metal door with a tiny grate for a window.

She must have drifted into sleep, because the next thing she knew, someone was outside the door, and a key was scraping in the lock.

The slight man entered, pushing the door shut behind him. He stood beside it and watched Dana, like a zookeeper who had come into the enclosure of a fierce animal to give it medicine or some such thing. "Get up."

When Dana didn't move, he strode over to the side of the bed and grabbed her arm. "Get up!" He dragged her up and off the bed, and the room became a careering imbalance of confusion. The man pulled her back out through the door. Blood sang in Dana's ears and she couldn't see straight, but she made out a corridor with other doors leading off it, like a prison ward. The barred door beside the one to the room she had been in revealed a similar cell, and somebody lay on the bed within, a boy, and the instant she saw him she sensed something familiar, not of his appearance, but a signal...

"Peter?"

The boy swivelled to face the entrance at the mention of his name. Dana caught sight of him only for an instant, his eyes wide in an emaciated face. He was so pale, a spectre of who she remembered, pallid skin taut over scrawny wrists and hollow cheeks. His hair, which had once been bright red curls, had become matted locks.

"Peter!"

Before Peter could reply or Dana could discern anything more, the man pulled her out of view down the corridor. Peter's signal vanished, blocked off by the dense walls. They reached a flight of stairs and he began to climb. Dana's legs didn't have the strength for the ascent, and every step made her feel weak and lightheaded. The man didn't care, and several times Dana slipped forward and crashed her knees painfully against the concrete steps, and the man swore or cursed and yanked her arm hard.

The stairs ended in a small concrete room filled with stuffy heat, a skylight in the roof and a weathered door in the wall facing the steps. The man opened the door to outside air, and then Dana was out on the roof of the building, where Gamma and the man with the hawk stood, near some chairs and tables and equipment.

The air was loaded with the sickly smell of putrefaction, and Dana at first thought it must be from the abattoir heap in the courtyard, but as her eyes adjusted to the bright sunlight after the dank corridors, she realised there was some enormous thing lying across the surface of the roof, filthy wings of ragged brown feathers extended like a sun-basking bird, a ruff of steel quills surrounding a cruel metal beak protruding from one end. At the other was a tail with a dark tuft on the tip and an expanse of motheaten dun fur, balding in places and with holes in it through which metal bones showed and decomposition fluids oozed. The creature rolled its head to one side to observe her, raised a steel lid over a camera-lens eye, and shifted slightly to reveal a heaving mass of maggots on the damp concrete where it had been lying. Dana swallowed back watery vomit as the man led her past, and shoved a plastic chair into the backs of her knees. "*Sit.*"

Where Dana had been positioned, the sun was full in her face, and she had to squint to get any impression of Gamma and the other man. Gamma wasn't looking at her and seemed to be preoccupied with him. The hawk was shuffling its feet in an agitated manner. It tried to launch itself, but the leather straps around each of its ankles were held firmly in the man's gauntlet, and the bird pounded the air with its wings, beating the man over the head and straining on its anchor, until it relented and let itself dangle instead, swinging back and forth with its wings half open.

The man very carefully slid the palm of his free hand under the bird's enormous breastbone and lifted it back up onto his glove.

Gamma shouted, "Prendick, what is that you have in your pocket?"

The burly man slowly withdrew something from his trouser pocket, an air of defeat hanging over him. Gamma took it from his hand; a metal key.

"We've had to tell you about this before. I gave you your Sight. I can just as easily take her away from you again!"

The eagle spread its wings over the man's scarred head and screamed in Gamma's direction, its golden eyes intense. Gamma turned away from it in disdain, and flung the key over the parapet. It disappeared in the glare of the sun over the south-west side of the building.

"Now pick up that box!"

The eagle turned its head to focus on a plastic box with a carry handle and airholes on the floor, the sort of box small pets are taken to the vet in. The big man, Prendick or whoever he was, bent down and picked it up with his free hand, as deftly as though he had see it with his own eyes.

Dana's breath quickened. That was the signal she had sensed. The bird was connected... to the man. He saw through the eagle's eyes.

Why did he have a key, and why had Gamma thrown it away? And if he could see via a connection to the eagle, why had he acted as though he didn't know she was there when she'd encountered him in the corridor?

Gamma faced Dana. "You will answer our questions."

"Gamma, I'm Epsilon. Don't you remember?"

Gamma was unmoved. Her voice remained steady. "Yes, I remember. They all said you weren't real."

Dana stared at the girl's face, older than she remembered her, sensing for her signal and trying to connect to the person she knew from the dreams. "Well, I am real." She couldn't come up with a better way to answer. "My name's Dana Provine."

"Prendick, open the box."

Prendick opened the grid at the front of the box and put his hand inside, and when he brought it back out he dragged out what at first looked like a tabby cat with its back arched like it didn't want to come out, and when it did there was something dreadfully wrong with it. Its head was covered with coarse dark hair and did not have the triangular ears a cat should, and when Prendick turned it round to stand it on the table it made a hideous croaking sound as though its vocal cords weren't compatible with its lungs, and she recognized its face as being that of a monkey. A monkey's head, sewn onto a decapitated cat in place of its own.

"You will answer our questions." Gamma repeated. "If you lie, the Sphinx will know, and the Sphinx will suffer on your behalf."

The catmonkey looked at Dana as Prendick tied the chain on its collar to the table, and she averted her eyes to look at the bandages on her forearms in shame and pity. It was giving off a signal of utmost misery and dejection. It wanted to *die*.

"How did you find this place?" Gamma demanded.

"I found a wyvern," Dana answered, not wanting to look at the Sphinx. "I tried to use the information it gave me to find out where it had come from."

"I sent the wyvern to search for and bring back those who give out a signal, those who can influence things with their minds. They have something in their blood that can be extracted and used to bind living nerves to computer chips. We found the imbecile boy, and we found a grave of another child."

"Alpha's grave!" Dana's lightheadedness didn't lessen the hot outrage at the revelation. Alpha had died as an innocent in the Information Terrorism attack, because of the mistakes Jananin and Ivor, and Dana herself, had made in their failure to keep her safe. She had been laid to rest in an unmarked grave, and her rest had been violated on top of what she had suffered in life.

"You know them?"

"And Peter's not an imbecile! He's just a boy with ADHD!"

The Sphinx fidgeted on the table. "She's holding something back," said the man behind her.

"Sanderson." Gamma indicated for him to do something, and he came forward with a plastic lighter in his hand and grabbed the Sphinx's front leg and put his thumb on that lighter with it held against its foot. Immediately the Sphinx screamed and fell down on the table, writhing helplessly, and at the same time an agonising dry heat started up in Dana's right hand. She gasped and curled her fingers into a fist, staring at her unharmed hand, yet still she could feel the skin blistering.

Gamma's consciousness was pressing against her. She was trying to pry open her mind, read her just like Dana could read information off any computer she wanted to. "What is it you know? Where is my wyvern?"

"We took the collar off it. We gave it to a scientist."

Sanderson interrupted. "I told you we should have destroyed that thing. It's uncontrollable, a liability. We should never have made them capable of independent thought in the first place."

"Shut up!" said Gamma. "Did someone come here with you?"

Dana tried not to think of Eric, of his name or what he looked like.

"Someone did." She turned to the rotting abomination lying near the door. "Search the area. Kill any trespassers."

The creature heaved its forequarters up onto the wall surrounding the roof's edge and hauled off with a flurry of wings.

"Who did you give the wyvern to?"

Dana squeezed her eyes shut and tried to hold off Gamma's assault while she simultaneously tried not to think of his name. He might be in danger if Gamma found out his identity.

"It starts with an O," said Gamma. "What is it? Osric. Ah, Rupert Osric. Write it down, Sanderson. Now what else is there you don't want me to know. You know something about the moiety, don't you? What is it?"

Dana didn't know what the moiety was, but she remembered hearing the word before, in the room somewhere below, after Sanderson had stabbed her, just before she'd lost consciousness. *Blood.* Everything that had happened came back to her in a rush of emotion: Jananin, explaining Pilgrennon's theft of her gametes and her invention. Ivor lying to her. Ivor breaking down and admitting the truth. Hiding in Roareim when the police sent helicopters to look for them...

"What are you getting?" Sanderson asked.

Gamma shook her head. "It's just disorganised visuals. I can't make any sense of it."

Dana clenched her teeth. "It's private. You're not having it."

Upon hearing these words, Sanderson went back to the Sphinx on the table and grabbed it by the neck, pinning it down. A choking sensation gripped Dana's throat. She breathed in hard, but it seemed to make no difference.

"A name! Anything!" Gamma goaded.

Dana's vision went fuzzy. She might pass out again. She might die. She would take it with her.

The Sphinx made a strangulated noise, and the eagle screamed again. Sanderson held up the Sphinx upside down, his other hand holding its head. "Say it or I'll kill it and make you know how it feels to die!"

The Sphinx croaked, its cat legs flailing weakly. Its life was torment and death would be a kindness, but Dana couldn't stand the thought of it being snuffed out and her feeling every sensation of it.

"*Ivor Pilgrennon!*"

Sanderson dropped the Sphinx, and it lay gasping on the table, too pathetic to try to get away. His eyes had gone wide, his face drained of blood and his mouth rigid, as though she had admitted to knowing someone she shouldn't.

"Who is Ivor Pilgrennon?"

The question evoked a fierce hate in Dana. Gamma had never met Ivor. She would not know him. She could never appreciate what he meant to her, the experiences they had shared. "It doesn't matter!" she shouted. "Because he's *dead!*"

The Sphinx shrieked on the table.

Gamma leaned forward into Dana's personal space. "You *lie!*"

"He's dead!" Dana shouted in her face so forcefully she took a step back. "The helicopter blew up! He fell into the sea and never returned!"

The Sphinx made a strangulated gargling noise, and Dana knew the real reason it protested. She did not truly believe, herself, that Ivor could be dead. She had never come to terms with it.

"I think this should stop now."

It was Prendick who had spoken, for the first time Dana had heard him. His voice was soft, lispy from thickened lips and the stiffness of the skin grafts over the muscles that moved his mouth.

"I'll do what I like," Gamma dismissed him.

"Think of what happened with the boy."

"She's not the boy."

"No." Prendick's hawk was watching Dana once more, its golden eyes keen. "She is much more powerful. Something far worse could happen."

Gamma scowled at him, and yet she had backed away from Dana. Something bad must have happened with Peter and she'd lost control.

"Sanderson, take her back. We'll finish this later."

As the man pulled her back up from the chair and towards the door, it occurred to Dana that she should have thought this through, tried to work out what was going on, but all she could think of was her wish to get away from the Sphinx's pain and to sleep.

*

When she woke, the sun had set and day was fading into twilight. The bats in the corner were twittering amongst themselves and growing fidgety. One by one, they flitted out the window and away into the dusk.

Dana got off the bed and gulped down some of the food that had been left for her. She went to the window and looked out upon the grassy fields and marshes sinking into shadow, and she searched for a wLAN and found nothing. And then, as she stood staring out into the gathering dusk, she picked up *something*, a tiny heartbeat of some electronic life.

A Bluetooth signal, from a phone. Below the window,

in the long grass, Dana thought she could make out a hunched shape and slight motion, barely discernible.

Eric?

The relief at his recognition came with a rush of embarrassment about the circumstances in which they'd parted. At least he was someone who might be able to do something to help, if she could contact him. She might not have a phone, but she could use the Bluetooth on his phone to alert him.

She composed a message in her head. Whenever she tried to fix on it to send the message, the feeble signal would become too weak to latch on to. Dana closed her eyes and leaned her forehead against the bars, and concentrated.

Eric it's Dana move closer to the building but don't make noise or try to look for me. I'm trapped and I need you to help me.

She thought she saw the dark shape in the shady grass shift, and then a brief square of light, from the display of a phone, became visible. She waited for him to read the message, anxious and thinking all the time of the griffin that Gamma had sent after him. Where was it now?

Where are you? Have you got a phone? Howcome you didn't call me before? I called your phone and I looked all over for you.

Dana quickly composed a message in reply. *I haven't got a phone, I've just got a thing that does Bluetooth and it only works when you're near it.*

A pause. She could detect Eric fiddling with his phone two storeys below the window. *What thing has Bluetooth but no phone?*

It doesn't matter. I'm trapped here and you need to get help. I've found the place where the wyvern came from. There's another thing, a griffin. It's been sent after trespassers. If it finds you, it'll kill you.

A long pause.

What is it you want me to do? Do you want me to go home

and tell your parents and get the police?

Dana considered this. If Pauline and Graeme found out what was going on, if the police and the authorities found out what was going on, people would find out about Ivor Pilgrennon's experiments, and they would realise that Jananin Blake's synapse was being used for this, and she might be implicated as well. Jananin had not wanted Ivor's experiments known to the public, not ever. And Dana didn't want people finding out what she could do.

Dana are you still there?

Yes. Dana thought it through again. She couldn't keep Eric waiting here. There was a real risk the griffin or some other security measure the Emerald Forge employed would find him, with dire consequences. She thought to Eric's phone, *Do you remember Rupert Osric, the man who took the wyvern away, who lived in Radford Smelly? You need to go back to his house, and I want you to tell him everything, you understand? And I want you to tell him to tell Jananin Blake that I'm being held hostage at the Emerald Forge, and they have her synapse and they're using it to make monsters.*

Another long pause before the reply came back.

You want me to tell that nutter, to tell Blake, *the Spokesman?*

Yes, Blake the Spokesman.

This sounds really intense.

Dana blinked back a hot moisture that had suddenly welled up in her eyes. She couldn't tell Eric, but it was so hard. *It is.*

What about your parents?

You can't tell Pauline and Graeme.

Don't you think they've got a right to know?

Pauline and Graeme would be worried. When Dana didn't come back from the fake field trip, they would ask the school, and when they found out the school trip was fake, they would ask Eric. Perhaps Jananin or Osric would be able to do something to make it look reasonable, if the message got to them on time. *They can't find out.*

So I'm just supposed to leave you here, and go home, and tell your parents I don't know anything when they ask me?

There was one thing. *There was a spare key they threw off the roof. It landed in the grass somewhere.*

If I can find it, perhaps I can bust you out.

She thought of him coming up here, wandering around, blundering into Prendick or Sanderson. If Eric got caught, they would both be stuck here, and there'd be no-one to get help for either of them. *No, don't try to come in. If they catch you, you'll just be trapped here as well.* They might not even imprison him. They were holding her here because they wanted to harvest her blood for Jananin's synapse. He had no such use to them, and Gamma had told the griffin to kill any trespassers. It wasn't safe for Eric to stay here.

Perhaps I can throw it up to you or something. I'll see what I can do.

Without warning, the Bluetooth signal went out of range. Strain as she might to detect it, Dana could sense nothing, and the ground below the building had by now become so dark she could make out nothing against it. She would just have to hope he would do as she'd asked him, and that he wouldn't get caught, or worse.

-12-

DANA woke intermittently during the night, sweating and parched. Weakness and vertigo overcame her every time she sat up on the bed to take a sip of water. The bats returned as the first predawn pallor bloomed on the horizon. The hot, dry summer was continuing, and the night was neither long enough nor deep enough to shed the heat of the day.

Getting up and trying to act was too tiring, but she could still think, and as she slept off her exhaustion, things began to make sense. She stared up at the dark ceiling and listened to the chitter of the bats and the sounds of birds outside in the marshes and long grass. Osric had looked at a sample of the wyvern's blood — or that black stuff in it that seemed to serve the same purpose as blood — and found Jananin's synapse. Jananin's synapse must be the same thing Sanderson and Gamma called the moiety. And they were collecting it from her blood, so they could make more wyverns, or things like that.

Because the synapse was inside her body in an active state, transmitting signals from the nerve cells in her brain to the transceiver that allowed her to communicate with wireless devices, that must cause live synapses to be loose in her bloodstream. Jananin had said something about the synapse being able to replicate and repair itself, a long time ago, in her car on the way to Scotland, and so had Osric when he'd seen the dormant synapse under the microscope. She recalled in the dream, Gamma saying to a doctor that her blood had *things* in it.

One day, someone must have checked and realised Gamma was telling the truth, and then Sanderson, or somebody, had thought of a way to exploit it, and Jananin's invention that she had never wanted used for such things had been used to make the wyvern, and that disgusting rotting griffin-thing, and the sphinx.

When she thought of the sphinx, she ached. She should have let Sanderson kill the thing, end its pain, but she'd been too afraid. And now it was still somewhere in the Emerald Forge, still suffering.

Dawn came. Dana rose and tried to stretch her legs, but everything was so tiring, and if she tried to ignore it and push herself, all that happened was that she got dizzy and her eyesight started going fizzy, like the static effect when it's too dark to see.

She was lying down again when Sanderson and Gamma came past. She heard their voices as they approached, and lay still with her eyes closed in the hope that they would think she was asleep and not bother her.

"Get her out," said Gamma. "I want to know what she knows and where she found it out."

"That may not be wise. She's not like the boy. She's weaker."

"I thought Prendick said she was stronger than the boy."

Sanderson paused before he answered, and when he did his voice was low and ponderous. "Mentally, perhaps. Not physically. I may have drained too much from her. Any more interrogation may be too great for her to cope with. If she dies, it will slow us down. We would be back to just the boy and you as sources of the moiety."

"I sent the griffin to the GPS coordinates the wyvern disappeared at to look for more."

"You think there'll be more of them, in the same place? When the three we know of so far have come from entirely different locations?"

"The intel suggests there's another one, a boy. We won't know until we've identified them all. At least not until we get her to tell us who this Ivor Pilgrennon is and what he has to do with everything."

Dana heard no more conversation for a minute or so after this, so she opened her eyes very slightly to see if they'd gone. Gamma had, so far as she could tell, but Sanderson was still there, standing behind the door's grille.

"Do you really believe Ivor Pilgrennon might still be alive?" he said.

Dana kept still, eyes shut and hoping he would think she was asleep.

"You keep playing your game and I'll play along. For now."

The sound of his footsteps retreated, and when she opened her eyes again, he'd gone.

Sanderson returned once much later in the day, to leave her a tray of food and a fresh jug of water. She pretended to be asleep this time also. After they had locked her door again, they went into Peter's cell, and she heard him fighting and protesting as they dragged him out. The noise he was making grew fainter and fainter as they took him downstairs, to the room with the basin.

Dana slept fitfully, and the sleep she did get was filled with broken fragments of dreams muddled together. She dreamed of the hospital where Gamma had been held prisoner, but these were not the lucid, rational dreams she'd previously had, and Gamma wasn't there with her in them. This time, it was she who was trapped inside the hospital, and no-one was there to help her, and the doors didn't respond when she told them to unlock.

The still heat in the room became stifling; the long stretch of hot dry weather was building into something torrid and thick, gravid with a tension that could only be broken by an explosive storm that never came. Sleep and wakefulness began to segue together into a feverish delirium in which Dana lay caught between flashing nonsensical visions and the reality of sweat-damp clothes on the bed in the stuffy cell. One time, only half aware, she shouted Peter's name over and over, convinced they had taken him downstairs and bled him to death, until he shouted something back from the next cell.

It was evening by the time she came fully awake. When she went over to the window and looked out, she noticed a red light flash briefly in the bushes some distance away from the building.

Another of the monstrous machine-creatures going about its inscrutable nocturnal business? Gamma had sent the griffin away, so it couldn't be that.

The light flashed on again.

Dana sat on the stool by the window and ate the food that had been left for her. There was not much else to do. Probably looking out of windows had been what people had done for entertainment before televisions and computers had been invented.

The sun set. Dana felt for a signal, but none came. The light flashed on and off, here and there intermittently. Someone or something was moving about in the undergrowth down there with some kind of LED device.

The sky began to darken. The light stopped flashing, and shortly afterwards the brush shook and parted, and a figure crept up through the grass.

Eric?

Eric I told you to go and get Osric! It wasn't safe here for him.

There came a pause while Eric entered a text message into his phone. *Chill. I sent Osric a letter.*

Letter?

You know, those papery things that go in a red box, that old people use because they can't understand email?

But how did you know where to send a letter?

I remembered Osric's street name and house number from when we went there. Anyway, I've found the key. Well, I've found a key.

How did you find it?

I went by an archery club and borrowed their metal detector.

Of course. That must have been what had been making the flashing red light. *How are you going to get it up here? You can't just throw it.*

Can you make a rope out of something up there that you can dangle down so I can tie it to it?

Dana looked around the cell. *There's not anything like a rope.*

You could rip up a bedsheet and tie it together or something.

There's not a bedsheet. The only soft furnishings in the cell were the grimy old brown pillow and a coarse blanket that didn't look rippable.

Maybe I could go and find a helium balloon from a card shop. Then I could tie the key to it and you could catch it as it floated up.

Dana thought about this. *That's a silly idea. If I missed it, it would float off and we wouldn't have it at all!*

I'm only trying to think of ideas! Have you got any better ones?

Dana looked again around the cell. The bats had not yet flown off for the night, and they still hung up in the corner like balls of fluff in leather cocoons.

There had been three bats there all the time Dana had been here. Did bats have a home? Did they always come back in the same place to roost?

Wait, I might have an idea.

She went to the bed and peeled the pillowcase off the pillow. The exertion of moving the chair over to near the bats and standing on it made her feel dizzy and breathless again. She grabbed the bat who looked to be the biggest, thrust the squeaking thing into the pillowcase, and tied a loose knot in the open end.

Dana went back to the window and carefully passed the bag between the bars, dangling the bat-containing pillowcase over Eric. *You ready?*

I can see something.

I want you to catch it really gently. There's a bat in it.

A bat? Like a cricket bat?

No, like a real bat that flies and uses sonar. If you tie the key to the bat, it will come back in the morning to sleep in the same place.

I don't see how that's any less silly than tying it to a balloon.

Dana waited and didn't send anything back.

You'd better chuck it down, then.

Catch it carefully, then, Dana reminded him. *Ready?*

She let go of the pillowcase and it fell lightly down to Eric.

Okay, got it. Gunna take it somewhere else and use a torch, though. Can't see to tie anything to it.

All right. Please be careful with it. After you do it, I want you to go home. It's not safe here.

A pause. What is it that's going on in there? Who are they?

They're bad people.

What, are they paedophiles and stuff?

No, they're nothing like that. They're doing experiments, bad experiments. You need to get out before they find you.

Another long pause followed. I don't like this.

Please just do what I ask.

Is this because of what happened? Will you not let me help because of that?

Dana tried to think of something to say in response to this, but nothing came to her.

I'm sorry about what happened, she sent at last.

After a long pause, Eric sent a reply. *I'm sorry too. I guess I'm a male chauvinist pig. The only women I know are my mum and my grandma. If you're a lesbian, or you just think I'm minging, it's none of my business.*

The signal from Eric's phone went out of range.

Dana lay awake that night, listening for any sound of bats returning, and wondering about Eric. What if he threw the key away out of spite? Even if she did get out of here, even if she went back to Pauline and Graeme's house, and got the message to Osric and Jananin so something could be done about what was going on here, she would still be going back to being someone who would never fit in, not even with other misfits like Eric.

*

You're in a dark room with the drone of a fan, and with a sinking feeling of dread, you realise you've seen this before.

"They tied me to the bed again." My voice is a plaintive whimper. "I wouldn't take the medicine they tried to give me."

I flex my arms, strain my legs and arch my back with all the strength left in me, but it's all to no avail.

Don't think about it, you tell me. There's nothing else you can do. The straps binding us to the bed are made of leather, not electronics, and you can't affect them.

"I don't know what time it is. I don't know how long it will be until they will come and let me off the bed!" Panic rises, overwhelming.

Do you remember when I said this world didn't need to be real? That we could make another world that's more real?

"Yes."

We can do it, and we can hide there. Close your eyes.

I obey. For several minutes, my breath shudders in and out of me, the black static behind my eyelids no less of a revelation than the dark ceiling I see with my eyes open.

I need to ignore all the stimuli I'm feeling, the noise of the fan, the sensation of my own breathing, the pressure of the straps on my body and the feel of the mattress under my back. You help me, and slowly we sink into concentration.

I think of empty green fields, and now I'm standing there, soft grass under my feet. I turn to scan the horizon, and nothing is to be seen, no people, no buildings. I let out a shout and begin to run, free of the world of tormentors. When I stop, you suggest we add some more features to the world. You explain to me how I can adjust the topography, making hills and valleys, and how to make trees and boulders.

As an example, you make as a present for me a clear lake with Koi fish in it and rafts of water lilies in deep, rich colours on the surface. All around the edges of the lake you add spring trees, their dark branches bare of leaves but festooned like candelabra with spear-shaped, soft pastel flowerbuds that glisten with dew, trees you draw from some memory you can't quite recall.

But I don't like the trees and the lake. *This is my world, and I'll make it as I see fit!*

The lake explodes, throwing water and dying fish and sodden clumps of water lilies all over the landscape, leaving only a crater in the ground and the serene trees as flaming stumps.

*

Dana woke at the break of dawn, and when she rolled over to look at the patch of ceiling where the bats roosted, there were once more three of them hanging there.

Dana got up and found the biggest bat. It had small piggy eyes and a body covered in dense fuzz, but a piece of string tied around its neck had marked a line into its coat, and when she turned it over and eased open one wing, the key had been secured lying along its front with string passing through the key's hasp around the neck and around the bat's legs at the head.

Eric hadn't failed.

Dana quickly unknotted the string and put the bat back. She would have to keep the key hidden, but what if Gamma started interrogating her again? Gamma could see certain things from inside Dana's memories. How could she keep this hidden?

Perhaps Gamma could only get at visual things. She hadn't been able to pull Ivor's name out of Dana's mind. In the dreams, she had been able to communicate mentally with Gamma, but perhaps that was different, in dreams, and when she consciously or unconsciously wanted to let her. Perhaps in waking moments, Gamma was limited in what she could pry from Dana's mind, just to images.

Dana shut her eyes and groped at the lavatory until her hand found the grubby space behind the U-bend. She slid the key under it and turned away without looking at it.

Today she felt much more alert, although if she stood up for any length of time, it made her dizzy. It made her restless to lie still on the bed and feign sleep, but this was what she did, out of fear that someone would come past and see her awake. It wasn't like there was anything else to do in the cell.

Sanderson came past twice with food on a tray. Both times she stayed still, and he did not loiter. All day, from somewhere deep within the forge, came the distant clamour of hammering, of great machinery turning and pounding and air blasting through a furnace.

The day passed slowly, the square of sunlight cast by the window slowly waning and sliding across the floor as the sun climbed, and waxing as it slid further as the day sank into afternoon and evening. The air in the cell was hot and stuffy, and outside the fields baked in bone-dry heat under a cloudless sky. Even though she barely moved from the bed, her back and scalp were constantly sweaty from the heat.

Finally the sun set. The steady noise from the forge fell silent, and the square of light from the window faded.

Dana sat up by the window in the gathering dark. The bats had long flown, and Eric's phone signal had not come into range again. Now was as good a time as she was going to get.

She got up and recovered the key from under the toilet. By now it was so dark she could barely see it. The key fitted to the lock, and turned, and the door was open, and she was out in the corridor.

She sensed a signal. The door next to her; Peter's cell. Unsure if it would work, Dana tried the key. It did work.

"Peter?"

Peter grunted and rolled over on his bed. He seemed to be asleep.

She went into the cell and shook him. He whined and pulled his arms over his head. He was asleep, or delirious, and she couldn't get through the visions he thought were real to pull him back into reality. Beneath his clothes his body was wasted, skin and bone.

"Peter! Come with me. You can't stay here."

But he wouldn't wake, and she had to go back out into the dark corridor without him.

She fumbled her way to the stairwell, the darkness impenetrable. As she felt for the handrail, she sensed something, heard a half-imagined susurration. Faint signals, originating from somewhere within the Forge. Others were trapped here.

Dana hesitated at the top of the stairs. The more time she wasted here, the greater the risk she would be caught. Yet she couldn't abandon captives who might never get another chance at escape, not after what she'd seen here. Peter had refused when he'd had the chance, but others might not.

She turned away from the stairs and began to follow the direction the signals felt to be coming from. They led her into a corridor totally unlit, where she had to hold out both hands in front of her and feel with her feet as she walked. The signals became more intense, and it began to feel as though her head was filled with bees.

She came upon a wall and had to fumble for the outline of a door, a handle. When it gave way, the door opened to a room full of sounds: the rustling of thousands of bodies and the squeaks and whispers of many inhuman voices. Light came from windows on one wall, illuminating the silvery lines of cage bars, piled against the walls and on tables before the windows and in the middle of the room. A musty pet-shop smell scorched Dana's throat... and the signals. The signals were so many, such an urgent cacophony in her head, she couldn't separate them nor make sense of any one. They were uncontrolled simple emotions, not the steady, logical signals computers transmitted, and not the complex signals given off by people like Cale and Gamma.

Dana tried to focus and identify a single signal to interpret, but they would not wait in any kind of orderly fashion, each of them clamouring and vying for her attention. She put her hands on her ears and turned full circle in the moonlit, stinking room, but they would not get out of her head. They had Jananin's synapse in them, not that they had any right to it, nor had asked for it. Her blood and Peter's had paid for this.

She heaved the nearest cage off the bench, and it crashed to the floor and disintegrated, spilling soiled litter and white things that scattered to the far corners of the room, mice or something. She repeated this on the next cage, and the next. Everywhere she sensed a signal she smashed, knocking down and breaking cages that set free birds who let off alarmed fragments of song and took flight for the holes in the windows, throwing glass containers to the floor where they shattered and spilled water and tadpoles that glistened and twitched among the fragments like frantic apostrophes.

After she'd pushed the cages off the bench in the middle of the room and the far wall, Dana stood in the centre, blood pounding in her ears and vertigo whirling around her. She breathed deeply for a few moments, keeping still and leaning on a table until it had passed. The signals filling her mind had started to disperse, and now they were fewer in number, she could identify individuals.

One of them was a transmission of pain and misery and self-pity that she at once recognised as the sphinx, although she couldn't see where it was. The other was also familiar. But no, it couldn't be. She was dead.

"Alpha?"

Dana had seen her lying on the ground with the paramedics crouching over. It had been in the midst of a crowd, but it had definitely been her. She had seen her legs spasm when the defibrillator discharged, and she had read on the Internet and in the papers about the girl who had died of unknown causes in the Information Terrorism attack in London, and how she had never been identified, and had been buried as an unknown. Alpha, the girl who had sleepwalked through her life, until Dana had forced her awake. Alpha hadn't understood the world, a child's mind trapped in a teenager's body, and Dana wondered sometimes if it would have been kinder to have left her sleepwalking in the unfeeling twilight. Some doors are locked for a reason.

But now she could sense the signal she had always been able to recognise as Alpha's, the same as she'd recognised Cale's and Peter's, and more recently Gamma's too. And from the intensity of the signal, she was somewhere in the room.

As she moved closer to the signal, it became apparent something was not right. The signal came from a bench in the corner, and there was nothing beneath it. It was just a carrier wave, not a signal with the steady thrum of consciousness behind it, nor even the slow brainwaves she sensed from Cale when he slept deeply.

On the bench, by the moonlight that came through the window, she could discern something pinned down on a mat. Wires from either side of it connected to the terminals of a battery.

It all made sense. *Compton girl dug up by a lion.* The griffin, it had the forequarters of a lion. They had robbed Alpha's grave to take this, so they could find out how it worked and copy it for their own ends. The people who investigated the burial site found nothing missing because — and gruesome imagery came to Dana's mind — people's remains don't usually have bits of computer devices rattling around inside their skulls.

Dana tore the connections away from the device. Alpha's signal disappeared at once. She put the device into her pocket, and with all the force she could muster, swept the equipment off the table to the floor. She had by now identified the source of the sphinx's signal from an animal carrier under the bench, and she grabbed the handle and pulled it out.

She looked around the broken cages and the glass on the floor in the moonlight flooding through the windows. All of those creatures had fled. Right at the back of the room, moonlight shone on what looked like a big box, like an enormous safe, built into the corner of the room. Glass and sharp pieces of stuff on the floor stuck through her socks as she moved towards it. Although the door was made of metal, it felt heavy, crinkly and almost soft, when she put her hand on it.

This looked like somewhere to keep something dangerous, and yet the dangerous thing could at its heart be just another animal, turned to something it wasn't. Or even a human. The prison was made of dense metal, and no signal from whomever or whatever occupied it could she detect.

Certainly, from what she had seen here, whatever might be inside had done nothing to deserve it.

She grasped the handle and turned it. A thick metal catch grated against the frame, and as soon as it gave way, something struck the door from within, sending it flying open and knocking Dana backwards. She shut her eyes and raised her arm to cover them at the blinding light that poured out, and as she stumbled backwards she dropped the animal transporter with the sphinx in it, falling over it on the floor. She sensed a living signal and felt the proximity of something bounding over her, and when she opened her eyes the bright light had gone, and there was just the moonlight shining on an empty lead-lined cell. That was what that crinkly, soft-feeling metal was. She remembered it now from a Physics lesson at school.

She got up off the floor, rubble digging into her hands, and picked up the sphinx in the box with its unending transmission of pain and misery. From somewhere distant, within the Forge, she could hear noises had started up. Were they from whatever she'd just released, or had the noise she had been making alerted Gamma and the two men?

Dana ran back into the corridor, but the debris caught up in her socks stabbed painfully into the soles of her feet, and she made the last few steps to the door with a limp. She leaned against the doorframe and tore off one sock after the other, feeling blood on the skin as she brushed her feet off. She ran down the corridor, relying on memory not to trip or hit the wall, and back into the stairwell. The air was hot and close, and she was starting to feel dizzy again. Light came from downstairs. Someone was there, and she couldn't go that way.

She grabbed the banister and began to haul herself up the stairs. The muscles in her thighs burned and she began to feel even more weak and dizzy. Grit on the floor dug into her bloodied soles. The weight of the sphinx made her arm ache. She reached the door to the roof at last. Perhaps she could hide up here.

She threw the door shut behind her and fell down on her knees, breathing rapidly. Pushing the animal transport box before her, she crawled out of the way of the door, up to the low barrier at the roof's edge. She might not escape this place, but she could at least give the sphinx the escape she'd not had the courage to give it before.

The door on the front of the box opened by two keys, one at the top, one at the bottom, that allowed it to swing open. She put her free arm on the wall and pulled herself up and slid the box to balance on the top of the barrier.

"I'm sorry," she said, although she wasn't sure what for. For what someone of her own species had done, perhaps.

Then she held the box by the handle and tilted it forward so the door swung open over the void at the side of the building. She sensed the sphinx's claws scrabbling against the plastic, and then the weight abruptly came off the box. She felt a short sense of panic, of falling, and then a crushing, suffocating impact that ended with a crescendo of pain, and the sphinx's signal disappeared.

Dana let out a choking sound and dropped the box over the edge. She heard it hit the wall as it fell. She breathed in and out hard, trying to get away from the dizzy weakness that came from her own body, and the stifling sensation of a broken chest squashing her lungs that didn't. The thick heat of the night was precipitating into dark clouds that were swallowing the moon. The air was charged with a storm ready to break. Behind her, the door shook with the sounds of feet hammering up the stairs. She didn't have the strength to move, and there was nowhere to hide.

As the first drops of rain prickled her face, a noise came from somewhere up above, something between the discordant notes of a bagpipe and a gut-reverberating pipe organ, and a current of air passed over her head. Something big alighted heavily just yards away from her, something all metal thorns and serpentine lengths that glinted in the dimming moonlight.

The wyvern...

She didn't know how or why it had come here, but that didn't seem to matter right now. Dana felt for it with her mind, reached out for it with one hand, and it came forward to her. She took hold of one of the metal spines on the back of its neck. Right at the point where its neck and wings joined its body, there weren't any spines. Probably it had been designed that way because they would interfere with its smooth articulation. She could sit there... that was where it meant her to sit.

It was a struggle to get up. Dana pushed against the wall and pulled with one hand on the spine and the other under the opposite wing. She got her foot up over the neck, and then her knee, and then the wyvern bent its legs and dipped under her, and slid her into place. When it stood upright again and began to walk, it felt horribly unstable to be sitting up on the shoulders of this half-mechanical thing, whose metal surface did not make a secure seat.

The wyvern crouched at the edge of the roof and jumped up onto the wall. Even though Dana had been ready for it, it still startled her and threw her forward on its neck, and she had to grip with knees and hands to stay balanced. The wyvern swayed as it adjusted the grip of its talons. Dana felt dizzy again, and sick.

Above her, the green face of the moon peered through the gathering clouds. The moon had slowly been turning green over the past six months. It was a project the Meritocracy were involved with along with scientists from the USA and Japan, to one day give the moon its own magnetic field and atmosphere. The verdant band slowly expanding around its equatorial regions was composed of lichens that grew on the rocks there. Below her, the green-tinged moonlight illuminated the texture of meadow grass a long way down. If she passed out again now she would fall.

The door flew open and a man burst out onto the roof. Dana froze.

With a sound like a hundred knives being unsheathed at once, the wyvern opened its wings.

The man turned and saw them there. It was Sanderson, and he let out a shout. She felt the wyvern's sides tauten, down where her feet were. She turned her head to face forward, aware of what was to come next. The wyvern crouched again, and pushed forward by straightening its legs. The motion threw Dana backwards and she clung on in grim desperation. The first stroke of its wings forced her down hard against its back. She crouched over its neck and wrapped both arms around as it began to beat its wings steadily, and to rise towards the massing stormclouds.

Fork lightning started from the dark skies to the horizon, and thunder followed a few seconds later. A squall of rain pummelled Dana's shoulders and trampolined upon the wyvern's wing membrane. The cold sensation and the fresh scent of rain-wetted undergrowth and soil carried in the updraught went some way to reviving Dana from her thick-headed vertigo. She adjusted her seating a little, settling her centre of gravity forward and finding chinks in the armour covering the wyvern's neck to use as handholds.

Light flickered upon the wyvern's silvery sinews for a fleeting instant as the lightning came again, and thunder was not far behind it this time. Dana thought she caught sight of something else in her peripheral vision, something at the lightning's source. At the instant of the strike, the flash had uplit something else, a dense clump at the heart of the storm, as though an enormous fortress floated up there.

Dana was getting dizzy again. She wanted to close her eyes and rest, just for a minute. She tried to stay alert, to keep focus on the clouds swirling ahead of the wyvern and the damp air that pressed thickly against her skin. When would they be able to land?

The wyvern didn't understand the question, but it was transmitting a fear that this place was not safe, that the greater the distance between them and it before they stopped, the better.

The next lightning strike came, followed by the crash of thunder, and behind it Dana fancied she heard distant squawks of crows, and the feeling of many signals. She sensed the wyvern's fear increase, its body tensing and wings beating faster. Dana held tight and chanced a look over her shoulder. She could make out many dark shapes, following them. Birds. What would the birds do to them?

One time Dana had gone to a farm, and a hen had flown up in the air and thrown itself at the back of her head. The farmer had explained that it was because the hen was a rare breed that was bred for fighting, and she had chicks and must have mistakenly thought Dana was a threat to them. Despite the explanation, Dana had never much liked chickens afterwards, excepting the ones that were roasted and covered in gravy. She could still remember the panic and the sensation of whirring feathers, and hard sharp claws on the back of her neck and scalp as she had fought to get it off.

When the lightning came again, she distinctly saw something this time in the clouds, a shape that was obviously man-made. Yet it wasn't an aeroplane, for it had no wings, and although she was sure any judgement of scale from this distance must be impossible, it looked *huge*.

Whatever it was, it clearly hadn't come from the Emerald Forge, and she wasn't picking up any bad vibes about it from the wyvern. She urged it to fly closer, to the point where she'd glimpsed it in the lightning's root.

The undersides of clouds glowed with a blue luminescence. A brief parting in the dark sky revealed the moon once more, and its light was enough to give definition to a silvery flank wreathed in towering stormclouds. As the wyvern made for it, she recognised an insignia engraved within a raised circular area: a stylistic representation of a pair of old-fashioned balancing scales.

The Meritocracy's symbol... and just as the recognition hit her, she sensed another signal, this time definitely from a computer, but far more complex than any ordinary computer. She tried to decipher it, but exhaustion and the signal's complicated encryption were too much for her. This had to be an ANT. She had heard of them many times, and how the Meritocracy relied on their raw computing power for analysing the many public referenda which without the country could not be run, but she had never before encountered one, for it was understood that ANTs were all kept in secret locations around the country, and only the Spokesmen and scientists with a licence to use them knew their locations and were able to access them.

Her attempts to decipher it were to no avail, and she thought directly to it, in desperation, *Please help us.*

Not far ahead, she spotted an open gap, a hole in the wall of the sky ship. Dana urged the wyvern towards it. The wyvern skimmed past the reflective surface and plunged for the gap.

Dana caught a brief impression of a sort of airlock

room, before the wyvern, struggling to stop in time, crashed into the wall and exhaled with a loud pipe-organ sound. She pushed herself back into position and looked around as the outer door slid shut, and an inner door opposite began to open.

Three men in dark uniform burst into the airlock. The one who had entered first stared, wide-eyed, at the wyvern and then at Dana sitting on its back. His ancestors must have come from India or some distant place of that sort, because his keen eyes were very dark brown, and his hair was as black as a panther's pelt. Something about him jogged a memory at the back of Dana's mind that she couldn't quite pin down.

He trained the nozzle of a heavy black gun supported by a shoulder strap on the wyvern, and started to say something Dana couldn't make out, and mid-sentence his voice distorted to a squeaky pitch. Dana tried to hold on to the wyvern's neck, but her hands had gone numb, and when she looked down the bandages on her arms were stained dark red from the pressure of hanging on in flight. Her backside was sliding sideways and she was slipping, but she seemed to have lost all sense of balance and her legs didn't respond when she tried to grip tighter and right herself. The floor was coming up to meet her. The man dropped his gun and fell forward on one knee to catch her. Dana's last moment of awareness was the dim sensation of her head hitting his chest, and then she remembered nothing more.

-13-

DANA could feel a mattress under her, and bars of dim moonlight striped the floor and gave contour lines to the sheets and furniture. Were they back in the hospital? "Gamma?" she said, and her lips moved, and the voice from her throat, though hoarse, was her own. She was still in her own body, and Gamma was gone, at least for now. Out of her head. And she wasn't in the prison-hospital, she remembered, because the moonlight fell in vertical stripes there, from the bars at the windows. The stripes she could see now were horizontal, from Venetian blinds.

Gamma's gone, Dana told herself. *Remember, I escaped from the Emerald Forge.*

She pressed her head onto the pillow and crumpled the sheet in her hand, taking comfort in their ordinary, physical feeling. And yet, though Gamma was gone, she had been aware of someone else in the room with her ever since she had woken; perhaps from the implacable sound of breathing beneath the limits of her conscious hearing, or some other biological stimulus. She raised her head, and she saw him, sitting there on the side of her bed, in the gap where she'd bent up her knees. He was facing away from the window, his broad back contoured with zebra stripes, but even in the strange moonlight, she could not mistake his face; his straight nose with his spectacles halfway down it, his curly hair flattened into a neat centre parting.

She could scarcely believe it, and yet she clung to the moment, willing against all else for it to be real, for this not to be a dream. "*Ivor?*"

"Don't try to sit up, Dana. You need to rest."

"Ivor, is it really?" Dana tried to reach for him, but her

forearms were bound up in something, and movement set up a tense pain in the side of her wrist.

Ivor grasped her hand and pressed it back down. "Rest." She felt his weight shift off the mattress, and he lay down alongside her, putting his arm over her. His familiar smell, so memorable to her after the years since she'd last seen him, was still the same, although obscured behind some kind of aftershave or deodorant. She clutched his hand in both of hers, although his fingers didn't feel quite so big compared to hers as she remembered, and the strap of his watch felt cheap and plastic, and she could tell from its signal that it was just a mass-manufactured digital one, not his real one that she remembered.

The mess she'd made at the school and with Eric, the wyvern, what Gamma was doing in the Emerald Forge, everything that had happened, it no longer mattered. All she wanted was to be here, right now, because Ivor had lived and he had not made the wyvern or the other horrors in the Emerald Forge, and he was safe, and nothing bad could happen any more now he was here with her.

"Don't ever leave me alone again!" she gasped.

His fingers tightened gently on her hand. "You have to rest. You're making yourself agitated."

"Keep talking to me."

And so he spoke to her softly in Gaelic. Dana couldn't understand a word he was saying; perhaps it was a story, perhaps it was just gibberish, but the sound of his voice after all this time was so very reassuring. A deep sense of peace descended over her, and as she sank back into sleep, his voice filled her dreams, dreams that were strange and wonderful, and so safe and secure.

*

Dana woke in a cool, fresh-sheeted bed in a bright, unfamiliar room. The walls and ceiling were painted a clean white, and there was a closed door in the wall facing the foot of her bed. Another bed, empty, stood to the other side of the room. An expanse of bright blue sky showed between the slats of the Venetian blinds. Through the open windows came the sound of birdsong and the slightest breeze.

She turned her head to see a bag on a stand next to the bed, with a tube coming out of it that reached down into the bandage on her arm. The bandages were fresh, without blood seeping through, and the cuts and scratches on her hands had been washed. A disjointed flurry of recollections tumbled through her mind. The Emerald Forge, the wyvern...

Dana sat up in bed. "Ivor?" she called. "Ivor!"

The door opened, and in came a broad middle-aged woman with a big bottom and a big bosom. She had short hair of an artificial red colour, and wore a lab coat with a stethoscope draped around her neck. Dana looked past her into the corridor. "Ivor!" she shouted.

"Well, good morning!" The lady greeted her in forceful, cheerful voice. She picked up a clip-board hanging from the end of Dana's bed and wrote something on it with a green pen from her lab-coat pocket.

"Where's Ivor? The man who was here in the night" Dana pointed to the crumpled sheets. She looked at the floor, and at the table beside the bed, where a tray held two fuses, a watch with a cracked face, and a small nondescript electronic device.

The lady frowned, considering for a moment. "There've not been any men come in, not since the *Stormcaller* landed and the Commodore brought you in."

"The what?" Dana looked in confusion at the bandages covering the wounds Sanderson had put on her forearms, and the small plastic tube that disappeared under the edge at her elbow. She tried to recall what had happened, but she couldn't clearly separate what had been real from what had been dreams.

"Air Commodore Rajani? He's the one who brought you in. He said he found you and that... thing... when he was out on the *Stormcaller*."

It came back to Dana hazily. Air Commodore Rajani must have been the man in uniform, and the *Stormcaller* — that must be the thing in the thunderclouds the wyvern had flown up to.

"I'm Jane Tarrow. Everyone calls me Tarrow." The woman reached over the bed, offering her hand. Dana grasped it weakly, and then let go.

"I'm Dana Provine; everyone calls me Dana."

The woman laughed.

"Has there been *someone* in here? Anyone?"

Tarrow frowned, not taking her eyes away from the vigorous strokes she was making on the clipboard with her pen. "Only Professor Blake in the night."

Dana's heart jumped. "Jananin Blake?"

"Yes, she arrived shortly after you did. Seems she felt sorry for you. The Commodore told her you'd passed out, and you looked very pale, and when we tested your blood you were anaemic." Tarrow's pen stopped moving momentarily. "That means you didn't have enough red cells in your blood. We're an experimental unit and we didn't have any blood on hand, and Blake volunteered, out of the blue, to donate some of her blood."

Tarrow lowered the clipboard and fixed Dana with a stare that showed whites all around the edge of her eyes. "I mean, Blake of all people. I don't know how much you know about her from the news, but she's a cold fish, and not an easy person to work with. Never saw her to care about kids, or anyone, really, except for herself and the name of science. I'd have expected to have to test everyone else in the building and not find a match before she'd let me test her blood. But, there you have it, and by an odd coincidence, it turned out you and she share a rare blood group."

Dana thought again of her blood running into the basin at the Forge. Perhaps she meant something about Jananin's synapse. "What rare blood? This is some other thing that means I'm not normal, that makes me *different* from everyone else, right?"

"B Rhesus negative." Tarrow finished writing and hung the clipboard back on the foot of the bed. "You think you're ready for some breakfast now?"

"Where's the wy— the thing? And where's Jananin Blake?"

"The thing's safe. And I've told Blake she's not to talk to you until you've been cleaned up and had some breakfast in you."

Dana shifted the pillows behind her and shuffled her backside to allow for a more upright posture. "You mean Blake wants to talk to me?"

Tarrow grimaced. "How does a bacon butty sound to you?"

*

Tarrow went away to find someone to make Dana breakfast, leaving Dana to get washed in a shower room adjacent to the ward she'd been sleeping on. Dana's clothes had been left washed and folded on a chair, along with a donated pair of socks and a pair of white canvas shoes. The shoes reminded her unnervingly of what the doctors and nurses who had staffed Gamma's dreams had worn.

After she had dressed, she leaned on the windowsill and looked out. Some distance away, a cluster of steel-and-glass pyramids rose against the clear sky, the sun striking a harsh glare from the apex of the tallest. Below spread geometric fields of stumpy trees and feathery crops, and farther from this there was a mast with a gantry constructed around it.

Dana switched on the television on a bracket in the corner of the room with a mental prompt. The news channel showed an elderly man in an expensive-looking costume and tall hat, speaking into a microphone from a balcony in a foreign language. The voiceover explained, "In the wake of the Republic of Ireland's declaration of meritocratic law and exit from the European Union, the Pope in Rome today expressed disapproval and described meritocratic systems as an unholy alliance of pagans and atheists." A scrolling banner on the bottom of the screen announced: *Breaking news: Ireland declares meritocratic law*.

Tarrow returned, carrying a tray. The tray had fold-down legs on it, which allowed her to set it up on the bed with Dana sitting upright against the pillows under it. Dana pointed to the television. "It says Ireland is a meritocracy now. Does that mean they're part of the Meritocracy, part of the UK?"

"No, it means they're still another state separate from us. They're just going to use the same system as we use to run their country."

Dana cut the corner off the sandwich and stuffed the warm bread into her mouth. "Like Fuyūtoshi? What's that cloud thing, what did you call it, a *Stormtalker*?"

"The *Stormcaller*. Can't tell you a lot about it. It's some kind of prototype aircraft. At the moment it mostly just runs up and down the east coast from here to Torrmede."

"And what's that rare blood thing you said about?"

"People all have different blood groups. Most people in England are either O positive or A positive."

"How does that happen?"

"Well, I can explain it to you if you want, but it's a bit complicated."

"Explain it, then."

Tarrow looked at her watch and sat down on the end of Dana's bed. "Well, your blood group is B, so that means the red blood cells in your blood have B antigens on them, follow so far?"

Dana nodded with a mouthful of bacon.

"What you aren't is blood group A, which means your red blood cells don't have A antigens on them. Still follow?"

Dana considered this for a moment, before nodding again.

"But because A is foreign to your body, your immune system doesn't recognise A and your blood plasma has antibodies in it that will attack A to stop your body being infected. So if we were to give you A blood cells, the antibodies in your blood plasma would attack the donor blood and it would clot and kill you." Tarrow made a grunt of forced amusement. "So we can only give you blood cells from either B or O blood groups, because O doesn't have any antigens on it and B has the same antigens as your own blood, so your immune system will ignore them. But if we need to give you plasma as well, we can't give you O or A plasma, because it will have antibodies against the B antigens and it'll make your own blood cells clot. So we can only give you plasma from AB and B people's blood."

Dana thought of Osric's rats in the lab, of the blood he had taken out of the wyvern, of her own blood in the Emerald Forge, and of the sphinx and the wyvern. All of this joined together in some way that didn't quite make sense yet.

"What about things like livers and hearts? The things you have a donor card for, so that if you die someone else can have them? Is that the same thing?"

"That's tissue typing. It's much more complicated than blood group. And if you need an organ transplant and there's an organ from a donor who matches, even then you have to take medicine for the rest of your life to keep your immune system suppressed, because if your body recognises the organ isn't yours it'll attack it. Unless the organ comes from your twin."

"I've got a twin," said Dana. "My brother."

"If he's a brother, he's a fraternal twin. It would have to be an identical twin, you know, a sister who looks just like you."

Dana thought it through to come up with something that would make sense without being too specific before she spoke. "So how about, if a cat needed an organ transplant, and you had organs for it, but only from a monkey?"

"Good grief, no, that would never work. Not even with immunosuppressants. A cat and a monkey are too different from each other. They did do some pretty awful experiments on animals during the Cold War, though. Grafting extra heads onto dogs and that sort of stuff. All the animals died and it's not very nice to think about, but it's how we learned the science that enabled us to do organ transplants and save people's lives in the first place."

Dogs with two heads. Or three heads. Cerberus. But Cerberus wasn't real. It was something out of a myth, that someone had named a computer after, and the computer had made a virtual world on the Internet and made itself look like the Cerberus from the myth in it.

"Is it all right to use animals in experiments and kill them?"

Tarrow stared at Dana with an expression of concern. "Of course it is, if the animals' welfare is properly looked after. We have much better rules for it in place now than during the Cold War. If we didn't do experiments, we wouldn't have any medicine or surgery for either people or animals." Her attention shifted to the knife and fork leaning on Dana's empty plate. "Well, since you've finished now, come to think of it Blake did want to have a word with you, if that's all right with yourself."

-14-

OUTSIDE, clouds had obscured the clear sky. A curtain of rain descended over the olive grove and the orangery. Long, wet streaks dashed the glass that spanned the length of the outer wall. The room appeared to be a cafeteria, with a pulled-down hatch as in the canteen at school, and empty islands of tables and chairs filling the long gallery that looked out over the fields and the suddenly-turned weather.

Jananin Blake stood leaning against the sliding door, her chin high and with her usual impassive expression as she beheld it.

"I'll leave you to it," said Jane Tarrow, and she went off into a corridor and the door fell shut behind her.

She wasn't wearing her katana, or her brown leather trench coat. Since Dana had last seen her, she had almost become an abstract figure in her mind, someone she'd studied avidly from afar, her face in the news every day, her thoughts reiterated over a network of a thousand blogs. Now she was here, and she was turning her head to face Dana, a towering storm filling the sky behind her, and it was as though no time had passed at all. Roareim, London, Nevada, Fuyūtoshi. Cape Wrath.

Yet there remained that awkward gulf between them. Jananin was Dana's genetic mother, but she barely knew her, and Dana's knowledge of Jananin was based almost entirely on information gleaned from the Internet and the news. Jananin had never even carried Dana inside her, nor given birth to her. That role had been taken by another woman, someone Dana had never even seen a photograph of, so there was not even that connection between them.

They stood there, and Dana couldn't think of what

to say, and apparently neither could Jananin, and all the time the room grew darker and the air more charged and oppressive under the gathering storm. Rain clattered against the window and a flicker of lightning glanced off the pane, and then a loud crack of thunder sent a violent reverberation through the room. At the heart of the storm Dana thought she could make out a dark nucleus, descending to the tall pylon at the far side of the fields, and forked lightning breached the gap between the clouds and the mast.

"The *Stormcaller*," said Jananin, breaking the silence at last. "Quite possibly the most remarkable feat of engineering since the sound barrier was broken."

"What is it?"

Jananin folded her arms and leaned back, silhouetted by another flicker of lightning, waiting for the thunder to pass before replying. "Experimental technology, a prototype of a new aircraft we call a gyromag. In the base of it is an enormous rotating cryomagnet with an engine that discharges electrostatically charged particles. The shape of the design of the craft at the base tends to trap the particles and funnel them in a particular way, whereas the magnetic field generated by the cryomagnet repels the ions and generates a downward thrust. It's extremely efficient, but it does seem to attract rather odd weather conditions."

After the last stroke of thunder, the sky began to lighten. "Did it leave?" Dana asked.

Jananin shook her head. "Earthed and grounded."

"Where's the wyvern?"

"It's safe." Jananin contemplated the scene outside for a moment. The storm clouds appeared to be thinning, evaporating into a mist. A bulky shape now appeared to be balancing on the top of the pylon. It didn't have wings or any other feature resembling a normal aircraft. "When I received the information that you had gone missing, I took a gamble and released the wyvern, and gave Commodore

Rajani instructions to track it. It made sense to me that if it had found you once, it might be able to do so again. Then Rupert Osric received a letter, and we had a reasonable idea where it might go."

Yes, that letter. Where was Eric? Dana hoped he had gone home. "Peter is being held prisoner in the Emerald Forge. We need to get him out."

"Would you mind telling me first where the boy it seems you dragged into this with you has ended up?"

Dana thought again with a sense of shame of the circumstances in which she'd parted from Eric. "We split up. We had a disagreement. He helped me get out of the Emerald Forge, but I think he went home after that."

She moved away from the window, to one of the tables scattered around the room, and found a chair to sit on. Jananin watched her. Dana could see vestiges of Cale in her still expression and dark wavy hair, despite the thick streaks of grey it had gathered at the temples. She could see resemblances of what she saw when she looked in a mirror in Jananin's face, made heavier and more severe by age. If she could not give Dana an answer that made sense, no-one could.

"You know if when you grow up and someone might like you?"

Jananin pulled out another chair and sat on it. "I think I know what you mean."

"How would you know if you like them back?"

"It's hard to explain. You would know it if you felt it."

"What does it feel like?"

A few extra years since Dana had last seen her had further exaggerated Jananin's strong nose and distinctive mouth, but her expression had remained mostly unimpassioned and cold, like that of a marble statue. Now, however, a frown managed to furrow her forehead. "Surely that would be a more appropriate question to ask your adoptive mother?"

"I ask her about stuff, but her answers are never any

help. She says I've got to become a *woman*. And if I say I don't like it, she just says everyone else has to put up with it, so why should I be any different? But I don't *want* to be a woman. It's bad enough just dealing with school and everything without having to be a woman as well. And I don't like men, or boys or whatever I'm supposed to like. Not in that way. Does it mean I'm a lesbian?"

Jananin pressed on, showing none of the embarrassment or indirect approach other adults usually did. "If you don't like boys, or men, do you instead like girls, or women?"

Dana tried to conceptualise what *girls* and *women* meant. The only examples that came to mind were Abigail and her henchgirls, foul sweaty bosoms squeezed into grubby bras, implacable sickly stench in school toilets where people had urinated, bloody sanitary products discarded on cubicle floors, grotesque bodies and the smell of shame and embarrassment crammed into a PE changing room full of steam and claustrophobia. She tried to think of someone less abhorrent, of Pauline, but even though Dana could see through Pauline's appearance to the person she was, she still did not think Pauline's body was attractive to look at, with lumps and fat in odd places under her clothes, doing her hair and make-up every day so she could go to work and look presentable. Jananin... Jananin was one of the few people Dana had met who seemed to be able to rise above having to *be a woman* to be something more ideological, but even she must have that same disgustingness going on under her clothes that the very idea of repulsed her so much.

"No, I don't like girls or women. What does it feel like, to like someone that way?"

Dana had once asked Pauline why she liked Graeme in that way. Pauline had told her the story about how she had met Graeme. Pauline had been having lunch in Coventry, in one of the quiet areas around the cathedral where there are trees and benches for sitting. Pauline had finished her lunch, and was reading a book, called *Three Men in a Boat*. Graeme had been passing by, and he saw what she was reading, and as he had read this book himself, he stopped and asked her if she had got to the part with the cheese yet.

Graeme and Pauline had started to talk about the book, and as their conversation progressed, Graeme had sat down beside her, and then with great fortitude, had asked her if she would like to have lunch with him the next day. And she had said yes.

When Dana asked Pauline why she had said yes when Graeme asked it, she said it was because he seemed nice and he had a good sense of humour. Dana hadn't been able to understand this, because if that was the only reason for it, then everyone would be bisexual. When Dana had asked Graeme why he had gone up to Pauline that day, he said it was because he noticed the book she was reading and that she had good taste, and also he noticed that she had a nice face and nice legs, which Dana didn't really understand either.

Jananin's frown deepened. "I'm not entirely sure this is appropriate for you to talk to me about."

"I want to understand what it's like!" Dana pleaded.

Jananin considered for a moment, her mouth twisting, as though she had just been served a plate of something extremely unappetising. "Have you ever noticed that most people look... *revolting*?"

Dana nodded, her eyes widening. Finally, an observation she could understand.

"Well, some of them, some men, are revolting, but in a way that makes me want to look at them, rather like a horrible accident. After I have looked at them enough times, I start to feel as though they are in fact, not quite so revolting. And then, sometimes, if I should chance to speak to one of these people, and he says something intelligent, something that perhaps shows he sees the world in some way, the same as I see it, it changes to *something else...*

"It is like... were you ever *obsessed* with something? Perhaps a particular topic? Perhaps collecting some sort of object? To the extent that you feel utterly at peace with yourself and engrossed when you are engaged in it?"

"Like making Airfix models? Or looking at carnivorous plants?"

"It's the same neurological pathways in your brain that are activated when you are addicted to a drug, or when you 'fall in love' with another person as people call it."

"And why is it just men?" Dana asked. "Why do you like men?"

Jananin shook her head. "I don't know. It just came out that way. I think it is something to do with how their voices sound, the shape of their faces. They are bigger, with big shoulders and big hands." She glanced at the door. "I think the medic likes women. Steve Gideon liked men. It is fine to like one or the other, or both."

Dana tried to think of how it would be to feel the same way she did about a person as she did when she sat down at her desk to make an Airfix model, with all the parts and her glues and paints arranged just how she liked them at her fingertips. It was ordered, secure. When she did that, she felt as though she was enclosed in a little bubble separate from reality, where things that went on in the real world couldn't get at her. When she read seed catalogues for the exotic plants she loved, she pored over the diagrams and read over and over the complicated Latin names until she knew them by heart, and she fantasised about the *Sarracenias* she could grow in the bog garden Graeme and Pauline were helping her set up, and about when she was older, she wanted to buy a house with a garden and build an enormous greenhouse and fill it with *Nepenthes*. She couldn't imagine how or why a person could make her feel that way. "But what if I don't like anyone? It's all just disgusting. Puberty, and what's happening to me and other people. I don't want to know about other people's private parts."

"Then by that process of elimination, you are not a lesbian, because the definition of being homosexual is being attracted to persons of one's own sex. You are also not straight, because being heterosexual is being attracted to the opposite sex."

"What am I if I'm none of those?"

"Possibly you simply haven't finished maturing and an appropriate sexuality will become apparent to you at some later point."

"But what if it *doesn't*?"

"Then—" Jananin Blake shifted in her seat and exhaled. Perhaps it was irritation, frustration, something like that. "It is not really anything worth mourning. In many ways, it's an advantage. That kind of thing is a bane, a distraction from the pursuit of more noble things. I lament how much more research I might have got done in my younger days had my attention not been swayed by certain men." As Jananin had been speaking, she had been staring at Dana's face, apparently finding some fault with it. "Have you been outside in the sun, wearing a hat?"

"No," said Dana. "I don't wear hats. Don't like them, after I had to wear one because of Cerberus. And I was locked up in the Emerald Forge. When I escaped, it was dark."

Jananin stared at Dana a few seconds longer, her eyebrows contorting behind her dark glasses. "You have what looks like UV burns, but only on the bottom of your face."

Dana had been aware of a hot itchy sensation in her face and one forearm since she'd woken up, although it had been just one of several aches and niggles in the background, along with the ache across her entire back and hips and shoulders, soreness in the soles of her feet, and the stiff discomfort where the drip had been inserted into the vein inside her elbow. Probably it was the sun, or an allergy to something after the sweaty, itchy time she'd spent camping with Eric.

"What is this place?" When Dana had checked on GPS, she could see very well where this was, but there was nothing to identify it. According to the maps she had in her head, there wasn't anything in this place, just empty farmland with not even the road leading off marked on it.

"It has no name as such, just the codename Site Twelve. It's a research institution. For research funded by the Meritocracy."

"Then what's Torrmede?"

Jananin started, her eyes widening behind the dark lenses. "Where did you hear that name?"

Dana took her hands off the table and leaned back against her seat, disconcerted by the sudden change. "Torrmede... I think I remembered it right. It was Jane Tarrow. She said that the *Stormcaller* travels between here and Torrmede."

"Then you had better forget it, and Jane Tarrow had better forget it as well."

"Okay," said Dana, thinking that now Jananin had drawn attention to it in such a way, she was unlikely to be able to forget it, whereas had she not reacted to it at all, the unfamiliar name would probably have slipped her mind by the next day. "What kinds of research get done at Site Twelve?"

"The main focus is technology that will enable this country to meet its own food and energy demands in their entirety, without it being necessary to rely on imports to any degree." Jananin gestured to the window. "Hydroponics pyramids, fuel crops genetically tailored to gain maximum productivity from the climate here. All projects of this nature are nominated by referendum, all public knowledge, although there are some private projects by independent research groups ongoing here that are in the development stage and have not been revealed to the public yet as funding candidates for further development."

The sky outside was lightening, the sun breaking through the clouds once more. Dana studied the distant shape of the *Stormcaller* on the mast. It looked to be shaped like a bivalve clamshell that had been taken apart at the hinge and put together back-to-front. She couldn't make out any other features over the glare of the sun on the reflective surface of its hull.

"It's necessary we press on with the subject I wanted to discuss with you," Jananin said. "This wyvern as you call it, and how you came to find it and where you have been, and what has happened to Peter, and what information you may have obtained there."

"I was in detention at the school, and—"

"I don't mean here. I suggest we go somewhere more suitable, such as my study."

They rose from the table. Jananin led Dana down several corridors, until they reached a suite of offices. Jananin's door didn't have her name on it or any other distinguishing features, just the number 57. Perhaps there was something significant in it, such as Jananin needing privacy and secrecy because of her status as a Spokesman, or something to do with the Meritocracy's ideal of people all being equal, but their ideas being what sets them apart.

The room inside was arranged around the desk in the middle. The far wall was taken up with bookshelves, and further shelving was also built in around the doorway. Of the remaining walls, one was taken up by a window, very modern in comparison to the ageing ones in the Emerald Forge, and the other was covered with a slick surface to which various pieces of paper had been pinned with small magnets.

Jananin took her seat at the desk and pressed a button on the front of it. The computer monitor flickered on.

Dana examined the things pinned to the wall while Jananin sorted out the computer. There was one photograph near the top of Jananin receiving the Nobel Prize, and Chemistry diagrams of molecules made of Cs and Hs and Os, and there was a map of an island, rounded and more or less featureless apart from a curling quill of a peninsula pointed towards a cluster of much smaller islands. Under this was a postcard showing a map of the smaller islands. Superimposed on each upper corner were the translucent heads and shoulders of two women, and between them a flag made up of the Union Flag and a shield with a sheep and a ship on it. One of the women was middle-aged with fastidiously styled hair and a prim, artificial smile. The other had short untidy hair and a friendly face.

"Wasn't she a politician or someone?" Dana blurted out.

Jananin glanced at the postcard, and then at Dana with a disgusted expression. "She was the Prime Minister of the United Kingdom. In 1982, Argentina invaded the Falkland Islands. Margaret Thatcher commanded the British Armed Forces to retake them. What History do they teach you in that school of yours?"

"I dunno. Just stuff about what date Henry the 8th married someone or other, and what religion people followed then. Who's the other woman?"

"She is Trudi Morrison, a Falklands citizen and a farmer who led the opposition during the occupation of the islands by the Argentine forces. A very courageous person who deserves to be celebrated rather more than she currently is."

"So what's the other map, and what's the Falklands?"

"It's a map of Antarctica. Do they not teach you Geography in that school of yours either?"

"It's the Meritocracy's school, and you're a Spokesman." Dana found herself laughing awkwardly. "If the school's crap, aren't you supposed to bring about reform to make it not crap?"

Jananin made an ironic grimace that might have been humour. "The Electorate are supposed to decide what reform must take place. The Spokesmen's duty is merely to ensure it is carried out. However, school reform is something that has been brought up in every referendum so far, and it's likely it will come to a head soon and some sort of action will be taken. The Electorate just needs to consider the alternatives that have been put forward and decide which one is most suitable.

"Anyway, the Falklands were a self-governing overseas British territory in the South Atlantic. When Great Britain declared Meritocratic rule, the Falklands elected to also, making them the southernmost province of the Meritocracy. The archipelago serves as a base for excursions into Antarctica, and the oceans around it provide sites for oil drilling."

"You know you had that alibi, that you were on Antarctica?" Dana said. "Have you actually *been to Antarctica*? Before and after then, I mean?" She hadn't done anything about Antarctica in school, other than once being told someone called Scott went there and died.

"Yes, I have. Many times." Jananin's demeanour and tone of voice suggested now that she thought Dana was being rather foolish. "A great deal of very important research is being carried out on Antarctica, by Japan and the USA as well as the Meritocracy, while Russia concerns itself with the Arctic, a place science predicts ten years hence will be nothing but open water every summer. When the ice caps eventually thaw, Antarctica will continue to have stable land all year round at its pole, whereas the North pole will not. There is an efficient way of moving material into orbit, using an ion propulsion system not unlike the one that powers the *Stormcaller*, but because it utilises the Earth's magnetic field, it's only effective at the poles. The Antarctic is rich in fossils. Once it was covered in forests and animal life capable of hibernating through the winter. One day it will be again, and probably people will live there, but in the nearer future, it will be a base for international research, and our port to the rest of the Solar system."

Jananin appeared to have finished setting up her computer now, and Dana found a chair and seated herself on the opposite side of the desk.

Dana picked up something that looked like an Airfix model off Jananin's desk. It was a gunmetal grey colour and looked a bit like a big fat millipede, with a segmented body and lots of bristly legs, and what looked like photovoltaic panels embedded along the top. "What's this?"

"It's a scale model of a machine."

"What kind of machine?"

"A machine whose job is to travel extremely slowly, collecting rocks rich in iron oxide and convert those rocks into iron and other trace elements, and release carbon dioxide and oxygen into the atmosphere."

Dana shrugged and put the thing back down. "It sounds like it just pollutes the atmosphere."

"Exactly."

"Isn't that bad?"

"Not if the atmosphere in question is on Mars."

Dana stared at Jananin. "Is that something the Electorate knows about?"

"The Electorate know the Meritocracy has a privately funded space exploration programme, but mostly not specific details yet."

"Why are you telling me, then?"

Jananin interlocked her fingers on the desk before her. "Because my past experience suggests you can be discreet, and because you're a child and it's highly unlikely anyone would believe you even if you aren't. To business." She pressed something on a keyboard.

She was looking at Dana as though she expected her to speak.

"Uh," said Dana.

Uh appeared on the computer monitor in red text.

"Just ignore it. It's more convenient than trying to write notes."

"Well, did you hear on the news, not long ago, about Alpha's grave?"

"Indeed. Naturally I made enquiries into it at once.

The undertaker and a forensic checked the remains before re-interring the coffin. They reported that nothing was missing. However..." Jananin's voice tailed off. "You're not going to be sick again like in New York, are you?"

Dana swallowed. "I'll try not to." Jananin's words had appeared on the computer screen in green.

"The body was in an advanced state of decomposition." She studied Dana's expression, apparently trying to interpret body language like Dana's therapist often tried to help her to understand. "That means it was, essentially, a smelly skeleton covered with slime from degraded organic material. Something appeared to have been inserted and withdrawn into what remained of the tissue in the eye socket."

Dana swallowed again, raising her hand involuntarily to her mouth. She put her other hand in her pocket, and in amongst the fuses she had there and Ivor's watch, found something else. She took it out and put it on the table in front of her.

Jananin reached over and took it. She turned it over in her hands, examining it. She lifted up her spectacles to peer at it from underneath them. It was about the size and shape of a large postage stamp, but with a thicker part on one of the narrower edges. Both sides of the wafer had a peculiar sheen to them, like a butterfly's wing.

"It was in the Emerald Forge, in a lab," Dana explained. "It's not giving off a signal now, but it was connected to a battery there, and it felt just like Alpha."

When Jananin continued to study it in apparent curiosity, and didn't reply, Dana asked, "Is that really what was in Alpha's brain? Is there really something just like that in me?"

Jananin raised her eyes to look at Dana for a moment. She turned the device again in her hand. "This part, to one side." She indicated the thicker part, electronics sealed inside plastic housing. "That's the transmitter-receiver. It likely sits, like this." She turned the object vertically, so the transceiver faced forwards to Dana, and held it up against the middle of her forehead. "With the transceiver on the inside of your skull, and the wafer positioned between the hemispheres of your frontal lobe behind it." She took it down again, holding it in her hand for Dana to see. "This surface you see on it. The iridescence is from microstructures. If you were to look at it under a powerful enough microscope, you would see many tiny connection points, that join up to nanocircuits printed inside the wafer. Each of these connection points is designed for one of my synapses. Even though the area is not large, there are many connections, and synapses are able to catenate. That means, to join up head to tail, in a chain, to reach more distant neurones. In this way, you are able to grow connections from the entire inside surfaces of both hemispheres of your brain to the transceiver."

Dana breathed unsteadily, looking at it. "And that was put into my brain, when I was a foetus?"

"Probably through the top of the skull," Jananin said. "I'm no medic, but I'm given to understand it ossifies very late in development."

This was inside her. And it felt like nothing, no pain or anything.

"Can you put it back? With the rest of Alpha's remains?"

"It's evidence of a crime. It will have to be examined and photographed, but I will see what can be done." Jananin opened a drawer. She took out a tin, and put the transceiver inside it, and she took a pen and wrote the Greek letter *alpha* on the top of the tin, and put it back in the drawer. "What about the wyvern? How did you encounter that?"

"I was in detention at school. This boy, Eric, I thought he was following me. Actually, he was the same person who helped me in the Cerberus game. Do you remember...?"

"Naturally. Continue."

"So I hid in the bogs until I thought everyone had gone, and as I was leaving it came down, from the sky. I tried to shut myself in but it broke the window and came in, and it went after me, but Eric was there as well, and he helped me."

"How did it know where to look for you?"

Dana frowned. "How do you mean?"

"Clearly it was sent to that location. Something of that nature could not just wander the country until it came upon you by chance."

Dana recalled a conversation she'd overheard Gamma and Sanderson having, about sending the griffin and the wyvern, something about *intel*. "I think it was. But I don't know how."

"Is there anything that could have happened recently that might have given away your location to someone trying to find you? Peter was living in a group care home, until he escaped, and it's likely if they've got him, the news report that was issued while social services were trying to locate him was what drew their attention and enabled them to identify him."

Dana considered this. "Cale was famous once, sort of. Well, Cale's pen was, really."

A vertical line appeared in the middle of Jananin's eyebrows. Her mouth twisted.

Dana tried to explain: "Cale has this pen, which he really likes. He once drew a picture of it, using it." Pauline had said the idea of a drawing of a pen, with the pen, was *profound*. "There was this local art exhibition, and it had a category for under 18. So Pauline took Cale's picture of his pen to it."

It had started off all quite fun and exciting, but then it had all turned rather unpleasant and stressful. First of all, a man, a journalist or someone who was paid to write rubbish, or something like that, had claimed that the picture was far too skilful, and a twelve-year-old boy, as Cale was at the time, could not possibly have drawn to such a standard. Then the name of Cale's school, and that he was autistic, had somehow leaked out. After this, it turned out some woman who wrote a blog, upon which she proclaimed herself to be 'an autistic artist' and 'a leading world authority on autistic art' wrote insultingly on her blog about Cale's drawing, claiming it had 'no artistic merit' and 'failed at creating a world on its own terms.'

Then Pauline and Graeme had taken Dana and Cale to the gallery for a prize-giving ceremony, because Cale had been awarded third place, after a scribble done by a three-year-old with crayons, and an anatomical illustration of lungs done with expired make-up on a piece of asbestos sheet encased in epoxy resin by a 17-year-old. As it turned out, the woman who wrote the blog had gone to the prize ceremony as well, and even Dana could recognise her because she had fluorescent pink punk hair and spectacles with enormous blue plastic frames, and had brought along a number of paintings she was hoping to sell there. Graeme had gone up to her and confronted her about what she had written. He told her she was a ridiculous windbag who needed to get a real job, and that it was disgusting that she should sneer at Cale's drawing in an attempt to promote herself, and a disgrace that she should show her face here.

After the ceremony, the local press had been there, and someone had held a microphone in Cale's face and asked him for a comment, and Cale had taken a deep breath, and had blown a very loud raspberry into it.

"I think it was only on the local news," Dana said, uncertainly. "But it might have gone viral." Possibly Cale's raspberry had become more famous than his pen.

"So, the wyvern, as we're calling it," Jananin continued. "Osric said it had something plugged into it, and you unplugged it and it became autonomous?"

"It stopped attacking us. I could communicate with it. It was confused, like it had just woken up, as though it didn't know what it had been doing."

"Possibly it was being controlled through a long-distance transmitter, something like a mobile phone, or the device was a program that determined its behaviour."

"We didn't know where to hide it. The only person I could think of was you, and I couldn't find where to contact you, anywhere."

"The ANTs protect information like that. They are extraordinarily good at it." Jananin arched one eyebrow. "Better even than you. Pilgrennon always claimed no computer would ever rival a human mind. Back before the revolution and the beginning of the Meritocracy, I would almost have agreed with him. Technology has of course advanced since then, and I think we finally have proof now that he was wrong."

The dream from last night tugged at the back of Dana's memory again. Jananin's biting comment was almost an insult, not only of her personally, but against Ivor and his life's work. The little experience she'd had with ANTs had confused her and she hadn't been able to access them, but maybe she could work them out with a bit more practice. She could always understand anything with enough time, even Cerberus. "Can I use the ANT here?"

"Certainly not. ANTs are for official Meritocracy business only. And unless the Electorate starts nominating you as a person with a worthy research proposal requiring ANT priorities, you are not Meritocracy business. I can fill in the part where you left the wyvern with Osric by myself. He told me of his discovery of my synapse in it, along with some sort of artificial immune system that's currently being analysed. What happened after that? How did you end up here?"

"Eric and I talked about stuff, and we decided to try to find where the wyvern had come from. Eric gave me a lift on his moped. We went to the east because when the wyvern came down from the sky, it came from the east side of the building, so we thought it must have come from that way. Eric said what if it was from France, but I thought if it was from France there would be French writing when Osric looked inside it, and there wasn't."

"But surely you did not simply *go* to a place you had no specific knowledge of aside from it being east of Coventry? You must have had another source of information to deduce it from."

"I—" Dana examined her hands on the surface of Jananin's desk. It would sound stupid. "I had these dreams. I never really remembered them until I found the Emerald Forge. It was all really vague, and I used to forget the dreams whenever I woke up. I just heard the name, the Emerald Forge. I don't think I ever went there in the dreams."

"What were the dreams about?"

"You know Pilgrennon said he originally implanted devices..."

"Transceivers."

"Transceivers in Alpha and four foetuses: Peter, then me and Cale, and then someone else he called Gamma?"

"They are all accounted for. I traced Gamma's signal to a psychiatric hospital after we... after Cape Wrath, and I made up an excuse and got access to her health records after I was made a Spokesman. Gemma Percival. Her mother was a career woman who left it too late and was told she couldn't have children, at least not using her own ova. She somehow crossed paths with Pilgrennon, who claimed he could give her a child that was genetically hers and her partner's. After the child was born, Pilgrennon disappeared and the child turned out to have severe psychiatric problems, and when they discovered she wasn't even genetically theirs as they'd been told, they abandoned her. She's severely mentally disturbed according to the health professionals. It's unlikely she'll ever leave their custody or live a normal independent life. A danger to herself, but not considered a threat to anyone else. Yet another of Ivor Pilgrennon's casualties."

Dana hesitated. *Mentally disturbed? Severe psychiatric problems?* That wasn't how it had felt. Gamma had seemed just like a normal person, trying to survive in an horrific situation. "In the dreams, it was in a hospital. It was her, I'm sure. But it was like I was her, inside her body. I was helping her when she tried to escape. They did awful things to her, like tying her to a bed, and forcing her to take medicine. I don't know what it means. Could it be that Gamma and I can communicate with each other, through the Internet, when I'm asleep?"

"I would say that was a logical inference, as it's unlikely you could have acquired the information about the hospital from elsewhere."

"But in the dreams, Gamma was much younger than she was when I found her in the Emerald Forge."

"Then it's likely the dreams were shared flashbacks, relived memories."

Dana considered this. She was sure she'd had at least some of the dreams multiple times, and that would account for it. "I wasn't sure of it at the time. I thought I was following something I'd picked up from the wyvern, something I couldn't translate into words or images or anything people could understand. It's like understanding machine code. You could tell me what machine code is, but I can't tell you what machine code feels like or how I understand it. Now I think it might have come from Gamma."

"You can sense GPS and navigate via some sort of self-developed instinct. It's entirely possible Gamma relayed raw coordinates from her position to you and you subconsciously remembered them and related to them when you later travelled towards the area."

Dana wasn't quite sure how she could remember something she didn't know about, but it did sound rather like the dreams she had. She hadn't even remembered the dreams before she'd set eyes on Gamma at the Emerald Forge. It was like her mind had locked it away until that experience had given her the key to reopen it.

"What is the Emerald Forge?"

Dana indicated the bandages covering the wounds

on her arms. "They've got Peter and he looks really ill. I tried to help him, but he wouldn't come with me. They're harvesting our blood, to get your synapse so they can implant stuff into animals. It's Gamma doing it and two men, Sanderson and Prendick they're called. There's a griffin-thing and a cat with a monkey head and a room full of rats and mice and things."

"Could you identify its location on a map?"

Dana shrugged. "I can try."

Jananin fetched a road map from a shelf. The page she first opened it on meant nothing to Dana, and she had to turn back to the page with Coventry on it and trace the route she and Eric had taken before she could find the place and recognise the pattern of roads and landmarks. Jananin marked the place on the map and wrote down the coordinates on a piece of paper.

Jananin took an ear-hook mobile phone out of her pocket and put it on. "Hello? This is Blake. I need a report on the condition of a psychiatric patient at Whaplode Hospital. Yes, I'll wait. As quickly as possible."

"I told you Gamma escaped from the hospital. She's in the Emerald Forge."

Jananin put her hand over her ear and said in a low voice, so the person on the other end of the phone wouldn't hear it. "One of us has incorrect information."

Dana synced herself to Jananin's phone signal and eased into a background noise of typing and people answering phones. *The number I have for Whaplode Hospital isn't working*, someone said on the other end of the line.

Jananin turned to her computer and quickly started a program and typed something in. A satellite image appeared of a building with a long train of smoke running from it. "It appears there's a problem."

-15-

HE heavy armoured car juddered over the rough surface of a minor road. The thick polymer alloy coating the windows made the interior dingy, despite the bright sunlight without.

Dana sat on the back seat beside Jananin, who now wore her familiar brown leather trench coat and sat in a slightly awkward position due to a knife she had strapped to her thigh beneath it, different to the wakizashi she'd lost in the sea off Cape Wrath, but with a design indicating the same Japanese origins. Dana couldn't recall that she'd ever seen her wear weapons when she'd been seen in public in any official capacity.

As it had been with Jananin's car on the journey to Lewis, GPS signals didn't penetrate the shielding. Dana wasn't able to tell how close they were to the hospital or how much longer it would take. The car was full of signals from various computer equipment and devices carried by Jananin and the driver and front-seat passenger. She couldn't work out what most of them were for.

"Thank you for the cards," she said. When Jananin didn't reply, she added, "You did send those cards on my birthday, didn't you?"

On Dana's last two birthdays, she'd received cards with the two kanji Jananin had once told her spelled her name handwritten inside, and nothing else, the envelopes printed with Graeme and Pauline's address by computer.

Jananin gave a slight noise of assent and a single nod.

She wondered if the hospital would be as she remembered it from the Gamma dreams, or if it wouldn't match up to Gamma's interpretation of it. Try as she might, she couldn't recall a lot at the moment, just the bars on the window and the ditch outside where they'd hidden. When did the dreams stop, and the reality of the Emerald Forge begin? Were the dreams fragments of a reality from Gamma's life, or mere hallucinations that had never happened, or something in between?

The car slowed, and Dana leaned forward to get a clearer view of what lay beyond the windscreen. Two police cars were pulled up at the side of the road beside a gateway into a wall, and beyond the wall smoke rose. Through the gap, Dana sighted the red and fluorescent yellow livery of a fire engine.

The vehicle stopped opposite the police cars. Jananin opened the door and got out. Dana followed, staring up at the rising smoke and the glowing embers drifting up into the summer sky.

The policeman at the gate saluted as Jananin approached. "Professor Blake."

"I assume you were informed of our visit?"

"Yes. I'm afraid we've not much to go on at the moment. The fire brigade have only just got the blaze out. What's she doing here?"

Dana realised with a jolt that he was talking about her.

"She has potential information regarding what went on here. She's helping us with our enquiries."

"You're not taking her in there, surely?"

"Of course we are taking her in there. She may notice or recall something significant."

"But there's dead bodies and all kinds of carnage in there." The policeman took off his hat and wiped his forehead on the back of his hand. A sick sensation floated upwards in Dana's chest. "I wouldn't want one of my green lads going in there and seeing that, not without a good talking to beforehand and the option of a counsellor afterwards. And she's just a kid."

A man who had disembarked from one of the other vehicles to stand close behind them overheard this, and he glanced sharply at Dana. "She's only a child." She recognised him as the man on the *Stormcaller*, Rajani or whatever Tarrow had said his name was, who'd caught her when she'd fallen off the wyvern and lost consciousness. Dana was sure she had seen him somewhere before, but she couldn't remember who he was or where it had been, and his presence made her uncomfortable. He had a machine gun cradled under his left arm, with a strap securing it over his shoulder.

Jananin turned to face Dana. "Are you prepared to go in there, or not?"

Dana looked at the forbidding gate, at the smoke rising from behind the wall. An ill feeling of apprehension knotted her guts. If Jananin wasn't afraid to see whatever was there, she wouldn't be afraid of it, either. She nodded silently, forcing saliva into her suddenly dry mouth and swallowing.

The policeman shook his head in a disgusted sort of way. "I'm not having it."

Jananin sighed. "She just consented to go in, of her own free will."

"She's not at the age of consent. I mean, she might say she wants to watch an eighteen-cert film; doesn't mean you should let her. I mean, that's what it's like in there. An eighteen-cert film, I mean."

"See here," said Jananin. "Your job is to enforce the law. My job is to uphold the will of the Meritocracy. Are you going to get on with your job and let me get on with mine?"

The man reluctantly looked away from Jananin and stepped aside to let them through. The pavement just beyond the entrance was all cracked and blackened, wet from the fire brigade's hose. The large industrial wheely bin Dana remembered Gamma hiding behind was now a charred lump of plastic slumped on the ground. Not far away, hidden from her previous vantage point by the wall, she noticed a prone human figure, lying with his back to them. His white uniform was filthy with blood and dirt, and one arm reached out through a torn sleeve. The skin was ripped and bloodied, and Dana suddenly recognised the white streaking in it as being the bones that joined the fingers to the wrist. She didn't want to see any more, but she couldn't look away. She forced her head to turn, looking instead at Jananin, who examined a flat computer slate that displayed a camera image of the world overlaid with luminous colours.

"What's that?"

Jananin pushed keys on the edge of the screen and mused briefly before replying. "Something that reveals evidence the eye cannot see."

Dana looked up at the façade of the building. The top floor on the left side had been obliterated, leaving only blackened, jagged remnants of walls that no longer joined together. Through the gaps in the ground floor wall, she could see the floor had fallen down. She closed her eyes and concentrated on her memory of the dreams, of the view from Gamma's window and how it fitted in to what she was seeing now. The destruction was centred right on Gamma's cell, she was sure of it. The view of the courtyard below had been from that position, although now the window had been destroyed without trace.

She looked back to Jananin's computer, where vivid purple picked out spots among the rubble where blood had stained the ground. When she reluctantly looked back at the corpse, she noticed clumps of dirty fur and bedraggled feathers on the ground around it; dead rats and birds: starlings. The realisation came to her with a crawling sensation up her spine and over the back of her neck. The animals had attacked the people and killed them, because of what Gamma and Sanderson had done to them. The lab in the Emerald Forge, where she'd sensed all the signals, where she'd released all those animals. They could be the same animals, and she had let them out. It could be she who had caused this. She'd done it to free them, but the damage must already have been done. She was Pandora all over again, and now these people were dead and this building was destroyed because of her.

The smoke from the smouldering wet ruin cut into the back of her throat and stung her eyes. The bodies of broken people and animals swam in her vision when she turned her head away. A weak, surreal feeling had come over her, and her legs became unsteady under her. She didn't realise she was falling until the man with the machine gun let out an exclamation and lunged to catch her by the shoulders and pulled her back upright. He turned to Jananin angrily. "I said you shouldn't have brought her here. This is no place for a child! Come with me, Dana, I'll escort you back to the car."

Dana was sure she had seen this man somewhere before, and it could have been in one of the dreams. He could be someone dangerous she shouldn't trust. She found herself staring at his uniform, and at the end of his gun and the hole where the bullets came out. "No!"

Rajani crouched in order to lower his face to Dana's level "Please, come with me. Blake has no right to put this upon you."

"No." Dana shook her head forcefully, as much in attempt to clear the feeble dizziness filling her head as to deter the man.

"There is no shame in not wanting to be here." He straightened, loosening his grip on her shoulder. "We can go out any time you like. Just say so."

Dana shook her head again and dragged her sleeve across her face. "Jananin, *they* did it. The birds and the rats."

Jananin looked at the ground, and gave a slight, almost imperceptible nod.

"The *birds*?" said the man in a low voice. Dana wished he would go somewhere else. She needed to tell Jananin that she had let the animals out of the lab at the Emerald Forge, and she couldn't do it with him there.

Jananin turned to some people dressed in white plastic

costumes who had entered through the gate behind them. "I need specimens collecting of these animals."

The people began to stoop over and poke dead rats and starlings into plastic evidence bags with hands clad in purple gloves. A policeman had come to stand in the doorway behind them, and he beckoned to Jananin.

"Perhaps he's found some evidence outside he wants us to look at," Rajani suggested.

Dana followed him and Jananin back to the entrance. With the policeman was another man, wearing a white jacket and trousers, and white trainers.

"This man says he works here," the policeman introduced the newcomer.

"I was on the other shift. If I'd been on the night shift, I..." He trailed off as his eyes wandered to take in the column of rising smoke.

Jananin interrupted his reverie. "What can you tell us about one of the patients, a certain Gemma Percival?"

He looked sharply at Jananin, and Dana noticed his pale, glacial blue eyes and a goatee beard on his chin, and some other memory she couldn't pin down stirred. "She had schizophrenia, or something, I don't know the official diagnosis: I'm just a care worker. She escaped months ago. It did make it onto the local news, although it was awkward trying to publicise it. She was understood to be a risk to herself, but probably not to others. Her parents didn't seem to care, they didn't want to go on and make an appeal or anything of that sort. To them, she was an embarrassment, and I almost feel they sent her here in the first place to hide her out the way."

Dana stared at the pattern on the man's shoes and the seams on his trousers. She had seen this before. A memory of raised voices came back to her, a struggle. Rough, heavy hands pinning her arms, forcing her down...

"You're one of them! You're one of the torturers!"

The man looked down at her and started, a look of worried panic coming over him. Perhaps he hadn't noticed her there before. He recovered himself quickly. "The patients here were ill. We did what we could to help them and keep them safe."

"You tied the patients to the beds and didn't let them go to the toilet!"

That same nervous startle again, that searching stare. And then Dana realised it. He was afraid he might have met her before, *inside the hospital*.

"Dana," Jananin interrupted, "there is nothing illegal about what this man does for a living. He has come here to furnish us with information. Your accusations are defamatory, entirely inappropriate, and utterly disrespectful."

Dana bit back the hot anger that threatened to rise from her mouth as another vehement outburst. She spun to face the gates at a heavy, muffled sound that she sensed as much through her feet against the ground as with her ears, the noise of something of great weight hitting the ground. A man in uniform — either police or military, she wasn't sure which — ran out and shouted breathlessly to them. "Someone's trapped inside the building."

There came another noise, a screech, like an animal and yet unearthly. The man from the *Stormcaller* pushed past Dana and ran for the gate, gripping his machine gun with both hands. Jananin went after him and Dana followed her.

She froze in the gateway. Part of the fire-damaged front wall of the building was leaning, slowly at first, but gathering speed as it surrendered to gravity. It hit the ground with a heavy smack and broke into bricks and a billowing cloud of dust and ash.

Something was clambering into the gap left behind, an odd shiny quality making it visible despite the dust obscuring the scene. It wasn't metal reflecting the sunlight. The thing gave off a light all of its own.

Something had started making a buzzing noise, and Jananin looked quickly at the screen of her computer slate. "I'm picking up radiation. Fall back!"

A mass of people rushed back to the gate. In the confusion, Rajani grabbed Dana's arm. He flung her down behind the wall and fell on top of her, his weight crushing her against the dry earth. "Shut the gates!"

Dana crawled out from under the man as the metal bars clanged back into place, and wormed across the dusty ground towards Jananin, who was shouting instructions into the mobile phone attached to her ear. When she'd finished, she picked up her slate, which had now become silent, and studied it. "The wall appears to be blocking it." She twisted her shoulders to examine the wall. "It's not particularly thick, so I think we can assume the emissions are alpha and beta radiation."

This was something from the Emerald Forge. When Dana had released the birds and rats, there had been something else as well, but she hadn't got a clear view of it. "Jananin... in the Emerald Forge, there was something they'd made, like some kind of bird."

Jananin turned to Dana. "Where exactly did you get those burns?"

"I let it out. I let the rats and birds out as well. I didn't realise."

"It's not a bird. You saw it yourself just now. It's too big."

"It's not a real bird. It's like the wyvern, something made to look like a made-up thing, like an animal that doesn't really exist, that comes out of myths. What kind of mythical birds are there?"

"A pelican?" Jananin suggested. "A phoenix?"

A phoenix. That had to be it. Phoenixes were meant to burn, weren't they? This phoenix burned with radioactivity.

"It's got a brain," said Dana. "I mean a brain from an animal. It's not just a machine."

After a pause, Jananin said, "So what we have here is a biomechanical construct plated with some sort of radioactive material, piloted by an organic brain."

The man from the *Stormcaller* made a grim expression and shuffled his gun under his arm, raising the muzzle and settling his fingers on the handle. Jananin shot a glare at him. "If you're thinking about blowing it up, all you will do is contaminate the entire site with radioactive debris."

Another screech came from behind the wall. The gate rattled.

"Any better suggestions?" the man asked.

"Oh, I have some." Jananin pointed to the car they'd arrived in. "The AV is covered with polymer alloy that can absorb or block pretty much anything with a wavelength below gamma rays. If we stay inside, we're more or less protected."

"How does that help solve the problem?" the man answered. "There's nothing to stop that thing flying away. It probably will have done by the time backup arrives."

Jananin considered before replying. "We've got two AVs. We could use them to herd the construct into the remains of the building and attempt to barricade it in there."

"In that case, someone has to get out to open the gate, and risk exposure, and then again to put up a barricade once it's trapped."

Dana had been sitting with the back of her head resting against the wall, half listening to the conversation as she tried to sort through what she could remember of her encounter with the phoenix. Now, thoughts of Cerberus and the Compton bomb in the Faraday bunker under the Amethyst building in London came back to her. "Why don't you put the phoenix inside the car — the AV or whatever it is — instead? If it can block the radiation outside, can't it block it the other way round, from coming out of it?"

Rajani turned his head to stare at her. An embarrassing incident in primary school flashed into her mind, when Miss Robinson had told the class how to do something on a computer, and Dana had put her hand up and told her a much quicker way because she'd thought she might like to know, and Miss Robinson had spoken to her harshly for being 'cheeky' and made her stand facing a wall while the rest of the class sniggered at her.

"I'm not saying it, like, to criticise. I just wondered why you wouldn't be able to do that instead?"

The man laughed abruptly. "Not at all. That's quite the best suggestion I've heard all week. And here we sit, me a trained tactician and an Air Commodore, and Professor Blake here a Nobel laureate!"

Jananin grimaced. Dana fancied she might have rolled her eyes behind her dark glasses. "There is the problem of how we are going to make the phoenix go inside the AV."

"The phoenix is attracted to signals," Dana explained. "All we need to do is put something in the car that emits a signal, like a mobile phone."

Jananin thought this over for a moment. "Very well. Even if it doesn't work, it should at least distract it for long enough to stop it from flying off until backup arrives. We should ask all extraneous personnel to leave and get everyone else remaining into the other AV in case it doesn't go to plan."

"I'll sort it out," Rajani volunteered. He gestured to another man in similar uniform to come and speak to him. "Jananin, take Dana to the other AV."

"Why do we have to wait here instead of help him?" Dana asked Jananin as they crept towards the vehicle, keeping close to the wall.

"Let the military deal with it. They're trained and it's their job to protect us." Jananin opened the passenger door for Dana. She climbed in and waited for Jananin to come round the other side and enter through the driver's door, looking up once more at a blue sky made dim through polymer alloy glass that could block alpha and beta radiation. She wondered where Eric had been the night this had happened.

"You can get hold of information on people and stuff

from all over the country, can't you?"

"Some information, yes. Not information the Freedom of Information Act exempts me from."

Dana put her hand in her pocket and fiddled with her fuse. "What information's that?"

"Unpublished research, people's private business that I have no right interfering in."

The car had an air freshener made from a piece of cardboard with spots in red, orange, and green like a traffic light, only the green light was a protruding, crystalline piece of plastic. She remembered Graeme having one like that in his car, on the very first day he'd brought her and Cale to his house. "Can you find out about people? Can you find out if Eric Cartwright has come home or not since we pretended we were going on a school trip, and can you tell Pauline and Graeme I am okay?"

"I've already got word to your parents. I'll look into the boy when we get back to the base."

Rajani and the other man were reversing the other car up to the gates.

"Who is that man?" Dana asked. "There's something about him I don't like."

Jananin scowled. "Don't be irrational."

"I think I've seen him before, something to do with Gamma and the dreams!"

"He's an Air Commodore in the Meritocracy's Sky Force. He is completely trustworthy. You cannot put faith in dreams. They are merely the way your brain processes the information it has gathered during the day. It's just your mind defragmenting to use a computer analogy. Steve Gideon studied it and tried to use it in his advanced computer design."

Dana didn't say any more, although she didn't believe Jananin. Jananin had made mistakes about people before. She had been wrong about Ivor, and she could be wrong in thinking this man was trustworthy. "But the dreams with Gamma in were real, or at least part real."

"They were generated via some kind of shared consciousness mediated by the Internet. You have picked up details from the consciousness you shared the dreams with via the dreams themselves, but this doesn't mean the dreams are true or give you any reliable way of gauging which parts of the information you have are accurate and which are not."

"I dreamed Ivor came to see me when I collapsed after the *Stormcaller*."

Jananin shifted uncomfortably in her seat. "Then that just shows how unreliable it is."

The men had by now opened the back doors of the vehicle and pulled the gates open. They hurried out the way and crouched down in front of the car. Movement flashed in the gap between the gates and the door, and the van's suspension dipped as something climbed in. The men leapt up and ran to slam the van's back doors.

Rajani came back to the car, a relieved grin spread across his face. He knocked on the car's window and Jananin opened the door.

"I like this kid, she thinks outside the box!" he said.

"You'd better arrange a helicopter with a transport crate," said Jananin. "Get it shipped to a secure area for decontamination. I need to get moving. You can handle it from here, I trust?"

The man nodded, and then he stepped back and saluted.

"What will happen to the phoenix?" Dana asked after Jananin had shut the door and the man was walking back to the other car. "Will you be able to make it unradioactive and keep it alive?"

Jananin didn't look at Dana. She kept her eyes fixed on the windscreen and the view outside, one hand resting on the steering wheel. "No. Something like that, we can't keep alive, not like the wyvern. It's too much of an aberration. The radiation it's emitting will probably kill it anyway, even if we don't."

"What happens now?"

Jananin reached under the steering wheel and started the AV's engine. "We go back to base. This counts as a crisis situation. I will need to consult the other Spokesmen, and a vote will need to be cast on what must be done next."

-16-

JANANIN crashed through the doors to the small ward where Dana had spent the previous night. She cast about the empty beds. "Where is that fat Scottish woman?"

The medic appeared through the side-door that led to the shower. "I'm here, and my name's Tarrow."

"This child came into your care in the early hours of this morning, and you failed to notice she was suffering from radiation burns!"

"*Radiation burns?*" Tarrow indicated to the bed. "Here, Dana, sit down. She had a bit of mild erythema, nothing I thought was significant. Kids go out in the sun these days and they won't wear hats."

Jananin reached across and raised Dana's arm in front of her face to reveal the exposed side of it.

"It's barely even visible now," said Tarrow. "Can't have been anything too bad." She rifled through a tray of medical instruments until she found a long-handled scope, and shone a light from it into each of Dana's eyes while squinting through a lens. "There's no sign of any permanent damage."

"What about the stuff radiation does to people?" Dana remembered making a table of the effects of the different kinds of radiation in a Physics lesson, although her memory of them and which did what was hazy now. "People get cancer and stuff off radiation."

"For that amount of radiation, and that short a duration, you're no more likely to get cancer than myself or Blake are."

Jananin flared her nostrils and twisted her mouth. "Statistically rather less likely, I should say, considering the sort of work I was doing in the lab during my postdoctoral years. I have to go now. I trust it you can get on with this? Dana, I want to see you later to talk about this *wyvern* as you're calling it."

She whirled about, her trench coat flaring out in the motion, and left the room.

"Off she goes." Tarrow rolled her eyes. "Official Meritocracy business." She unscrewed the lid from a shallow glass jar and dipped a wad of cotton wool in it, and thrust a dollop of greasy-looking chamomile-scented pink glop into Dana's face. Dana pulled back suddenly. She'd noticed face creams like this tended to cause acne outbreaks on her forehead. "I can do that myself."

Tarrow set the pot down on the bed and stepped back and shrugged. "You're a right funny bugger, you."

"Thanks," said Dana, unable to come up with a more appropriate retort. She dabbed some of the pink cream off the cotton wool on one finger and started to rub it on her nose.

"You'll certainly save the NHS money, applying it like that!" Tarrow sat down on the bed next to Dana. She leaned her feet back onto her heels and flexed her toes inside the white pumps she had on.

Dana paused to look up at her. "Are you a lesbian?" she said.

Tarrow stared. "That's rather a forward question to ask. But yes, I like lasses."

"How did you find out you were a lesbian?" Dana asked. "Like, how would I be able to tell if I am one?"

Tarrow shrugged again. "I'd have thought that was obvious. So, where've you been with Blake?"

"I'm not sure I'm supposed to tell you that," said Dana.

Tarrow made a loud blowing noise through slack lips. "Suit yourself."

The image of the mangled bodies clad in white came back to Dana, blood on the floor, broken bodies of rats and birds on the wet concrete. When she looked down at her feet, the white trainers she'd been given were dirty with ash, and reddish smears still marked the rubber of the soles. Her hand stopped halfway between the jar and her face.

"Now what's the matter?" Tarrow said. "You don't have to talk about it. It was just a joke."

"I did something wrong. And horrible things happened because of it."

"I did all kinds of stupid, horrible things when I was young. My sister had this expensive German teddy bear, and I jammed it down the bog one day because she got better grades than me and my parents made this big fuss."

"Who's that man, the one on the *Stormcaller*, Rajani or whatever his name is? What do you know about him?"

"The Air Commodore? He's a canny lad."

Dana screwed the lid back on to the jar. She could sense various signals for wLANs about the facility, but something blocked her every time she tried to access the Internet through them, something complicated upon which every decryption trick she could come up with failed. "What does canny mean?"

"It means he's nice, like he won't screw people over or lie. He even seems to get on with Blake!"

"What did he do before he was an air commodore?"

"Well, I don't know. Why didn't you ask him if you wanted to know? You've just been out with him, haven't you?"

If she could get to a computer, perhaps she'd be able to do an Internet search to find out more. "Have you got any computers here? I mean, just normal computers I can check my emails on, not the ANT."

Tarrow frowned. "ANT? Who told you there was an ANT here?" Her expression turned to one of dismay. "Was it *me?*"

Dana put her fists against the mattress where she sat and shuffled backwards uneasily. "You said something about a place called Torrmede as well."

Tarrow's eyes widened. "*Damn.* I'm always doing this. I engage my mouth before I put my brain in gear."

Dana and Tarrow stared at each other for a moment, and then both of them started laughing.

"Don't tell anyone about the ANT or Torrmede, right?" said Tarrow.

"What is Torrmede?"

"I can't tell you even *more.*" The medic turned and headed back for the door. "I'll see if I can find you a laptop," she called over her shoulder as the door closed behind her.

Dana got up off the bed and went over to the window. The sky was still blue and empty, and the sun beat down on the glassy pyramids.

She turned at the sound of the door opening again. It wasn't Tarrow with a computer, but Jananin.

"Something you will be glad to hear, first. The police in Coventry have informed us that Eric Cartwright returned home last night."

"Oh." So Eric had gone home, as she'd told him to, and he was safe and away from this chaos after all. Relief tempered the embarrassment accompanying the thought of him. Perhaps this would all have blown over when she eventually got back, and they might be able to go back to being friends. "Thank you."

"Now, to the matter of where we were this morning. The bodies of the birds and rats we found have been examined. Their brains were implanted with cheap mass-produced chips. That seems to account for why they attacked the workers at the psychiatric unit. The police have found twelve bodies so far. Some of them are of the staff there... others are of... patients."

"I let those rats and birds out. When I escaped from the Emerald Forge. I didn't realise they would do that! I thought they were being held prisoner, like me."

Jananin stared at her. "What are you raving about now? It's beside the point that you let them out."

"I let them out, and they went somewhere and killed

people! It's my fault the... the *doctors* and the children... the psychiatric patients are dead!"

"They had computer chips in them and radio transceivers to control their behaviour. They didn't go just *anywhere*, they went to a predetermined location that presumably was chosen as you said yourself because Gamma was interred there and escaped. That you released them does not matter, as they would likely have been released at some point anyway with exactly the same outcome."

Dana sat on the bed and breathed hard. After her mind had run through it a few times, it started to make sense. Eric was safe at home, and the people in that prison from the dreams were still dead, but from this perspective it no longer felt quite so much as though it was her fault.

"They're in the process of coming up with a way to examine that construct from the site."

"The phoenix?"

"Personally I don't see how it's a phoenix, but if you prefer."

Dana looked down at her feet and the hospital floor. "No, you have to understand it," she said after a pause, because she hadn't really realised it before, not until now. "That's the way of it. I like plants. Cale likes beetles and flies and stuff. Peter likes fish. And Gamma likes made-up animals out of myths."

"There's some more information on the leads you gave me. Gemma Percival as we know was a patient at the hospital. You mentioned someone else, Sanderson. There is an Archibald Sanderson of whereabouts unknown. He was a neurosurgeon who worked on patients with mental illnesses. He was found guilty about a year ago of illegally performing lobotomies and other dubious treatments outside the remit of the NHS, and struck off. Historically, he was also implicated in an embezzlement charge involving a *certain charity*."

Dana stared at Jananin for a moment as she worked

out what she meant. Ivor, reading a court judgement, throwing his wedding ring off the *Atlantic Sonata*.

"So he could have worked where Gamma was being held, and that's how she met him, and how I recognise him from the dreams?"

"Almost certainly. The other man, now, you thought his name is Prendick. There was a Norman Prendick, a highly skilled metalworker, who was blinded in an industrial accident six years ago. He lived as a recluse in the vicinity of Ely, until he apparently disappeared, his house abandoned and with nobody in the area knowing his whereabouts."

Norman Prendick. Blinded in an accident, his life ruined, his visage inspiring horror in anyone who set eyes on him, until Gamma and Sanderson found him and asked him for his skills in exchange for another sight. It had to have been Prendick who had so skilfully shaped the armour and joints of the wyvern.

"So what happens now?"

"All we can do for the moment is wait for each of the other Spokesmen to reply with their view on the situation and recommendation on how to proceed. In the meantime, let's take a look at this construct you found."

Dana got down from the bed. "It's kind of the other way round. *It* found *me*."

Outside in the corridor, the lift down to the ground floor had a large window that faced out through a glass wall overlooking the fields of exotic plants. "Can you really grow anything, and feed everyone in the country, and have fuel as well, with genetically modified plants?"

"To a point," Jananin replied. "Science is to all intents and purposes running only slightly ahead of a population tidal wave. All of this non-polluting technology — *Stormcaller*, nuclear engines — is just a means of stalling the inevitable. Much of the damage is already done, and there is no such thing as completely clean energy. The populace will always damage its environment through the process of its development. Ultimately the problem boils down to there being too many people and insufficient resources and land to generate more resources to sustain them if they continue to grow at the same rate. All we can do is hope science stays ahead."

The lift reached the base of its descent and the door opened. Jananin led Dana through a short corridor and out through a swipe-card controlled door and along a path that ran alongside the building.

"Perhaps you can provide some insight on it. I have to admit, every question I have come up with an answer for surrounding this construct has only engendered yet more questions."

They were soon approaching a fence made from galvanised palisades, much like the ones surrounding the school Dana attended. She sensed a familiar signal, and something moved on the other side. The wyvern adjusted its position so one eye was visible through a gap in the fence. It transmitted a reassurance of a sort. It had been concerned, while Dana had been gone, particularly as its last sight of her had been when she'd fallen off aboard the *Stormcaller*.

Jananin opened the gate using a swipecard. The wyvern stepped forward, transmitting a *happy* signal along with a sentiment something along the lines of it being glad to see Dana and to know she was well.

"I don't believe it to be dangerous," said Jananin, "but it does appear to be completely autonomous. It seems to eat only fish. I understand when you came across it, it was aggressive, as though being controlled remotely, and you removed the device by which it was controlled?"

"Yes, there was a collar on it. It has a brain, an animal brain, connected to computer parts like Gamma and I do. Well, Osric said it was an animal and not a human, but I don't know that for sure. Gamma and Sanderson might have kidnapped a very young child, or a braindamaged person, or something else like that."

The wyvern studied Dana as she spoke, and then it tilted its head and regarded Jananin quizzically.

"It's very unlikely," said Jananin. "It's an intelligent animal for sure, but all the observations we made of it before I released it were consistent with it not being human. It did attempt to communicate with the researchers, but it didn't demonstrate any behaviours specific to humans. I think the end guess was a dog or pig, but not a human and not any other primate. It's not possible to tell for certain without euthanising and dismantling it."

Dana gazed out upon the long grass beyond the compound fence. "I was afraid Osric would do that. I don't know if you can do this, but would you be able to make sure the wyvern was safe?"

Jananin closed her eyes and shook her head. "I'm afraid I can make no such promise."

On the concrete to one side beside the entrance was a sloppy greenish-brown pile with flies crawling over it. "Did it do that?" Dana pointed.

"Obviously," said Jananin. "Everything does *that*."

"Where did it come out?"

"Presumably from the underside of its body somewhere. If it has a brain and a nervous system, it needs oxygen and nutrients, and therefore has to have a cardiopulmonary system and a complete alimentary canal."

Dana stared at the wyvern and considered this. Jananin couldn't make any promise because her loyalty had to be to the Meritocracy, but Dana could make promises in her own name, and she made a silent promise to the wyvern that she would not abuse its trust and abandon it again. She tried to convey in her sincerest terms, that while it was safe here while she was with it, and that it must not under any circumstances harm Jananin, or indeed anyone else, escape was the ultimate and only end. She didn't know where she could hide it or what she would do after that, but she would have to find a way. She'd *used* the wyvern by contacting Osric, and she owed it to keep it safe after all it had done for her. She had shown it nothing but dishonour, while it had been loyal to her.

The wyvern's thought in response surprised her when she realised what it meant: She had been the one who had saved it from Gamma's control. It felt it was totally justified in returning the favour and rescuing her from the Emerald Forge.

Eyes blurring, Dana let out a gasping laugh, and reached out to put her hand on the metal plates covering the wyvern's neck. *I won't fail you again.* It was time to be responsible now. This was not school, where she could run away from her problems, or do her best to ignore them, and hide behind an adult. This was real life, and what she did here could have effects on life and death and what happened in the future.

"Perhaps you have some ideas about why someone would go to such lengths to make something so elaborate, so complicated, instead of something simple that would work the same way?" Jananin said.

Dana wiped her eyes. "You mean, why a wyvern?"

"Exactly."

"It's Gamma," Dana replied at length. "She's lived all her life in a fantasy, because reality was so bad she couldn't let herself believe it was real. So she has to turn her fantasies into a reality." The realisation began to unfold, and more understanding came to her, and after a moment she spoke again. "They need Prendick to make the actual, like, *hardware* for the constructs. Then Sanderson does the stuff with brains and nerves and living flesh. But Gamma's the one who controls them in the end. So she gets to say what they make, because if she won't control it, they can't use it."

Jananin walked a little distance away and seated herself on a metal container. The place they were keeping the wyvern in was a concrete-floored yard surrounded by a high fence, with a large locked gate at the end so lorries could back in. Various bottles and pieces of equipment were locked up in cages. "There's something more to it than that. There are too many features on that wyvern that don't seem to do anything. The part of it that bewilders me most is the helium."

"I thought the helium was put in for lift," Dana said. "To help it fly, like in a balloon. Osric said it didn't work like that, though."

"You would need a much larger volume of helium gas in comparison to the wyvern if that were the case. What it appears to have is a bottle of helium connected to a second pair of lungs. Any small advantage filling the lungs with helium would give to flight is rendered utterly pointless by the significantly heavier mass of the bottle with the compressed helium in."

"What do you mean?"

"I mean, the combination of the helium bottle and the additional lungs, minus weight from the buoyancy gained by the volume of helium when the lungs are full, gives the wyvern a greater weight than if none of these things had been included. Certainly it does use the lungs for ballast when it's flying, but it would fly much better had all of this simply not been part of its design."

Dana couldn't think of an answer to this. After a rather longer pause, Jananin spoke again. "The only solution I can come up with is that flight buoyancy was not the main design intention of the lungs, and in this case, the gas bottle must have originally been intended to be something else."

Dana turned away from watching the wyvern to face Jananin. "What something else?"

Jananin pointed to the wyvern's head. "You see those serrated edges on the back of the teeth?"

Dana studied the wyvern's metal beak. There were two fangs, upper and lower, on either side of the head, their surfaces meeting when the mouth was in its closed position. Each contacting surface was marked with minute closely-spaced grooves cut into the metal.

"It almost looks like an ignition source, designed to spark when the mouth is opened. That means this construct was meant to function as a flamethrower, and the bottle inside it was intended to contain hydrogen and not helium. So then why did it contain helium when we examined it?"

"Because it has to be true to the myth?" Dana suggested. "Eric said wyverns have four limbs, not six like dragons. Perhaps wyverns don't breathe fire either."

Jananin shook her head. "There is too much that doesn't add up. It has metal valves inside it that essentially function as a voicebox, allowing it to make different tones. And why make the control for it removable, as a collar? Surely it would have been a better design if the control mechanism had been an integral part of the brain, as it was in the birds and rats that attacked the hospital. It's almost as though it's a prototype that was built over a long period of time, with functions removed and added to its purpose as development went on."

Dana tried to query the wyvern. She tried to visualise fire billowing out of its mouth, but this didn't seem to stir any recognition. "Is there a way we could try to see if it actually *can* breathe *fire*? If it went wrong, would it hurt it?"

"I don't see that it would. Hydrogen won't burn without oxygen, and there seem to be certain precautions built in to stop it inhaling with the lungs connected to the gas bottle. It's worth a try, but you need to be sure you can control it. I do not think it is dangerous by its own intents, but if it panics and swings its head around, people could be seriously injured."

Dana considered the wyvern's state of mind. It understood about replacing the cylinder accessed by the hatch in its back, but it didn't really understand what it was they were trying to do, although it was curious about this image of glowing orange stuff coming out of its mouth that Dana had come up with.

"Let's try it."

Jananin and Dana undid the plate on the wyvern's back. Jananin took the bottle out and set it down on the concrete.

"It doesn't look very heavy," said Dana.

"This one's nearly empty. And these days they're made of polymer alloy, so the actual container weighs very little despite having extremely strong walls. What we do need to know is if we have a hydrogen one in the same size."

They examined the cages of bottles and cylinders until Dana found some a similar size. Jananin unlocked the cage and tilted a hydrogen bottle onto the edge of its base so it could be rolled out. She compared the circumference and the fitting to the empty helium bottle. "This looks suitable."

Dana helped her lift it up onto the wyvern's back. Jananin eased it down into the space and connected the hose that ran down through the thick plastic sheeting protecting the wyvern's organs. The hose stiffened with a faint hissing sound. The two of them fastened the panel back down.

"Now, let's get out before we try anything." Jananin headed back for the gate. Once she and Dana were both outside the yard, she closed it. "Make it turn away from us before it tries."

Dana got the wyvern to turn around. She tried to think of exhaling hard and opening her mouth quickly. The wyvern jerked its neck and made a snorting noise. Nothing happened.

"It's just breathing out. Wait a minute." Dana closed her eyes and concentrated on the sensory feedback she was getting from the wyvern. She tried to think of her chest, and the muscles in it that moved when she breathed, and now here she could sense other parts that didn't match up with anything she was familiar with. The wyvern coughed again, the sensation alien to her. She thought of when they'd risen from the roof of the Emerald Forge, chest expanding with lifting force. The wyvern exhaled and something gave way with the feeling of an enormous breath rushing up her throat, and something blinding bright startled her eyes open, and a jet of flame shot out in front of the wyvern. It let out a discordant bagpipe squeal and hopped backwards, flapping its wings with a sound like a cutlery drawer slamming.

An exclamation came from behind; a soldier on the path there was beckoning to Jananin. "Wait here," she said.

Dana went back to the wyvern while Jananin and the soldier disappeared from sight. The wyvern's fire breathing attempt had left a blackened deposit on the concrete, a dark smear with a long tail, and it reminded her of something she'd seen at the destruction site, at the hospital. The buildings had been on fire, but rats and starlings wouldn't know how to start a fire, would they? Even with chips implanted in their brains? If the wyvern *was* a prototype as Jananin thought, and a prototype was a simplified, scaled-down version of what it was ultimately intended to be, what might *this* construct look like?

When she tried to pry into the wyvern's thoughts, all she got from it was a mingled sense of confusion and alarm. It had never expected that sort of thing to happen. If it did have an animal brain, as Jananin presumed, didn't most animals fear fire by instinct? Perhaps that was why it had been fitted with a helium cylinder in place of hydrogen, because the brain and senses of a real living animal turned out not to be compatible with breathing fire.

Dana thought of the mildly suggestive idea of having another attempt, and the wyvern responded with a horrified balk.

Jananin reappeared behind the gate and entered once more, mouth set grimly and face inscrutable as ever.

"Some more information has come to light. The construct from the hospital, the phoenix, has just exploded."

Dana swallowed. "It *exploded*?"

Jananin nodded. "As it turns out, it was what's called a dirty bomb, designed to scatter radioactive contamination over an area. It was guided by some kind of organic brain that had been reprogrammed to seek out signals. Fortunately at the time it was still inside the car in a metal crate, securely contained in a hangar. The crate contained most of the blast. A few people were injured, and the hangar will now have to be decontaminated, but no-one was killed. The Spokesmen have voted that the Emerald Forge is a threat and that immediate action must be taken, without holding a public referendum."

"So, what's going to happen?"

"It has been decided that sending military personnel into the Emerald Forge in an attempt to gain control of it would be too great a risk. The *Stormcaller* will be deployed, with instructions to Compton bomb the area."

"What? What about Peter? Did you tell them Peter was there?"

"I told them they had a hostage, and that the hostage was a boy with no family, and developmental difficulties that meant he would be impossible to rehabilitate into normal society."

"What do you mean, he doesn't have a family? He's my half brother! Ivor was his father! You promised Ivor you'd see to it that he was safe!"

Jananin shook her head. "I'm sorry, Dana. There is only so much I can do. I did try to monitor what was happening with Peter. He was in an institution, but he wasn't doing well there, and since he ran away I've been unable to find what happened to him. From all the reports, he just wasn't coping, and as he tended to have violent outbursts, his prospects weren't good."

"What do you mean?" Dana demanded. "You knew Peter! You know what he was like! You called him a... *a perfectly personable*... something or other. You said you didn't mind if he called you Jininan!"

"Unfortunately it seems that Pilgrennon had developed his own way of managing him that worked. It probably helped him to have you and Alpha around. But without those supports, in a modern world filled with signals, he couldn't be helped. I am sorry for what happened. Ivor's suggestion of Peter staying with him, in retrospect, would have been the best outcome. But that wasn't the outcome we got, and there was nothing I or you, or anyone else could have done about that."

"But Peter's not a horrible boy! He's just a funny boy who likes nature and Vikings, and he needs someone who's calm and strong to be a dad to him! It's not fair!"

"You have seen the sorts of weapons they are fighting with. If we send military personnel in there and try to retrieve Peter, there is a strong chance we will suffer heavy losses, the loss of life of those military personnel, on the intention of rescuing one hostage and arresting three people. And Peter, if he is recovered, will have to go into a care home or probably even a secure institute."

"Someone might adopt him, like someone did me and Cale!"

"It's unlikely."

"Cale and I were in foster care and homes for years, but one day Pauline and Graeme came along, and we got to go and live with them, and—"

Jananin interrupted. "The only reason you weren't adopted sooner is because they couldn't separate you from your brother."

"What do you mean? How do you even *know*? You didn't have anything to do with me and Cale! You didn't even know we were born!"

Her mouth was tense. She mustn't have meant to say that, and when she continued her voice was low and uneasy. "I've seen all the records. You wouldn't be apart from him. When they separated you, you screamed. When you were large enough to move about by yourself, you sought him out. You would have been far more appealing as a single child for adoption. You did have clear problems, but you were much higher-functioning than Cale. Because they couldn't separate you and because of the high interdependence, social services insisted you be placed together."

Dana couldn't look at Jananin. Although something ached inside of her, she couldn't say what it was. All the feelings she had about this matter were tangled up together. She couldn't understand why someone wouldn't want Cale, Cale who was quiet and calm and, on the other hand, she couldn't accept that it might have been Cale holding her back all the time when they'd been shunted around foster homes constantly. And she couldn't imagine what life would have been like without Cale in it, and how anyone could even have thought they had the right to take her brother away from her. She couldn't work out if she resented Cale, or she resented herself, or she resented all the people who'd disapproved of Cale. She wanted to shut everything out and build Airfix models until this ache went away, but there were no Airfix models and this was not her home, and there were things going on in real life that were more important.

Finally she said, "Cale never spoke. He still never speaks, unless he really has to. I've always been able to tell what he feels, and I can speak for him. He's never felt he needed to speak. Cale isn't stupid... it's just when you understand the world like Cale does, a lot of the stuff that matters to other people just *isn't* important."

"It must have been the signals you gave out that allowed you to identify each other. You were the one constant in each other's lives."

When Dana did not add anything further, Jananin continued. "Peter functions at a level closer to Cale's than yours. He's also much older than you and Cale were when you were adopted, and has a tendency towards violence. It's extremely unlikely an adoptive home could be found for him."

Dana stared at Jananin, and then a realisation came upon her. "If he does go into care, they might find out what he can do. They might find out he was one of Pilgrennon's experiments, and that he has the synapse that you invented in his blood! That's why you want him to die! It would be convenient for you!"

"I don't want anyone to die. I'm a Spokesman. It's my job to enforce the will of the Meritocracy, or to act on behalf of the Meritocracy in instances like this. The other Spokesmen agree that the risk involved in storming the Emerald Forge is not worth it for the sake of rescuing one hostage who has no family to miss him. The soldiers we would have to send, have families who would miss them were they to be killed in the endeavour! You are allowing your emotions to dictate your reaction to this situation! Surely you must see the sense in this if you think about it rationally?"

A faint signal had just become noticeable, a signal with a primal quality to it that Dana recognised very well. "My brother."

"Your brother?"

"*My brother!* Cale!"

Dana sprang upright. She had sensed Cale's signal somewhere not far away, and there was another signal too, and this she also recognised. It was the griffin. She had known Gamma was sending the griffin to Coventry. It had never even occurred to Dana that it would go after Cale. The significance that he too was one of Pilgrennon's children had utterly eluded her. She'd never thought of him as having anything to do with Jananin or what had happened during the Information Terrorism attack.

"It's the griffin!" Dana pointed to a distant object flying in the blue sky above the base. "It's got Cale and it's taking him back to the Emerald Forge! Do something!"

Cale's signal was utter panic and terror. Dana couldn't get any visual information from him, just a sense of a horrible stench from the griffin's rotting flesh. His eyes must have been closed. The wyvern raised its head to examine the objects the signal came from. Jananin went back to the gate and called a soldier in. She pointed to the object in the sky.

"No, don't shoot!" Dana shouted. "You'll hit him, or he'll fall! You have to fly a plane or something and catch him!"

"Dana, I am forty years old" said Jananin severely. "I am not a stunt pilot and nor have I ever been one."

"But you have to stop it and get Cale back!" She faced the wyvern, and its head turned on its long neck to face her in turn, and the same thought passed through both their minds. "If you won't do something, I will!"

Jananin seized Dana roughly by the arm, turning her away from the wyvern. She pointed, squinting up at the dwindling speck in the sky. "This place is not on a direct flight path between the Emerald Forge and Coventry. We have weapons here. There is no reason for whatever is carrying Cale to fly in range. If you can see into Gamma's thoughts remotely, it's probable she can see into yours reciprocally. It's very likely she knows where you are, and this is a trap designed to lure you out, and by pursuing their bait you are doing exactly what they want you to do."

The thought of Cale, locked in a cell in the Emerald Forge, being cut, being *bled* for Gamma and Sanderson's experiments, that she couldn't stand. "But I can't just do *nothing!* If they take Cale to the Emerald Forge they'll use him, and he'll be killed because *you'll* still bomb it!"

"You can't say that with any surety," Jananin argued. "The acquisition of a second hostage would be considered a significant change in the situation, and the decision would have to be put before the Spokesmen for a second vote."

"Then would you vote differently?"

"I don't know. I would have to consider the ramifications thoroughly first. I have to approach this impartially, as a scientist, or a judge."

"Would you vote differently if I'd never escaped from

the Emerald Forge, and you had found out this information some other way, and I was still trapped there?"

Jananin's hesitation told more than any answer would.

"*Why?* Why would it be different?"

"Because you are the one and only thing Ivor Pilgrennon got right!"

For a moment, Dana couldn't decide what to do. Disgust and hurt that someone would think Cale did not matter as much as her overcame her mind. She could see aching emotion on Jananin's face that was beyond her faculties of analysis. Then she reached out a hand behind her and touched the hard metal plates covering the wyvern's neck, and the wyvern dropped willingly into a crouch to allow her to mount when she turned away.

"Dana, don't do this," said Jananin, but the wyvern sprang aloft and its wings drove down a buffet of dusty air as it launched itself to clear the perimeter fence, and anything else she said was lost to the roar of the wind and the shearing of steely pinions.

-17-

A STEADY succession of forceful wingbeats carried the wyvern higher into the clear sky. Dana held on, gripping its neck with her knees and squinting over the glare of the sun reflecting off the metal plates of its neck as the meadow rushing below grew more and more distant. Even if it was a trap, even if doing this was exactly what Gamma wanted her to do, she had to at least try. She couldn't leave Cale to be taken to the Emerald Forge, to be bled, and where the Meritocracy might even kill him because they thought the threat to the public outweighed the risk involved in rescuing him.

The wyvern's chest became taut with each breath, its second lungs expanded with hydrogen, breathing lungs working hard to power the muscles in its wings that bore them higher. Both of them could still sense Cale's signal, although it was weak from distance. He was still much higher above. What if the griffin was simply swifter than the wyvern, and catching up with it might turn out to be impossible?

No, the signal was becoming stronger, and now, in the bright heights above, there could just be discerned a darker speck with steadily beating wings. Dana urged the wyvern faster.

Wisps of cloud passed, brushing over them and penetrating Dana's clothing like cold, damp fingers. The ground was a long way down now, an articulated lorry on a hedged road tiny and distant. No sounds reached this far up, just the roar of the wind the wyvern's passage through the atmosphere generated.

The figure above by now had grown more distinct, and Dana could identify the shape of the griffin and the human figure dangling beneath it, clutched in its front paws. Cale hung with his back bowed, facing earthwards, arms and legs limp, but he was still conscious.

Dana thought to him. *Cale, open your eyes, please...*

It was only now it occurred to her: How on Earth were they going to get Cale off the griffin and back down to the ground? She hadn't thought that far ahead yet.

There came an insane thought from the wyvern, of driving the griffin higher still, of attacking and destroying, or otherwise causing it to drop Cale. It responded to Dana's sense of horror at this suggestion with a reassurance: Its metal body was denser than Cale's flesh and blood. So long as they flew up far enough and went after Cale as soon as he was dropped, the wyvern would fall faster and be able to catch up with Cale and carry him down. Dana would just need to hold on tight.

An instant of doubt: Dana herself must increase the wyvern's flying weight substantially. Would it be able to carry twice her weight? Again the wyvern reassured her: it might not be able to take off under the weight of two people, but it was strong enough that it could descend slowly so as to land without harming them.

What if the griffin refused to go higher? The wyvern responded by breathing out with its flight lungs. A jet of flame tore into the air ahead. The wyvern fought to maintain flight and shape the fire by controlling the force of the flow from its lungs and how much air from its other lungs was exhaled to mix with it as the griffin ascended.

Now was high enough. The wyvern shut off the breath from its flight lungs and beat its wings hard, striving higher still to bear down on the griffin's back. It gave the thought to Dana to keep low and hold tight, and they were falling through the sky, wings folded back in a dive that burst into a pipe-organ roar of flames in front of the wyvern's snout, to intercept the griffin. At the last minute, the wyvern pivoted its legs downward and slammed steel talons into the griffin's back, and the griffin squealed in pain. The wyvern clamped the griffin's wing in its jaws and fired again, burning feathers.

All four of them fell, locked together. With the wing pulled up out the way, Dana could see Cale hanging underneath the griffin, and he'd opened his eyes and turned to stretch up his arms towards her. She couldn't risk him being dropped and the wyvern not being able to catch him in time. She let go of the wyvern's neck with one hand and reached down for him. *Cale, grab my hand...*

In the same instant, the griffin desperately arched its back and bucked, and its hind feet hit the wyvern, the jolt throwing its whole body upwards, and Dana lost her seating and her grip on the wyvern's neck. She caught only a glimpse of Cale's face and the wyvern and the griffin as a tangle of bodies before she twisted over, and her ears were full of wind and her eyes watered from the force of the air as the clouds and countryside spun beneath her.

She was falling from a place people can only survive with parachutes, and she was going to die and Jananin Blake would have to take whatever was left of her back to Pauline and Graeme and apologise about what had become of her, even though Dana had deliberately disobeyed her, and they would have to bury her in the cemetery, next to their dead babies whom Pauline lost before Duncan was born. They would have to be told not to look at her remains, because that's what happens when people die in ways that make horrible messes of their bodies because it's too traumatic for their relatives to see them.

The wyvern's bagpipe-organ roar sounded from above. Dana found she did have some control over how she fell, and managed to turn herself so she was facing upward. The wyvern was falling after her, gradually gaining, its wings pinned back against its body. She spread her limbs out, trying to increase her air resistance so it could catch up with her faster.

The wyvern was closer now and it reached out for her with steel beak and sharp talon. Dana flailed with her hands, trying to get a grip on any part of it as the wind buffeted them. The wyvern lunged and caught hold of her forearm, and Dana cried out as its sharp claws penetrated the sleeve of her jacket and pressed in on the bandage covering the wounds that had been inflicted in the Emerald Forge. But now they were at least linked together, and she could reach up and take hold of the wyvern's other leg with her free hand.

The clouds were closing up above. They were falling back to Earth. Now was the time to stop diving, to start pulling back up so they could go after Cale again. And yet now, through her connection to the wyvern, she sensed panic.

When she tried to find out from it what was wrong, the only sensation she got was a pain, so cold it felt almost hot, right in the middle of her chest. She tried to think through the pain, but the wyvern was overwhelmed and reeling. The sensation was spreading outward, a feeling like wearing a jacket that was much too small and restricted the movement of one's arms. The wyvern wouldn't open its wings; indeed it wanted to curl up in a ball and wait for the pain to go away. There wasn't time. Dana looked over her shoulder to see the ground closing fast, a sandy field dotted with small rectangles expanding to meet them. She yelled a wordless, senseless exclamation at the wyvern. They had to react now, but the wyvern was falling with its neck hunched and legs and wings tensed, retracted into its body.

Gritting her teeth, she pushed her connection to the wyvern tighter, letting its pain spill into her and forcing its limbs with her own will. Agony exploded as its wings extended, not fully, but enough to slow their fall into an uncontrolled glide. Dana urged it to hold on just a little while longer. The ground below flew past in a blur, but Dana was hanging from the wyvern's legs facing upwards and back from the direction it was moving, unable to see clearly enough to steer. The wyvern was barely aware of what was going on, but it managed to flap its wings weakly.

A disturbance in the airflow told Dana the ground was getting close, and then something heavy and solid crashed into the back of her legs, and her hands slipped from their contact with the wyvern's legs. The world became a spinning haze of sky and dusty ground and blows to the shoulders and knees. From somewhere ahead came a loud clang, like a car crashing into a line of old metal dustbins, as the wyvern touched down.

Dana lay on the ground for several seconds before her senses resumed normal service. Sharp stalks scratched her hands and pressed into her shoulder as she turned over. Shorn-off straws of wheat stood up in neat lines from sun-baked stony earth, and all around cuboid bales had been deposited where the loose straw had been gathered by a baling machine.

The stubble and the bales were as dry as tinder.

She pushed herself to hands and knees, ignoring the ache that would surely turn into bruising. The wyvern had fallen across one of the bales and lay collapsed over it, tail sticking up in the air and wings sprawling. Its head moved sluggishly on its neck. Dana hurried towards it, rushing to impress upon it that it must keep its mouth closed and not breathe out from its second lungs. Any fire here would spread rapidly and burn fierce.

She had to urge it onto its feet, and all it wanted to do was lie there and succumb to unconsciousness until the pain had passed, but Dana made it stand, made it concentrate on one step and then another, until they made it to the edge of the field and to a tiny copse beneath which grew green grass and ran a small stream. It was only here that she allowed it to fall down in the shade and rest, and by this time it was in so much pain it fell into a delirious state, passing just below the surface of consciousness.

Dana knelt beside the wyvern's neck and slid her hand under its chest, to the place where she'd imagined the pain had started. Between the metal plates lay rough skin, icy cold to the touch. She frowned: the wyvern had mammalian organs, warm blood, she was sure of it. As she slid her hand either side of the cold spot, the skin warmed. Why was there this cold spot? Something must have gone wrong with the hydrogen cylinder. Dana recalled when she and Eric had fought with the wyvern in the classroom, and how the carbon dioxide fire extinguisher had got so cold it had burned her hand where she'd been holding it wrong. When gas depressurises, it takes the heat out of things around it. So much gas had come out of the hydrogen cylinder it must have frozen tissues deep inside the wyvern's throat.

Perhaps *that* was why it had been fitted with helium instead of hydrogen.

The wyvern was breathing more easily now, and the cold area in its neck felt to be getting less cold. Dana looked up at the sky between the gaps in the trees. Cale's signal was no longer in range, and there was no sight of the griffin in the sky. It was a disturbing thought that minutes ago they had both been way up there, in what felt like another world, and their descent back to Earth could have gone so terribly wrong.

The wyvern began to come to its senses, and gradually raised its neck. Dana encouraged it to have a drink from the stream. After that, it felt a little better, but the thought of filling its flight lungs and trying to take off was met with a reaction of fear and refusal.

Fine, we walk.

GPS told Dana there were no roads nearby. The farmland ended not far away, and the land sloped down towards the ocean. She fancied she could hear the waves breaking upon the distant shore.

She and the wyvern walked slowly together, following the edge of the thin line of trees dividing the fields, until they crested a low hill. Beyond this the soil became sandy and the scrub turned into dunes of harsh grass, and yet farther spread a grey stretch of beach, and beyond that, the sea. More distant along the shore there rose the dome of a nuclear powerstation. The sky had begun to cloud over, and the dome reflected its exact colours.

They moved down through the sandy paths among the dunes, where insects made their lazy songs and a tiny lizard scuttled out of the way. The beach was deserted and strewn with pebbles of many different sizes. The wyvern stood and looked out to sea, and the view stirred in it a strange emotion it didn't recognise. A little distance out in the sea, in deeper water beyond the place the waves broke, a raised platform stood on four rusting metal legs. Dark blobby strings of mussels trailed from the legs where the tideline reached, floating and sinking with each wave.

The wyvern expressed a wish to be on the platform, to have a better view. It was a short distance, and Dana needed to get the wyvern in the air again. Either they had to go back to find Jananin and get help, or she and the wyvern would have to continue to the Emerald Forge alone, and try to defeat Gamma and the men who worked for her unaided.

The wyvern responded to this with a thought, something along the lines of not wanting to see Gamma again, and that Dana wouldn't want to either if she had any sense. Dana agreed not to think of it again, at least until the wyvern felt better, and suppressed her fear of Cale being trapped in the Emerald Forge.

She climbed up onto the wyvern's shoulders. A test flight, to make sure no permanent harm had been done. The wyvern filled its flight lungs again and ran into a takeoff. It had to turn in to the platform to get its speed and altitude right for landing, and the sea passing beneath on the manoeuvre reminded Dana how much she hated the ocean with its wet, suffocating depths.

The platform felt unstable, and it wobbled underfoot when the wyvern landed and when Dana dismounted from it. Dana crouched in the centre, liking neither the height nor the dynamic sea below.

The wyvern stood looking out to sea, and it stretched its head over the edge of the platform and let out a noise — a *song* — of three notes.

Dana pressed for an answer as to why it was doing this, but none came, other than for the emotion the wyvern had felt when it had seen the sea.

A sudden blowing noise came from the sea below the platform. Dana leaned forward cautiously. An unpleasant smell of fish drifted up, and a flat tail appeared, and a back with nostrils in it that blasted out a spray of air and water, and another tail.

They were dolphins. Now, when Dana looked at the wyvern, it began to fall into place. The brain of an intelligent mammal, but not a human, not something that understood language in the way humans understood it. Gamma had made the wyvern from a dolphin.

You're one of them.

The wyvern looked back at her, grateful and regretful and sorrowful all at once, and Dana realised what it meant. "No! Don't leave me!"

But Dana had to understand. It needed to be with its own kind. This was where it belonged. She had saved it and it had saved her and now they were equal. It was time for it to go back and claim the life it would have had, had this not been done to it.

Dana got up on her knees and reached for it, but it turned away from her, and with a farewell thought of appreciation and affection, it dived off the edge and into the water with a force that shook the rickety platform on its spindly legs so hard that Dana threw herself flat on her stomach and gasped, fearful the thing would tip over. The surface closed over the wyvern, just a faint glint of metal visible beneath before it disappeared for good.

Come back!

But the wyvern was gone, and Dana could no longer feel its signal. A burning ache filled her eyes and face as she lay there, feeling the tremor of each wave as it passed through the legs of the platform, and her breath broke apart into wracking sobs. Why could she not belong, anywhere? Why did it never work, not with her own kind and not even with others altered to be different as she was?

It began to rain, soaking her hair and clothes and trickling down her neck. Dana raised her face to the sky and let the cool water wash away the heat and tension and stickiness the outburst had left on her face. She put her hand in her pocket to touch Ivor's watch, and she closed her eyes against the falling rain and tried to visualise his face and the sound of his voice. Sometimes these days she could barely recall either, and she wished so much she had been able to find a half-decent picture or a recording of him speaking, but despite all her searches on the Internet, she never had. Jananin must have used all the influence she had to erase all trace of him.

She drew a deep breath. Ivor as an abstract concept wouldn't come back to her this time, but she could remember the dream she'd had last night and the memory of Ivor as an entire physical presence taking up all of her senses, and she drew support from that memory and the comfort and security that came attached for it. She could just about reach that reassurance everything was going to be all right.

Time to stop this, now.

When Dana opened her eyes and sat up, a figure picked its way among the dunes back on the shore, a person mounted on a horse, perhaps a policeman? As he drew closer, Dana realised he was looking up at her. He was the air commodore, Rajani, she was sure of it. She recognised his uniform and dark hair. The large black horse he rode wore heavy, technical-looking tack with webbing and straps that reached down its legs.

As the horse reached the tideline, the man kicked his feet out of the stirrups and swung his leg over the back of the saddle to slide on his stomach over the side of the beast. He turned away from the horse's shoulder and looked up at Dana. "I think you need to come down."

Dana looked down upon the heaving, queasy sea, and did not speak in return.

"Can you swim?" he called up.

"A bit." Dana stared at the surface, the waves trying to escape for shore. Ivor had taught her to swim. "Aren't there strong currents and things that pull you under and drown you?"

The man waded into the sea. When the water reached above his waist and he was not far from the place below where Dana perched, he stopped and raised his hands. "No strong currents." He glanced about himself. "Perhaps a few weak raisins, but that's all." The waters heaving around the man made it look as though he was drifting out of control against an amorphous background. A sick salty taste came into Dana's mouth, the memory of the cold water, stranded on Roareim, the plunge into the sea off Cape Wrath and that icy, penetrating grip freezing her breath in her lungs.

"I can't do it."

"You can. Sit on the edge and hang your legs over."

Dana slowly bent her knee and lowered first one leg and then the other over the edge so she sat there, head aswirl with vertigo. Her fingers gripped the weatherbeaten edge of the platform.

"Now slide off. Feet first. I'll catch you the moment you land in the water."

Dana closed her eyes and breathed in and out a few times. After a moment, she heard the man calling up to her again. "Take as long as you need, but please consider, the more you think about it and the more you delay, the bigger a problem it's going to be."

He was right. She couldn't stay up here indefinitely. This would be so much easier if it wasn't *him*, if she hadn't this unnerving instinct they'd met somewhere before and that there was something more to him, and not in a good way.

Don't think about it, just do it.

Dana straightened her legs and slid off the edge. It was only afterwards that she opened her eyes and allowed herself to think about what she'd done, and to panic. Her feet plunged through the surface and the water rushed up at her face. Immediately, she felt a hand on her shoulder.

"Gotcha!"

An arm reached under hers and around her chest, and before she'd worked out what had happened, she was being supported with her head above the water and her legs drifting out as the man towed her back to the shore. Soon, her heels struck sand and stones, and the sea's grip released her shoulders, and she and the man were wading up, back to the shore, he still holding her arm.

Dana sat on the stony shore away from the tideline. Her breath was coming very fast and the shock of the cold water and the weight of it on her clothes had left her dizzy. Rajani dropped to one knee in front of her. "It's not so bad. Try to breathe deeply. You're taking lots of little short breaths and that's probably not making you feel very well. You need to breathe slowly, with your stomach." He spread the fingers of both hands over his diaphragm to demonstrate.

Ivor used to squeeze Dana firmly when she got herself worked up into a state, and it had always helped, but she didn't have him any more. It took a lot of effort to breathe normally. Dana leaned backwards until her back was flat on the ground with her knees bent, and concentrated on breathing with her stomach. From this vantage point, the rain appeared to be easing off, the sky lightening. It was only now she noticed there was a *signal...*

Dana sat up and turned to face the source. It was the black horse with the high-tech armour Rajani had been riding. Dana examined it, expecting the signal to come from some gadget the horse was wearing, but no, this was a living signal that came from a brain modified by Jananin's synapse, the same as Cale and Peter, and Gamma and the *wyvern...*

She shuffled away from the man as he turned to her, an expression of incomprehension dawning on his face. "Who are you? Where are you taking me?" she demanded.

"My name's Rajesh Rajani. I'm an air commodore of the Sky Forces, in the service of the Meritocracy." The man pointed at the symbol on the breast of his jacket, an emblem very similar to what used to be called the Royal Air Force. "I'm taking you to Jananin Blake."

"How do I know that? How do I know you're not a double agent, that you aren't spying on the Meritocracy for the Emerald Forge?"

"What are you talking about?"

"The horse! That's what they do at the Emerald Forge! They graft cybernetic implants into animals' brains!" Dana chanced a glance away from him to check what the horse was doing. She broadcast a signal of hate and anger, and it pawed at the ground and tossed its head with a snort, eyes flashing.

Rajani held up his hand. "Please don't do that. This horse was developed by the Meritocracy for military situations. She doesn't feel fear, and that means anything that does agitate her is going to turn her to fight and not flight. Please, you mustn't make signals to try to upset her."

Dana got to her feet and pointed at him. "You know I can make signals!" she shouted. "You wouldn't know that unless you were in league with Gamma!"

"*Gamma?*" He frowned.

Dana took another step back. "You think I'm stupid." She turned and searched the dunes; where should she run to? And what chance did she stand when he had a horse, even an electronic horse she could affect, and perhaps weapons, that she may not be able to affect?

"Wait." Rajani began to undo the fastenings on the front of his jacket. "I wear the Meritocracy's badge because I work for the Meritocracy, but there's another badge I wear closer."

Dana took another step away, unsure what he was about to do and at a loss at what she could do to prevent it. Behind him, the horse paced up and down at the edge of the tide's reach.

Rajani shrugged so his jacket came loose from his shoulders and slid down to his elbows. Underneath it, he was wearing a plain white vest. He turned, hands restricted awkwardly by the sleeves, to display something on the skin of his upper right arm... something etched into the skin... a *tattoo*. The lines of black ink were not immediately discernible against his brown skin. It took a moment for Dana to work out the trunk of a tree, with symmetrical geometric branches, and in the fork in the centre of the tree, a bird, an *owl*...

Immediately as it dawned on her what the symbol meant, she remembered when she'd heard the name Rajesh before, and where exactly it was she remembered seeing him before. Cape Wrath. *Eagle Owl calling Tawny Owl...*

"Now do you understand?"

After Rajesh had stared at Dana and Dana hadn't answered, he shrugged his jacket back onto his shoulders and began refastening it.

"You can ask me any questions you like, but please don't try to interfere with my horse again. If you do that, it's dangerous to both of us. And it's not fair on the horse."

She didn't know what to say. Dana wasn't supposed to talk about Pilgrennon's experiments or Jananin's involvement. The symbol on Rajesh's arm meant he knew this information, that Jananin herself trusted him. When she had contacted Osric, she had known he was safe because of this sigil, and she'd understood it would be permitted for her to mention these things to him, because she was doing it in order to pass necessary information to Jananin. Did Rajesh's possession of the same sigil mean she could speak openly to him? And what should she ask?

Dana turned away from him and sat down again. "I'm making a... a Spitfire."

"A *Spitfire*?"

Dana glanced back at the look of incredulity on his face. "Sorry. It's kind of a code. It's a kind of aeroplane you can get Airfix models for. I mean I just need a bit of time to think."

"I know it's a kind of aeroplane," said Rajesh proudly. "I flew one once!"

Dana turned around fully. "You flew a Supermarine Spitfire?"

"Yes. The one I really want to fly is the Lancaster. There's only one left in flying condition left in the country, and they're understandably very selective about how often it can fly and who can pilot it."

"B I *PA474*?"

"Yes. I used to have all the Airfix kits as well, when I was about your age. You know on the Spitfire? Is the landing gear still so bloody awkward to stick on?"

"Yes!" Dana exclaimed, and both of them burst out laughing. It would have been very easy to forget about things and talk about Airfix and World War II planes, but more pressing matters needed to be dealt with. Something did come to mind, although not the sort of topic she expected Rajesh to be thinking. She hadn't realised how thirsty she was. "Can I have a drink of water, please?"

"Of course." Rajesh went back to his horse and withdrew a plastic water bottle from a pouch at the front of the saddle. He handed Dana the bottle and sat down on the shore. "I'm under orders to rendezvous with Jananin once I find you, but I'm not going to try to make you go under duress, or until you're ready to go."

Dana swallowed water and sat down again. "You know Blake? How much do you know?" She took another swig and thought back to a long time ago. "That picture of the owl in the tree. Rupert Osric had it as well. Jananin said it was a sort of code." Dana hesitated. "Do you know about

Ivor?"

Rajesh dark eyes met Dana's and he nodded discreetly, as though even speaking that name might be an act of blasphemy.

"Do you know *everything*... about what happened? At Cape Wrath?"

Rajesh exhaled forcefully and leaned his elbows on his knees. "I think you know as much as I do on that. I was there. I saw, probably, less than what you saw."

"What about last night, when you brought me in? Was there anyone else there?"

"A doctor, I believe. I had to go back out, so there could have been someone else."

She hadn't dared bring it up with Jananin, but some instinct told her this person would react differently, although it was still hard to risk it. "I thought I saw, I mean, I think it was a dream, but, I thought I saw my father. Ivor."

Rajesh glanced at her, and back at the pebbles littering the beach.

"You don't believe me?"

"I believe you. If your father was with you last night, it's because you needed him. It doesn't matter if he wasn't corporeal, if he was in a dream, or you saw him as a spirit, or an hallucination. People who die do stay with us who remember them, whether you believe that they remain in spirit form, or they go to an afterlife, or they simply persist as memories that serve as psychological support for us."

"So you're saying that Ivor's still with me, even though he's dead, and that's why I saw him in the dream?"

"Indubitably he's still with you. His influence has shaped part of who you are. Something like that always leaves a mark. You wouldn't be here, the same person you are today, had you not known him. You have the memories you made with him to guide you. Our memories and the people who have influenced us make us ourselves."

"Is that a religion or something?" Dana thought of

Isaiah Redwood, in Nevada, and how he'd once said that only God was perfect, and how it seemed to help him accept life's imperfections.

Rajesh smiled. "Philosophy, perhaps. I suppose I am culturally a Hindu, although my parents looked upon it as meaningful teaching stories and not something deadly serious."

Dana could remember very vaguely doing something about Hinduism at school, although they had taught about that many different religions that she tended to mix them up. "What do Hindus think?"

"There are lots of different versions of Hinduism, but in the version I grew up with, there are three central gods: Brahma, Vishnu, and Shiva. Creator, preserver, destroyer."

"So the creator's the one who made the Universe, and the destroyer's like, the baddy?"

"You're probably thinking along the lines of the three Abrahamic religions. They all have a similar origin in the Middle East and teach of a god who embodies everything positive, and often an antigod who embodies everything negative. Hinduism is one of the Dharmic religions that come from India. There aren't any villains, just gods with good and bad inside them like everyone. Destruction is a necessary part of reality, as much so as preservation and creation, and without all three of them in harmony no progress can be made."

Rajesh contemplated the stones before him for a moment, picking one up and examining it. "Very soon after I met Jananin, it was clear to me she was one to follow Shiva's path. It was so strong in her, I suppose I made the error of automatically assuming any child of hers would be the same." Rajesh paused, studying Dana's face cautiously, like a big jungle cat gauging a pounce. "But now I meet you, I think you may be more like Vishnu."

Dana gazed out to the flat horizon of the sea, where the wyvern had gone and she couldn't reach it. Somewhere, under that mass of sea surrounding the British Isles,

Cerberus lay in bits, and whatever was left of Ivor, burned from the Compton bomb explosion, smashed to pieces, flesh eaten away by little carrion fishes...

But why would the dead wear digital watches and deodorant?

Some questions would not be answered.

Dana rose stiffly from where she'd been sitting. Her wet clothes were making her cold, despite the warm afternoon. Perhaps moving would help.

"I'm ready to go to see Jananin." Dana could feel heat building up in her face when she said the next bit, despite the chill of the sea. "Rajesh, I'm really sorry I thought you were working for the Emerald Forge and I tried to frighten your horse. I knew I'd seen you somewhere before, but I couldn't remember. You did all this stuff to help me, really, and I was ungrateful."

"It's no problem," Rajesh replied. "You didn't know, and now you do, and no harm has come about because of any of it."

He stood up and went to his horse, and spoke into a device. "Eagle Owl calling Tawny Owl."

A voice came back, the words indistinct.

"I've recovered Little Owl safely. I'm heading back. Over and out."

"You're Eagle Owl?" said Dana.

Rajesh smiled. "It was originally supposed to be *Bengal Eagle Owl*. The Bengal got dropped for brevity."

<h1 style="text-align:center">-18-</h1>

RAJESH Rajani had a large band with a screen on it strapped around his left forearm. He tapped a few controls and studied it for a moment.

"What's that?" Dana asked.

"It's my feedback for the horse, that lets me check it's okay and what it can sense. A bit like a systems report."

He put his foot into the stirrup and heaved himself into the saddle. "You ready?" Rajesh offered Dana his hand, and leaned the other way to help her up. Dana got hold of the back of the saddle and slid her knee over.

She held on to Rajesh around the waist, and the horse set off over the dunes, winding its way through sandy paths between hummocks of thick scrubby grass.

"You see the wood up ahead?" Rajesh pointed. "That's where Jananin will meet us."

A narrow strip of copse had become visible where the dunes ended. Rajesh checked the band on his arm and pressed the horse's sides with his heels, and it broke into a trot. Rajesh bobbed gracefully with the motion of the horse, apparently supporting his weight with his thighs. Dana held on to him and bounced uncomfortably in her seat.

As they approached the trees, however, an inexplicable feeling of dread began to take over. Dana looked up at the forbidding canopy of dark leaves with an irrational sensation of being watched from the heights. As Rajesh guided the horse in through narrow paths worn by deer and rabbits, the trees closed ranks around them and the sunny afternoon dwindled into a claustrophobic gloom. The wood was alive with a kind of malice Dana could neither pinpoint nor identify.

"There's something wrong. There's signals here. Lots of signals."

Rajesh shifted his weight in the saddle as he looked around. "There won't be any signals out here. There's not even a road nearby. Jananin tracked you as far as the woods and we couldn't get any closer, not even in the four-wheel-drive. That's why I brought the horse down. Perhaps it's the horse's systems you can feel?"

"No, it's not the horse. I know what the horse feels like. It's all around us. There's something in the trees... in the ground." She found her attention drawn to the bank below where the horse walked. The soil there looked freshly scraped around the entrances to tunnels, and dried grass had been thrown out on the ground. A stronger signal had risen above the unnerving background sensation, and that was where it originated. "It's something down there."

Rajesh checked the computer on his forearm and stopped the horse. "Are you sure?"

"I can still feel it."

"Okay. Slide your right leg over behind you, and come down on the left side of the horse. I want you to wait by the horse and I'll go down and investigate."

Dana did as he asked and waited by the horse as he dismounted. He went to the edge of the bank and started to climb down, placing his feet cautiously. Dana was now getting more feedback from the signal, and she sensed behind it a mind that meant no good. "Rajesh, please be careful! I don't think it's safe."

Rajesh removed a small gun from a holster at his hip. He held it in both hands and aimed down the bank, scanning steadily over an arc.

"No, *it's in the ground!*" Dana realised.

A black-and-white-striped blur flashed out of the soil at Rajesh's ankle, and before Dana had registered what was happening, he was on the ground. "Rajesh!" She slid down the bank to try to help him. His right leg had sunk into a hole, right up to the hip. He held on to Dana's arms and braced with his left leg, and with a forceful grunt through gritted teeth, he pulled his leg out of the hole. His boot had disappeared and his sock was dark with blood.

Rajesh stumbled forward from the force of the exertion and fell on his knees.

"What's happening?" Dana searched the trees above for the sinister eyes she could feel upon her, but could not see, stared into the empty mouths of the holes in the bank.

Rajesh's eyes were wide. "A badger! A badger attacked me!"

The signal she had sensed before was rising again. "Oh no. It's coming back! Let's get out of here!"

Clutching at each others' arms for stability, they slithered down the bank. The soil crumbled and slid under Dana's feet. She couldn't get away fast enough. A low, guttural sound came from the hole, and a large grizzled shape with a striped wedge-shaped snout erupted from the ground and lumbered down after them. Dana screamed.

A dark figure sprang over the summit, too big and upright to be another animal, a long coat flapping behind. It flailed down the bank and fell upon the badger.

Dana let go of Rajesh and got up from where she'd slipped over on the ground. "Jananin."

Jananin Blake got off the badger; it lay motionless on the ground, and the braided leather handle of her Japanese blade protruded from between its shoulders, the steel running straight through its heart and into the soil beneath. Its death hadn't made a sound. Right in the centre of the badger's head, buried in the fur between and just above its eyes, something caught the light: a plastic gem like what is found at the pointing end of a television remote control.

"It's implanted. The wood's full of implanted wild animals that have been programmed to attack us!" Dana realised.

Jananin leaned her foot on the badger's back and pulled the bloodstained blade out of its body. "I suspected so. They're drawn to your signal. We must leave at once."

"Perhaps we should take a sample from the badger to compare," Rajesh suggested.

"There's not time." Jananin raised a hand and turned to face up through a gap in the trees. "Look."

A grainy texture hazed the blue of the sky, rippling like a gauze curtain in the wind. It appeared to be made from hundreds of small, distant objects all moving together. Rajesh narrowed his eyes. "What is that, a swarm of insects?"

As Dana watched the mesmerising folding and unfolding, the sliding densities of many lives moving as one, a deep sense of unease began to clutch at her stomach. "No. They're birds."

Rajesh and Jananin exchanged glances. They'd both been there and seen the bodies of the birds lying with the bodies of people at the ruins of the hospital. "I suppose it would be wishful thinking to presume that might be a natural phenomenon?" Rajesh said.

"They've made a network," Dana said after a long pause. "A network out of animals they implanted and released. They've been alerted to us and they're coming."

Rajesh took a step back towards the horse. "Go to the vehicle and get the engine running. I'll load up the horse."

"The car's not far away," said Jananin. "Come with me."

Dana followed her back up the bank and through some undergrowth. She could still sense many primitive and malevolent minds around her, although none of them showed themselves. The only living thing she sighted was a toad sheltering under a tree root, and there was no sign of an implant on its head. They reached a clearing where an off-road vehicle with a horse trailer had been parked. Jananin made for the driver's door while Dana stumbled around the front of the car, grabbing at the roo bars to stabilise herself, unable to look away from the swarm of birds drawing nearer. Immediately when she got in and shut the door, nearly all of the malign signals from the wood disappeared. A sense of relief came over her. The car was coated in polymer alloy. They wouldn't be able to sense her here.

Jananin took the driver's seat and slammed the door shut. She turned the key in the ignition, but there was no click of electronics coming to life, no lights on the dashboard, and no whinny from the starter motor turning the engine over. There was only a dull scrape of the key moving in its slot.

Jananin swore.

She opened the door and got back out. Dana stayed still in the car, her hands clutched together in her lap, but she heard Jananin say outside, "Rajesh, the engine won't start."

Dana opened the door and got back out as the two of them came around to the front of the car. She could sense no signals from the car, but the air around was filled with sinister thoughts, repulsive little minds pressing against her own.

Rajesh hooked his fingers under the edge of the car's bonnet and pulled it up. A sudden deluge of sharp signals protested at the sudden ingress of light, and a fuzzy mass of small, dull, grey-brown bodies *poured* off of the engine and through the gaps in the car's undercarriage. Dana let out a small cry and stepped backwards, away from the fleeing mice, and Rajesh took hold of her arm to steady her.

"They've eaten the electrics!" Jananin exclaimed.

Dana wanted more than anything right now to get away from these horrible thoughts from minds that meant her harm. In the car, she hadn't been able to hear them. "The car is still safe! It's a Faraday cage, and they're still just birds and they're not going to get through glass and metal. They won't be able to detect my signal and we can hide there until help comes."

"No," said Rajesh. "There's a problem." He pointed to the car's open passenger door, and the window that showed a gap of several inches between the edge of the glass and the upper rim. "The windows are electric. We can't close them. The birds will be able to get in."

Jananin pointed to the horse. "That leaves one option remaining, but it can't carry all three of us. These constructs are attracted to signals. We saw it with the phoenix, and it would seem with the badger you just disturbed. We can hide in the car if we turn off all our electronic devices, but Dana and the horse can't simply be switched off like everything else. Therefore, it makes the most sense for the safety of everyone involved that Dana take the horse and go as fast as possible to Site Twelve, while you and I stay in the car and await retrieval."

Rajesh let out a sharp exclamation. "Without one of us? She's not an experienced rider. A fall could kill her."

"I can't ride a horse!" Dana interjected.

"Dana, you have the ability to interface directly to the horse." Jananin turned to Rajesh. "She will not fall if she is in control of the animal. It doesn't matter that she is not trained to ride."

"Please, at least let me ride with her. Or accompany her yourself."

"No. The horse will be swifter with only one rider."

"No, let someone come with me," Dana pleaded. "Either of you, I don't mind who. I don't know how to control a horse."

"You just controlled a wyvern as you call it, did you not? And in that instance, there was much farther to fall. How is this different?"

"The wyvern was my friend. I wasn't *controlling* it. It let me ride on it; it wasn't just doing what I told it to."

"There is no time for any more discussion. This is what is happening, and if you are not ready for it, you had better prepare yourself now. Rajesh, give me the console for this horse and send out a call for help."

Rajesh unfastened the band from his forearm and gave Jananin a disapproving glower as he handed it over. He walked back to the car with what looked like a big mobile phone held to his ear. "Mayday, mayday."

"I'm going to disconnect the horse from this interface now, and I need you to make the connection and synch yourself to it. Ready?"

Dana did not like this idea, but she could think of no other, and the birds were coming, and all around in this wood she could feel the conspiracy against her. She nodded, her mouth dry.

Jananin pressed a button that switched off the armband, and simultaneously she put her hand to the armour on the horse's forehead and adjusted something. Another signal appeared, searching for something to connect to. Dana hesitated for a second, and then adjusted the frequency of her concentration to mesh with that signal.

Consciousness shifted. She could feel damp soil and leaves under her feet, the heavy beat of a powerful heart and breath in great lungs. She could hear the drone of flies in ears that twitched and turned restlessly, see the world in a flat, panoramic rendition that encompassed both sides of the horse and was oddly drained of the red portion of the spectrum. The horse didn't filter which parts of its experience of the world were shared with her as the wyvern did.

"Ready?"

Dana let out a shuddering gasp, and nodded again.

Jananin offered her the stirrup. "Put your left foot in here and hold on to the saddle at the front and back."

Dana did as she was told. Jananin caught her right leg and pushed it up over the horse's back, and now she was sitting up high with the horse's long neck and twitching ears in front of her. The horse was smelly, but it wasn't an unpleasant or excessively strong smell. Jananin hurried to adjust the stirrups and get Dana's feet into the right position. She pressed a leather strap into Dana's hands. "You may not be able to use the reins, but try to keep hold of them or they'll cause problems if they go over the horse's head and get in the way. Don't stop until you get to Site Twelve. Now go!"

Jananin gave the horse a push and it began to move down the bank, its body swaying with each stride. And with each step it took, Dana began to understand more of it, what each group of muscles felt like and what it did. Jananin was right. With this connection, even though it had a mind of its own, the horse was an extension of her own body, the same as any unliving device or machine.

She felt for it, finding the point in its neural connections that would trigger the thought of moving faster. The horse was accustomed to taking instructions, if not normally in this way, and responded. Increasing its gait to a trot brought an uncomfortable bounce to the horse's pace, although now with Dana able to anticipate the rhythm of it through the horse's muscular memory, it was less jarring than it had been when Rajesh had controlled it. Dana pressed her knees in tight and urged the horse faster. They came upon a clearing in the trees and the horse broke into a rolling canter. Dana aimed for a gap in the trees, planning to stick to the wood to hide them from the skies for as long as possible.

The horse thundered through muddy ground wet from the recent rain, splattering its legs and undercarriage, and charged up into the trees. A rush of adrenaline hit home. This animal exulted in running. It was what it had been born to do, what it was alive for. The horse had by now accelerated to a flying gallop that shook Dana's eyes in her head so much the view ahead became a blur. Shafts of light between the trees flashed by, sending her eyes into blinking spasms. The breath rushing through the horse's nostrils, the pounding of its hoofs and its green-blue view of the trees rushing past on either side were overwhelming, and Dana struggled to keep focus on the sensations from her own body and to hold on and duck from the branches passing overhead.

They reached the edge of the wood and the horse galloped out into an open space. Dana forced it to slow to give her a chance to reorient herself and get a better seating. They'd reached a meadow of grass going to seed, teeming with purple-crested thistles that blended into a lavender haze over distance. Insects buzzed and chirped in the warm sun. Motes of fluff from the thistles drifted up from the passage of the horse like a cloud in a dream. Dana looked over her shoulder, up into a still blue sky. Nothing. Perhaps they hadn't followed her after all.

Then a dark cloud reared behind the trees, and she sensed signals. She turned her head, trying to locate their source: one in front and two either side and slightly behind, coming in to converge on her. She shouldn't have slowed. Dana gave the signal for the horse to run again, aware it would bring them towards one of the signals, but unable to think of any alternative. As it charged forward, a russet shape somewhere between a dog and a cat leapt from the thistles in front of them. Dana flinched but the horse didn't shy or balk; it ran straight into the fox and trampled it. A stringy electric fence was fast approaching, and Dana had no time to compose herself before the horse jumped over it. She fell forward in the saddle and had to cling to the horse's mane while she struggled to get her legs back into position and recover her seat in the saddle. No sooner had she regained control when the horse jumped a stream and landed running in a grassy field. The speed seemed dangerously out of control, but she couldn't risk going slower. Dana leaned forward over the horse's neck, trying to lower her centre of gravity and reduce the wind whipping past. As they passed what she calculated to be the halfway point between the wood Jananin and Rajesh had been trapped in and Site Twelve, the horse galloped along the bank of a river, and it was only now she stopped feeling overwhelmed long enough to notice the grass rushing past a long distance below, and felt able to chance a look over her shoulder.

The sky behind had fallen dark, not with clouds or an oncoming night, but by the bodies of an innumerable number of birds.

Dana urged the horse faster. Jananin had told her not to stop, and she'd been right. The open field was running out, and more woods approached. She crouched lower as the horse's course plunged them into the shadows between trees. There was no proper path here, and pushing up a steep slope through nettles and undergrowth slowed the horse. Their pursuers in the air would face no such impediment. They emerged from the woods at a summit that sloped down through fields of crops, to the distant vineyards and orangeries bordering the squat, fortress-like monstrosity that was Site Twelve, with the shining glass pyramids behind it.

The horse charged down the edge of a field of wheat. As they reached the end and jumped through a gap in the hedge into a vineyard, Dana became aware of a pressure on her ears, from the beating of thousands of wings, and a draught behind her despite the wind in her face generated by the horse's speed. She kicked and clung on as the horse ran for the concrete cliff rising ahead. She struggled to think past the signals of animosity, to find the nearest entrance to Site Twelve and work out the fastest way to it. She mustn't look back, not now. It took all her concentration to stay balanced and keep the horse at speed.

They turned into a grove of genetically modified figs, and there in front of her stood the heavy metal gate she'd only left this morning with the wyvern. Two men in uniform stood behind it. "Open the gate!" she bellowed over the horse's head as it galloped towards them. The gate didn't open, and the horse struggled to slow. Gravel sparked under its iron-shod feet.

Dana kicked her feet out of the stirrups and slid to the ground. "Let me in!" she shrieked, running for the gate. The men were gawking at the enormous flock of birds behind her. The rush of wings came louder now, and mixed with it were the shrill voices of the birds, growing closer.

"This is private property and you've no permission to come in here," one of the men told her.

There was a sign on the gate, something about the Official Secrets Act, rather similar to the one Dana remembered on Gallan Head. She didn't have time to read it. "Please, let me in. These birds are dangerous. I'm here on Jananin Blake's instruction. She and Rajesh Rajani are trapped in a wood."

The two men exchanged glances.

Dana turned around. The sky overhead was dark with bodies, and the birds were falling from the air towards her. The rising pressure broke over her like a tidal wave. Light feathery bodies pounded against her back and sharp beaks and claws flurried around her head. She covered her face with both hands, but something struck her cheek and drew blood. Dana crouched down and tried to cover her head with her arms. She reached within herself, trying to find a horrible memory, and she recalled how she'd felt after Abigail had hit her and she'd found out there was a device implanted in her brain: shame and hopelessness and incomprehension. She forced the feeling outwards and pushed the birds back, but she couldn't hold them off for long. Somewhere nearby the horse whinnied, and she caught sight of it rearing and thrashing, birds swirling around it.

A woman had come out of the building to the gate. She gesticulated, her eyes wide.

"Tarrow!"

"Dana!" Tarrow reached through the gate and grasped Dana's hand. "Why are you all wet? Open the gate!" she shouted at the guards.

One of the men pulled out a device. "I'll just call the supervisor and ask." He began tapping the screen hurriedly.

"Supervisor my arse! This is the Meritocracy! Open the

gate man, can't you see those birds..."

Tarrow's voice trailed off. She stared up past Dana into the sky, her face filled with horror.

Dana turned to see what it was. Way up in the glare of the sun, a huge shape that must be a bird of prey plunged earthwards, cleaving the flock in two like a sword through a billowing sail. She threw herself to the ground, face down in front of the gate, waiting, imagining the feel of sharp talons raking into the flesh of her neck and shoulders.

There came a heavy rattle of metal on metal, and someone grabbed Dana by the upper arm. She raised her head to find the gate open, and Tarrow pulling her in towards the building. She scrambled to her feet and the two of them rushed for the door. Just as they reached it, Dana looked back to see the big bird, surging up, carving the flock into disarray. Could it be the wyvern? Surely she would sense its signal from here if that were so. And it definitely looked like a bird, with a blunt bird tail and short neck. It must be a wild hawk that had happened upon the swarm of birds by coincidence.

Or...

She had seen one bird like that before. Prendick's eagle.

-19-

TARROW led Dana back into the building where the metal in the walls blocked out the signals from the birds.

"Please get someone to bring the horse in. Jananin and Rajesh are stuck in a car that's broken down..." Dana began.

"There's someone gone out to get them, and someone will sort out the horse. Come in here and sit down." Tarrow pushed open the door to the medical ward. Dana sat on the bed and Tarrow wiped the scratches on her cheek with a wad of cotton wool wet with an alcohol-smelling substance that stung the raw wounds.

"Dunno what the hell Blake thinks she's doing, dragging you into whatever's going on and sending you home on your own."

Dana wanted to argue, but the chase had exhausted her, and she didn't know what she could say that would be believable while at the same time not revealing anything about the history she shared with Jananin.

"Now you get some rest. I'll go and sort out a drink and some dinner for you." Tarrow fished some pyjamas out of a drawer and lobbed them at Dana. She threw the cotton wool into a bin as she went out the door.

Dana got changed out of her wet clothes and rearranged the pillows on the bed so she could sit up against the wall. She needed to wait until Jananin and Rajesh got back. Cale would now be in the Emerald Forge. She had to do something. Yet her body ached from staying in place on the back of the horse, and her mind was numb from the strain of concentration. Try as she might to focus, she was sliding towards sleep, heavy muscles slumping and eyes refusing to stay open. If she could close her eyes and rest for just a *moment...*

*

The moonlight tonight is so bright the landscape is visible for miles around. We can even make out the distant sliver of the sea when we look to the east.

I look down at myself. I smell. My clothes are dirty. But they're my clothes, not lunatic asylum pyjamas.

There's a car parked nearby where I stand outside. Possibly it's red, or orange, or something like that. It looks greyish-black in the moonlight that makes everything else look slightly green. There's a man as well, who has come to visit me in the car. You know who he is, although you can't recall his name, and you know he is a bad man.

The man steps away from the car, towards me. "Gamma. We've been fortunate so far in that they've given up the search. This factory is remote, and people avoid it, but when it becomes apparent something is happening here, they will come looking."

On the west horizon, a cluster of lights marks out the position of the nearest town. How I hate people. How I loathe their interfering curiosity, their intolerance of anything that is different to themselves. How I wish I could snuff out those lights, be alone in the world without all the people who would come poking and prodding, to hurt me and tell me what's wrong inside my head.

"What's that you have in your car?" I say.

The man obligingly raises the boot door of the hatchback. A cage takes up the entire bootspace and the folded-down back seats, and inside the cage is an enormous bird, settled on a thick wooden perch. It's a bird of daytime, subdued by the night, but as I look at it, it looks back with feral eyes, its wings slightly opened. An empress from the skies, defying her captors despite the cage containing her and the leather straps binding her ankles. There is something odd about her. She emits a signal.

"Release her," I say.

"No. This is a gift, a bargaining chip with great value to someone who may be able to help us. I can't protect you here, not by myself, not from what may come, but there is another way. With this man's skill, and my skill, and your ability, and the moiety in your blood, we can use animals to defend ourselves. This bird will be loyal to you. Bend her to your will, and she won't betray you as a human would."

"And this other man?"

The moon is behind the man, and I can't make out much of his expression, but then, I never was much good at understanding expressions. "He's an outcast, like us. Someone who has been betrayed by the world isn't going to betray those who come to him offering allegiance."

Something about him unsettles you, but I won't see it. This man is the only one who listened to me.

This man is not kind...

I know nothing of kindness. What use is it?

This man does not love you.

This man respects me. He knows my true name. He doesn't tell me that the truth of my eyes and my ears is a lie. He doesn't force me to take medicine that makes me ill. He doesn't tie me to the bed.

Memories you can't quite grasp flicker at the limits of your reach: contemplating in the car, quiet and calm as he drives beside you, not speaking, but *together* all the same. Being hugged tightly, the feel of his broad chest against your face and his thick arms around you. Something on a boat, with the white foam the motor churned up spreading behind. Being silly, jumping into a swimming pool with someone else, with your clothes on.

This man is not a father to you.

I once had a father. He abandoned me. I have no need of another.

I helped you escape. I'm only trying to protect you. Please, don't trust this man.

The moon is green and sickly. The mottling spreads from its equator like mould. Its light illuminates green-tinged walls, stained from rainwater and coloured with lichens and moss that begrime the ageing concrete. The buildings and the abandoned industrial site surrounding them are sunken in decay, broken gaps where windows once were, cracks spreading up the walls, brutal weeds thrusting through the shattered paving. The edifices are grotesque in the moonlight.

A terrible accident once happened at this place. The owner of the factory stood accused of negligence for not taking more precautions, for allowing it when he should have known better, and in his guilt, he came here alone one night, jumped from the roof, and met his end.

"It is beautiful," I say aloud, even though it's not.

In the hospital, things were clean and hygienic. The hospital was built to be architecturally attractive, to resemble a faux Victorian building, with gardens all around it that were supposed to be to help the patients rehabilitate. But the only people who used the gardens were the gardeners paid to maintain them, and the visitors who came, to be reassured about the patients. The patients who didn't have relatives who came to visit got put in the rooms that overlooked the car park and the deliveries entrance, and the dustbins.

This place might once have had a name, although it's been forgotten. If the people who live in the area know it by anything, it's probably 'that monstrosity'. A cursed place where people were hurt and died. Something that should be torn down, ugly grey-green blight upon the landscape that it is. The Emerald Forge. It's mine, my sanctuary, my haven, and that's the name I choose for it. The ghosts of its past will not bother me here, and neither will those of mine pursue me here.

*

The next thing Dana noticed was the light in the room had grown dim. When she turned her head to look at the window, the trees on the horizon stood in gloom. The sun had already set; she must have fallen asleep.

"Tarrow!"

Dana got up from the bed, the insides of her thighs aching as soon as she moved her legs. She winced and hobbled towards the door.

It opened before she reached it, and there stood Tarrow with a tray.

"Why didn't you wake me? Where are Jananin and Rajesh?"

"They're fine. Came in not long after you did. They're coming to see you as soon as you're rested and you've eaten this." Tarrow set the tray down on a hospital table on castors.

"No! You don't understand! I need to speak to Jananin now!"

Tarrow's eyes widened. "Dana, last night you collapsed and needed a blood transfusion! Today you went out who knows where and came back injured and drenched, clinging to the back of a horse much too big for you and being attacked by birds. Whatever is going on between you and Blake, your health has to take priority! Now sit down and eat your dinner!"

Behind her the door opened, and Jananin Blake appeared.

"What's been happening?" Dana demanded.

"Since the recovery vehicle brought us back, I have been in touch with the other Spokesmen discussing the matter of the recent turn of events."

"And what did they decide?" Dana waited anxiously for the answer.

"That the Emerald Forge must be disabled by Compton bomb, tomorrow."

"No! You can't! Cale and Peter are there!"

"Dana, calm down," said Tarrow. "When people talk about a Compton bomb, it doesn't mean a *real* sort of bomb that explodes and kills everyone in a big mushroom cloud. It's just a device that emits a powerful signal that disables things like computers and televisions. It doesn't hurt people."

"It will hurt my brother!" Dana shouted at her.

Before Dana could say anything else, Jananin interjected a false explanation. "Dana's brother was born with a heart condition that resulted in him needing a pacemaker. The Compton radiation will affect the device he needs to live on. It could kill him."

Tarrow looked from Dana to Jananin, and then to Rajesh, who had entered after Jananin and stood with his back against the door. "But... what... Then *why* are you Compton bombing there? Didn't you tell the other Spokesmen? Good *grief!*"

Jananin glanced at her. "Don't you have work to get on with?"

Tarrow muttered something before excusing herself and leaving, Rajesh stepping out of the way and opening the door for her.

Jananin came further into the room and sat on a chair near the end of the bed. "The Meritocracy has a policy of not negotiating with hostage takers. If we try to storm the Emerald Forge and take the hostages back, there will be real risk to the people we send in there. Two hostages do not warrant that risk. There is a very good chance a Compton blast will take out their defences and make it far easier for our forces to seize the Forge."

Dana couldn't believe she was hearing this. This wasn't what happened, this wasn't the sort of thing that got reported on the news. Cale had been with her through her whole life, and now Jananin was saying they couldn't get him back, that he had to die in a Compton bomb, because of what Gamma had done?

"Ivor wouldn't let you do this! He'd say we had to think of something else!"

"If Ivor were here, no doubt he would walk in there expecting to be able to reason with them, and end up changing his mind and in league with them, or dead, or used to make a merman or some other ridiculous thing.

But he is not here, and making plans on the premise of what he would do is therefore a waste of time!"

"But you can't kill my brother! Talk to the other Spokesmen again!"

"And tell them what? Unless you have any suggestions of alternative plans for stopping what's going on at the Emerald Forge, there is little point."

Dana sat up on the bed and thought. "It's the birds and things, the constructs and the animals they've implanted stuff in that's the problem, aren't they?"

"They appear to constitute their main defence, and they seem to be what they intend to do damage with. There was no evidence of any other weapons being used at the hospital. That's why a Compton bomb is a very effective solution with very little collateral."

"But there's other ways of stopping them. They must all be controlled by Gamma. The transceiver Pilgrennon implanted in her — if it's the same as mine — can't broadcast over long distances. It's just short range. I have to connect to a wLAN or some other piece of equipment that can transmit long distances if I want to access the Internet, and Gamma is the same. She would have to use something to carry her signal out there when they send the animals outside of the Forge, like when they attacked us and at the hospital."

"Or it could be that there is no such transmitter, and the birds communicate through a network of sorts, with some birds in range of Gamma and each other acting as a relay chain to carry instructions out to the main flock."

"I suppose so." Dana hadn't thought of that, but if there were enough birds, it would make sense. "But even so, that means Gamma is still controlling them all from the Forge. And that means if we can stop Gamma, we stop them all as well. It's like a hive of bees, and Gamma's the queen."

Rajesh spoke up. "I can just about see where you're coming from, but that will not be easy when everything she controls is all around the Forge, strategically placed to defend her. It would be like playing a game of chess with the intention of taking the king without damaging any of the other pieces on the way."

"But there must be some way of making a diversion and sneaking someone close enough to the Emerald Forge so they can break in and try to get at Gamma. I mean, when those birds came, they chased me and didn't hang around and try to get in the car after you, did they? If we could make a big signal or something to distract them, and I could get in..."

"No, hold on there." Rajesh held up his hands, palms towards Dana. "You can't get involved in this. It's a dangerous situation and you're just a child."

A spike of anger rose in Dana's chest. "Nobody told Cale or Peter they couldn't get involved in it because they're children! Or Gamma! And now Cale and Peter are stuck there and they can't do anything to help themselves, anything apart from sit there and die in a Compton bomb." She turned imploringly to Jananin.

After a few seconds of thought, Jananin interlocked her fingers and leaned back on the chair. "Hear her proposal first, Rajesh."

Rajesh gave Dana a disbelieving look, but didn't voice any further protest.

"I know Gamma," Dana said. "I've seen everything about her in my dreams. There's this connection we share, although she won't let me in when she's awake. They did awful things to her at the hospital. She's just a person like me who has been treated in a way that has made her hate everything. If I can get in there, if I can get her alone, I think I can reason with her."

Jananin studied Dana for a little while. "Rajesh, I want to put an alternative suggestion to the Spokesmen. We will have the *Stormcaller* on standby ready to deploy, however, we will send in a small task force first, a group led by you to attack the Forge and cause a diversion, while I will attempt to get Dana close enough to enter and defeat Gamma. If this strategy proves unsuccessful within a reasonable time limit or it looks as though we will incur heavy losses, we will use the Compton bomb."

Rajesh stared at Jananin in horror. "If you deploy the Compton bomb while Dana is still in the Forge, she'll be killed as well as the hostages and Gamma!"

"But that risk is worth taking to save Cale!" Dana shouted.

Rajesh shook his head. "You don't understand what you're saying! Jananin, I can't believe you're prepared to even consider this! She's a child! She's not capable of understanding the risk and making an informed decision!"

"Rajesh, this child is rather more capable than you might think. She managed to follow Pilgrennon's beacon to its source alone."

"I know that very well, and you should never have allowed it! She couldn't possibly have understood the risk. You exploited her to further your own agenda."

"I understand the risk!" Dana interrupted. "Really what it is, it's the choice of just the hostages dying, or the hostages and me as a gamble, to save all of us. Because you can give the command to use the Compton bomb as soon as things start to get too dangerous, if it looks like someone could get hurt or killed."

A deep unease had come over Rajesh. He looked again to Jananin, who again did not respond. "In theory, yes."

Dana couldn't imagine going back home to Pauline and Graeme's house, without Cale. She had come into this world with him, and he wasn't leaving it without her. "Then that's what you must do. Because I can't and I won't stay here and rest because Tarrow says I'm ill, while you go out and kill my brother and Peter. Even if it means I end up dead as well, at least I will have tried."

Nobody spoke for what seemed a long time, and then Rajesh said, "I am an air commodore in the Sky Forces, and it's my job to act on the Meritocracy's orders. If the

Meritocracy orders me to do this, then I must do it, no matter what I think."

Jananin said to Rajesh, "I will speak with you in a moment. I want to speak to Dana in private first."

He looked away from her and his mouth groped for words. "Pilgrennon did you a severe wrong, and I still believe you were right in your actions to stop him, although I often thought at times vengeance played more of a part in it than I was comfortable with. I gave my word to support you in this to the best of my ability, and I have always upheld it, even when it put my career and my own life at risk. You are one of my oldest friends. However, if we do this, and it fails, and she is killed... then... we are through." Rajesh saluted loosely and left the room.

Jananin stared at the door where he had gone for a moment, stony faced, her posture rigid. "Before you accuse me of it, I shall say that I will stand by your decision, and I am not tempted in the remotest by the prospect of destroying the evidence of Pilgrennon's illegal research. My objection to this plan is based not only on the concern for the safety of all involved, but also on the likelihood that you will throw away your own life in your attempt to realise an unrealistic ideal. Ironically, you are the only one of Pilgrennon's experiments that was a success. Peter is potentially a liability and a danger to society, and Cale from the reports I have read barely functions in society at all."

Dana glared at her. "Your reports are wrong! All of them! Cale is my *brother*. He is your *son*. Just because he doesn't care about the economy or being social or other stuff like that, and he'd rather think about beetles, that doesn't make him any less than other people."

"No. But you have a future ahead of you. These people do not. You are not sacrificing your own life for theirs. You are not making any kind of exchange. What you are doing is risking throwing away your own life in the pursuit of something unlikely and not worthy on the bigger scale of things."

"You would understand it, if you'd ever bothered to come and meet Cale! The Meritocracy says all people are equal, but they're not. Not really, are they? If all people are born equal, why do some people have votes that are worth more than others? Why isn't everyone's vote worth the same?"

Jananin folded her arms. She made a disparaging expression. "Direct democracy has been trialled before, on computer models. In a few small countries. It might be honourable in intention, but it doesn't work in practice."

Dana shouted, "And why do the Spokesmen get to decide to do this to Cale and Peter, and not the Electorate? What would the Electorate think, if they knew what the Spokesmen had agreed would kill two boys who have done nothing wrong?"

"This is a national emergency, and a military situation. There is no time to organise a referendum to determine how we should act. Doing so and making what is going on public knowledge would only serve to warn the people we are trying to stop!"

"Why do you do it? Why did you agree to be a Spokesman, and to make decisions to kill people on behalf of other people? Just because they voted for you, because you lied in a stupid video about doing research in Antarctica, and it went viral?"

"I serve because the Electorate ask me to." The room had by now become completely dark, and Dana could not make out her face. "You had better sleep now. Tomorrow will be hard, and it may be the last tomorrow you see." She paused. "And do not tell that medic about what we intend to do. The last thing we need is her interference on top of Rajesh's disapproval."

-20-

OUTSIDE the stable block, the *Stormcaller* rested on the tall pylons that provided a landing site for it. A stream of people clad in blue Sky Forces uniforms moved incessantly up and down the gantry to it, like a line of ants coming and going from a nest.

"Put this armour on." Jananin pointed to a tangled mass of interlocking plates spread out on a hay bale. "It's intended to be made specifically for the wearer, but there wasn't time, so I borrowed a set from the smallest woman I could find on the base."

Jananin already had her armour on and was strapping tack and equipment to a black horse much like the one Rajesh had ridden. Another horse, more heavily built, skewbald, and with a shaggy mane and dense feathering on its ankles, stood quietly at the back of the loose box.

Dana held up what she hoped was the chest piece and tried to work out which way round it was meant to go and how it was supposed to be put on. "Why is this horse different from the other one?"

"Horses are social animals, but the fearless nature of this horse means it's liable to fight if it's housed with other fearless horses. Thus, the necessity for a rescue horse companion."

She gazed outside, at the fields of unnatural crops, at the malevolent bulk of the *Stormcaller* blocking out the sky and the glass pyramids. "Isn't all of this technology bad for the environment?"

"Quite the opposite. The crops absorb carbon from the atmosphere, and the *Stormcaller* is a carbon-neutral mode of transport."

Dana continued to stare at the *Stormcaller*. There

was something disturbing, almost shocking about its even being there at all. It was not like an aeroplane, or a helicopter, or even an enormous ship; it was like nothing on Earth that had ever been seen before, made either by nature or man. "Don't you think it looks horrible?"

Jananin heaved a saddle onto the horse's back and adjusted its position. "No, I think it is a marvellous feat of engineering. And I daresay all the Luddites thought the steam engine Stephenson designed was *horrible* when they saw it steaming and screeching through the countryside. Yet these days we tend to view such things as quaint and romantic."

"It's like, no other species in the history of the planet affects its environment as much as humans do."

"Who told you that?" Jananin said sharply.

"I don't know. Lots of people. I thought it was a well-known fact."

"Well-known, possibly, fact certainly not."

"Is there another species that affects its environment more than humans?"

"Oh, there have been several. This planet is not some static environment with a fixed number of species that must be preserved in its current form no matter what. Ecosystems and whole planets are evolving, developing entities that change over time and ultimately will be destroyed. In the beginning, there was no life. The first organisms that evolved started photosynthesising and affecting the constitution of the atmospheric gases. That's a pretty drastic change for a species to cause to its environment, don't you think? Then we had the Carboniferous, when plants evolved lignin to sequester carbon, and atmospheric carbon dioxide plummeted. After that evolved the first fungi that could break down lignin, bringing about a mass extinction event as oxygen levels fell."

Dana considered this. Photosynthesising organisms. Fungi. "But they're all... *natural.*"

"And what makes humans *not* natural? Did we not evolve on this planet too? What sets humans apart from any other species that is or has been here? How can you make the claim that humans are an aberration when there are no other separate ecosystems at the same stage you know of to make a comparison? Perhaps in this galaxy there may be a great many planets all with a species on them in exactly the same evolutionary niche as people. Species like our own could be a normal and natural part in the development of a planet in the stage this one is at. Humans are just one of a long succession of species shifting the equilibrium of an indifferent ecosystem. It's happened before our species evolved, and it'll continue to happen after our species goes extinct."

Dana found a hole in the armour and decided to chance putting her head through. It was made up of narrow, indigo-coloured laminae that flexed slightly when she pressed them. "Is this made of polymer alloy?"

"Naturally."

What *wasn't* made of polymer alloy these days? Dana watched Jananin as she fastened straps and made adjustments to the horse's equipment. It was easy to see why she had won the Nobel Prize. She had invented something that had, in its various forms, become part of everyday life for nearly everyone. And she had invented the biomechanical synapse that allowed Dana to communicate with computers just by thinking, the same substance that had been implanted in the horse's brain, and in the wyvern's and in the birds and rats. Images of the dead rats broken on the blackened ground at the hospital flashed through her mind, followed by a memory of living rats, in cages, where she and Eric had taken the wyvern.

"In Osric's work there were rats being killed to find out if drugs were harmful. What gives him the right to do that to rats if it's wrong for Gamma to use animals?"

Jananin turned away from the horse and rested her elbow on the saddle. "Pilgrennon did not know when to stop. The future will be in grave peril if you too do not know where the line must be drawn."

"Osric tried to kill the wyvern! He's a sadistic coward."

Jananin's eyes flared. "I'll not have you speak of him like that! There are things about Osric you don't know. Claims like that are unfounded and ignorant!"

"What *things*?"

Jananin hefted up what looked like two pairs of trumpets connected with a thick strap and covered in black-and-yellow hazard warning marks, and slung it over the horse's withers. "None of your business."

"How do you expect me to understand if you won't tell me anything?"

"Years ago, Osric was young and idealistic. He was fresh out of university and he had a job in a research laboratory. He did something that would later turn out to be very foolish: he made a blog about his experiments on animals. He wanted to show the humane reality of the work he did and how important it was for making medicines to save lives, and dispel the malicious myths about his profession perpetuated by extremists. Somebody who read the blog traced his IP address through it, and after that a terrorist group began to target him. He received death threats, had a bomb planted under his car, poison sent in the post, people lurking near his house and spreading a hate campaign against him. At the time he lived with a partner and had a newborn son, but the stress of what was happening caused them to part. Osric moved out and his partner and son kept the house. Unfortunately it was too late. The night after he left, someone put a petrol bomb through the letterbox. The fire brigade found the woman and the child trapped together in an upstairs bedroom, both unconscious. She recovered, but his lungs were too young and the smoke had overcome him. If my memory serves me right, he would be about your age now."

Dana's mouth was dry. She had never considered what might have happened to Osric in the past, or how it was

Jananin might have got to know him. If she ever saw him again, she would see differently.

"The terrorist group on the Internet wrote an insulting obituary, saying Osric's son's death was no more significant than the deaths of the rats Osric studied, that the boy deserved to die because humans are a plague upon the Earth." Jananin hesitated before continuing. "Then I did something that could very well have turned out to be foolish as well. I offered Osric sanctuary in my house. I taught him things, I introduced him to people. I gave him the means to track down the terrorist who murdered his son and to have his revenge."

Dana forced saliva into her mouth and swallowed. "And then what happened?"

"That is between Osric and the terrorist." Jananin grimaced. "I have said too much. Do not repeat what I have told you. To *anyone*."

The hospital all that time ago. Osric had spied on Dana for Jananin. Doctors weren't supposed to do that. Their patients' details were meant to be confidential, and Osric would probably have lost his job if it had been discovered he had helped Jananin kidnap her. "And that's why Osric helps you?"

"It formed a bond of trust between us. I needed people who would take an oath of silence that they would never break. I had realised by this time I couldn't stop Pilgrennon alone."

"But if you had stopped Pilgrennon... if it wasn't for him, I wouldn't exist. So if what he did was wrong, it must be wrong for me to exist."

"That's not how it works. You are not wrong. You are just someone who was brought into existence in a wrong way."

"But if something that's not wrong came of it, that must mean it wasn't entirely wrong."

"There is no such thing as entirely wrong, or indeed entirely right. You have to look at the whole picture. The way Pilgrennon acquired material for his experiments was immoral and illegal. Most of the results of his experiments were braindamaged or deranged; we have him to thank for what we are currently going outside to fight. The overwhelming majority of Pilgrennon's work had extremely negative consequences. The fact there is an errant data point, that one small facet of it did not, is immaterial compared to the overall trend."

Dana took a deep breath and tried to keep her voice calm. She did not want this to become a fight, and she was aware that her questions would probably come across as provocative, but she truly could not see where the difference was. "How is making a horse like this one different to making a wyvern? Why is what the Meritocracy does better than what Gamma does?"

Jananin exhaled loudly, irritated. "Do you think life is like a children's story, and that the hero triumphs through use of a white horse with bells on it and a shiny magical sword, even though his adversaries have monsters and guns, and engines of destruction? There are no such things as good and evil. There are only things that are done for the greater benefit, and those that are not, and there are forces that can be controlled and can be used, and there are forces that cannot be controlled and should not be used."

It was all very well for Jananin to say Ivor's experiments and the wyvern were wrong, but she didn't have firsthand experience of it. Jananin wasn't one of Pilgrennon's children, and she hadn't made mental contact with the wyvern, so she had no idea what it felt like to be either of them. Yet this was vitally important. Dana had to understand and be able to justify to herself why they were going out to stop Gamma. She needed a reason to believe she was right and Gamma was wrong, or when they confronted each other it would be hazy and ambiguous like in the dreams again, and Dana feared she would forget why she set out and lose her way. She fought to concentrate, but she couldn't see it.

"But... I *can't*. Is there something the matter with me?"

Jananin's face tensed for a moment, and then her shoulders relaxed. "Perhaps I lay too much responsibility on you. It is easy to forget how young you are when I am thinking all the time of the ramifications of what he did to you. It may be, a better understanding of the issues at stake here will come to you when you are older."

She had finished equipping the horse now, and she handed Dana a helmet.

"It's got aluminium foil inside it," Dana commented.

"It worked well enough last time we needed to hide your signal. Wear it."

Dana fumbled with her armour, which seemed to have come together as intended, despite its ill fit. "Will you come with me?"

"I can take you as far as the Forge perimeter. I can't go in with you. If it becomes known I, as a Spokesman, have interfered with the proceedings of the armed forces when they are acting under a veto from the Spokesmen, that will look very bad." Jananin put her foot into the stirrup and mounted the horse.

Dana put on the helmet reluctantly, trying not to show that the sudden disappearance of GPS and all the other minor signals to which she was accustomed bothered her as much as it did. The world felt very empty and sinister without them.

"What's that on the horse?" Dana stared at the reflective black-and-white webbing and the trumpet-like apertures pointing forward on either side of the animal's chest.

"It's a sort of cannon developed for use against rioters, that causes disorienting shockwaves from blasts of sound. It's unlikely to kill anything, but it should be some use if we come up against any constructs from the Emerald Forge." Jananin reached down to pull Dana up by her arm. "Now, keep your feet away from the horse's flanks, and hold on."

Dana held on to Jananin around her middle. She had

her katana at her left hip, and the armour covering her torso made her feel more like a machine than a living thing. Jananin checked the screen on her arm, and the horse started to move forward. Outside the stable block, the morning sun cast a long, looming shadow from the *Stormcaller*. Dew glistened in the grass, the fields of crops grown bright and fresh from the previous day's rainfall.

"I'm going to keep to the cover of the trees for as long as possible," Jananin explained. "We move quickly now!"

She touched her feet to the horse's sides and they sped alongside the hedge, up the incline of the land towards the wooded line Dana had ridden through alone, fleeing the birds. The birds wouldn't be able to sense her now, not with this helmet blocking her signal. Or at least she hoped they wouldn't. The motion in the saddle hurt muscles that ached already from the ride yesterday.

Soon they were moving through wood, slowly down banks and through streams, and faster through breaks in the wood and open areas between widely-spaced trunks. It was a long while before they reached the edge of the woods and stopped to look out upon an open field, and beyond it, more fields, and beyond that, a blocky shape on the horizon that might be the Emerald Forge.

Jananin raised a communicator to her ear. "Tawny Owl calling Eagle Owl."

Dana could hear or sense nothing of the reply Rajesh must have given her.

"We are in position. We need the distraction now. Over."

"Do we go now?" Dana asked, impatient to get this over with.

"No, we wait. If they perceive Rajesh's attack to be a threat, they will start summoning their forces to the front. Watch."

Birds started to rise from the trees, all flying off in the same direction. Dana stared up as they darkened the sky, and hoped Rajesh would be okay.

"Now do we go?"

"No." Jananin was studying the screen strapped to her arm. "There's something coming."

A faint tremor ran through the ground. Out in the distance in the dry field, four or five pale shapes became visible, horses. As they drew closer, running at full gallop, Dana could scarcely believe what she was seeing. Each of them had welded in the centre of its forehead a single long spine of metal that flashed in the sun, and ran with its neck arched and head lowered, so the horn pointed forward level with the ground, like a lance. Jananin waited for the horses to pass by, the thunder of their hoofbeats diminishing as they moved to the front to defend the Forge.

"Now we move!"

Jananin kicked the horse urgently and it took off at full speed. Dana did not try to move with it or hold herself down in the saddle properly, and all she could really manage was to cling to Jananin and try to look forward and make sense of a rattling view of the dry, wheat-stubbled ground tearing past beneath the horse. They passed down the side of a field of maize, perhaps the same one she'd hidden in when she'd first approached the Forge, and jumped a dyke. The shape of the Emerald Forge grew upon the horizon, and at last they reached the meadow surrounding it. The dry blades of grass whipped around the horse's legs as they galloped for the perimeter fence, Jananin turning the horse to line up for a gap where one of the high wire panels had come down. The horse leaped the full length of it, and then Jananin was pulling the reins and leaning back, and the horse was digging its hoofs into stony earth and cracked concrete coming apart along seams of rampant weeds, slowing as the wall of the Forge loomed before them.

"Now hold my arm and get down."

Dana dismounted and waited for Jananin to get off. High above, a large bird of prey turned on a thermal.

"We don't have much time," said Jananin, noticing the bird. "I can go no further with you."

Dana gazed up at the stained concrete under the cavernous sky with mounting trepidation. "Can't you give me anything? Something that will help me?"

"You mean a weapon? Do you remember what the Samurai said, about using weapons you don't understand?"

Dana recalled a room in a B&B. Jananin's katana lying in the boot of her car. She had once asked to look at Jananin's sword...

"A wise man gives life with a sword. A fool kills himself on another's sword."

Jananin said, "That was it. And yet... The Samurai had another belief, that a sword is more than just the steel it is made from. A sword is believed to be imbued with natures from its maker and its owner, to have a soul in its own right. While that is plainly fantasy, there is in such beliefs some deep psychological inertia... and what are war and weapons apart from psychology?

"What do you think?"

Dana looked once more at the blank, forbidding face of the wall. She was afraid to go in there again, into that dark, dirty labyrinth abandoned for whatever its original purpose had been, alone, deaf and blind to the familiar reassurance of GPS and computer signals.

Jananin considered for a moment. Then she leaned to unstrap the knife from her thigh.

"This is called a tantō. I wish I had taken photographs and made exact measurements of my wakizashi, because I can't say I particularly like it or anything else I've tried since. I fear by giving it to you, I will only be providing it to be used against you, but on the other hand, having it might be able to do something for your state of mind."

Dana took the knife, a short leather-braided handle and a blade hidden inside a lacquered sheath.

"Do not think of trying to do this in a pacifist way. There is unlikely to be time, even if you do manage to free the prisoners, for you to get out of range. As soon as you get in there, your job is to stop Gamma as quickly as possible, by whatever means necessary."

Dana squeezed the handle of the tantō and nodded, her mouth dry.

Jananin put her foot into the stirrup, pushed off, and swung her leg over the horse. "If you see the *Stormcaller* in the sky, run *away* from it. The electromagnetic field that keeps it up there, if we drop and detonate a charge into it, will create an EMP far more powerful than anything Ivor and I made from TNT and household electronics." With a quick adjustment of the controls on her arm and a flick of her heels against the sides of the horse, she and the horse were away, Jananin glancing over her shoulder just once as the horse tore back through the perimeter and made for the cover of the woods.

Dana looked back at the sky, but the bird had gone. She pushed the scabbard of the tantō through her belt, but she felt sick at the thought she might have to stab Gamma with it. *By whatever means possible.* She thought again of her brother Cale. Jananin's reports had been wrong about Cale and Peter. The report about Gamma didn't seem to fit what Dana had seen either.

Dana had got herself into this, and she couldn't just abandon it and leave Cale to die. It was time to get on and act. She could do this. She had Jananin's blood running in her veins, literally and not just by genetic descent. She had Jananin's knife that had gone everywhere with her, imbued with her courage so now it could imbue it in turn on Dana.

Cale and Peter mattered more than Gamma, whatever had happened in Gamma's past. She had brought this upon them. If that was what it took to stop her, that was what Dana would have to do, the same as Jananin once had to do to the yakuza.

Jananin could do this. So she could do this too.

Keeping close to the wall, she began to make her way

around the perimeter, searching for an opening. It wasn't long before she found a boarded-up window with a loose panel.

She pushed it aside just enough to squeeze through the gap, splinters scraping dully against the protective carapace of polymer alloy encasing her chest. The contrast from the bright sunlight outside and the near darkness within was impossible for her eyes to adjust to, and she stumbled blindly over something on the floor, possessed by a helpless horror at the loss of her eyesight on top of the signals she could usually sense.

Another body collided with her. Dana screamed in the dark. Hands grappled with her arms, pulling them behind her back, out of reach of the tantō.

"I thought you would be back eventually," said Sanderson.

-21-

SANDERSON hauled Dana through the corridor and into another room, lit by a dim electric bulb. He shoved her into a seated position on a wooden chair, and dragged up a chair for himself. "Tell me what you know about Ivor Pilgrennon."

The instant he'd pushed her down into the chair, he'd let go of her arms, but the unexpected question stayed her hand from reaching for the tantō. A seed of doubt had taken root in her mind: this man might not be the enemy she knew him to be. He could have information she needed.

"He was my father. Sort of."

"Yes, and you were his fifth and final issue, Epsilon. He made you from one of only two ova he obtained from Jananin Blake, yes, Jananin Blake the Spokesman and Nobel laureate, and one of his own cells that he gene edited. Now, we both know that, me because I was there; you because someone, probably Ivor Pilgrennon himself, told you, but you know something I don't. Where is he?"

Dana stared at him, scarcely able to believe he'd just summarised in a loud voice information she'd dared not speak about to anyone. There were only supposed to be a very small number of people who knew about how she'd been conceived, and all of them were people Jananin trusted implicitly: Rajesh, Osric, Takahashi. There could easily be more of them she hadn't met, but surely Sanderson couldn't be trusted by Jananin; she would have known when Dana had described him, and more importantly, if he was loyal to her, he would have found a way to help her get Cale and Peter out of the Emerald Forge.

"What do you mean, you were *there*?"

Sanderson raised his palms to her and spread long, delicately boned fingers. "Pilgrennon isn't a surgeon. He wasn't trained nor skilled enough to carry out the procedures he wanted to do. I am. Now, it's imperative I find him, so tell me what you know."

Dana had never thought of there having been people Ivor had trusted, although she'd been aware of Jananin's confidants, and thinking of it now it did make sense. Yet whereas she'd felt greatly relieved to discover Rajesh's allegiance to Jananin when before she'd been distrustful of him, with Sanderson her reaction was very different. Something about the idea of this man being there when she and Cale were conceived made her deeply uneasy. Whereas Rajesh's connection to Jananin had made him safe and trustworthy, Sanderson's connection to Ivor made him an unknown impossible to predict.

Dana couldn't understand why she felt this way. Sanderson might have some idea where Ivor had gone. If she helped him, he might be able to help her. "Two years ago, a helicopter blew up while Ivor was flying it at Cape Wrath. We looked and looked afterwards, but we couldn't find him."

"Where did you look?"

"I don't know." Dana could only remember the cold air, the surreal storms that ravaged the edge of the world, and the utter desolation she had felt after that point. "I think everyone just went home after we looked in the sea."

"Do you know where he had been hiding after he disappeared in the first instance? Perhaps he could have returned there?"

A sudden, desperate hope ignited. She had never thought of that. "He was in a disused military base, in a cave in an island called Roareim, off the coast of Lewis in the Outer Hebrides." Surely Jananin must have looked, or sent someone to look. After all, she'd wanted him dead from the start. But then again, her mind might have changed after what had happened off Cape Wrath. She'd agreed to let him go once Cerberus was destroyed, and might have chosen in the end to draw a line under the whole business and leave him be.

"Interesting." Sanderson rubbed his cheek. "Now, you came here to stop Gamma, did you not?"

Dana didn't say anything, so Sanderson continued. "Gamma, of course, remotely controls one side of the war going on outside. She's the only one who can."

Disliking his self-assured manner, Dana locked eyes with him. "The Sky Forces are coming. The Spokesmen for the Meritocracy have voted to destroy everything in the Emerald Forge with a Compton bomb."

"I *say* she is the only one who can. There are only five children known to be implanted with Pilgrennon's devices. The first girl was brain-damaged in the attempt to implant her transceiver, more of a learning exercise than a result. It appears she died in the information terrorist attack on London. We exhumed the grave and retrieved the transceiver, so we know for sure it was her. The boy here does not have the mental proficiency to mentally control an army, and my assessment of the other boy recently found suggests that whether or not he has the proficiency, he is utterly disinterested and unmotivated to work for us. You, however..."

His voice had tailed off, as though he expected her to make a logical inference. Dana felt sick, remembering the thought of people digging in Alpha's grave, stealing from what should not be disturbed. "Those *boys* have names. They are Peter and Cale. You want the Sky Forces to win the fight outside against the animal machine constructs *you* helped to make?"

"Oh, I do not wish the blood of intelligent men and women spilled. Not under any circumstances that can be avoided. Perhaps you will understand my situation better if you see for yourself."

He reached into his pocket and took out a flat, black, rectangular object. It took several seconds before

Dana realised it was a phone. Because of the helmet she still had on, she couldn't sense the signal that normally accompanied one. Like most modern phones, the full face of it was a screen with a few basic buttons to control it on the edges and back. Sanderson set it on the table in front of her, and a video began to play.

A man and woman looking to be in their late forties sat on chairs in a room. They looked stiff and formal, their expressions serious. Facing them and leaning in a much more casual manner on a desk, was a man, and recognition sent a bolt of adrenaline through Dana's heart. He was a young man, smooth-faced, his curly and neatly parted hair a bright sandy brown, his broad-shouldered physique looking not quite at ease in a white shirt with the sleeves crumpled up around the elbows and a badly done tie with cartoons on it fastening the collar, but *undeniably* he was Ivor Pilgrennon.

The woman spoke, her face sceptical. "I have talked to six different consultants. All of them told me the same thing: that I could not have children of my own. The eggs in my ovaries are all used up. But you are saying you can create an embryo that will really be ours?"

Ivor's face was intense. "Yes. The technology we're developing allows us to make germ cells, eggs and sperm, from normal cells taken from the body." His voice, although rendered flat and thin through the phone's meagre speakers, sent an electric prickle up Dana's back. "There will be no hormone injections, no painful procedure to collect ova, just a simple cheek swab. The child will be genetically yours and your husband's."

The conversation continued, the woman leaning forward in fascination, as Sanderson spoke over it. "Mr and Mrs Percival. Career people. People who didn't stop to think about when to have a family until it was too late. Pilgrennon is lying, of course. The embryo he implanted in Mrs Percival was not from an ovum generated from her cells, for no such technique exists or has been developed since, and while there is a procedure to generate proto-sperm from normal cells in a laboratory that can be used to fertilise an ovum, he certainly didn't use the sperm of her husband or anything else derived from his cells. The ovum came from one of his patients; fertilised with material derived from his genetic engineering project. The Percivals were nothing more than a free surrogate for an experiment to him. Of course, I had to provide the surgical expertise to implant the transceiver in it when it was large enough, under the pretence of it being a routine test to rule out Down's syndrome. Pilgrennon wrote the Greek letter Gamma on the container the zygote was cultured in. Mrs Percival seemed rather taken with it, because when a daughter was born, she named her Gemma.

"When Pilgrennon disappeared, I never found out what happened to the children. Pilgrennon set off a Compton bomb and destroyed the computers with all his records on, so I couldn't find the Percivals' address. When I did eventually track them down, they were childless once more. I managed to get hold of Gemma's NHS health records. As it turned out, she was not growing up normally. She had autism, certainly, but there seemed to be some kind of psychotic condition in addition that none of the experts could agree on a diagnosis for. Some said it was schizophrenia. By this time, Gemma had grown to look nothing like her parents, and the Percivals must have realised Pilgrennon was a fraud, and had a genetic test done to find out if they really were her parents. When they discovered they weren't, it seems they disowned her and abandoned her in an institute."

Abandoned. Dana considered this. She'd considered herself and Cale to have been abandoned by their real parents, before she'd hit her head and Jananin Blake had found her outside the hospital, and another truth had been revealed to her. But that Gamma should be abandoned by these people who'd said they really wanted a child, put into that awful hospital where they used to tie her to a bed, that seemed far worse.

"You do realise," Sanderson narrowed his eyes, "that you have to be autistic for the technology Pilgrennon pioneered to work?"

Dana stared back at him, transfixed, not knowing what to think.

"Oh, Ivor was brilliant, but he was held back because he always had to frame himself as being a bleeding-heart humanitarian saviour of the autistic. His sister was some sort of Physics-whizz chess champion who blew her brains out playing around with electricity because she never had any friends. That's why he made the transceivers, to help the autistic to communicate; some computer scientist called Steve Gideon helped him with the design because that wasn't really his forte either, and of course the moiety needed to connect it to brain cells and make the whole thing work was purloined from Blake.

"One of the nurses who worked at his institute persuaded me, without Pilgrennon's knowledge, to attempt it on him, possessed with the power it would give him, having seen its effects on you and your brother, mere infants. But when it was done, the signals to him were incomprehensible; the sensation of them intolerable. I couldn't remove it. He ended up sectioned under the Mental Health Act, and so far as I know spends his days now sedated into oblivion.

"After Pilgrennon absconded and took you and your brothers with him, the hooker he'd used as a surrogate for you all came to me, desperate to trace you and him. I told her what had happened to the nurse, but she begged me to implant her, believing it would give her the ability to find you. I eventually agreed, but the results only confirmed the first attempt. She died by heroin overdose a year or so later, probably intentionally."

Jade Cooper. Ivor had told Dana that was the name of the woman who had given birth to her and Cale. Jade Cooper had *looked for them*? Jade Cooper was *dead*?

"It's possible to make a simple implant that a neurotypical can use, like the one in Prendick's visual cortex that allows him to see with his bird." Sanderson's expression tightened. "But the complex, high-fidelity connection you and Gamma have, will not work on a neurotypical. The genes involved in autism, which Pilgrennon identified, are necessary to allow proper interfacing. Those genes were all catalogued and investigated in his thesis, and all trace of it has mysteriously disappeared. Without Pilgrennon or a copy of his thesis, I cannot find out if *I myself have enough of these genes to be able to take the implant*, were I able to find another neurosurgeon with the skill to perform it on me."

Dana remembered. Jananin and the ethics committee had rescinded Ivor's work, hidden all trace of it from the public record. Perhaps people like Sanderson were the reason why.

"Gamma is functional, but she's damaged. I don't know if she would have turned out that way whatever the circumstances, or if it's more a result of the way she was brought up, and her obsessive parents dragging her in and out of hospitals constantly. It is very difficult to work with her when she insists what we make be made to look and function like imaginary animals she reads about in mythology books. If Prendick and I refuse, she refuses to control the finished products. You seem rather more reasonable."

Dana stared at him. "You want me to help you make animals into intelligent robots, and *control them?*"

Sanderson leaned back in his chair. "For the greater good, of course. We wouldn't have to fight the Meritocracy. All I ask is that you call off the battle and tell them Prendick and I have already left. We can rendezvous somewhere else later."

"And what would happen to Gamma?"

Sanderson shrugged. "Either leave her to the Meritocracy to deal with, or do to her what she did to you:

use her as a source of the moiety."

Dana tried to solidify what she felt about this into something meaningful, but what she felt about Gamma didn't make sense. On the one hand, she had felt the misery and self-pity of the individual trapped in the hospital. On the other, she could not reconcile this with the ruthless person who tortured and maimed and had no compassion for anyone, inflicting that same suffering on others. "But why do you need an army made of mechanical animals?"

Sanderson leaned toward her, eyes wide and bright. "*Don't you see?* This is Pilgrennon's work. This is the sort of breakthrough that started the revolution that destroyed the old ways and brought the Meritocracy to power. The Meritocracy has ANTs, powerful computers that have transformed the function of society. Think how the function of society could be improved with this technology at its disposal."

"But Jananin Blake stopped Pilgrennon. It was her that supported the Meritocracy. Pilgrennon said he didn't agree with it. And Blake said Pilgrennon's work would lead to autistic people being exploited if it went public."

Sanderson shook his head dismissively. "*Blake is a genius*, but she won't see things through all the way. She's too besotted with the equality side of the Meritocracy and the idea of everyone having a say no matter how insignificant they are. The null tier was an excellent idea — that people who can't support themselves can forfeit their right to a vote in exchange for benefit money — but they should have pushed it harder. Is it right that someone on null tier should be able to sit in social accommodation doing nothing, making a career out of breeding more null tier people? The stupid and the worthless will always outnumber the intelligent and the constructive, unless we end this subversion of Darwin's laws and let the natural equilibrium rebalance itself."

Dana wasn't sure how this fitted with what she understood; something about the first-tier people being so numerous that if all of them voted one way on any particular referendum, they would outnumber the higher-tiered people no matter how they voted. Jananin had said nothing about the null-tier people. Dana knew who they were, of course; people living in social housing who couldn't find jobs, and didn't vote in referenda because they'd been given money to live off and a house to live in by the Meritocracy. Did that mean Jananin thought they were worthless, as Sanderson seemed to? How many null-tier people were there, compared to how many first-tier people, and people in the higher tiers?

"And the Meritocracy's stance on the threats from foreign powers is deeply lacking. America. *Land of the free.*" Sanderson scowled and turned his head to spit on the floor. "Land where a minority of intelligent people work in state-of-the-art facilities to advance scientific understanding, so their majority of obese illiterate religious-fundamentalist rednecks can have weapons of mass destruction to go with their fast food meals. We could put an end to that. The European Union, for too long has that foreign power axis been a thorn in our sides. Before the rise of the Meritocracy it robbed the public coffers, flooded us with immigrants, and interfered in the affairs of private citizens and businesses; now the Meritocracy has come to power, the bureaucrats sit in Brussels making hollow threats and clogging up our trade routes with their red tape. We could destroy it."

"But those aren't part of this country." America was a place from the television, where a black man with a photogenic smile sat in a white temple, under a stripey banner with a rectangle of stars in one corner. But Dana had been there, once, with Ivor. The people she had met there didn't seem anything like what Sanderson had just described. There was talk in America of becoming a meritocracy, to give the states more autonomy.

The European Union was some kind of government that controlled a lot of countries in the east. She didn't know who led it, only that it used a symbol that was a circle of stars, and it made lots of laws and the emblem was stuck to a lot of imported things made there. Ireland had recently left it, and so had the UK when the Meritocracy had risen to power, so if countries could leave as and when they wanted, surely that was up to them. "Isn't it up to the people who live in them how their country is run? It's not up to the Meritocracy to go there and change how they do things."

"It is if those places interfere with the Meritocracy's freedoms, if they obstruct the rights of the Electorate." Sanderson paused, his face intense. "We could raise an army out of the birds in the sky and the beasts of the land. We could make machines more powerful than anyone else can. We could build an alliance of life and technology that would stand undefeated. We could destroy corrupt governments and remake the world in freedom. We could *finish* what Pilgrennon *started*."

With these words, something that made sense leapt from Dana's confusion, the memory of the moment in the helicopter before the fall, the icy water below, and the explosion high up in the sky above. Perhaps Ivor hadn't really been there with her in the hospital room, but it was immaterial now. What that memory did give her was a feeling of surety and security, and she held on to it, the touch of his hand on her arm, the sound of his voice, his smell.

Ivor Solomon Pilgrennon had died off Cape Wrath because he had made a choice, because he had made the right choice, to end what he had started. If Dana made this choice now, then Ivor's death and everything he had done for her would be in vain. His sacrifice would be rendered meaningless.

"No."

Sanderson straightened in his chair, moving his face away from hers. "No what?"

"No, I won't help you."

Sanderson apparently considered this for a moment, rubbing his finger between his top lip and his nose. Then he took hold of Dana's arm and rose from his chair abruptly, pulling her with him, back out of the room. He grabbed her other wrist as they emerged into the corridor and held her up by both arms, hauling her along sideways. "There's no more to discuss," he muttered.

Dana had become disoriented from the loss of signals, but from her memory of the building, she estimated he was heading for the long, high room where they collected the blood. Where was he taking her? To Gamma? It occurred to her that if she'd gone along with what Sanderson had said, it might have been a much quicker and easier way to stop Gamma, stop the Compton bomb, and free Cale and Peter. She'd thrown it away by letting him confuse her.

"Okay, I'll do what you say!"

"You're lying. You've had your chance and made your choice. If we're to work together, we need to be able to trust each other. The decision has to be made of your own free will."

Sanderson reached the door to the hall and kicked it open. The long room was filled with sunlight, stained green from the filters of the filthy windows, but shadows flickered, betraying great flocks of birds in the sky without.

"I shall say I cut too deep, I waited too long. She'll be angry, but she'll get over it." He dragged Dana to the basin and kicked her feet out from under her. Her kneecaps crashed into the concrete floor so hard it felt like they'd shattered, and the pain was so terrible she couldn't move to resist or fight back, only gasp for breath and struggle to think through it. Sanderson forced her down over the basin.

"Get off of me!" Dana managed to force the words from lungs seized with pain. She thought frantic distress signals, but nothing would transmit through the foil inside her helmet. After everything, was this how it would end? That she would die here, unable to do anything, and Cale and Peter would die for her failure?

A blur of movement flashed into her peripheral vision. Something large crashed into the side of Sanderson's head. The weight bearing down on her ceased. She pushed herself off the basin and fell on her back on the floor, drawing up her knees and pressing her palms against them to try to stop the pain. A buffeting draught from enormous wings rushed over her.

She looked up to see Prendick's eagle fly across the room, towards the windows, before she lost sight of it. Dana rolled onto her side, but her knees hurt too much to roll onto her front. Sanderson and Prendick were fighting, but Prendick's bird couldn't look where it was flying and watch for him at the same time. The bigger man threw a clumsy punch. Sanderson ducked, and Prendick lurched, unbalanced.

With a grating screech, the bird launched itself back across the room, flying with its talons outstretched at Sanderson's head. He flailed in desperation to defend himself, he and the eagle spinning like a hurricane of limbs and feathers. Dana put her weight on her elbow, trying to sit upright. Prendick hurled his fists into empty space, searching for the attacker he couldn't see.

Sanderson by now appeared to have got hold of something. The enormous bird still pounded its wings, but he held it aloft, by the legs, his arm shaking under the weight of it. A triumphant grin spread over his face.

"Don't hurt her, please." Prendick's voice came out thick and lispy through unyielding lips.

Sanderson turned to face Prendick, so his back was to Dana. He held the bird higher and grasped its head with his free hand, bending it back like Ivor had done with the rabbits he meant to have for dinner.

Dana seized the handle of the tantō from her belt and threw herself forwards onto her stomach. She slashed as far as her arm could reach for the back of his legs, and the blade tore through sock and tendon and cartilage at the back of his ankle, just above the level of his shoe. Sanderson staggered and lost control of the bird. It started to flap as though it was trying to take off, dragging him in the direction of the door. He lost his grip and fell. Dana caught sight of his face, full of anger and pain, through the flurry of the bird attacking his back. Sanderson struggled on hands and knees out of the room, blood spreading in a great stain across his sock and up the leg of his trousers. The bird refused to follow him into the corridor, flying back to land on Prendick's gloved fist.

The huge man reached down, offering his free hand to Dana. The skin was rough with scars and calluses.

"Please help me, Prendick" she begged him. "I must stop Gamma, or the Meritocracy will set off a Compton bomb and you and I and Peter and Cale will all die!" Dana was up on her feet. It hurt to bend her knees, but she could stand, and probably walk. "Where is she?"

"I'm not sure," said Prendick.

It was time to face this and get it over and done with. There was one way to find Gamma.

Dana took off her helmet and threw it on the floor. As signals flooded back into her consciousness like warm sunlight into a cold, dark dungeon, she waited and searched for that one she couldn't mistake, the one Gamma gave out.

-22-

PRENDICK'S hawk flapped over to the window and perched cumbersomely on the concrete sill. Prendick's mouth tightened. "Something approaches."

Dana stepped around him and looked out through a missing piece of the dirty window. A storm gathered on the horizon, and in the midst of it lay what looked like a large solid mass. Lightning flickered over the undersides of the cloud as she watched. Almost without thinking, she started counting. Fifteen seconds later, the concrete reverberated with thunder.

"It's the *Stormcaller*. We don't have much time." As she spoke, she noticed other things in the sky, large, shaped like elongated spheres, zeppelins maybe. She could see three from her position, drifting up into cloud and towards the *Stormcaller*. Dana shielded her eyes with her hands and squinted at the closest, trying to see what it was. Long crane-like appendages reached from below the main bulk, and gouts of flame blossomed in the distance. The wyvern was a prototype, Jananin had said, and surely this was the fully developed version, a bag of hydrogen with a dozen fire-breathing necks. A dragon for all intents and purposes.

She turned to Prendick. "Did you make that?"

He nodded, not looking very proud of his work.

Dana caught sight of motion in her peripheral vision. A dark horse galloped, pursued by a flock of birds, a man in the uniform of the Meritocracy's Sky Forces leaning forward in his saddle, urging his mount faster. It might have been Rajesh. The horse swerved about, doubled back on itself to face its pursuers, hoofs tearing up the dry ground. The air *distorted* in front of the horse's chest where the four trumpet-like devices were arranged, and most of the birds fell to the ground as a dull crack echoed over the landscape. They spun and flapped, while those that had not been downed by the shockwave swarmed over the horse, which began bucking wildly, lashing out at its attackers with its hind feet while its rider fought to stay in position.

"I have to find Gamma and stop her, now." There was no time left to look for Gamma. Dana would have to make her come.

Dana closed her eyes and put her hands over her ears to keep out as much distraction as possible while she sought Gamma's signal amidst the noise. She had to be here somewhere, so were the walls blocking her position, or was Dana just not looking hard enough?

At last she found it, weak, from somewhere above. Making the connection instantly gave away her position. Anger oozed out of the walls. Prendick too seemed to sense it, his eagle shrinking her head down into her shoulders and hunching her wings to form a protective mantle. "If Gamma finds me here..."

"Send your bird away."

Prendick pushed the bird out through a window on the side of the hallway. Now Gamma couldn't threaten him, but without her he would be next to useless in anything that might follow.

A shadow formed in the corridor. Dana faced it, the tantō ready in her hand.

Gamma entered the room with slow, deliberate steps. Her eyes were locked with Dana's, and she did not look away. The claustrophobic control room, deep within the rock of Roareim came back to Dana. Alpha had faced her like this, Alpha unthinking, her actions controlled by a program Cerberus had written into her. Gamma wasn't unthinking. She wasn't like Alpha, but her mind worked in the same way, the same as Cale's and Peter's did. Peter had once tried to push his thoughts into hers, and she had pushed him out. Many times she would push into Cale, usually when he was daydreaming about beetles and she wanted to join in, and he would push her out. If she could push into Gamma without being pushed out, she might be able to make her see sense.

Dana concentrated on all the anger and hate that flowed out of Gamma, focusing on that point and trying to press through to what lay behind it; to reach the person she'd once been when Dana had tried to help her. Gamma pressed back. This was not like the push and pull with Cale or with Peter, annoying each other without malice. Gamma meant harm.

Dana tried to think of the hospital, of the escape, but in return found her own mind being probed, Gamma forcing her way into private memories of Ivor, lifting her up on Roareim to see the sea, Ivor driving with her beside him, in the car on the road up the west coast of America. *That's private.* By her lapse in focus, she lost the control she had and succumbed to Gamma's intrusion. Her last thought was of the *Stormcaller* readying destruction in the sky above, and that she had failed Jananin, and Cale and Peter with her.

*

The sun is setting over a flooded garden. Poking up out of the water are bits of Greek statues and funny effigies, and imitation monuments on pillars that are too small to really be what their grandiose forms suggest. You've been somewhere like this before. A made-up place where there lived a dog... with three heads. There had been someone with you, a boy, you think, but something had happened, your fault, and trying to remember only brings a feeling of embarrassment and self-disgust.

There is someone else here with you, although it's not the boy, but a girl. When you try to speak, your mouth won't respond, but this doesn't bother you a great deal. You've always been able to get by just by *thinking*.

Where are we?

Lips that aren't yours but feel like them move in response. "We're safe, Epsilon. Remember? The other place isn't real. This is real, this is better. Let's stay in this place. We don't have to go back to the other."

You don't remember how you got here. You know you have a life outside of this, that you have a name you just can't recall. This is a dream, but you're not sure if you've had it before, or if you've just dreamed you had it before.

Not far away, where a grassy bank rises from the clear water lapping around the bases of the stones, there is a muddy crater in the ground, surrounded by blackened sticks that might once have been trees. It is ominously familiar.

I'm supposed to be somewhere else. There's something I have to do.

"There's nothing you have to do. You're not real. You're just someone I made up."

Dark clouds are beginning to gather on the horizon, obscuring the sunset. Lightning pulses, but thunder never comes. A dark nucleus lies at the centre of the storm. Without understanding why, you are afraid. You have something to do, and something terrible that can never be reversed is going to happen if you can't remember what it was.

I am horrified. "What's that? It's not supposed to be here!" I turn away, refusing to look at it, and you can no longer see it. Several birds flit across the sky in succession. "They shouldn't be here either!"

The birds are flying up, joining with more birds to form a giant swarm that moves together as one. You know birds aren't harmful to people, but something makes these birds malevolent. Their motion is disturbing. You want to hide, so they can't see you.

Another, larger bird has come, a predator. It dives like a spear into the flock, carving it in two. The halves fly apart like rippling curtains.

"No! This is my world! I'll not let you spoil it!"

I'm not!

Spite and anger boils over. My voice comes out as a hoarse scream. "You are! You're not real. If I don't think about you, you'll just cease to be."

The feeling won't take form, won't turn into a conscious thought, no matter how you try, but you know somehow this isn't all there is and that you must be able to break free from this.

I am real, and I don't need you to exist. Memories are starting to come back to you now. There is a boy with curly hair whom you have known as long as you can remember. His name... his name is Cale. There is another boy, with red curly hair gone all matted. Peter. There is a family, a man and a woman and an older boy. The man is all hairy and weird with hands like tarantulas, and the woman is short and her body is lumpy, because the boy, the only child she had who survived long enough to be born, had to be cut out of her to save her life. You didn't like them when you first met them, but they were not what their appearance made them seem, and they became your family. There is a scheming woman with dark hair all shot through with grey at the temples, who used to live in Japan a long time ago when she was a girl, and there is a man, very tall and strong, who once held you in his arms and reassured you, and then he went away...

My limbs don't respond to your struggles at first. The memories are what you must hold on to as you fight to take back control. You have done this before, and you can do it again. Last time, I allowed you do it; now, I fight with every fibre of my being.

One foot moves from the ground, followed by the other, and we're facing back towards the clouds. Something else has appeared, a building. "What is *that*?" I scream. Walls crowned with barbed wire surround more walls, a prison within a prison. Blank windows stare down at us from the heights. Now a man is walking out from the gate, clad in white. He holds something in his hand, but you can't see what.

I am shrinking, crumpling to the ground, needing to be away from this world that has turned against me. You stand taller, refusing to collapse, and as I fall you break away as a moth shrugs its chrysalis.

You stand alone at last, looking down on someone who is not what she pretends to be: a broken, withered child dressed in a hospital gown crouching in the mud and snivelling with its arms clutched around itself. You feel pity, but then you remember who you are and why you're here. And you realise your eyes have been closed the whole time.

*

Dana opened her eyes. Gamma crouched on the floor in front of her, knees bent against her chest and head leaned forward, as though she was trying to take up the least space possible. It was only now she noticed Gamma was wearing something on her head, a thin metal band, almost like a crown. This had to be how she was controlling the animals outside. She reached down and removed it. Without thinking, she put it on her own head.

A thousand thoughts and visions exploded into her consciousness. Every single animal outside was transmitting its view of the world back to her. Initially she could make no sense of it, but slowly she began to recognise things.

Rajesh stood over where his horse lay unmoving, a few snakes' heads and the hindquarters of a Komodo dragon crushed underneath it. The soil was black with blood.

"Rajesh!" Dana cried. "Eagle Owl, this is Little Owl!" She struggled to understand the interface, trying to find the frequency of the radio transceiver he must be wearing to let him communicate with the *Stormcaller*. "Eagle Owl, can you hear me?"

"Little Owl, this is Eagle Owl, receiving you loud and clear." Rajesh's fingers were pressed to his ear, and he shouted urgently into a microphone on his cheek,

"*Stormcaller*, this is Eagle Owl! Abort and stand down! I repeat, abort, abort!"

The man diminished as the disorganised horde of birds rose skyward. The sensation was *incredible*.

She could have rescued Cale and Peter and stopped the attack without the Meritocracy. She didn't need this army here, this engine of dread hanging in the sky above. She could feel its prickling threat in the air all around her, in the creeping of every follicle on her body. She could have gone back to Lewis and looked for Ivor. That was what mattered most, wasn't it? Finding if Ivor was still alive, and at least getting closure if he was not? How had she come to forget that? Sanderson had been right... and she'd said no?

You don't remember.

Something about the Meritocracy and Jananin Blake. But Ivor had never liked the idea of the Meritocracy anyway. He'd said it wasn't right that some people's opinions should carry more weight than others'. Jananin Blake had tried to murder Ivor, and once she'd almost tricked Dana into helping her. *Her own father!* How could she have been so stupid? What was the Meritocracy to condemn the experiments of the Emerald Forge, when it made horses that could not fear, and machines like the *Stormcaller* that could end everything with a blast of Compton radiation? Why had she trusted Rajesh and Rupert Osric, who were spies for Jananin, when Sanderson had been Ivor's confidant?

She could take these birds and these rats and horses to the school they'd made her attend every day. They could do to those horrible teachers, and that bully Abigail Swift, what they had done to those people in the hospital, and no-one would be able to stop her or punish her for it. This could make her untouchable, safe from those who would do her harm. She could *demand* the answers she wanted, and people would give them to her on pain of death.

Out of the riot of signals that had overwhelmed her,

the clamour of voices filling Dana's head, a single signal rose that she recognised. *And it recognised her in return...*

A shadow blotted the light; Dana turned, sensed the signal growing closer fast. Prendick shouted something. She ducked under a bench an instant before the tall window caved inwards with a terrific noise, shattering into a thousand green fragments that cascaded to the floor around what appeared to be a mass of metal limbs driven in by a blade of bright daylight.

As the sound of falling glass faded away, Dana turned around and pulled herself back upright against the pain in her knees. Hard rays of bright light flared from the jagged hole in the window. A long neck made of segmented metal plates rose from the destruction in the middle of the floor, and the wyvern lifted its great cruel head, setting more glass jangling on the stone floor with every movement. Streams of tiny shards trickled off when it stood up and flexed its wings.

Dana's last memory of the wyvern flashed through her thoughts, a silvery tail disappearing beneath a grey frothy surface. It came back? What had happened since then?

The wyvern as ever didn't seem able to convey answers as such, but it did manage a narrative composed of visuals and emotions. Streamlined silhouettes in the water, familiar from a deep, primal memory: first came elation and recognition, curiosity and novelty, but then, disgust, ridicule, the sting of rejection. The wyvern no more belonged with them than Dana fitted in with the children at the school. With the realisation came shame and guilt from the wyvern. It had abandoned her in pursuit of something inferior, false.

Confused, Dana reached up for the object on her head. What had come over her? With a sudden urge of revulsion, she dropped it on the floor and trod hard on it until the metal crumpled and lost its form.

A rush of motion and a bagpipe roar, and the wyvern was standing on top of something... someone... one great metal claw pinning down the chest of... *Gamma*. Its jaws were clamped around her head, and she struggled ineffectively.

"*No!*" Dana commanded it.

The shrill sound of a dentist's drill pierced the air. An agonised scream echoed through the empty hall, and Gamma's signal abruptly went out.

The wyvern stepped back with a heavy clank, spark-teeth rasping. Gamma lay on her back, blood trickling from a wound in the dead centre of her forehead, staining honey-coloured hair that splayed untidily where she had fallen. Dana saw in that pathetic figure not the one who had taken Cale, had forged monsters from living animals, had held her and Peter hostage, but the girl in the hospital whom she'd been so terribly sorry for, so broken and desperate to help escape. Her eyes moved to look straight at Dana, before they rolled back and her face became inert.

Dana staggered back, raising her hands to her face. A dizzy, sick feeling filled her head. This was Alpha all over again. The wyvern could have done it to any of them. That could have been her, had things turned out differently the afternoon the wyvern came to the school. "What have you done?" she shouted. "You killed her!"

The wyvern shrank back from her outburst with a broadcast of guilt and shame. It turned and bounded onto the windowsill, and launched itself into the air and was gone, dislodging yet more glass that jangled on the floor.

Prendick's eagle must have come back at some point during what had been happening, because now he had it as he came quickly to her side and bent over Gamma's body. He pressed two knuckles to her throat, under her jaw.

"She's still alive."

"What's that?" Dana sniffed. She wasn't sure if she was imagining it, but there was a sharp, burning odour in the air. "Do you smell it?"

"I lost my sense of smell the day I lost my sight." Prendick turned to the door. The corridor held a soupy density that it hadn't before, and Dana was by now certain of a smell of burning penetrating the room.

-23-

DANA and Prendick hurried to the doorway to look out into the gloomy corridor. The air out there burned Dana's throat and made her eyes sting. Thick fumes drifted up the stairwell.

"Sanderson must have started it to get rid of the evidence," Prendick said.

Dana looked from the smoke, down the other side of the corridor. "Please, help me find Cale and Peter."

Although Prendick did not move, the eagle on his shoulder shuffled itself about so it was facing the opposite way. "What about *her*?"

Dana looked back at Gamma's body sprawled on the floor. If she was not yet dead, medically speaking, she surely must be as good as dead, for she no longer emitted any signal. Jananin's haunting words from a long time ago passed through her thoughts: *A breathing corpse.*

Yet even if Gamma was dead for all intents and purposes, it would feel wrong to leave her body here for the fire to devour before her breath had ceased. "Can we bring her?"

Prendick passed the eagle from his shoulder to a stool. He bent down and hefted Gamma's limp form up from the floor, and slung her over his right shoulder, wrapping his arm around the backs of her knees. He offered his gloved fist to the bird, who stepped back onto it. "The two boys are upstairs on the next floor."

Dana went first with Prendick behind her, his breath heavy from carrying the weight of both the enormous eagle and Gamma. Soon they reached a corridor Dana recognised. The cell she'd been in had been here, so Peter must be nearby.

She sensed his signal, and then there he was, lying face-down on the bed, the soles of his thin bare feet protruding from ragged trousers and pointing to the door. "It's locked." Dana rattled the heavy metal door. "Where's the key?"

"Gamma had it." Prendick turned his back towards Dana and bent his knees so she could see something on a piece of string caught around her neck. Dana hurried to disentangle the key. "I think you'll be wasting your time, though. I've tried to help him escape before."

Dana got the door open. "Peter, you have to come. The building's on fire!"

"Go away!" Peter roared into the mattress as soon as she came into the room.

Peter stank. His clothes looked like they hadn't been changed for months, and his hair fell in grimy locks felted together with filth. "Peter it's me, Dana, Epsilon. Remember?"

Peter curled his arms under his chest. "You're not having it!"

"Having what?"

"His blood," said Prendick.

"We're not here to have your blood. We're here because you need to come with us, otherwise you're going to die!"

"Let's at least find the other boy first," Prendick suggested.

Cale was easy to find. They'd put him in Dana's old cell, although the bats were no longer sharing it, perhaps having smelled the smoke and departed already. There was a nasty smell in there that wasn't either the bat guano or the smoke, or the normal smell of dirty bodies. Dana's brother lay on his side on the bed. His signal suggested he was in a very deep, dreamless sleep.

"Cale?"

Cale's body lolled unresponsively when she shook him. His face was burning hot with fever.

"Cale! What's the matter with him?"

"I don't know." Prendick slid Gamma's body down onto the floor. He heaved Cale up from the bed. "We need to get him out of here. You see if you can get Peter to come. We'll have to come back for Gamma afterwards."

Dana went back into Peter's cell. What would tempt him to move? Peter had only ever known one place, and a small number of people. Dana would need to try to use that for leverage. "Peter, you need to come with us. We're going back to Roareim now."

Peter at last turned his head away from the mattress to look at her. "Where's Ivor?"

"He can't be here now. He's going to meet us when we get to Roareim. But you have to come quickly!" She suspected Peter would be able to sense she was lying. He could sense things from her signal as much as she could sense things from his, but hopefully he would also be able to sense the danger in staying here.

"All right," he said after a moment, and got up from the bed.

Dana led the way back to the stairs, but by now a thick funnel of smoke was flowing up through the stairwell. Dana pulled her sleeve down over her hand and spread her fingers to make a mask with the fabric over her face, but even so she could only manage to descend a few steps before her eyes were streaming and she was choking from the smell that got inside her lungs, although she fought not to inhale. As she climbed downwards, she must have passed some structural part of the building shielding the lower floor from her, because she sensed the agonised signals of animals panicking and dying in a burning laboratory. Behind, the eagle screeched in protest.

"We can't get out this way," said Prendick.

They turned back and retraced their steps. Smoke was beginning to fill the corridor, and the only escape was to keep moving upwards. Dana could barely see, but GPS and her other senses guided her to the stairs that led up to the roof, and up they struggled. Dana forced open the door and smoke plumed up and away, where dark oppressive clouds dominated the sky. Somewhere up there floated the *Stormcaller*. The birds had all flown away. Without Gamma's control, they were just ordinary birds, despite the transceivers implanted in them.

Prendick bent over to lower Cale to the ground. The eagle hopped off and landed on the wall. "Stay here," he said. "I'm going back to get Gamma."

Prendick's eagle didn't accompany him as he disappeared into the doorway filled with billowing smoke. It was by now so thick that surely eyes of any kind would not be able to see in there, and a person with their full eyesight had no better chance of finding their way than did a blind man anyway. All they could do was wait, wait to see if he would return, or succumb to smoke or fire. Neither Peter nor Dana could stop coughing. Peter's body looked so thin and weak where he crouched, as though the hacking coughs that had overcome him might break his ribs. The smoke had settled in Dana's lungs, and no amount of coughing seemed able to dislodge it.

A signal. A flash of metal above. The wyvern alighted on the roof beside Dana. Perhaps they didn't agree with each other right now, but the wyvern wasn't going to stand by while they were trapped up here.

"Peter, climb on." Dana pushed Peter towards the wyvern, who lowered itself into a crouch to allow him to mount. For once, Peter did not argue, apparently awed by the appearance of this strange metal saviour who could hear his own thoughts. In the meadow below, figures in dark uniforms rushed forward to meet them; Rajesh's squadron.

"Rajesh!" Dana shouted, waving both arms from the roof.

The Commodore saw her and waved back, and then came more coughing from the doorway onto the roof behind. Dana turned, expecting to see Prendick returning, but saw instead the tall form of Sanderson staggering from the smoke.

"Go!" Dana said, and the wyvern climbed up onto the wall and opened its wings to fall into a glide earthwards.

Dana dropped her hand to the handle of the tantō and drew it, pointing it at Sanderson and putting herself between him and Cale. He scowled, wiping his streaming eyes on his sleeve, and lurched away from her on his injured leg. A waft of rotting stench mixed with the odour of smoke, and the griffin landed on the wall at the corner of the roof. Sanderson staggered to it and flung himself on its back. It turned as though to drop off as the wyvern had done with Peter, but its descent came as a thrashing, out-of-control fall that terminated with a jolting crash into the ground and a sudden broadcast of horrible pain.

Prendick appeared from the smoke, coughing violently. Dana was relieved to see him back, but there was no body over his shoulder.

"Where is she?" Dana demanded.

"She's gone," he choked out.

"*Gone?*" How could she be gone? Her signal had gone out. She couldn't possibly be capable of getting up and moving. "Are you sure?"

"She wasn't in the cell."

"Are you sure it was the right cell, and you were looking in the right place?" Dana didn't believe he was lying, but it must have been hard for him to find his way in the smoke.

"Yes. I'm sure. We need to get off this building, now."

Dana looked back at the smoke pouring from the doorway. If Gamma was still alive and in there, that could only lead to one of two things. Either she would escape and there would be a risk she would start again what she'd tried to do here, or she would die inside the Forge. Neither of them were good for anyone.

The wyvern landed on the wall, flapping its wings awkwardly for balance, Peter safely deposited with Rajesh below.

The wyvern could carry a child's weight, and it at least

thought it would be able to glide down with both her and Cale, but the griffin hadn't been able to carry Sanderson. Prendick was a big man, and Dana didn't want to risk him or the wyvern by trying that. "I can get down. But what about you and Cale?"

"Those men down there. See if they have a rope."

Dana stepped up onto the wall and swung her leg over the wyvern's neck. It turned to drop off and carry her down, and at once hands were grabbing her and lifting her off, and she was back with her feet on the ground in the fresh air, the Emerald Forge looming over her with smoke pouring from every orifice and all its windows ablaze with the heat of the fire within, intense in the darkness of the towering storm-swept sky.

"A rope! My brother and a man are trapped up there, and we must take them a rope!"

"We can get a rope," said Rajesh, "but I'm not sure how we can get it up there."

Dana pointed up above, to where an enormous bird circled. "Give it to the eagle!"

Rajesh looked at her, like he thought she was mad, but he and the other Sky Forces personnel ran back to the body of a fallen horse and retrieved a coiled rope made of some sort of lightweight polymer alloy. The eagle came down when Dana signalled it, and it took the end of the rope in its claws when Rajesh offered it, and carried it back up to Prendick.

The smoke was becoming much worse, but through it Dana could just make out a bulky shape abseiling clumsily down the wall. As it got closer to the ground, she could make out Cale slung over Prendick's shoulder. Rajesh and another man ran forward to help Prendick down and lift the boy off him.

Prendick was coughing violently. Someone offered him an oxygen mask to ease his breath. Cale's breathing was rapid, yet raspy and shallow. Dana could just sense his signal, and it was weak, with no hint of consciousness behind it. "What's the matter with him?" asked the other man. "Has he succumbed to the smoke?"

"No, we found him like this. He's hot, like he's got a fever."

Rajesh knelt beside Cale and touched the boy's face. He lifted his hand and examined the smelly bandage on his forearm.

"His hands are getting cold. He could have developed blood poisoning. He needs immediate medical treatment and antibiotics."

Dana looked at him. "Have you got any?"

Rajesh frowned, studying the bandages on Cale's arms that were stained brown and pale yellow where his arms had been cut. "The *Stormcaller* is directly above. It has medical supplies on board. Can that construct of yours get him up there?" He glanced at the wyvern. Of course. Dana imagined the plan to the wyvern at once: it was to fly up to the *Stormcaller* with Cale on its back. Immediately it came forward and dropped into a crouch.

Prendick and Rajesh lifted Cale up and arranged his legs either side of the wyvern's neck, but he couldn't sit upright or hold himself in position.

"Dana, you're going to have to hold on to him," said Rajesh.

"But the wyvern won't be able to take off with both of us on. It's hard enough for it to get airborne with just me on it."

Rajesh lifted Cale off again. "Can it carry him with its feet, like a bird carries things?"

Dana translated this into a thought the wyvern would understand, but the response was that it wasn't possible, although it took a moment to work out why. "It needs its legs so it can jump when it takes off. It's not going to work. Can't you contact someone and get an ambulance to come out?"

"I already have done. But it isn't here yet."

Dana knelt in the damp grass beside her brother. "Cale?

Cale, please wake up." She tried to think of all his favourite things: beetles in the museum, that bland tapioca pudding he insisted Graeme make him all the time, calculating Pi and converting it into musical notes to play on a keyboard. The raspberry he blew into a microphone when someone tried to get him to make a comment on television, and how they'd laughed and gone home, and forgotten about the stupid art competition and all the problems it had wrought after that.

The wyvern rose from its crouch and snaked its head under its chest. Dana stared as it opened its mouth and sank the sharp point of its beak into the skin on the inside of its leg, where there was a gap in its armour. When it carefully removed the point, the steel tip glistened with a black substance, and a thin rivulet of dark ichor tracked slowly down the wyvern's leg.

It had just bitten itself. Dana's probing as to why was rejected without answer. The wyvern refused to reveal anything to her about what it was doing. It reached out, straight past her with its long neck, and bit Cale's arm.

"Get off him!" Dana reacted immediately, hitting the wyvern in the neck and cutting her own hand on the sharp edges of the metal plates. Rajesh, who had been standing a short distance away discussing the medical situation with the other man, turned at her outburst and pointed his gun at the wyvern.

"Get away from them! Both of them!"

The wyvern didn't understand Rajesh's words, but the gesture held meaning enough. It slunk away and crouched down in the grass.

"It just bit itself, and then it bit Cale!" Dana pointed out the puncture hole in Cale's flesh, just above the bandage, stained with blood and what looked like black ink.

As she and Rajesh knelt beside the boy, Dana sensed from Cale's signal that something was changing. The fever was not quite so great, his sleep not so deep, consciousness not so far away as it had been. He was getting better.

"You say the wyvern bit itself?"

Dana looked up to see Prendick standing over them.

Prendick continued. "The constructs like the wyvern couldn't have natural immune systems. They were made out of organs from different individuals, often entire different species that weren't compatible. They had artificial immune systems instead, nanomachines, to protect the body from infection. The boy has a blood infection, and it looks as though the artificial immune system in his blood is fighting it for him."

Dana stared at Cale, and then at the wyvern, who stared back at her with its head lowered. Of course. The things Osric had seen with his microscope. She shouldn't have doubted what it was doing... but after what it had done to Gamma...

The other man made a signal to Rajesh and pointed to something. "Dana," said Rajesh grimly, "you'd better come and look at this."

Not far away, the griffin and Sanderson had fallen. Sanderson lay still on his face in the grass, and from the unnatural angle of his neck it was obvious he was dead. The griffin lay broken, struggling to raise its head. As soon as it saw Dana, an appalling torrent of pain hit her.

"Please, make it stop," she gasped.

Rajesh nodded. He went over to the griffin and took aim, settling the butt of his gun against his shoulder. Dana looked on, not wanting to see this but unable to turn away.

The gun jumped in his arms with a single shot that made Dana start violently, even though she'd been waiting for it. The griffin's signal disappeared and its neck immediately collapsed. An unearthly shudder spread over its limbs, and then Prendick had her by the arm and was leading her away, back to Cale.

-24-

CALE had still not regained consciousness, but the signal coming from him was not so dulled, so weak. Rajesh moved him onto a blanket and wrapped the sides of it over him, and claimed his hands were getting warmer.

Dana looked back at the now-still bulk on the ground that was the griffin's corpse. Sanderson's phone must have been on him when he'd fallen, because she could sense its signal. He had kept the footage all this time, while Jananin, or someone else in league with her, had been erasing every public trace they could find of Ivor Pilgrennon from the Internet. Dana had been looking for years and had found nothing, and this phone might be the only chance she had of some evidence of him that was more than just a memory.

Where was it? She crept away from the people surrounding Cale. She could make out Sanderson's body lying on the ground. She didn't want to touch him, trying to get it out of his pocket. She glanced at Rajesh, crouching over Cale still. Would it be safe to ask him, or did his loyalty to Jananin run too deep?

Then she spotted a flicker of firelight reflecting from something in the grass near Sanderson's feet. It must have fallen from his pocket when they'd hit the ground. When she picked it up, it appeared to be in standby mode, inert yet still transmitting a low signal.

She turned at the distant sound of an engine. A Land Rover pulled off the road and lurched through the meadow towards the gathering of people before the burning Forge. By now, the roaring of fire filled the evening air and long plumes of flame tore up into the dusk sky from the many windows. Whenever Dana turned to face it, the great heat radiating from the concrete walls was so intense it was close to painful.

The engine of the Land Rover stopped and the doors flew open. Out came two women, one tall and thin, one short and plump. Jananin and Tarrow. Dana put the phone in her pocket.

Tarrow rushed to them, a bulky box clutched in her arms. She fell on her knees beside Cale. "All right, laddie, what've you been getting yourself into?"

While she attended to him and Rajesh explained the situation to her, Jananin came over more cautiously, and indicated to Dana to come away from the others.

"Well done," she said. "I have to admit I wasn't convinced, but you've done everyone proud." She looked at the body lying in the grass and at Prendick. "I have to ask one question, though..."

Dana slumped her shoulders. "The wyvern attacked Gamma and we thought she was dead, but she wasn't, and we don't know if she's still inside or she got away."

Peter had noticed Jananin's approach. He got up weakly and came towards them. "Where's Ivor?" His face was tense with suspicion.

"Of course," Jananin continued, "your success has unavoidably brought about yet more problems." She turned back to Tarrow and the other medics. "Can we have some medical assistance for this boy over here."

Dana looked up at Prendick, whose face did not now appear anywhere near as horrific as it had when she'd first glimpsed it. "Thank you so much, Prendick."

"My name's Norman."

"Norman, what kind of a bird is Sight?"

"She's a martial eagle, from South Africa."

Prendick lowered his hand to let Dana see the eagle. She cautiously put up her hand to touch the soft feathers of the bird's chest.

Jananin indicated to the wyvern. "Did you make *that*?"

"The metal parts of it," Prendick replied.

"He only did it because Gamma and Sanderson gave him this bird," Dana explained.

Jananin scrutinised the bird and Prendick's scarred face for an uncomfortable moment. "I may have work for someone of your talents, that is, if you are interested."

A shout from Rajesh interrupted the conversation. He came over from where he'd been helping Tarrow with Cale, pointing up at the burning building. "Look! On the stack! There's someone trapped up there!"

Dana squinted, trying to discern a figure against the blank walls and the darkening sky over the glare of the flames and the billowing smoke. Somebody was there, clinging halfway up the chimney. There was only one person it could be.

"It's Gamma."

Jananin stood beside her and stared up at the figure on the stack, and for a while said nothing.

"It's not safe for anyone to enter that building. Probably it is best that we take no action."

Dana watched the figure struggling, trying to climb the stack to escape the flames. Could she have escaped if she'd wanted; had she only stayed in this building because it was the one place she'd felt safe? Dana could no longer detect any signal from Gamma, but just because she couldn't feel her, that didn't mean she wasn't there. She was still the same person, the child who had been trapped in the hospital. The thought of the heat, the pain, of life fading away, she couldn't bear it. She looked to the wyvern crouched in the grass, reflections of firelight flickering over its body. The only response it gave was anger and hate directed at Gamma, that she deserved death, that its only regret was its failure to kill her when it had snuffed out her signal.

"You think she should die?" Dana said to Jananin in a low voice so Prendick and Rajesh didn't overhear.

"She's a danger to everyone, including herself. Things will be a lot simpler if she does not walk away from this."

"You are wrong," said Dana. "You were wrong about Ivor, and you were wrong about Peter, and Cale, and you are wrong about Gamma."

She disentangled the cord holding the tantō to her belt. The sun had set and night was closing in, the pattern engraved in the leather of the sheath unseen, the intricate fretwork on the guard and weaving on the handle barely visible. She had always looked up to Jananin and, although she may not always have trusted her, there'd been this understanding that everything Jananin did, she did for the greater good. Jananin might have won the Nobel Prize for her contribution to science, but she wasn't always right.

Dana stared at the tantō in her hand. This wasn't hers. She held it out.

"Have your knife back."

Jananin took it, and Dana walked away, towards the wyvern. Dana's legs ached, but she ignored them, and pulled herself up onto the wyvern's shoulders. Its thoughts were mutinous, and it refused to take off. Dana reminded it that it had decided itself that it owed her a debt, and if it would do this one last act, she would consider the debt repaid.

Then we're through.

The thought was as much a realisation to herself as it was an assurance to the wyvern. While she would always remember the deep connection she'd felt to it as a fellow creature born out of similar circumstances, and it might be an intelligent animal, an animal it was. She now realised her idea that she could somehow keep the wyvern hidden from the world was hopelessly naïve. This animal had its own needs, it didn't belong in human society, and she couldn't have it for a pet. If it would help her this one last time, she would make sure it could go somewhere safe, where it would be free.

Although the idea of doing what she'd done to Gamma again to another living being repulsed her, she gritted her teeth and forced her will upon the wyvern. It launched angrily into a rough takeoff and flapped up. As they climbed higher, the heat rising from the burning forge provided an artificial thermal to give them lift. The wyvern couldn't land easily and had to circle the chimney twice in order to gauge the appropriate altitude and speed.

Dana pressed her knees in and gripped hard as the wyvern descended, wings braking and talons outstretched, braced for the impact. Below, the roof where she and Prendick had not long ago stood was on fire. The impact threw her forward and hard metal armour pressed into her, but she managed to stay in place. The air was full of choking smoke and a dry, awful heat radiated from the concrete and up from the flames below.

"Gamma!" she shouted. She could see the girl just below where the wyvern's talons gripped crannies and edges in the masonry's surface. She reached down past the wyvern's neck. "Gamma, hold on to my hand!"

Gamma didn't answer. It was frustrating being unable to tell what she was thinking.

"*Gamma!*"

"I'm not Gamma any more! You destroyed me!"

Sweat was soaking through Dana's shirt. It was difficult to breathe and every time she did inhale it made her cough. "Who are you, then?"

"I'm not going back into hospital and being Gemma again. I'm not being *that!*"

The wyvern couldn't stay in this position for much longer. "You define who you are. Choose a different name. Start again and be someone new. We'll tell people what happened in the hospital. There's people who know about the experiment that made us able to do what we can. They'll understand and they can make sure you go somewhere else."

Gamma didn't respond.

"You can choose whatever name you like to be called and take as long as you like. But you're going to have to come with us, because if you stay here you're going to die!"

"Who says I'd not rather die?"

Dana looked down at the flame tearing through the roof. It wasn't like death was easy to avoid in this situation. "Because you climbed up here."

Gamma said nothing, and for what felt like a long time Dana feared she would just stay there, holding all three of them in limbo and refusing to respond any more. Finally, she reached up with a weak, trembling hand. No sooner had Dana got hold of her wrist than the wyvern lost its grip and slipped off the side of the stack. It got hold of Gamma's leg with one of its feet as they fell, its wings fighting gravity but not doing enough to keep them away from the flames below. Dana held on with her arm, wrapping her legs hard around the wyvern's neck and shutting her eyes against the stinging smoke and heat. The next moment, the wind on her face had cooled, and they made a poorly controlled descent for the people on the grass.

They hit the ground heavily, but without any injury Dana could detect. As soon as the wyvern was down, soldiers took hold of Gamma. Someone pushed Dana off the wyvern. She looked around in confusion to see Peter restrained by two uniformed men. In the red light of the inferno, his eyes blazed with righteous indignation. "You said we were going back to Roareim!"

"Jananin!" Dana shouted over the throng of military men. She pushed between them to get to her, and while they restrained Peter and Gamma, they did nothing to impede her. "Jananin, where are they taking them?"

"They will both go to a secure unit for psychiatric testing. The construct…"

"The wyvern!"

"The construct will go to a secure laboratory for study."

"But what will happen to them there?"

"That's up to qualified specialists to decide, for the good of themselves and the good of society."

"You mean Peter will go into care, and Gamma will go back into a hospital like that awful one she escaped from?

And the wyvern will end up dead?"

"Dana, it is not up to me to decide these things!"

Dana glanced again at Peter struggling. She had to think quickly to come up with an alternative. "Please, let Peter and the wyvern go to Roareim and live in the military base Ivor hid in. They won't be in anyone's way there, and they can look after each other. Nobody will even know they are there. They're both too wild to be part of society. Gamma can't go back to a place like where she came from. It's what made her ill in the first place. There must be another place she can go."

"That child is a serious risk and a threat to the entire nation!"

"But she can't do harm any more! The thing — the transceiver..." Dana pointed frantically to the centre of her forehead. "It's broken. She can't interface with computers any more."

Jananin's head turned slightly. She must have been taking in the blood on Gamma's face. "It's still too great a risk."

"Jananin, I never told anyone about Ivor Pilgrennon, or what happened in the Information Terrorism attack on London, or at Cape Wrath. I could have done, but I didn't. You promised him you would make sure Peter was safe! You say it's not up to you to decide, but I know you could do something if you wanted to. The people who are supposed to decide don't even need to know that Peter and Gamma and the wyvern came out of the Emerald Forge alive!"

Jananin appeared to think about this for a moment. A tension had spread over her. Dana's breath came in ragged gasps. She was starting to feel weak and dizzy.

"Are you attempting to blackmail a Spokesman for the Meritocracy?"

Dana stared back at her. "I kept your confidence! If it became public knowledge *who my parents were*, they would think... that you were *carrying on with him*... that it happened the normal way. You would have to tell them the truth about what he did to you, and how you destroyed all the evidence of his research, or let them believe that!"

It was only after she said it, that Dana realised how utterly *offensive* it was.

Jananin and Dana stood, staring at each other, and it seemed a long time until Jananin spoke again. "Rajesh?"

The Air Commodore turned around from where he'd been speaking to the other men.

Jananin glanced away from Dana to draw attention to where Gamma sat hunched up on the damp ground. "Get both the children medically assessed, and then take them and the construct to Torrmede. Guard them closely and see that the girl in particular does not have access to computers. I will send precise instructions later."

Dana felt greatly relieved as the soldiers marched Gamma over to the Land Rover, but Gamma threw a look of disgust over her shoulder at Dana as they pushed her inside.

Jananin's jaw was set rigidly. She spoke in a low voice so only Dana would hear it. "Pilgrennon intended you as a weapon. As he does not wield you, I have decided not to interfere as yet. If you make an enemy of me, you may some day find yourself in the situation Gamma was heading for."

Dana had noticed many people make meaningless threats: *You'll wish you'd never been born*, Dana's old teacher Miss Robinson had used to say. People say *I'm going to kill him* when they are angry with someone. *I'll have your guts for garters*. Jananin's threat did not feel that way. Could she really have Dana taken from her home? She had the influence to do it, but would she really do that? Despite their blood connection, Dana did not really know Jananin.

She watched Peter fighting weakly, spitting. When that car drove away, its occupants would be gone from her life, and she might never know how their stories continued. Although Jananin seemed to have little concern for the lives and wellbeing of others when they conflicted with her own intentions and what she saw as being morally just, Dana had never known her to lie outright or renege on her word. Quite possibly it went against the personal code of honour she upheld with people like Rajesh and Osric. She believed Peter and Gamma and the wyvern would be treated in the way she'd asked, and hoped her feelings were not merely wishful thinking.

"Your ambulance is here," said Tarrow. Blue lights flashed over where the road was.

"Good-bye, Dana," said Jananin.

"They'll be leaving base tomorrow morning if you want to visit," Tarrow suggested, but Dana knew Jananin would deliberately avoid proximity to her and Cale until they went home.

Rajesh carried Cale back to the road, Dana and Tarrow walking beside him. Dana's legs ached terribly, which hadn't mattered so much when there'd been problems to deal with, but now the pain and the exhaustion were too much, and she had to hold on to Tarrow's arm for the last bit of the walk to the ambulance.

Rajesh lifted Cale in through the back doors of the ambulance and put him on a bed, while Tarrow settled Dana on a chair, with a blanket over her and a plastic cup of cold water. Rajesh saluted to her and smiled before getting out.

Tarrow put a pale blue blanket over Cale. She rolled up his sleeve and set about putting a drip into his wrist, like the one Dana had in the hospital. He wasn't awake yet, but Dana knew he would be soon. In his dream, he happily wandered a gloomy half-lit museum, after all the staff and the other visitors had gone home. She wasn't about to spoil it by waking him. There was an oxygen mask on his face and a big, squishy plastic bag full of liquid hanging over his bed and flowing slowly through a tube into the vein in his arm, to help him. Looking at it was reassuring in a way. She knew Tarrow could keep them safe now, and they were going to a nice hospital that would make Cale better, not like the awful hospital in the nightmares.

An urge of worry fidgeted briefly over the calm she felt: what about at the end of the holidays, when she had to go back to school and face Abigail Swift and Eric, and having to turn into a woman? Thinking about them like this, these concerns suddenly seemed rather less important. If she could face a man like Sanderson who was bigger than her and more experienced, and a bully like Gamma who was older than her and could get inside her head as well, surely stupid bullies the same age as her could be defeated? And if she'd made an embarrassment of herself with Eric, surely it was no worse than any embarrassment she'd made with any other person, and surely plenty of other people make embarrassing mistakes with their lives. Having to become a woman might not be as bad as she expected, if Tarrow and Jananin could still be themselves despite having done it. At any rate, it was no use worrying about things before they'd even happened.

Tarrow's voice interrupted her thoughts. "I'm going to sit in the front. Keep your brother company and we'll be back at Site Twelve soon."

Dana nodded. Tarrow got out and set about closing the back doors, shutting out the starry sky and the cool night air.

She put her hand into her pocket and took out Sanderson's phone. She switched it on, silencing it with a thought so Tarrow and the ambulance driver wouldn't hear it. It didn't take long to find the video. Ivor, or a brief moment of him preserved in the tiny LCD screen, the Ivor before he came face to face with the products of the chances he'd dared to take. She wished she'd had time to ask Sanderson more questions, but at the same time she knew no answers he could give her would be any use. Nobody could answer her questions about Ivor, because nobody else had known him like she had, not at the end. The Ivor Sanderson would have known was not the same person.

Dana wiped away a dampness that had formed in her

eyes as the ambulance's engine started. She put the phone back in her pocket. Life went on.

-End of Book Three-

THE LAMBTON WORM

MANDA BENSON

-Book four of Pilgrennon's Children-

"They made me sit my grammar school entrance exam in a Faraday cage, and that's why I failed! Because when you take away what Ivor Pilgrennon gave me, there is nothing left! That's why I can't do the exams and I'm going to fail my GCSEs, because I'm stupid, and the transceiver and the computers are the only way I can hide it!"

Disillusioned with the new order, Dana is failing academically and socially. But someone's about to come into her life, the sole survivor of a family destroyed by a cycle of abuse. And she's determined to atone for her part in it and, more than anything, to prevent history from repeating itself again.

Meanwhile, something is evolving in the Meritocracy's computers that can't be contained, and could bring to an end an international peace that was never particularly stable...

www.tangentrine.com

PILGRENNON'S CHILDREN

THE TETRALOGY

PILGRENNON'S BEACON

PILGRENNON'S GAMBIT

THE EMERALD FORGE

THE LAMBTON WORM